First Comes Love

Christie Ridgway

FIRST COMES LOVE

AVON BOOKS
An Imprint of HarperCollinsPublishers

AVON BOOKS
An Imprint of HarperCollins*Publishers*
10 East 53rd Street
New York, New York 10022-5299

Copyright © 2002 by Christie Ridgway
ISBN: 0-7394-2215-4

Printed in the U.S.A.

Acknowledgments

My deep appreciation to the following people who helped me during the research and writing of this book:

My mom, Marilyn Fritz, who whisked me from the San Francisco Airport to the Gold Country, where she led me on a grand tour. She even volunteered to make the greatest of sacrifices (no stopping at antique shops), though she knew, of course, I'd never agree to that!

Thanks also to Michael and Lisa Pundeff, friends extra-ordinaire. Michael for his patience with my "legal" questions and Lisa for her willingness and enthusiasm for brainstorming. But most especially, thank you just for being our friends.

Maureen Caudill and Teresa Hill deserve chocolate and roses for their always insightful comments and undying support.

And finally, thanks to my "men." My husband and sons are everything a writer could wish for. They are the inspiration for my happy endings.

Chapter One

Running a brothel was hot, sweaty work.

Awaiting the arrival of her next round of guests in the overheated parlor, Kitty Wilder figured she should know. She'd been doing it for the past seven summers, ever since her great-aunt Catherine was hospitalized with her first stroke. Before that, everyone in her hometown of Hot Water, California, including Aunt Cat, thought Kitty was too young to dress in satin and feathers every day. Of course, they expected she *would* eventually—after all, there had been a Doc Watson and a Judge Matthews in town for over one hundred and fifty years, so who other than a Wilder woman belonged in the local bordello?—but modern mores had postponed Kitty's debut at The Burning Rose until it was absolutely necessary, when she was nineteen years old.

She hadn't been what you'd call "eager" to take on

the work. It certainly wasn't a conventional summer job—and conventional was Kitty's soul-deep desire— but in Hot Water, where the past was so tangled with the present, there wasn't much point in bucking century-old traditions. Though at nineteen Kitty had already been coveting minivans, wanting nothing more than a super-size white one with wood side panels, a stroller spilling out the back and a bronzed male forearm propped in the driver's window—oh, she especially longed for that bronzed forearm and the rest of the family man that went with it!—she had accepted the responsibility and donned a floozy's dress and some feathers with fatalistic calm.

This seventh summer was little different from her first. Though Kitty was now twenty-six, the brothel's parlor smelled as always of old wood and lemon oil. The sluggish air conditioner battled against Hot Water's late-July heat with minimal success. The black lace edging the low-to-the-point-of-embarrassment neckline of her gold satin costume itched.

This summer the only difference was in Kitty. What was missing was her fatalistic calm. That was why, when the town's Gold Rush-era living-history district closed its doors on the summer tourist season, Kitty was going to quit playing madam. For good.

Heat had nothing to do with it. Sweat was a mere inconvenience. But six months ago Kitty had seen how futile that soul-deep ambition of hers was. Though for three-fourths of the year she held the responsible position of "head" of the one-person advertising and PR department of the Hot Water Preservation Society, she'd realized she would never be considered conventional. She'd realized that the two thousand residents of her hometown would always see her as a Wilder—would *only* see her as a Wilder.

That was why it was a sadder but wiser Kitty who now pushed a damp lock of hair off her forehead with the back of her wrist, then consulted a mental calendar, ticking off time by touching thumb to forefinger, tall man, ring finger, pinkie, forefinger once more. After today's last tour, she had five weeks left as Hot Water's madam. In five short weeks she'd be pointing her packed car north, because the only way to escape her past was to leave home behind.

The brothel's front-door hinges squealed. Kitty pushed herself off the parlor's stiff Victorian settee and smoothed the skirt of her off-the-shoulder dress. She tugged up that black lace at the décolletage too, even though the dress's sewed-in stays couldn't manage to thrust her meager breasts into immodest prominence. Its low cut might make the garment cooler than the high-necked, long-sleeved costumes the other women in the living-history district wore, but she never felt completely at ease in it all the same.

"Kitty?" Sally Sloan, owner of Sloan Tours of San Francisco, poked her head through the front door.

"Coming," Kitty called. As she hurried across the parlor rug, the wilting black ostrich feather that was poked into her loose topknot of hair waved at the edge of her vision. Kitty batted it back. "Is your group ready?"

Every Wednesday, Thursday, and Saturday, as part of Sloan Tour's "Golden Age, Golden Country" tour, a 747-sized bus stopped in Hot Water, discharging a bundle of chilled tourists from its luxurious, partly refrigerated confines. Once Kitty led today's group through the brothel, she could leave the madam's clinging dress behind for the day—if not the madam's reputation that clung to her as stubbornly—and curl up in her little house for a quiet evening with a book and a cold glass of lemonade.

As Kitty reached the wide archway between the parlor and the entry hall, Sally stepped completely inside, shutting the front door behind her. Clutching her customary clipboard and water bottle to her chest, she leaned back against the door and released a long, tired sigh. Her eyes closed.

Kitty stopped short, surprised by the exhaustion etched on the face of the usually energetic woman. "Sally, what's wrong?"

One of Sally's eyes opened and she grimaced. "That obvious, huh?"

Kitty nodded. "That obvious, yes. What's the problem?"

Sally grimaced again, then pushed her shoulders off the door and met Kitty's gaze squarely. "I hate to tell you this, but I have forty untamed rugby players out there."

Kitty groaned. "Not today." Not today when it was so hot and so late and she'd already been dreaming of lemonade and her book. "Not *rugby players.*"

But Sally was nodding her head. "Rugby players."

"Women rugby players?" Kitty asked hopefully.

Sally shook her head.

"A rugby team of retirees, then?"

"You're grasping at straws, girlfriend. They're male. College age. I hesitate to label them something so grown-up as 'men,' however. You'll see what I mean. You're going to have your hands full."

Kitty shuddered. "Can't you tell them The Burning Rose is already closed?" she asked, even as the sound of forty untamed rugby players' feet rumbled on the wooden sidewalk outside.

"No can do." With a sympathetic smile, Sally moved to pull open the door. "They've been looking forward to visiting a brothel all day."

Kitty groaned one more time as she retreated to the parlor, dreading what lay ahead. She'd experienced tour groups like this before. Young men titillated by the legendary, infamous goings-on at the old brothel. Young men who asked brazen questions and who made outrageous proposals. But she really wasn't serious about refusing them entrance. With temperatures and gas prices at record highs this summer, the Hot Water Preservation Society, which ran the living-history district, rejoiced over each and every admission fee.

Resigned to the coming ordeal, she flipped the switch on the player piano. The plunking notes of "Clementine" tumbled into the room at the same rate as the rugby players. They were big men, with big, crew-cutted heads and big grins. They jostled one another with big elbows and stomped on each other's big toes with their big shoes as they made room for their entire party in the small parlor.

Only a couple of them inspected the souvenir "passports" in their big, meaty hands, the passports that gave a brief history of the town and listed all of the restored businesses and homes that made up the six-block tourist attraction. The rest inspected her.

Inhaling a calming breath, Kitty resisted the instinctive urge to tug again on the black lace at her plunging neckline. The trick to handling this kind of crowd, and to maintaining her dignity as well, was to talk fast and to talk all the time. Once she started her spiel, she'd give them as few opportunities to heckle as possible. By keeping her concentration and her word count up, she'd keep the situation under control.

Rugby players were still cramming into the parlor when the first foray on her composure was made. With a teammate pushing on each side, one young man squirted forward, nearly bowling Kitty over.

Instead of stepping away or even just apologizing, he widened his grin into a varsity-caliber leer. "Want to go out tonight . . . madame?"

Madame. Now *that* was original. Mentally rolling her eyes, Kitty shook her head. "I don't think so, sonny." Unabashed, he leered once more, then moved back, taking elbow jabs to his mastodon-sized ribs while wearing that same half-wit grin. Then his oh-so-mature buddies launched into a game of rock-paper-scissors. Probably, Kitty thought with a sigh, to decide which of their charming comrades would ask her out next.

The fact was, she rarely met a man who wanted to go out with *Kitty*, the flat-chested, ordinary-faced woman whom she greeted in the mirror every morning. Too often, men wanted to go out with Kitty the "madam," or—especially in the past six months—they wanted to date one of the notorious Wilder women.

Just as another grinning player stepped forward, Sally caught Kitty's eye and nodded, indicating the tour could begin. With a grateful smile, Kitty crossed to the player piano and switched it off. The audience automatically quieted, and before the boys could get rowdy again, she dragged a low footstool to the center of the room and stepped up.

Now. Kitty inhaled and—

Something distracted her. *He* did. Beyond the boxily built men gathered in the parlor, she spotted a tall, lean shadow framed by the open front door. She narrowed her eyes, trying to make out the features of the so un-rugby-shaped last arrival. But against the bright yellow sunshine outside, he was only a silhouette, a dark figure centered in the doorway as if determined to prevent an escape.

Ignoring an odd sense of alarm, she raised her voice. "Sir? Please come in and shut the door. It's time we get going."

As it happened, though, it was much too late for Kitty to go anywhere.

Because, after a brief hesitation, the black shadow obeyed. The front door shut and he stepped through the arched entry to the parlor. Behind all those collegiate grins and bristling haircuts, the shadow turned out to be a lean, tough-looking man in black jeans and a black T-shirt, with black, nearly shoulder-length hair.

Holy bad news, Batman.

As if her skin were allergic to her sudden, excruciating panic, it broke out in goose bumps like a bad rash. Her bare skin, hidden skin, secret skin, it *all* prickled in horrified reaction. Her head spun in woozy circles like an ill-weighted merry-go-round.

Because she knew him. She'd been barely eighteen when she'd last seen him, and on that occasion she hadn't been at her . . . best. But there was no doubting who he was.

The man was Dylan Matthews. Those were his dark eyes, his sexy-sulky mouth, his square-cut chin with just a hint of a cleft. Looking as cool as a cucumber and about a zillion times more dangerous.

Cool as a cucumber, but not the least bit green. No, that was her. Kitty supposed she looked green anyway, because her head and now her stomach were reeling. Dylan was back. Back in Hot Water.

Worse yet, he was here, in Kitty's place of business.

Self-protective instincts kicking in at last, Kitty wrenched her gaze off him. Her stomach calmed, but then pitched again as she took in what else was happening around the room.

There were other people in it. People looking at her. Expectantly. Kitty gazed about, baffled. Then it hit her. The tour!

She closed her eyes, opened them. *You're fine*, she said to herself, drawing in a deep breath. *Just fine.*

In a second she would be, surely. Dylan—no! Head starting that queasy spin again, Kitty resisted even thinking his name. He was her One Silly Mistake. But even with her One Silly Mistake—her teenage, eight-year-old mistake—in the audience, she could get through this tour. With dignity.

She straightened her shoulders. Rubbed her palms against the satin of her skirt. Cleared her throat, then started her spiel.

"Welcome," she said—more words tumbled out, as easy as creek water over smooth stones, because she'd said them hundreds of times before—"to this entertainment establishment built for the men who came to Hot Water, California, seeking gold. It was called The . . ."

On a roll, she darted a glance at her One Silly Mistake. He still stood in the rear, his face expressionless, his stance relaxed. Certainly nothing more than mere chance had brought him into the brothel, she assured herself, trying to stifle her nagging worry. Most likely he didn't even recognize her as someone he'd known before. Eight years ago she'd been a towheaded beanpole of a girl. There was no reason for him to see any resemblance to the towheaded beanpole of a woman she was now, right?

She swallowed. "It was called The Burning . . ."

Her OSM crossed his arms over his chest.

Kitty stared. ". . . Biceps."

The crowd guffawed and Kitty blinked. "Rose," she quickly corrected herself. "The Burning *Rose*."

Swallowing again, she hastily focused her gaze on the front row of rugby players, far away from the man behind them who stood out like a lean, lethal dagger in a field of plump Iowa corn. "And my name is—" *Wait.*

Think. No matter if his reason for being in the brothel was mere happenstance, it would be safer for her to remain anonymous. She searched her mind for an alias, a nom de guerre of sorts, but the man at the back of the room must have taken another long silence as proof of her complete idiocy.

"You're Kitty," he called out, with a sort of grim helpfulness. "Kitty Wilder."

Once again her equilibrium fell, sad but swift, straight onto its overly optimistic fanny.

She wasn't sure how she got through the next few minutes, struggling as she was to deal with the fact that not only was her OSM in town, he was in The Burning Rose, and perfectly aware of her identity.

Judging by the college boys' heh-heh-hehs and cat-calls, though, she assumed she rattled out her usual description of what went on in the parlor circa 1850: the musical entertainment, the serving of exorbitantly overpriced drinks, the purchasing of wooden disks in the shape of roses that were stamped "Good For One" and allowed a man upstairs for a more private visit.

The idea of a "private visit" set the rugby boys off again. They laughed. They elbowed one another. They asked, "Good For One is good for what, exactly?" Several wanted to know if Kitty gave out free samples of the house wares like the bakery did.

But their obnoxiousness didn't even make her blink, not when her brain was so frantically preoccupied with the problem of Dylan Matthews. It wasn't until she was preparing to lead the group to the brothel bedrooms that her agitated mind finally latched onto a sensible, calming thought. Just because her OSM knew who she was, *it didn't mean he knew what she'd done.*

As a matter of fact, the more she considered it, the more she could believe that he'd joined the tour out of some offhand, nostalgic curiosity. Likely he was merely reacquainting himself with the town's history following his long absence. After all, Hot Water was his heritage as much as it was hers.

On that happy thought, she managed not to hesitate before stepping off the footstool and pushing her way through the towering walls of rugby chests in order to reach the narrow stairway. Once at the bottom of the steps, she pinned a gracious smile on her face and lifted a hand. "Gentlemen, please proceed."

Like a herd of hungry cattle, the boys hurried from the

parlor, eager to check out where the "butts hit the bed," as one silver-tongued young man referred to it. When the first size 16 shoe hit the bottom stair tread, Kitty collared Sally. She dragged the tour director toward a far corner of the front hall, removing them both from the proximity of the visitors as if to discuss important business.

Because even if Dylan's appearance at the brothel was perfectly innocent, when it came to her OSM, Kitty wasn't. So there was no good reason to risk an encounter with him, however casual. Aloof should work. If she treated him like any other tourist, as if *she* didn't recognize *him*, then she might encourage early ennui and thus an early—maybe even immediate?—departure from The Burning Rose.

A wishful hope that Sally instantly dispelled. "Who the heck is that?" she demanded, her finger quivering as it pointed to a figure in black climbing the stairs, *not* heading out the front door.

"I don't know," Kitty lied.

"But he knows *you*."

Those panicky goose bumps prickled her skin again. "He used to live in town."

Sally frowned. "You just said you didn't know him."

Kitty turned her back to the stairs and fiddled with her dress. "He hasn't been home in eight years," she mumbled, vainly tugging upward to add more coverage. "I *don't* really know him."

It was an honest answer. Although she'd recognized him at once, the tough-looking Dylan ascending the brothel stairway right this minute little resembled the handsome, good-natured young man the entire town had always admired and loved. Eight years ago he had already been changing, understandably affected by the tragedy that had marked them all that June, but the hardness Kitty saw in him now made her stomach knot.

Either that, or it was her guilty conscience.

Sally propped her hands on her hips. "What is this? Are you holding out on me?" she huffed. "I demand the scoop. Right now."

Since the "scoop" was something Kitty had managed to keep to herself for the past eight years, she edged away. "I've got to get upstairs," she said.

Sally grabbed her arm. "Come on. Give me something. Does he have a job? Kids? Wife?"

"Yes, job. No, kids." Kitty slipped free of her friend's hold and hurried to the stairway.

Sally's loud whisper drifted after her. "Okay, but what about a wife?"

Kitty pretended not to hear.

Keeping a close eye out for the dangerous man in black, she followed the last of the rugby players upstairs, then lingered at the top landing as the men shuffled in and out of the five bedrooms on display. In each were feminine toiletry articles, lingerie, and hand-lettered lists of the men purported to have taken their ease at The Burning Rose.

The first madam herself had entertained two governors, a future senator, and a banker who went on to build a prestigious university. Of course, there had also been a passel of customers identified only by bawdy nicknames like "Long Owen," "Handy John," and "Quick Pete." Despite vigorous appeals from the crew-cutted crowd, Kitty, as usual, refused to speculate about such nicknames.

"While they aren't original to The Burning Rose," she commented instead, "the furniture, wall coverings, and curtains are in keeping with the period. They're similar to those described in letters the Hot Water Preservation Society has in its collection."

As she suspected, the rugby team didn't seem much interested in the bedrooms' decor, only in the bedroom doings. For herself, Kitty liked to imagine that Rose, the first madam, had possessed better, less obvious taste than the red velvet bed hangings and matching, gold-embroidered curtains. But the committee in charge of decorating had, when it came to The Burning Rose, opted for sex over subtlety.

From the corner of her eye, Kitty caught sight of her OSM exiting one of the rooms and heading straight for her. Her voice squeaky with anxiety, she immediately urged the young men to follow her back to the parlor. To hasten them along, she grabbed the nearest brawny forearm and dragged the young man attached to it downstairs with her.

In minutes they were all back in place, Kitty standing on a stool up front, the man in black in the rear, and that comforting, wide buffer of beefy college boys in between. Just a moment more, she thought, and the tour would be wrapped up.

She risked another glance at her OSM, and though he still appeared steely, she decided he didn't look stormy. Regardless of that, her quivering sense of danger in the offing didn't entirely disappear. Not until she got through the good-byes and got him out of here would she know her secret was one hundred percent safe.

"Well, that's it." Kitty pasted on a smile. "Unless

there's anything else I can tell you, I'd like to thank you and—"

"What's that?"

Her here's-your-hat-what's-your-hurry speech was interrupted by a rugby team member she hadn't noticed before. Understandably, because he was a spider monkey to their standard King Kong size. His hair was styled in the prerequisite crew cut, but apart from that, he was short, skinny, and wore a pair of wire-rimmed glasses. He took them off, using one stem to point at a gilt-edged frame sitting atop the player piano.

"That?" Kitty repeated. Inside the frame was a needlework piece dated 1852. She thought it really belonged in her great-aunt's house, preferably buried in a box in the attic, but Aunt Cat always insisted it be displayed in the brothel parlor.

"Yes, that," the young man said. "What is it?"

Kitty cleared her throat against a tide of rising nervousness. She was so close, so close. "It was stitched by one of the original owners, named Rose," she answered quickly. "She was the older of a pair of sisters who came to Hot Water from New Orleans."

Her heart started banging harder against her breastbone as all eyes swiveled to read the words stitched on the square of buff-colored linen. In precise and delicate embroidery, they stated: *Wilder Women Don't Wed And They Don't Run.*

"But what's that saying mean?" Mr. Persistent asked. "They 'Don't Wed'?"

Kitty didn't dare look toward the back of the room as she carefully picked her words. "The miners were desperate for wives." No reason to mention how desperate, or the little custom they'd devised to lure women into matrimony.

"And, um, despite their reputation as 'soiled doves,' " she went on, "the women of The Burning Rose received their share of proposals. Marriage, though, would have meant surrendering their lucrative livelihood and their independence. So Rose indicated right up front how things stood."

The room went silent and Kitty held her breath. Then, as the silence continued, she started to relax. If her OSM had been planning to say anything . . . awkward, that would have been the perfect opening.

Finally, the forehead of the young man next to Mr. Persistent pleated. "That doesn't explain the 'Don't Run.' "

"Oh. That." This part was even easier to explain. "As the West became more stable, the miners' mothers and sisters arrived from the East. They weren't as enamored with Rose and her sister as the men were. Several times they tried to run the ladies of The Burning Rose out of town. Apparently Rose had a definite opinion about that too."

And both opinions had been passed down, daughter to daughter, until they'd taken on the weight of a family creed. *Wilder Women Don't Wed And They Don't Run.* Biting her lip, Kitty sent a silent, guilty apology to her antecedents.

C'mon, ladies, she thought, *you forgive me, right? You were never any good at following rules either.*

"Well, if that's all . . ." she began.

From the back, one of the largest of the players half raised an arm, a souvenir passport clutched in his big fist. He was tall enough that Kitty could see the slogan "I Do It My Way" stretched across his chest, and instinct warned her not to look closely at the accompanying cartoon. There was a gleam in his eye that she recognized all too well.

"It says here the town is chock-full of descendants of the first residents," he said, waving the passport again. With a smirk, he jerked it toward the ceiling. "Any of those who worked upstairs your grandma?"

It was inevitable, Kitty told herself. Natural. And it wasn't as if that question hadn't come up hundreds of times before.

"One of the most special things about Hot Water," she responded, "is just how many of our current citizens can trace their family tree back to an early town resident." Sometimes just that one comment was enough of an answer.

But not this time. "What about you?" the rugby player insisted.

Though she wished it away with all her might, telltale heat crawled up Kitty's skin. Her undeniable feeling of discomfort—she refused to call it shame—wasn't this man's fault. He couldn't know how integrally one's Hot Water identity was tied to who one's original Hot Water ancestor had been. He couldn't know that around these parts, and it had become even worse over the past six months, she was looked upon as something of a soiled dove herself.

"Rose Wilder is my great-great-great-grandmother," Kitty said.

"Yeah?" The young man's smile was lewd. He leaned forward with new interest. "So besides passing down her genes, did your randy great-great-grandy pass down any tricks of the tra—" His yelp cut off the rest of the question.

Kitty nearly smiled, swearing she'd kiss whoever had halted the smart aleck's remark. Then the smart aleck shifted, and she could see exactly who had caused the young man's cry.

Oops. Scratch that idea. Kissing the man in black would become her *second* silly mistake.

But that bad kissing idea, darn it, refused to disappear. Instead, it operated like an eraser on the blackboard of her mind, rendering Kitty not only speechless but motionless until Sally hurried to the rescue. She barked orders to the players and then, hands to shoulders, guided Kitty out of the parlor and into place behind the narrow table by the front door.

When Kitty's consciousness finally reemerged, she found herself with red ink pad ready and rubber stamp in hand, prepared to mark each visitor's guest book as he exited. *He!* Mind once again at full alert and heart rising in her throat, she peered up the single-file line of men, dreading who might be waiting to confront her.

But her OSM wasn't there.

She checked a second time, almost unable to comprehend that she'd sidestepped the final hurdle. But there was no scary, dark-haired, dark-eyed man in line. Once again she was free! Free to pretend, as she had since she was eighteen years old, that her One Silly Mistake had never happened.

Taking her first full breath in over an hour, she motioned the lined-up rugby players forward. *Thwat . . . thump . . . thwat . . . thump . . . thwat . . . thump.* Right hand moving mechanically from ink pad to paper, Kitty focused on the table top, stamping the books of the men shuffling past. As each one exited, she breathed even more easily.

Challenging tour completed. Man-from-the-past dodged. She'd done it!

Lost in that happy thought, Kitty enthusiastically continued her automatic stamping of the last few souvenirs. *Thump. Thwat. Thump. Thwat.* As a matter of fact, her thoughts were so far away and her movements were so automatic that it took her several moments to register that the very last guest book she stamped with a blood-red rose wasn't a book at all, but the back of a man's hand. The hand had slapped down, flat and commanding, on the tabletop in front of her, and she'd simply gone right ahead and stamped it.

Now she stared at that wide-palmed, long-fingered, very male hand, her panic resurging. Dylan's hand, she thought, the panic curdling into clumps of just plain fear. He hadn't left the brothel after all.

As before, she tried telling herself that the odds he'd found out her—their, really—secret had to be infinitesimal. But looking at that big, no-nonsense hand, she couldn't shake the conviction that he had. And the idea that he knew their secret was bad. Terrible. Nothing short of disaster.

Her gaze skittered away from the tanned flesh branded by her rose, shifting downward to take in black jeans and a pair of black leather motorcycle boots. When she sucked in a shallow, panicky breath, she also sucked in the smell of that leather. Of him.

Funny, she thought woozily. She'd always associated

the smell of leather with Dylan. But it had been the All-American, leather-and-wool scent of a letterman's jacket, not this new, dangerous scent of hot engines and animal skin.

"Damn you, Kitty Wilder," he said softly. Menacingly. Oh, God. Yes. He knew the secret.

Kitty kept her gaze on his boots and tried with all her might to pretend this was just a dream. No, a nightmare. "C-can I help you?"

"Yeah." He paused, then leaned forward, one hand still on the table. With the other, he grasped her chin and forced her to look at him.

Kitty shivered as she stared into his face. His features were the same as she remembered—the sexy mouth, the almost dimpled chin—but so different too. His black hair was rock-and-roller wicked-looking, and his eyes weren't just dark brown, they were burning.

Swallowing hard, she had the distinct, unpleasant suspicion that even if she made it out of Hot Water five weeks from now, she wasn't going to entirely escape her past. Because it looked as if six feet two inches of it had just caught up with her.

He cemented that suspicion by tightening his grip on her chin. "Yeah, you can help me, Kitty Wilder," he said, his voice still prey-stalking quiet. "You can tell me when the hell we got married."

Chapter Two

In Dylan Matthews's thirty-one years of experience, every debt ultimately exacted its price, and for some debts you kept on paying.

So he wasn't as surprised as one might expect to find himself secretly married to a woman with a face like a Sunday-school teacher, but who dressed like a harlot and worked in a whorehouse. But though he wasn't entirely surprised, he *was* furious.

He'd ridden all four hundred miles from L.A. to Hot Water with the angry words of an FBI assistant director still ringing in his ears, decibels louder than the whine of his Harley-Davidson Heritage motorcycle. The Bureau frowned on FBI agents—even FBI agents on involuntary leave due to unused stockpiles of overtime and vacation hours—who possessed secret wives.

Even if, until a week ago, the marriage had been a se-cret from the aforesaid FBI agent too.

But his anger had made his return to the rolling, oak-dotted hills of northern California easier. As he'd crossed the county line, a particularly large and nasty bug had flown into his mouth. Just when he'd expected to feel sharp stabs of guilt and remorse, he'd thought about his "wife" and crushed the bug between his back teeth.

He'd sworn to do the same to her.

Yet, rather than facing down some duplicitous, double-dealing doxy—he'd held onto his temper for half of the trip by coming up with alliterative insults— the woman on the other side of his ire hadn't changed that much. She was still Kitty.

Little Kitty Wilder.

Well, not so little anymore. Although she'd grown into those miles of legs she'd loped around on as a teenager, she hadn't been transformed into a vixenish villainess. She still had the Ivory-soap scrubbed look of a preacher's kid, with a wide brow, big blue eyes, and straight, blondish hair. The only jarring note to a face perfectly fashioned for the front row of Bible school was her small, plump-looking mouth.

His fingers tightened on her chin as he remembered staring at it eight years ago, fascinated by the paradox wrought by those puffy lips in their perpetual half pucker. For all Kitty's wide-eyed, innocent looks, the Wilder genes had bred true when it came to that cathouse mouth.

Dylan jerked his suddenly tingling fingers away from

her skin and shoved his hands in his pockets, pissed at himself for even thinking *Kitty* and *innocent* in the same sentence. He narrowed his eyes and pinned her with a hot stare.

"Well?" he demanded. "Apparently we're married and we've been married for some time. Aren't you going to say anything?"

She swallowed. Then her lips parted and the tip of her tongue darted out to wet the shiny undersides of her rosebud mouth. "Welcome home, honey?"

Dylan saw red, and not just the red velvet on the walls of the damn brothel that had been decorated like the inside of a tacky jewelry box. Maybe this unwelcome marriage wasn't going to be a problem after all, he thought, because at this rate he'd be a widower before nightfall.

To give his temper a moment to cool, he took his hands from his pockets and ran them over the hair he'd let grow as a personal protest to his involuntary vacation. Then he leaned closer to her.

"Do you realize," he said softly, in a voice that had been known to make federal prisoners quake in their leg shackles, "that I'm trained in martial arts you've never even heard of? I know over six hundred ways to do you in. One hundred and thirty-seven of them just with that god-awful ostrich feather you're wearing."

She blinked, dark, curly lashes falling slowly over those big, pseudo-sweet blue eyes, then lifting again. "One hundred and thirty-seven?" she murmured faintly. "Wouldn't that be . . . overkill?"

The edges of his vision turned red again. "Number eighty-eight is my favorite," he said through his teeth.

"And I'm prepared to use it, Kitty, unless you tell me how the hell this happened."

Flushing, she gave a one-shoulder shrug. The slight movement caused the inch-wide sleeve of her clinging costume to slip from the curve of her upper arm toward her elbow, revealing the strangely vulnerable-looking juncture of shoulder and breast.

She picked something off the table separating them and pushed it into his hand. "Heritage Day, of course," she said.

He jerked his gaze off that distracting cleft of bared skin to stare at the brochure between his fingers. Full-color and glossy, it proclaimed HOT WATER HERITAGE DAY . . . RELIVE THE PAST. The front photograph showed a long queue of couples lined up at city hall, waiting for their Hot Water wedding. The very trap that had so neatly—and secretly—snared his ass.

Originally intended as bait to attract women to wife-hungry miners, an 1849 city ordinance allowed that on August 31 of each year, couples could marry without any preliminaries besides a hefty fee to the town fathers. The trick—inspired by the ancient tradition of handfasting and put in place to make marriage in those unstable times more attractive—was that the blushing bride had a year's time to register the wedding, and it wasn't legal until and unless she did. In times when the fortunes were fickle and in a place where the living was hard, this had given a Hot Water wife a way out if her miner husband, his mine, or just the marriage itself proved a disaster.

In this century, Hot Water used that leftover law as an end-of-summer tourist lure. Marriage certificates were handed out like flags on the Fourth of July. Visitors weren't even told of the potential legality of the wedding, because once California had become a state, the certificates were meaningless unless registered in Sacramento.

So while the elementary-age kids at Hot Water School learned the story in their fourth-grade Gold Rush unit, as far as Dylan knew, no one had taken the whole thing seriously in a hundred years. No one except the young woman standing before him.

He shook his head. Why the hell she'd done so completely baffled him, though he didn't claim to understand women. Before that last summer in Hot Water, he'd probably been too young to figure them out. After, he hadn't tried very hard—or at all—which likely explained why his last girlfriend had hissed her final goodbye, stating that the only thing he was good for was sex. The one before that had screamed pretty much the same thing, all the while using her fresh French manicure to shred the sweater she'd knitted for his birthday. But what Kitty had done made her the most incomprehensible of all.

Dylan tossed the brochure back down and looked at her again, refusing to be softened by her guileless face and yards of flawless skin. "All right. So I remember there was a six-pack and then a wedding."

But he'd never even dated her, for God's sake! Their one and only social contact had been eight years ago, on his last night in Hot Water. A fresh-out-of-high-school Kitty had found him hanging around the creek, feeling sorry for himself. She'd handed him a beer. And then another. Some beers later, they'd both gotten a little silly, and then gotten "married" in one of those Heritage Day weddings. It was supposed to be a joke, a last Hot Water hurrah. Not a lifetime!

He tamped down another flare of temper. "And it doesn't explain why you made it legal—"

The trill of his cell phone interrupted.

Setting his back molars, Dylan fumbled in the front pocket of his jeans for the phone, which apparently gave Kitty the idea she could slip away from him. But just as she skirted the table, wearing a fake, let-me-give-you-some-privacy half smile, her mistaken impression was quickly and effectively corrected. He grabbed her wrist.

"Not so fast, *wife*," he said, ignoring that odd tingle in his fingers again. Then he flipped open the phone with one hand and brought it to his ear. The voice coming through the receiver was as familiar as Dylan's own face.

"Judge," Dylan acknowledged. It was his father.

At the sound of the older man's undeniable pleasure, a sudden pang of guilt added to Dylan's lousy mood. For eight years he'd been as detached from D. B. Matthews as he'd been from the women who had come into his life and then gone.

Worse, that detachment was almost the only damn thing Dylan was glad about when he woke up in the mornings.

"Yes, sir, I made it," he assured the judge. Apparently Dylan's former first-grade teacher had spotted him on his way into town and called his father. Though how the hell she'd recognized him under his helmet and tinted visor, he didn't know. That was Hot Water for you.

"Tell Mrs. Macy I appreciate her phoning you, Judge. Yes, tell her I noticed those True Heart roses growing over her front trellis too. Sure. That I'm not surprised she won first place in the county fair last month."

He listened again, then gave a little squeeze to the slender wrist in his hand, putting the woman whom it belonged to on notice. "I'll stop by the courthouse as soon as I conclude a little . . . business," he said, smiling down at Kitty wolfishly. Plucked nerves usually provided quicker answers.

Then he thumbed the phone off and slid it back into his pocket. Still holding Kitty's arm, he rocked back on his heels and gave her his full attention. "Now, where were we?" He smiled again, the wolf still prowling.

The pulse at her wrist kicked up, beating against his thumb like frantic but useless moth wings. "H-how's your father?" she said quickly. "I'm sure he's glad you're home."

Dylan shook his head. "No, babe, that's not where we were at all."

"Still." She tried tugging her arm from his grasp, but he hung on as a faint breath of warmed rose perfume tickled his nose. "You have to know the whole town will be delighted by your visit."

Which was the reason in a nutshell, Dylan thought, that he'd never visited before. He didn't want them killing the fatted calf, thank you very much. He didn't deserve it. "I'm only here because of you, Kitty."

Her baby blues widened a fraction. "I'm, uh, flattered."

He ground his teeth. "I take it back," he told her. "Number eighty-eight is a method for wusses. Three-thirty-two is much more satisfying. So unless you want to learn firsthand *how* satisfying . . ."

Her gaze hastily fell to a point just below his throat, and, smart woman that she was, she started talking hastily too. "The thing is, Dylan, I'd like to explain everything, I really would, but I can't discuss this right now."

Not so smart after all.

Yet she valiantly pressed on, at the same time trying again to ease her arm from his grasp. "Perhaps some other time, some other day, but, well, now, you see, I need to lock up and—"

"The front door's already locked." He halted her sly attempts to get away from him by hauling her close, so close that he could feel the heat from her body and almost taste the spicy-sweet perfume rising from her flesh. "It's just you and me, Kitty. So talk."

He could see the wheels spinning inside her head, searching for another diversionary tactic. "What do you want?" she finally demanded. "An apology? Okay. So I'm sorr—"

"An apology!" he exploded.

She jerked, causing the stupid ostrich feather in her hair to catch on his afternoon whiskers. He reached to brush the thing aside at the same instant she did, and their hands met, merged. This time he felt more than a tingle. Like a hornet's sting, her touch pricked him, sending a heated buzz speeding up his arm. Ignoring the sensation, he latched onto her fingers and forced her hand down.

They were both breathing hard, and with their fingers entwined, hand to wrist, chest to chest, the only thing between them now was Kitty's secrets. "I don't want an apology," he bit out. "I *want* an explanation—"

He broke off, distracted, as the lace at the neckline of Kitty's dress grazed his T-shirt like a sexy tickle with each of her breaths. Focusing hard, he started over. "I *want* reparation—"

His mind spun off again. That carnal scent of full-blown roses intensified and he tensed, anticipating her next breath and the next erotic caress of lace on cotton. Her gaze glued to his face, Kitty again wet her pouty bottom lip with her tongue. Another sharp sting of . . . something pierced his body. Hot and dizzying, it pulsed like truth serum through his bloodstream.

"I want . . ." He closed his eyes. *Jesus what-the-hell-was-wrong-with-him Christ.*

What he all at once wanted—was this more pay-back?—was her. At this inappropriate time, with this in-appropriate woman, he was turned on! Kitty, with her devious ways, her innocent eyes, and her take-me mouth, turned him on.

He was turned on by . . . his wife.

No. Shaking off the ridiculous reaction, he snapped open his eyes and stared down at her. "Now, dammit," he said, making his voice cold and insistent, "tell me why you did this."

A flush spread from her throat to her cheeks and it seemed to make her lips rosier too. Despite a new, un-welcome rush of hard to his hard-on, he forced himself to remain still as, on her long breath, the lace of her dress once more slowly stroked his chest.

She opened her mouth.

Now, he thought. Now he'd get the answers he wanted.

"I—"

"Kitty!" *Bam. Bam.* "Kitty!" Just a few feet from where they stood, the front door of the brothel was shaken by heavy knocks. The voice outside sounded young, loud, and anxious. "Kitty!"

Her eyes darted to the door. Her body tried to do the same thing.

"Forget about it," Dylan said, hanging onto her. "I've traveled four hundred miles and eight years. This comes first."

Her eyes widened. "Dylan—"

Another barrage of impatient knocks cut off whatever she intended to say. So instead, she glared at him. Those blue eyes and long, curly lashes weren't the least bit effective against his intent to strangle her for answers if he had to.

"Kitty!" Both the voice and the knocking sounded more anxious and more urgent. "*Kitty!*"

Once more her eyes darted from Dylan's face to the door and then back again. Shit. What blue eyes and long, curly lashes couldn't do for a glare, they could sure as hell do with a plead.

He groaned. If his prick weren't still so damn hard, he'd swear he was going soft.

Then he sighed. The truth was, with all that yelling and with his own spawned-by-the-devil arousal, he wouldn't be able to concentrate on what she said right now anyway. Cursing himself, he threw up his hands. "Go ahead, answer it."

At her release, she dashed to the door and pulled it open. On the other side stood a gangly, freckle-faced teenager dressed in old-fashioned clothes and cap. "Kitty! You've got to come. There's an emergency."

Her hand crept over her stomach. "Jeremy, what is it?"

"I hate to tell you this, Kitty, but it's the sheriff again," Jeremy said. "He's naked and he's asking for you."

A bead of sweat rolled down Kitty's spine as she contemplated "Sheriff" Beau Caruso, sprawled on the wooden sidewalk in the shade outside the restored jail. Twenty years ago the citizens of Hot Water had wisely decided to preserve the past while ensuring a tourist-filled future. By creating a living-history district as well as an area of restaurants and specialty and antique shops, the town had maximized its attraction to sightseers. Although the sidewalk overhangs a few streets north were strung with yard after yard of misting hose to cool off the visitors sipping their Lola Montez iced lattes or licking their Mark Twain Mango frozen yogurt cones, in Hot Water's Old Town the atmosphere was kept as authentic as possible.

Meaning there was no relief from the ninety-plus degrees, though Sheriff Beau didn't seem the least affected by the heat. Propped against the jail's sturdy front door without an apparent care in the world, he wiggled his fingers at her in good-natured greeting. He wore nothing but a hand-tooled holster—fitted with two twenty-four-ounce cans of beer instead of revolvers—an astonishing pelt of body hair, and a drunken grin. A white straw hat, on his lap instead of his head, was the only thing keeping him decent.

And Kitty wanted to fall to her knees beside him. She wanted to throw her arms around his burly, bushy chest and kiss him.

But due to the small knot of other Old Town reenactors around her, she resisted the impulse.

"You're going to have to fire him," said Mrs. Shea, of Shea's Dry Goods. The long skirt of her beige calico costume twitched in disapproval. "You only gave him one more chance, Kitty Wilder."

"I don't know, Mrs. Shea." Not only was Kitty willing to kiss Beau, she was willing to give him a thousand more chances, just in case one of them might rescue her from another confrontation with Dylan Matthews. "If I fire Beau, who will be sheriff?" She eyed the others around her.

"I'm committed to the livery stable," Jeremy said. "Nobody else knows how to drive the wagon."

"And you know I won't do it," Spenser Marsh added, his quavery voice anxious. "I'm only in the assay office until Friday. After that I'm visiting my granddaughter in Oregon for a week. I have a great-grandson to meet."

Kitty patted his liver-spotted hand. "I know, Spenser. It's on the schedule." Along the way, somewhere, somehow, her duties as "head" of the Hot Water Preservation Society's one-person advertising and PR department had also come to include hiring the reenactors and arranging their hours.

Some reenactors, like Spenser and her own great-aunt Cat, worked just enough to make them feel like they were contributing to the community's history and to minimally supplement their pensions. Others, like Jeremy, counted on the summer job to help pay for college tuition.

"By the way, we're nearly out of souvenir passports," Mrs. Shea said. "And someone stole the gold nuggets from the display at the assay office." She cast Kitty a sidelong, suspicious glance, as if the culprit might be Kitty herself.

Even other reenactors made it their life's work to try her patience as often as possible, Kitty thought, sighing inwardly. She smiled, though. "Thank you, Mrs. Shea. There's an order of passports ready at the print shop. I'll pick it up in the morning and take care of the display in the assay office after that." With the help of a handful of rocks and the can of spray paint she kept in her utility closet, she could easily replace the missing "gold."

Then a pop-hiss, signaling the opening of Sheriff Beau's next malt and barley beverage, refocused Mrs. Shea's displeasure. Her skirts twitched again as she pointed to the inebriated reenactor. "Fine. But what are you going to do about *him*?"

Kitty knew the older woman meant the beer-guzzling Beau, but that didn't stop her mind from leaping to the very same question. Regarding Dylan.

Another round of breathless panic dizzied her again, and she gulped in a breath. That Dylan had finally discovered she'd legally registered their marriage bee-lined beyond embarrassment on a straight path toward humiliation. If she faced him again, he was going to want to know why.

Her stomach churned. How could she describe her

state of mind? Eight years before, she'd been barely eighteen when she'd woken alone in a strange bed—*his* bed—nearly naked and with the first and only hangover of her life. She'd registered the marriage certificate she'd found on the floor beneath her discarded blue jeans because . . .

God. She didn't know a non-humiliating way to explain the impulse. Partly it had been a way to keep hold of some of that night's magic. Of the magic night the most handsome, most sought-after, most *respected* young man in town had talked to her, one of the notorious Wilders. Really *talked* to her. He'd laughed with her, kissed her. Married her, and then—

"He's going to keep causing problems," Spenser predicted, giving his head a mournful shake. "You better get rid of him."

Kitty's eyes widened. "You think I can just tell him to lea—" She cut herself off, remembering they were talking about Beau, while she'd been thinking about Dylan. She was *still* thinking about him. What was she going to do when he caught up with her again?

Biting her lip, Kitty glanced up the steep rise of dusty Main Street. For six blocks, gingerbread Victorians sat cheek by jowl beside more rustic buildings of hand-shaped brick and native stone. Most of the buildings were narrow, with second-floor balconies hanging over the wooden sidewalks. Iron shutters stood ready on either side of the windows of the oldest buildings—the best fireproofing from a time when fire was a common, deadly enemy.

Her roots on these streets went all the way back to 1849, when men were pulling a pound of gold a day out of Piney Creek. They'd named their camp Hot Water for the steaming spring that bubbled to the surface in the crotch of the nearby hills. Unlike many boomtowns, though, after the gold panned out, prosperity didn't.

Thanks to its central location, the early residents of Hot Water had made their fortunes the way most successful people in the Gold Rush times did—by selling goods and services to the thousands of miners who came chasing a dream. The profit on the sales of provisions, picks, pans, and, yes, sex had built a small but thriving community.

But maybe now was the time for Kitty to yank up her over one-hundred-fifty-year-old roots. Right now. Instead of waiting until summer's end, she could pack in the middle of the night and go, avoiding Dylan and—

"Kitty?" Spenser's silver brows connected over a nose that had convinced her years ago that some features of a person never stopped growing. "Is something the matter?"

Kitty sighed, her hopefulness dying. Leaving right away was no solution at all. Creeping out of Hot Water at midnight would leave the Hot Water Preservation Society in a lurch, right at the height of a less-than-stellar tourist season. People she cared for deeply, like Spenser, like Aunt Cat, would be not only hurt but affected financially. Spenser's part-time work as assay officer paid for his cherished visits to his granddaughter in Oregon. The money Kitty made at The Burning Rose would repay the college debt she owed Aunt Cat, something she'd vowed to do by summer's end.

She sighed again. "Everything's fine, Spenser."

As if Beau agreed, he let out a loud, bullfrog-worthy

belch. Then he grinned proudly, his eyes focusing some-where around Mrs. Shea's knees. "Wherz Kitty?" he asked. "Here, kitty kitty kitty kitty."

"I'm here, Beau," Kitty said.

He swigged another gulp from his beer can. "Kitty kitty kitty kitty kitty," he called again.

"What is it, Beau?" she said more loudly. "I'm right here."

He looked up, blinking as if dazzled. "I'm no good," he replied morosely. "No-good sher'ff, kitty kitty kitty kitty kitty."

"No, Beau, you're good," Kitty corrected hastily. "You're a good sheriff." Not strictly true, because he was actually better at beer drinking than he was at any-thing else.

"Kitty—" Mrs. Shea began.

"A fine sheriff." Kitty spoke over the other woman. On the weekends, it was the lawman's mock arrests that really drew the crowds, and the bottom line was there wasn't anyone besides Beau to do the job.

"Wanna drink. When I drink I don' remember. Don' wanna remember they're coming back."

Mrs. Shea made a disgusted sound and Kitty sighed. A month ago a roaring-drunk Beau had visited the real county sheriff's office with a garbled story about a fly-ing saucer and his temporary abduction by aliens. They were coming back, he'd insisted.

He'd struggled even harder with staying sober since.

Kitty sighed again. "Beau, we need you to stop this behavior if you're going to be the Old Town sheriff."

Beau held up his beer can, eyeing it with love. "Don' wanna be sher'ff no more."

"Aha!" Mrs. Shea smiled triumphantly.

"No, Beau—"

"He quit, Kitty," the older woman interrupted. "You can't ignore it."

"He's going to change his mind," Kitty countered. "Right this minute. Aren't you, Beau?"

The clatter of Beau's empty beer can hitting the wooden sidewalk made it clear he'd changed his mind, all right. About remaining conscious. As the drained can rolled toward Kitty's toes, Beau's eyes closed and his chin dropped to his chest.

"He's through," Mrs. Shea declared.

"No, no." Kitty nudged him with her foot, managing only to awaken a series of rumbling snores.

"Through," Spenser agreed.

Kitty looked at Jeremy, but even he just shrugged in apology.

Accepting defeat, Kitty recruited the young man to help her half drag, half carry Beau back inside the jail. Spenser followed with Beau's hat, and after debating, they left him sleeping in the middle of the floor. Tsking for all she was worth, Mrs. Shea draped his clothes over him. Kitty took his car keys; Spenser, the rest of the beer. Then the four let themselves out and locked the jail behind them.

By the time they'd finished with Beau, it was well past the hour of closing and the last visitors to Old Town had departed. The other reenactors had already locked up their buildings and left for the day as well. Spenser and Mrs. Shea hurried off, leaving Kitty and Jeremy in a virtual ghost town.

Kitty hesitated before returning to The Burning Rose,

rubbing her temples to banish the headache threatening to bloom. How was she going to replace Beau?

She inhaled a long breath, capturing the mingled scents of home—hot, orangey dirt; crisp, curling oak leaves; the trace of mossy-wet left in the summer-low creek beds. All the elements she'd breathed her entire twenty-six years lingered inside her, including just the barest undertone of the clean, tangy scent of the pine trees that grew profusely a few miles up State Route 49 as the elevation climbed toward the Sierra Nevada mountains.

If she managed to solve her sheriff dilemma and duck Dylan, in mere weeks those particular problems and this particular scent would be only a memory. Her heart gave a strange little squeeze, and Kitty breathed in deeply again. Yes, she'd miss the smell of home. Still, she couldn't stay in Hot Water anymore.

If nothing else, Dylan's return underscored that. Achieving a conventional life in Hot Water was as much a fantasy as her eight-year-old memory of his tenderness the night they'd married. His dark, angry eyes and his ruthless grip on her today were proof of that. Everything about him was hard and unforgiving now—his words, his hands, his body. She shivered.

She'd done that earlier this afternoon too. Shivered against him despite herself and his obvious anger, her breasts suddenly aching and her nipples tight. As on their wedding night when—

"Kitty?"

She blinked, startled to find Jeremy still standing beside her. "I'm sorry. Did you say something?"

His gaze skipped away from hers as a flush threatened to overtake his ginger freckles. "I was wondering, I was just thinking . . . would you like to go out for a—for a drink?"

Unsurprised by the invitation, yet still uncomfortable with it, Kitty responded with a stern frown. He was younger than she and not of legal drinking age, though that was the least of it. "You know your mother would give you heck for being out with a Wilder, Jeremy." That was the most of it.

Instantly, his cute freckles were completely lost in an even deeper blush, and Kitty felt a pang of sympathy. No one knew better than she the powerful influence a mother could have on one's life.

"I don't care—" he began.

"I can't go anyway," she interrupted gently. "I need to check on Aunt Cat tonight." The hardest part of leaving Hot Water would be leaving her great-aunt. When Kitty's seventeen-year-old mother had run off, the elderly woman had raised Kitty in true Wilder-woman tradition—without anyone else, especially a man. "I'll see you tomorrow, Jeremy, okay?"

Though he sent Kitty a last mournful look, he obediently clapped his old-fashioned cloth cap on his head and turned away. She sighed. A scarlet woman's lot was a lonely existence.

Jeremy's departure left her alone with her thoughts too. What a mess. The Beau problem ran a pale second to Dylan's knowledge of their marriage. From the moment she'd impulsively sent the certificate on its way to Sacramento, she'd never said a word to anyone about it, half appalled and half thrilled at her daring. The marriage had been her secret, maybe even her secret rebellion.

Though eighteen, she'd been childishly convinced that she was owed something, something just for herself, after what had been the best and worst night of her life. As time went on and Dylan never came back to confront her, she'd worried about how the secret might affect his career. But then, after even more time had passed, she'd buried her guilt as best she could by living a blame-free, good-girl life.

But how was she going to save herself now? She couldn't explain what she'd done and she couldn't run away. The only solution lay with Dylan. Okay, so maybe it wasn't a likely solution, but she was latching onto it all the same. After all, he'd been gone for eight years. The only hope she had was that he'd go away for another eight.

Chapter Three

Walking the few blocks from the living-history district to her great-aunt's Victorian cottage, Kitty skulked from one long late-afternoon shadow to the next. Though she had every finger and every toe crossed that Dylan had departed Hot Water, it did seem a bit of a stretch. And while anyone would agree she possessed an extraordinarily positive nature, even this quality was having trouble giving credence to her other vain hope that if he still was in town and happened to pass by, he wouldn't recognize her out of the madam's costume and in her own T-shirt and cutoff overalls.

Luckily for her, in this part of Hot Water the mature trees—sycamores, oaks, and sugar maples—were tall and lush, casting shade on the meticulously painted, pastel-hued Victorian homes, their front gardens, and the narrow sidewalks bordering the winding streets. As she neared the last corner undetected, she smiled, visualizing a cold glass of Aunt Cat's iced tea.

For sanity's sake, she'd make up some sort of excuse and bed down in her old room at Aunt Cat's too, just in case Dylan knew the address of her own place. By tomorrow, surely, she would have figured out a way to handle him, their marriage, and whatever she was going to do about it.

Rounding the corner, she dug her thick-soled sandals into the asphalt. Strangers. Three doors away, on the sidewalk outside Aunt Cat's waist-high white picket fence, stood four thirty-something women. They were wearing the kind of matching city-chic, linen-and-silk shorts outfits that screamed Chardonnay at five and the occasional midweek getaway at an elegant spa or a picturesque bed-and-breakfast. Of course, with The Stafford House Bed & Breakfast just a half block past Aunt Cat's home, guests like these wandered by all the time. Frowning, Kitty shook off her momentary fluster and strode on.

Except these ladies weren't wandering, Kitty realized as she got closer, her nerves jangling another warning. They were standing. Gawking, really, right in the direction of her aunt's front door. Kitty's heart jumped. Was something amiss with Aunt Cat?

Then one of the Chardonnay ladies shifted, and beyond her, Kitty glimpsed a menacing-looking machine parked against the curb. A motorcycle. The kind of motorcycle that would drive off by itself with a snide snort of laughter unless its rider was dressed in black clothes—all black—and wore his black hair loose and dangerous.

Her mouth tightened. Dylan wouldn't have gone to Aunt Cat, would he? Afraid to answer her own question, she continued toward the group of giggling women. "Can I help you?" she called out.

Their heads whipped toward her; then they looked at one another and giggled again. Darn it, Kitty recognized that giggle. It had followed Dylan around since he was thirteen years old. Even at eight, she'd noticed it and understood on some deeply feminine level what the sound meant.

Her temper rose. Darn *him*. Dylan *was* at Aunt Cat's.

Brushing past the women, she put her hand on the gate latch.

"Excuse me?" This Chardonnay lady wore her shorts outfit in a tasteful mauve, her lipstick matching its exact shade.

Kitty paused. "Did you need some help? Directions? A restaurant recommendation?" Yeah, right. She knew what they wanted.

"We thought . . . we thought we recognized the man that just went inside." The woman pointed toward Aunt Cat's one-story house, its Victorian styling nearly hidden by the front yard's flourishing greenery.

Kitty sighed inwardly. Hot Water wasn't a cave. Of course she'd read newspaper accounts of Dylan's exploits. One night she'd accidentally happened upon the E! channel when it was profiling him and the story of a French model-turned-actress he'd saved from a stalker the previous year. At first she'd felt sorry for the childlike, scrawny woman, until she'd spied the model's *un*childlike breasts and the way her scrawny fingers clutched Kitty's husb—*Dylan's* arm.

"Is it . . . ?" the woman prompted with another breathless giggle. Obviously she didn't live in a cave either.

But that didn't mean Kitty had to encourage her interest. She widened her eyes, pretending alarm. "We hoped no one would spot him. He won't hurt you, though, I swear. He's on medication and the probation board insists—quite rightly—that he wear an electronic ankle monitor twenty-four/seven."

"Medication?" The lady blinked. "Probation?"

"Ankle monitor?" another echoed. All the giggles subsided.

"He's not Dylan Matthews?" a third questioned. "You know. The FBI agent."

Kitty plastered her backside against the gate and took a white picket in each fist, as if barring the way in. Why spend seven summers acting the madam if she couldn't portray a moll when need be?

"What's that about the FBI?" she said, faking more distress. "They've had their chance at him. He paid for *all* his federal crimes. All of them, I tell you."

Then, lifting a hand to tap forefinger to cheek, she pretended to reconsider. "Well, except maybe for . . ."

The rest wasn't necessary. The Chardonnay ladies had already hightailed their now-silenced giggles and their fancy-schmancy manicures halfway down the street. Squaring her shoulders, Kitty forgot all about them as she shoved open Aunt Cat's gate, determined to do whatever was necessary to stop Dylan. If someone was going to break the news that Kitty was the first Wilder woman to wed in over one hundred and fifty years, it better not be the guy she'd married.

The front door let out its usual loud squeal. It swung straight into the living room, so Kitty didn't have far to go to face the man she'd hoped never to see again.

He looked just as lean, dark, and gorgeous as he had at The Burning Rose. She suppressed a little hiccup of reaction as he met her gaze from his place on the couch. Then he unfolded his tall body and got to his feet.

Kitty blinked. Did he realize he was thwarted so soon and was leaving already? But his mean-looking motorcycle boots didn't move.

"Good afternoon," he said, nodding, his feet still not moving.

She blinked again. Then, suddenly understanding, she felt goose bumps rise on her arms. He had stood for her. As a signal of respect for _her_. Okay, fine, it was just a dose of old-fashioned good manners, but still, it was manners a man showed a _lady_.

"Hello, dear."

Kitty turned her head toward her Aunt Cat. Even at eighty and after two mild strokes, her aunt was like all the Wilder women but Kitty; she had beauty, a _presence_, and was ultrafeminine and completely at ease with herself. "Hi."

"Look who came by to visit me, of all people," Aunt Cat said, sounding pleased. "Dylan Matthews. Sit down, Kitty, and let me get you a glass of iced tea." She was already walking toward the kitchen, not one silver hair out of place, not one wrinkle in her long, flowered skirt and round-necked white blouse.

Glancing down at her own overall shorts and clunky sandals, Kitty felt like a female character from a _Dukes of Hazzard_ rerun, only without the prerequisite centerfold bosom. "Thank you, I'd love a glass."

She smiled sunnily and took a seat on a nearby cushioned armchair. The instant her aunt disappeared from the room, however, Kitty transformed that sunny smile into a vicious scowl. "Why are you bothering Aunt Cat?" she whispered to Dylan. "This is between you and me."

He settled back on the couch, obviously not the least bit put out by her unwelcoming tone. "Exactly. And I suspected you'd try hiding from me here. Gee, seems I was right."

Kitty scowled again. "How did you know where my great-aunt lives anyway?"

Dylan's deep-set eyes couldn't hide his surprise. He raised his dark eyebrows. "C'mon, kid. I'm with the FBI."

Her scowl deepened. *Kid*. Then she swallowed, appalled by a sudden, new thought. "Are you telling me the FBI has a . . . has a file on me?"

He shrugged. "*Now* they do."

Kitty froze. Swallowed. Tried to think. Couldn't. With a wave of her fingers, she flicked away the whole disturbing idea of an FBI file and whatever the heck that might mean. "Just swear to me," she said fiercely, returning to the crisis at hand. "Swear to me you didn't tell her."

"I haven't got around to it yet."

Kitty's heart leaped in relief and she launched herself from her chair to fall on her knees in front of his place on the couch. She took each of his legs in a desperate grip. "Don't say anything. Please." Breaking the Wilderwoman tradition was something she could maybe explain, someday. But having kept it a secret for eight years . . . Aunt Cat would never understand.

He regarded her with a spark of new interest in his eyes. "You know what? I kind of like you in that position."

"Ooh." As if burned, Kitty shoved away from him to stand up.

"What's the matter, dear?" Aunt Cat held out a tall, icy glass.

Kitty took it and returned to her seat, shooting a quelling look at Dylan. Then inspiration struck. She smiled sweetly. "I was just expressing my sincere disappointment that Dylan must be going. Right away."

It was Aunt Cat who looked sincerely disappointed. "But he just arrived."

Dylan grinned at Kitty. "Yeah, but I just arrived."

Kitty speared him with another pointed glance. "Yes, but he has so many people to see while he's here."

Aunt Cat sighed. "I'm sure you're right about that. Did you know this is Dylan's first vacation from the FBI in almost eight years? He was just telling me he has so much time saved up they made him take three months off."

Almost eight years ago, on the night he'd married Kitty, his bags had been packed for the FBI Academy. Though he'd arrived home that summer with the intention of returning to Berkeley in September for his second year of law school, the tragic events in late June had brought him to the attention of some federal agents. Almost eight years ago, sitting on the banks of Piney Creek on his last night in town, he'd confessed to Kitty, and to Kitty alone, his secret decision to leave law school and attend the Academy instead.

Her heart squeezed, feeling a nostalgic pang for the naive teenage girl who had been so flattered and thrilled he'd chosen to confide in her. "Eight years?" she echoed, as if she didn't know exactly how many days and months had passed. "He's been very busy, I suppose."

"Oh, yeah," Dylan said. "I've been busy catching up with all the bad guys."

His dark good looks were no less brooding and romantic than they'd been that night, and Kitty could almost forgive herself for the foolishness of marrying him.

"The world is full of dishonest people," he continued. Then smiled. At her.

Dishonest people, he'd said. Meaning *her*.

She bristled, her sentimental recollections evaporating. "Dishonest?!"

He raised his eyebrows. "What would you call it?"

Young. Silly. Starstruck.

She took a calming breath. "I'd call it a conversation we should have some other time." And never in front of Aunt Cat. "But it's getting late now, and I'm sure you're hungry—"

"Oh, forgive me," Aunt Cat interjected. "I should have set something out. It will just take a minute for crackers and cheese . . ." She was bustling toward the kitchen before Kitty could stop her.

So she glared at Dylan instead. "I don't want Aunt Cat involved in this, I told you. So just go now, Dylan. I'll make your excuses."

He shook his head, and the late-afternoon light flashed on the links of a thin gold chain hanging around his neck. "And never catch up with you again? I don't think so. Not until we set a place and a time to talk this out."

Panic rose in Kitty's chest again, clogging her throat.

She never wanted to talk it out. "I'll take care of . . . the problem," she said hoarsely. "I promise."

"When?" he asked bluntly. "In another eight years?"

Kitty flushed. He'd backed her neatly into a corner and she didn't like the feeling. "What's the emergency?" she grumbled. "Afraid you'll feel guilty about your swinging bachelorhood?"

"Kitty, you beat me to it." Aunt Cat was back in the room, a platter in her hands. "Pass this to Dylan, won't you, dear?"

"I beat you to what?" Kitty obediently took the platter and walked it over to Dylan.

Aunt Cat smiled mischievously. "Dylan's bachelor status, of course. I've heard rumors about a wedding."

Kitty's hands jerked.

Dylan's reflexes were quick enough to catch the edge of the plate as it dipped. He held it steady and looked beyond Kitty. "Excuse me, Ms. Wilder?"

Kitty's mind whirled. "Redding," she said quickly. "Aunt Cat wants to know if you've ever been to Redding, California. You know, farther north." She had no idea what Aunt Cat was talking about, but with Dylan's cooperation, maybe they could redirect the conversation so it wouldn't go into what sounded like dangerous territory.

Dylan's lip curled. "She asked me about a *wedding*."

So much for cooperation.

"Kitty, are you all right?" Aunt Cat asked. "I certainly did say 'wedding.' " Her mischievous smile broke out again. "Forgive my nosiness, Dylan, but I read a tabloid at the hairdresser's that said you were marrying Honor Witherspoon."

Kitty's jaw dropped. "Honor Witherspoon?" That

was the name of the heiress the FBI—starring Dylan—
had rescued from a kidnapping a few months before.
She'd read the newspaper accounts, but apparently there
was more to the story than what *USA Today* and *The
Sacramento Bee* had reported.

Dylan's face went blank. Careful, federal-employee,
G-man blank. "Honor and I are just friends."

Kitty stared at him. *Just friends*? Not "friends,"
which could actually mean friends, but *just friends*. Her
throat tightened. Still holding the untouched platter of
cheese and crackers, she walked stiffly back to her chair
and sat down.

"Ah." Aunt Cat nodded. "Of course I don't believe
everything I read, but it does sound as if that young
woman's father wants you in the family."

Honor Witherspoon. Of course Dylan would want to
end his marriage to Kitty so he could be free for someone with a pedigree like Honor Witherspoon. The
woman's father had taken his old money and invested it
in new technology, along the way making his daughter,
Honor, one of the filthy-richest heiresses in the world. It
was said her bedroom was papered in stock certificates
and her platinum card was, well, platinum.

Kitty felt strangely . . . something.

"Dear? Kitty?"

She looked over at Aunt Cat. "What?"

"Dylan just asked you a question."

She didn't want to look at him. "What question?"

Aunt Cat frowned. "He asked you out to dinner."

"No." It was stupid to feel . . . betrayed, but there it
was. "I don't want to."

Aunt Cat blinked at her rude tone. "Kitty . . ."

That sense of betrayal, of hurt, put fire in her voice. "I bet he can handle it, Aunt Cat. I'm sure women must have said no and even 'I don't' to Dylan before."

"As a matter of fact, it's the 'I dos' that have been causing me trouble lately," he murmured.

Kitty narrowed her eyes, but forced herself to keep it polite for Aunt Cat. "Maybe some other time, okay?" she said, pasting on a smile.

His nostrils flared. "I'm afraid to let you out of my sight. You can't keep running from it, Kitty. From me."

She winced. *Wilder Women Don't Wed And They Don't Run.* "Cut me some slack, will you? I've had a really rough day."

Aunt Cat's puzzled expression was suddenly wiped clean with sympathy. "Oh, dear," she said. "I didn't know about your day. What's the trouble?"

Kitty's heart, still stinging from that irrational feeling of betrayal, was soothed by her aunt's genuine concern. "Men," she mumbled.

Aunt Cat leaned forward. "What did you say?"

Dylan leaned back, crossing his arms over his wide chest. "She said, I believe, 'Men.' "

Kitty slid him a quelling glance. "I had to let the sheriff go."

One of Dylan's dark eyebrows rose in casual inquiry. "Would that happen to be the naked sheriff?" he asked.

Kitty glanced at him again. "Yes, the naked sheriff. So I'm going to be busy tonight making phone calls or juggling schedules or something. We need a replacement."

Aunt Cat made a sympathetic noise. "We certainly do. Old Town won't be the same on the weekends if the sheriff doesn't drag you down the street and lock you up."

"*What?*" Dylan straightened, his dark eyes focused on Aunt Cat.

She looked at Dylan in surprise. "Oh, that's right. You wouldn't know." She sipped from her tea. "About five years ago Kitty concocted an idea to liven up our living history with a little playacting."

He blinked. "I see. I think."

Sighing, Aunt Cat shook her head. "The tourists are going to be very disappointed if we can't provide some exciting Old Town melodrama. We definitely need a sheriff." She glanced down at her glass, then up, then let her gaze travel first to Dylan and then to Kitty.

Oh, no. Kitty saw the idea dawning in her great-aunt's busy brain.

The elderly woman opened her mouth. "How about—"

"No," Kitty blurted out.

"But it would be perfect," Aunt Cat protested. She turned toward Dylan. "Right?"

"Right, what?" he asked warily. "What are you talking about?"

Aunt Cat smiled, the Wilder smile that had enchanted men for generations . . . until Kitty's. "I'm thinking *you* could be our sheriff," Aunt Cat said triumphantly.

Kitty took in Dylan's stunned expression and her panic subsided. Surely he wouldn't agree. *Immediately* he wouldn't agree.

Instead, after that initial moment of shock, he ran both hands over his head to smooth his long dark hair. Then he looked at Kitty, speculation, amusement, and—oh, no—*satisfaction* in his eyes.

A smile tugged at the corners of his full, sexy

mouth. "What was that you mentioned?" he said to Aunt Cat, though his gaze never left Kitty's face. "Something about dragging Kitty down the street and locking her up?"

Planning to return and put Kitty out of her misery after she'd had a chance to stew for a while, Dylan left his motorcycle at Cat Wilder's house. On foot, he wandered aimlessly through the residential streets, glad for the camouflage of the deepening dusk. After leaving the brothel that afternoon, he'd visited the judge at the courthouse. His father had grabbed him by the arm and paraded him past dozens of old friends and acquaintances. Dylan had shaken hands with men he'd known his entire life. He'd been peppered with old-lady kisses.

But despite—because of?—their welcomes, the homecoming pained him. It was still Hot Water, with the people who had witnessed all his triumphs and all his disgrace, and it didn't make it any easier that no one seemed to hold the latter against him.

Their blindness to his failure was what he couldn't accept. It seemed so damned unjust. He rubbed his chest, his palm finding the gold St. Barbara medal he wore beneath his shirt. For God's sake, he knew better than most that life wasn't fair, but there was something . . . unforgivable in all the forgiveness he'd found here eight years ago.

They'd called him a hero, when he'd known he was a fraud.

It was why he'd left. It was why he hadn't ever come back. It was why he'd do whatever it took to break the

ties of this insane marriage to Kitty, because it tied him
to the town.

He took a deep breath of the warm, clean, weed-
scented air, so much lighter and invigorating than the
heavy ozone and toxins that passed as oxygen in L.A.
The scent of roses from someone's nearby garden
drifted by his nose, reminding him of Kitty, and a smile
pulled at his mouth.

She'd stomped into her aunt's living room, farmer's
daughter cum Valkyrie, her long golden hair held back
by a knot halfway down her back. He hadn't been able
to look away from that for a minute—the astonishing
sight of that silky hair *knotted* like a hank of rope.

But the only thing on Kitty's mind had been keeping
her secret. He didn't know why she worried about her
aunt learning about their so-called marriage, and he was
trying not to care. Not that he was particularly eager for
anyone else to know either, but his curiosity about
Kitty's motivation was even more dangerous.

When you grew up in a town the small size of Hot
Water, your fellow residents became like extended family. Since he'd watched her grow up, he found it hard to
resist turning the puzzle of her character into a crossword he knew most of the answers to. But detachment
and distance had worked for him for eight years and
would work best for him now.

Which was why he hadn't for a minute seriously considered playing the part of sheriff, though he hadn't
been able to resist pulling Kitty's tail about it. For God's
sake, she deserved a little torture after what she'd put
him through.

It had been a hell of a shock when Warren Wither-

spoon had taken him to lunch the week before and asked
him about his wife. Of course, he'd already been reeling
at the idea that the man had investigated him, but that
was nothing compared to the bombshell that he'd been
married for nearly eight years.

Warren had suggested siccing a lawyer on her, but Dylan believed a man cleaned up his own messes, at least as
well as he could. That was the reason he'd joined the FBI.

Besides, he figured taking a day or so to clear up the
marriage was his ticket out of the rest of the worthless,
three-month vacation he'd "agreed" to. Even before the
sticky marriage issue had come up, the supervisor of the
L.A. FBI field office had claimed Dylan needed the time
away as a cure for his increasing tiredness.

But what L.A.'s Special Agent in Charge, David
"Deuce" Ducent, didn't know was that Dylan couldn't
sleep at all unless he worked his caseload to the point of
exhaustion. The clincher to Dylan's decision to come to
Hot Water was that he figured if he returned to L.A.
unmarried—or nearly so— Deuce would prove his sal-
vation by waiving Dylan's remaining vacation. Dylan
didn't want more time to think.

A Siamese cat dashed across his path. Startled, he
nearly stepped on its tail, and it gave him a reproachful
look from its wide blue eyes, then stopped directly in
front of him to clean its foreleg. Time was, Dylan had
known every citizen of Hot Water, and nearly all the
cats, dogs, and horses by name as well.

"Hey, buddy." He crouched to rub the Siamese between the ears in apology. It stretched into his hand, its
warm fur as soothing as a pleasant memory.

Okay. So he missed the animals. What was wrong

with that? His sterile condo complex in L.A. didn't allow pets. There was probably some regulation against person-to-person socializing too, because he couldn't think of the name of any one of his neighbors.

"That's Tinkerbell," a voice said.

He looked up. Kitty. Somehow she'd found him, and he couldn't tell if she was happy or sad about it. Standing in the twilight, she had her hands jammed in the front pockets of those cut-short overalls. Her endless legs flowed from ragged threads to sandals with thick soles that looked fashioned from old snow tires. Her stance was belligerent. Her shoulders were squared.

Her harlot's mouth was sulky.

He went hard.

She shifted, affording him a quick peekaboo glimpse of one breast beneath her overall bib. Though now covered with T-shirt cotton instead of half bared by her madam's dress, he remembered exactly how their slight mounds had been pushed up and forward earlier that afternoon. Years ago one of Dylan's frat brothers had evangelized that a woman's breasts need be only large enough to fill a champagne glass or a man's mouth. Well, hallelujah. For the first time, Dylan could call himself a true believer.

Slowly straightening, he captured her gaze with his so she wouldn't have a chance to notice the telltale bulge in his jeans. He couldn't afford the sign of weakness.

She shuffled her feet restlessly against the sidewalk, and Tinkerbell the cat beelined for her legs, twining itself against her long, smooth calves.

Dylan's gaze followed its movements. "Lucky cat," he said.

"What?" she asked, her eyes widening.

He slanted another look at her drool-worthy legs. "Lucky cat."

This time Kitty twitched.

Interesting. Dylan kept his smile to himself. His job had prepared him to observe, deduce, to find which buttons to push when. It seemed that sexual talk, even the mildest observation, made Kitty nervous. Good.

He moved closer to her. She moved back, Tinkerbell leaping to keep up with her.

"Were you looking for me?" Dylan asked.

A light breath of ripe roses drifted through the air. "I . . . I wanted to talk you out of the sheriff thing." A flush bloomed on her skin.

"Why would you want to talk me out of it?" He was quite willing to needle her. "You need a sheriff."

She bent to fondle the cat's ears, her hair in that improbable knot sliding over one shoulder. She looked young and uncertain and he thought of that crossword puzzle again and the blank squares he couldn't fill.

Kitty straightened, then started moving backward down the street to leave the cat and him behind. "You don't want to be sheriff," she said.

He caught up with her. "How do you know that?"

"You're on vacation." She turned around and continued walking. "I'm sure you want to be with your father and get reacquainted with old friends."

He winced, thinking of that afternoon and how the familiar, smiling faces had clawed at his conscience.

"You'll want to talk over old times."

God. That was worse. Thinking about the past nearly

suffocated him. Talking about it—he forced the idea
away. "What about you and me, Kitty?" he said, an edge
to his voice. "*We* have old times to hash over, don't we?"

Her footsteps quickened. "Not . . . not really."

He lengthened his stride to keep up with her. "There
was that night—"

"I don't want to talk about that night." Even though
she was walking, he could almost see her squirm.

"But—"

"I *said*, I don't want to talk about it." She made that
squirmy movement again.

He frowned, baffled. "But—"

"*No.*"

His frown deepened. "Kitty." He stopped, putting his
hand on her arm to halt her.

That sexual sting pierced his palm like a dart and he
saw her shudder with a similar response. "Hell,
Kitty . . ." Maybe they should talk about this, address
the obvious, unexpected chemistry. He turned her his
way, then froze as he noticed the sight over her shoulder,
directly across the street.

The cemetery. He dropped Kitty's arm and his heart
constricted, shriveling into a small, hard stone inside his
chest. As was common for many small towns, even
though Hot Water's graveyard had originally been situ-
ated on the outskirts, the town had grown toward it. Established by the Independent Order of Odd Fellows, a
brotherhood made popular in Gold Rush times, the
cemetery was operated by the still-thriving fraternal or-
ganization. In an ironic twist, the Odd Fellows had
deeded the adjacent land for a city park. Ever practical,

Hot Water had accepted the gift with gratitude, and despite its proximity to the dead, the park had become the center of every town celebration since.

But now, in the dinnertime almost-dark, the park was deserted. No children played on the swings; no oldsters took a stroll under the shade of the giant oaks. The only ones around to enjoy the summer night were in the cemetery, buried six feet belowground.

Except for the lone man standing beside a simple marker on a prominent knoll.

Kitty's voice was hushed. "Bram visits her every evening. Never in the day, never in the night. Always at dusk."

His heart shrinking even smaller, Dylan didn't doubt for a second that Kitty—or anyone else in the small town, for that matter—knew Bram Bennett's rituals, even rituals of grief. Inhaling a long breath, Dylan stared at the figure in the distance, his eyes burning. They were second cousins of sorts, he and Bram Bennett, and they'd been best friends since the day Dylan had learned to ride a two-wheeler, though the other man was two years older. Of course, they hadn't been best friends for a long time, because they had another, even stronger connection.

It was Dylan who had killed Bram Bennett's wife.

Chapter Four

Kitty had sought Dylan, determined to talk him out of playing sheriff, but now his attention was riveted on Bram. "Nothing changes, does it?" he said softly.

She didn't know exactly what he meant by that, but she couldn't disagree. For herself, as always, she felt hyperaware of Dylan, sensitized to his very presence. For as far back as she could remember, she always knew when he was nearby. Passing through the halls in their K-12 school, shopping in Kemper's Market, or standing in line at the post office, her skin would suddenly tingle and she'd look up, as certain who was near as if he'd whispered his name in her ear. My God, her nerves would be at a nonstop jangle if she were forced to play soiled dove to his Old Town sheriff.

Dylan continued staring across the street. "Bram's . . .

still hurting, then?" he asked, his voice strangely dispassionate, despite the concerned question.

Kitty half turned to look again at the solitary figure in the cemetery. "It's hard to tell what Bram's thinking and feeling," she said. "He's cut himself off from everyone." Not that Bram Bennett didn't have good reason for his pain and grief. Eight years ago, driving three neighborhood children into town for ice cream, his young wife had been stopped on a country road by a gun-wielding, would-be carjacker. From some distance away, Dylan had witnessed the scene, riding to the rescue on his motorcycle.

Dylan's pursuit had ultimately saved the children, making him a bona fide hero, but the gunman had managed to drag Alicia into the hills. She'd been found three days later in an abandoned cabin in the woods, dead from a gunshot wound. Federal agents had found the killer a week after that. Though the perpetrator had died in a shootout with the FBI, it hadn't brought Alicia back. And after that summer, Dylan had never returned to Hot Water either.

But he was here now, threatening the rest of Kitty's summer. Refocusing on that crucial issue, she mentally girded her loins. "Listen, Dylan, about the sher—"

A truck cruising by braked suddenly with a harsh shriek. The driver threw the car into reverse, bringing the vehicle alongside them and then slamming to an abrupt stop.

"Hot damn!" Tony Kula threw open the door, his smile overjoyed, and launched his bulk in a mighty leap in Dylan's direction. "Matthews, you son of a bitch, when were you coming to see me?"

Dylan staggered under the other man's weight, trapped in a bear hug worthy of the linebacker Tony had once been to Dylan's quarterback on the high school football team. "I was getting there, Tony," he said. "Give me a break. I've only been in town a few hours."

Still grinning, Tony released him and stepped back. "Yeah, but instead of hanging with me, you're with"— his eyes widened as he recognized her—"Kitty Wilder?"

No, Kitty thought, *nothing ever changes*. A Wilder with a Matthews . . . that was a match made for shocked expressions.

"Hi, Tony," she said, pretending she hadn't noticed his reaction.

"What's new, Tony?" Dylan asked. He nodded in the direction of the fancy truck at the curb. "The last time we talked, you didn't tell me about that."

"It's been a while, Mr. Too Damn Busy for Old Friends. What's new is that Bram finally convinced me to join his company, Enigma. The whole town's on economic high ground, thanks to the high-tech security devices we make." Tony grinned. "I tell you, Bram's a genius."

At the mention of that name, the warmth on Dylan's face fled. Kitty thought for a moment he looked agonized, but then she blinked and the expression was gone.

In the small, awkward silence that followed, she strolled over to the truck and leaned into the passenger window. "Hey, sweet thing," she said brightly to Amalie, Tony's three-year-old. "I haven't forgotten you, even if Daddy has."

Amalie smiled back, her teeth like little white pearls

against the dusky tone of her skin. Amalie was born and bred of true Gold Rush stock. Her mother, Sylvia, was descended from the Mexicans who were the very first to mine La Veta Madre—the Mother Lode—while Tony's ancestors were among the many Hawaiian people who had sought their fortunes in the area as well.

"That's right, that's right." Tony latched onto the new topic and hustled over to open the passenger door. "You've not met my girl." He unbuckled Amalie from her car seat and carried her over to Dylan. "Isn't she the prettiest ever?" With one swinging movement, he deposited the child in Dylan's arms.

Kitty's breath caught. Rather than looking awkward or uncomfortable, as she expected he might, Dylan hitched the little girl against his chest. His distant expression was banished by a slow, warm smile. "Hi, there," he said softly. "I'm Dylan."

The little girl appeared to melt. She let out a very recognizable, very feminine giggle, the oh-my-is-this-a-man-or-what? giggle that must be the theme song to Dylan's life. "Me's Amalie," she said. Then her gaze sharpened and she reached out one pudgy baby finger to hook it under the gold chain at Dylan's neck.

"What's dis?" she asked, pulling free a small medallion from beneath his shirt.

He cupped the gold circle in his palm, holding it up to her. "It's Saint Barbara."

"Church lady." Amalie nodded wisely.

He smiled again, and a sweet shiver rolled over Kitty's skin. "That's right. A legendary church lady. She was given to me by the mother of a very pretty little girl like you. A very lucky little girl who I found when she was . . . lost."

Amalie frowned, looking uncertain about this mention of other little girls. "My mommy's Sylvia," she said.

"And Sylvia is going to be just as mad as me if you don't stop by soon, Dylan," Tony declared. "We'll throw a party for you. A welcome-home party."

Amalie wriggled and Dylan set her down. "I'm only going to be here a very short ti—"

The shriek of another set of brakes interrupted. An SUV screeched to a halt behind Tony's truck, and this time two men jumped out to, by turns, curse Dylan's long absence and pound his back in exuberant welcome.

Edging away into the shadows, Kitty sat on the low wall encircling a nearby house and smiled as she watched the meeting of the old friends. It was full dark now, but the tableau of Dylan and company was well lit by the headlights of Tony's truck. She wasn't surprised when another vehicle pulled up and a passel of teenagers piled out.

In a small town, excitement was where you found it, and even the youngest of the newcomers had heard of Dylan Matthews. Of course, there were the athletic trophies inscribed with his name in the glass case at the school, but his exploits as an FBI agent were no less fodder for town pride.

Nothing ever changes, he'd said, and he'd been right.

After a few minutes, he was still encircled by men and Kitty figured she'd lost her shot at him for the evening. There was talk of that welcome-home party, of a game of poker, of meeting for billiards and beer the next evening. Relief ran through her. With the kind of calendar-filling his friends were doing, he'd be too booked to be sheriff.

Rising from her place on the wall, Kitty managed to catch Amalie's eye and give the little girl a one-fingered wave good-bye. Then, with a last look at the knot of excited males, she smiled to herself and silently started past them toward Aunt Cat's.

A hard hand snaked out and caught her wrist. She was reeled backward, until her shoulder bumped against Dylan. "Where are you going?" he asked.

All the men were looking at her, questions in their eyes. They wanted to know why the heck Kitty Wilder was with Dylan, of course. Even Tony still looked puzzled by the notion.

She cleared her throat. "I'm going back to Aunt Cat's."

"Not in the dark. Not by yourself."

She half smiled, trying to slip her wrist out of his grasp. "You've been living in the big city too long, Dylan. I'm perfectly safe here."

"No," he said. Then he looked at the men around them. "Sorry, guys, but I have to go."

"But, Dylan—"

"The lady needs an escort home."

Kitty felt her face heat. *The lady.* "Really, I'm fine—"

But he was already bidding his friends good-bye. They made polite noises to Kitty too, but saved their last comments for Dylan as they climbed into their vehicles.

"Kayaking, definitely," one said. "Just like old times."

"Don't forget poker," said another, jingling the

change in his pocket. "Unless you've gotten any luckier at cards, Dylan, I see good fortune coming my way."

Tony's truck was still at the curb as the others drove off. He leaned out his window. "It's great to see you, Dylan. Why don't you come to Bram's tomorrow? We'll show you around."

"I don't think I can," Dylan said pleasantly enough, but the hand holding Kitty's wrist tightened. "Things to do tomorrow."

With one last wave from Tony, the two of them were alone again.

Kitty cleared her throat. "Uh, 'things to do tomorrow'?"

"Hmm." He turned her in the direction of Aunt Cat's and started walking, still grasping her arm.

Kitty pulled, and he released her. She let out a little sigh, a little sigh cut short—cut to a stifled gasp—when he took her hand. A hot current jolted her palm and the hairs on her arm stood up.

She must have made a little sound.

He looked down at her, in the darkness his eyes just darker pools. "What's wrong?"

She licked her lips. "You, uh, shocked me."

He laughed. "Just that one time? Then we're not near even."

Kitty couldn't think what to say. His hand was still sending electricity up her arm. Her muscles tensed. "I, um, I could have made it home just fine, you know."

A couple of cars passed them and he had to raise his voice. "I thought you wanted to talk to me."

Kitty blinked. *That's right, that's right.* Really, this

haywire overreaction of hers only proved the obvious one more time. "You can't be sheriff," she said, stating it.

"I can't?" he asked mildly.

"Well, I mean it's really not necessary. And you can see how disappointed your friends would be."

"What about my friends?"

"I already told you. You just saw it too. They want to spend time with you. Kayaking, poker, whatever."

"Yeah." He didn't sound all that enthused.

"So you see," she said in a bright voice, "there's no need for you to be stuck with me day in and day out."

"Stuck with you?"

"And everyone else in the living-history district," she added hastily.

"That's right," he said softly. "I could be stuck with you, or stuck . . . entertained by talking over old times with all my old buddies."

"Exactly," she said, pleased he was seeing it her way.

"But, Kitty, honey," he murmured, "what if I'm afraid to let you out of my sight?"

Kitty swallowed. A subtle edge in his voice, just like his touch, was sending some kind of sexual Morse code to her nerve endings. She swallowed again, trying to ignore all the buzzing, pulsing, dash-dot-dot-dashes. "Why would you be afraid of that?"

His shoulders moved up and down. "I've been thinking. First I discover we're married. What the hell might be next? I find out I'm a daddy?"

Every inch of Kitty's skin burned. "Oh. Oh, no," she reassured him quickly. "I wouldn't have kept something like *that* a secret. I promise you. If *that* had happened that night . . . well, I'm sure you took precautions . . ."

Somewhere mid-jabber, he'd halted. Stricken with embarrassment, she noticed only when her quick strides took her to the end of the length of their joined arms and she was snapped backward.

". . . didn't you?" she finished lamely, stumbling against him.

But he wasn't listening. A series of catcalls and lewd hoots from a car passing by would have drowned out his answer anyway. The car slowed and some rowdy young men leaned out the windows, their attention focused on the sidewalk. Kitty froze.

Their attention wasn't focused on *her* sidewalk, but on the one across the street. There, a blond woman was walking in the opposite direction of Kitty and Dylan, her tall height accentuated by her self-assured, graceful posture. Playboy Bunny-sized breasts thrust forward, she strolled along in a dark skirt and low-cut tank top, the intermittent streetlamps spotlighting the gentle yet seductive sway of her hips. If she heard the boys' "Baby, baby" or even realized their car was reversing down the street to keep pace with her, she gave no notice.

Dylan's jaw was just an inch short of banging against his kneecaps. "Who—" He swallowed. "Who the hell is that?"

That was the reason Kitty was leaving Hot Water. She'd lived with the Wilder reputation her entire life, gritting her teeth through summers in the brothel and the occasional flare-up of ancient rumor or new speculation. But she'd loved her town and been determined to make over the Wilder image. Six months ago, however, *that* woman had returned. Gossip about the Wilders had flared again—and refused to subside. During the past few months Kitty had learned once and for all that some things never, ever could change.

"That," Kitty said, "is my mother."

Judge D. B. Matthews whistled tunelessly as he pushed open the door of Bum Luck. The cool, low-lit interior of the bar smelled of popcorn, beer, and scotch, in that order. Over the masculine rumbles of the patrons, it was easy to make out the feminine tones of Bum Luck's owner-bartender. "Oh, I don't believe in second chances, Red," he heard her say as she set a draft beer in front of Samuel "Red" Morton. "Once is all you get."

D. B. couldn't help himself from grinning when Samantha glanced his way. Though she didn't do anything more than reach below the bar for a glass, he knew she'd spotted him. He pulled out one of the two chairs at his usual table and settled himself against its faux leather back.

On his first visit to the bar a few months ago, he'd deliberated over the proper place to sit. A fifty-year-old Superior Court judge needed to exercise circumspection. He'd almost talked himself out of going altogether, but his curiosity had gotten the better of his scruples. As he did tonight, he'd arrived at the newly opened establishment only an hour or so before closing time.

It hadn't been as quiet as he'd hoped even then, and Bum Luck had only gained in popularity since. But on that occasion he'd hesitated in the doorway, debating among the bar, the booths, and the small tables between the two. Sizing up the situation, he'd decided the bar was too casual, the booths too comfortable, but the tables were just right. The citizens of Hot Water wouldn't begrudge the judge a drink, as long as he didn't appear to enjoy it too much comfort.

"Good evening, Judge." Just as he'd known she would, Samantha Wilder appeared at his table, a round tray balanced on one palm and his usual vodka martini balanced on the tray. She wore her blond hair in a soft twist at the back of her head, and a dark skirt. When she leaned over to place the long-stemmed glass on his table, he allowed himself an eyeful of her truly spectacular breasts, their luscious cleavage exposed by a black, sleeveless blouse.

He refused to feel guilty about looking. The fact that he was a judge, a midlife judge at that, didn't mean he was dead. Yes, martinis might be his drink of choice (she'd kidded him over that, teasing him about choosing something that was at best yuppie and at worst stodgy) and it was true a few gray hairs silvered his temples. But he had all his own hair, by God, and the rest of him was in pretty damn good shape too.

He gifted himself with another peek of cleavage before Samantha straightened. No, he was nowhere near dead.

"You're looking especially pleased with yourself tonight," she said, cocking her head.

She usually didn't initiate chat with her customers. Even the men who sat at the bar were forced to pull conversation out of her, so D. B. felt favored. "My boy came home today." He grinned again; he just couldn't help himself.

Samantha smiled back. "I know. It's been the talk of the bar tonight. You're pleased?"

"Pleased" didn't come close to describing his mood. "For the past eight years I've had to chase Dylan around the country to get in a visit. Even though he's been assigned to the L.A. office for the last three, he's never come to Hot Water."

One of her golden eyebrows winged up. "He's been avoiding home?"

"I don't know about that." To dodge Samantha's gaze, he turned his attention to his martini and took a sip, hoping the vodka's heat would burn away a cold niggle of uneasiness. Of course Dylan had been avoiding home. D. B. didn't know exactly why, and he wasn't sure he wanted to find out.

"Are you all right?" Samantha touched the back of his hand.

D. B. jerked, alcohol sloshing out of the glass and onto his fingers. Cursing his teenage reaction, he grabbed the small cocktail napkin she held out and daubed at his hand. "I'm fine. Just fine."

Samantha leaned one hip against the empty chair. "What brought him back now?" she asked.

Staring at that womanly, sexy curve, he almost wished she'd go away. The other men in the bar would be sure to notice her lingering at his table, and then there was his rookie reaction to her nearness. Her breasts, her hips, the sensuality in every one of her movements, made him sweat. Christ, if she knew she made him feel like a fifteen-year-old with a girlie magazine, she'd be appalled.

Or worse, she'd laugh.

"Judge?" she said softly.

He realized he hadn't answered her. Taking another swallow of his martini, he considered what to say. Why *had* Dylan returned? He shook his head. "I don't know." That niggle of uneasiness threatened to deflate his good mood again.

A round of boisterous laughter broke out. Samantha looked over her shoulder, then back at him. "Well," she said, an impersonal smile turning up her full mouth, "I've got work to do. It's good to see you."

From the corner of his eye D. B. watched her walk away, the subtle swing of her hips nearly causing him to spill his drink again. His fascination with Samantha Wilder had started six months ago, the first day he'd spotted her back in town. As she'd crossed the street, a brown grocery sack in each arm, her dancer's posture and her centerfold body had struck him like a one-two punch in the gut.

Not examining his reasons why, he'd headed for the store she'd just exited, where the whispers were already rampant, just as he'd counted on. *Samantha Wilder.* He hadn't really remembered her, though he knew her aunt and her daughter, Kitty, of course. When she'd left town at seventeen, he'd been miles away, a twenty-four-year-old widower trying to get through law school while taking care of his five-year-old son.

That day he'd learned she was now forty-three. Nobody knew where she'd been exactly, all those years she was gone, but the rumors were as salacious as they were unsquashable. The only confirmed facts were that she'd bought the old Bum Luck, a sleazy dive closed for years, and that she was classing up the place. As a local judge, he'd decided right then it was almost his duty to visit the new establishment and view it up close and personal.

View Samantha up close and personal.

"D. B.!" Red Morton had managed to tear himself away from the bar. He plunked his mug of beer beside the judge's martini and pulled out the opposite chair. "Heard Dylan's back."

D. B. nodded, satisfaction running through him like another hot swallow of vodka. "You heard right."

"Well, where is the boy?"

D. B. shrugged. "Here or there." He wasn't going to start worrying that his son had only briefly stopped by the courthouse before taking off again. Dylan had accepted D. B.'s set of house keys, hadn't he? That Dylan had said he was unsure how long he might be forced to stay wasn't going to disturb D. B. either, though admittedly "forced to stay" wasn't the most positive spin on a long-postponed visit home. "He's probably hooked up with some old friends."

Red looked down at his beer. "Heard he was with Kitty Wilder tonight."

D. B. straightened, then shot a glance toward Samantha, who was taking an order nearby. "Kitty?" he questioned, keeping his voice quiet.

Red nodded. "Was holding her hand or had his arm around her or something."

D. B. relaxed and picked up his martini. He didn't believe Dylan and Kitty even knew each other, let alone were friendly enough to touch. Hot Water's gossip mill was untiring, but it wasn't infallible.

"Seems pretty strange, a Matthews and a Wilder together," Red said.

D. B.'s fingers tightened on the stem of his glass. "I—"

"What's this about a Matthews and a Wilder?"

D. B. twisted around to find Samantha standing behind him, a faint smile curving her mouth. "Has the judge been sweet-talking my aunt Cat again?" she asked, placing one hand on her hip.

Red inspected the bottom of his beer mug. "Kitty and Dylan," he muttered.

Samantha stilled. "What, Red?"

"Somebody told me Kitty and Dylan were together tonight." He drained the dregs of his beer. "Probably just a rumor, though."

"Mmm." Samantha's pleasant expression flickered and D. B. felt another cold twinge of dismay. But then she directed her gaze at him, looking calm and composed as usual. "Can I get you another martini, Judge?" She smiled again.

As it often did, her beauty struck D. B. like a blow. He froze, paralyzed by the curve of her mouth, her breasts, her hips. Lord, she was gorgeous. His mood soared once more. It wasn't every day a man's son returned home. It wasn't every night he could share his pleasure in it with the sexiest woman he'd ever seen, even if she spent most of the evening on the other side of the bar. Mentally he threw off the last of his looming disquiet.

"Why not another?" he said. "A martini for me, another beer for Red. Hell, a round for the house. I'm celebrating." He grinned as the room erupted in a cheer.

The next martini went down in a slow, warm glow. Everyone in Bum Luck was jolly, a free drink a welcome end to the evening. Dylan's name came up over and over, along with retellings of his most memorable exploits. One of the men at the bar claimed to have taught Dylan his baseball swing, and another his forward pass. D. B. just smiled. The entire town had always taken credit for his son, reveling in Dylan's accomplishments, but D. B. didn't resent it. On the contrary, it only made him prouder.

"Another, Judge? Last call." Samantha was standing before him again, looking like a wet dream a middle-aged man like himself shouldn't remember.

He shook his head, curling his hands together to keep from reaching out and stroking the round, tempting curve of her rear end. "Two's plenty for me, thanks." Usually he stuck with one, afraid to press his luck by letting his inhibitions loose.

She was lingering beside him again, and he smiled, enjoying her out-of-the-ordinary nearness. Little tendrils of blond hair had escaped her temples to caress her faintly flushed cheeks. D. B. imagined himself touching those tendrils, then pulling her hair completely free of its confines to let it fall on her naked shoulders.

The ends wouldn't quite reach her breasts. They would be bared to his gaze and he would put his palms on her curving hips and draw her toward him. Draw her breasts toward his mouth.

As if she could read his mind, Samantha's breath

suddenly caught. "I—I have to start cleaning up," she said, stepping back.

D. B. just barely stopped himself from preventing her retreat. Instead, he leaned back in his chair to savor the last drops of his martini.

Samantha moved gracefully around the room, retrieving empty glasses and wadding paper napkins. Though she bade a friendly good-night to each customer, she never lost her cool reserve.

In another fifteen minutes the barstools were empty. Red left too, assuring D. B. that he was walking home instead of driving. A foursome of young men in the corner booth argued good-naturedly over who would pay their tab. They finally settled it with an arm-wrestling match, breaking two beer mugs but netting Samantha reimbursement and a big tip.

D. B. slid lower in his seat, unwilling to stir himself. He rested his head against the back of his chair and closed his eyes. The young men left and he hoped they were walking as well, but he knew by now that Samantha was very careful about her patrons. She wouldn't let anyone leave the place with his keys in hand if the situation seemed dangerous.

Over the past few months, he'd come to realize she knew drinkers, and more, she knew men.

He thought he heard the sound of her locking the front door. He should move. Get up, take his martini glass to the bar. Something. But instead, he sat there, basking in the satisfaction of a good day and a pleasant evening.

All over the world, men his age were having midlife

crises. They felt useless or used up or disappointed in what had become of their lives. They asked themselves what the meaning of it all was. More than one of his friends had been floored by the feelings.

D. B. didn't know if he was there yet or if he'd somehow bypassed that dirty trick that age could play on a man. While seeing his grown son could have made him feel old, he'd felt happy instead. Maybe he'd failed Dylan somewhere in the past, but now, perhaps, man to man, he could make amends. That was one of the blessings of being at this stage in life—dealing exclusively with adults.

A beguiling organ riff tumbled from the bar's speakers, followed by the shivery cymbal-drum-cymbal backbeat of The Doors' "Light My Fire." His eyes still closed, D. B. was instantly caught by the driving rhythm. A smile curved his mouth. God, if he didn't feel twenty again, his mind alert, his body primed.

A throaty, feminine voice sang along with Jim Morrison.

D. B. slowly straightened in his chair and opened his eyes.

As he'd imagined earlier, Samantha stood in front of him. Her blouse was off, her bra was gone. Her hair was up in its twist and her skirt was still on, but not for long.

He reached out and drew her to him, his fingers digging into the sexy curve of her hips. Her breasts brushed his mouth.

"I've been waiting all night for this," he said.

Her neck arched as he licked a tight nipple. She moaned softly.

He sucked, the taste of her, the feel of her, delicious against his tongue. The night was burning, all right. "It's been four months," he said. "And it gets better every time."

Samantha Wilder had put the "life" back into "midlife."

Chapter Five

Kitty stared, unseeing, into the darkness out the bedroom window of her tiny rented house. If tonight's bad news was her being forced once more to observe the reaction her mother had been inspiring since she returned to town six months before, its good news was Dylan's shock had allowed Kitty to break free of him for the evening.

She needed the respite.

Of course, "good news" was relative, because he'd still been grounded enough to extract her promise to breakfast with him the next morning. And to add more weight to the bad-news side, breaking free of Dylan had freed her to tackle some long-overdue accounting, not a happy task.

The cursor on her laptop computer blinked insistently, nagging her to get on with updating the financial files. Somewhere, somehow, keeping the books had become another responsibility of the "head" of the one-person advertising and PR department of the Hot Water Preservation Society. Though Kitty had earned a minor in accounting as an accent to her advertising degree, working the numbers was her least favorite duty.

And right now, her most depressing one.

Sighing, she reran the balance sheet. Dismal. Though she'd been aware that admissions were off in Old Town, she hadn't been considering how much energy the air-conditioning units in the restored buildings were using to keep up with the uncommon heat. The higher utility bills were a further blow to the bottom line.

While the area that preserved Hot Water's roots was actually owned by a descendant of one of the town's founding fathers—Bram Bennett, to be precise—the reenactors were paid a percentage of the profits. This summer's low ticket sales might not mean the difference between filet mignon and the soup line for the reenactors, but it made a big mental difference to Kitty. Leaving Hot Water with a clear conscience meant using her share of this summer's proceeds to wipe out her college loan from Aunt Cat. Her aunt wouldn't hold her to it, of course, but running away from the woman who had loved and raised Kitty was bad enough without running away and leaving something behind.

Her mother had done that—left Kitty—and the last thing Kitty wanted was to resemble her mother in any way.

She was going to fulfill her obligations.

Then she was going to leave Hot Water and never return.

Samantha's homecoming had forced that. The return of that Wilder woman had served up another plateful of gossip and innuendo about their family. Before that, Kitty hadn't gone so far as to consider herself *respectable* per se, but she had reached the point where she didn't feel completely tarred by the tart brush. Then, reenter Samantha and exit any designs on conventionality Kitty had ever dreamed of.

Thinking of the stunned expression on Dylan's face this evening just confirmed it. She was paying off Aunt Cat and then she was outta here.

Elbows on the desk, Kitty dropped her head toward her fisted hands and rapped gently against her skull. "Think, think, think," she whispered to herself. She'd graduated with honors, for goodness' sake. Surely her ad-trained brain could dream up some spicy draw to attract the tourists to Hot Water despite the record heat and the price of crude oil.

But with her eyes closed she could think only of Dylan. His dark, intense eyes, his rock-and-roller hair, his masculine charisma that had strange women lining up at her aunt's gate.

Dylan, who was a national hero.

Kitty's pulse fluttered as a delicious but dangerous idea floated to the surface of her mind. Well, "floated" was a misstatement. This idea was waving both arms over its head and shouting, like a swimmer who needed saving.

And it was Dylan to the rescue. He was going to be Kitty's savior. He was going to be her ticket out of town.

Every scrap of media product about him she'd seen or read whirled in her mind. *Entertainment Tonight*, the tabloids, *Time* magazine. The man was a gold mine of publicity.

She'd need a press release, of course, Kitty thought in growing excitement. Advertisements taken out in the Stockton, San Francisco, and Sacramento papers, not to mention L.A. and San Diego. A banner stretched across the entrance into town. DYLAN MATTHEWS KEEPS OUR STREETS SAFE!

Kitty bit her lip. Letting Dylan play sheriff would mean she must overcome her embarrassment about their marriage. It would mean she'd have to face him every day and hide the shivery truth of what one look from his dark eyes could do to her.

It would mean that in a few weeks she could leave Hot Water and her Wilder reputation behind, once and for all.

Kitty pushed away from her desk, the decision-that-was-no-decision-at-all made. Now that she thought about it, however, she wondered if he'd really been serious about taking on the sheriff job. No matter. By tomorrow she'd find some way to convince him to go along with her plan.

Forty minutes before his breakfast appointment with Kitty, Dylan slumped in a corner booth at Pearl's Cafe, located a few blocks from Old Town and across the street from the I.O.O.F. Hall. It was just his luck that this was the day the Independent Order of Odd Fellows held its monthly breakfast in Pearl's small banquet room, so he'd been forced to endure an early-A.M. dose of backslaps and handgrips from the movers and shakers of Hot Water.

Nearly every town in the Mother Lode had its Odd Fellows Hall and fraternity of Odd Fellows, because the group dedicated "to improve and elevate the character of man" had provided a sort of social security during the Gold Rush. Nursing the sick, providing for widows and orphans, and burying the dead had been essential social functions in the wild boom times.

In twenty-first-century Hot Water, the Odd Fellows continued to do good works, everything from operating the town cemetery to running a summer camp for under-privileged kids in the nearby mountains. Dylan shook his head. He'd likely be an initiated Odd Fellow himself if he'd stuck with his original plan of establishing a practice in Hot Water after law school.

Regret started pounding like a headache at the base of his skull. Dylan winced, then gulped a scalding mouthful of coffee, letting it burn away the feeling. Those long-ago plans were best forgotten. It was now that mattered, the now of confronting Kitty and getting the issue of ending their marriage resolved.

Dylan gulped more coffee, staring at the cafe walls covered with wallpaper of trailing ivy. Nearly every green leaf was hidden by some Victorian-inspired knickknack—wreaths of silk flowers, paintings of rosy cherubs, and lace-embellished ladies' hats. It wouldn't surprise him if he had enough time to count them all before Kitty showed. As a matter of fact, because of yesterday's hedging and stalling, he wasn't convinced she'd arrive at all. And everything he'd learned about human nature warned him that if she did turn up, she'd turn up late.

But this time he refused to let her put him off or distract him. Hell, he'd track her down if necessary. His bike was parked outside, already gassed up and packed for the return trip to L.A. Once he extracted Kitty's promise to immediately begin the termination of their marriage—he'd wring it out of her if he had to—it would be adios to Hot Water. Good-bye forever. Then, if his stubborn boss refused to be moved on the vacation issue, Dylan would simply stare at the soulless walls of his condo for the rest of the summer.

Pain throbbed in his head again, made even worse by the cheerful jangle of the bells hanging from the cafe's front door. Dylan took another fortifying swallow of coffee, then glanced toward the newcomer.

He blinked. It was Kitty. She was early.

Her silky hair was knotted to smoothly hang over one shoulder, a shoulder made nearly naked by a dress about thirty degrees more outrageous than the one the day before. Its shiny fabric laced up the center of her body from belly to cleavage, and the skirt ended at her ankles in a froth of ruffled petticoat. The dress was red, the petticoat black, yet the sunny smile of the woman wearing them had him thinking of church choirs.

Hell. At the sight of all that skin, he knew something of his was rising up and ready to belt out a hymn anyway.

"Oh, good," she said, sliding into the seat opposite him. "You're early too."

Every instinct on alert, he regarded her warily. He didn't trust chameleons, and Kitty's ability to go from harlot to farm girl and back again was unnerving. Interesting, but unnerving.

His mind flashed to that woman—Kitty's mother!—striding through the darkness. Definitely interesting.

"Kitty?" There was a wealth of surprise, and maybe disapproval, in Pearl's voice as she walked up to their table, steaming coffeepot in hand. "Are you . . . are you sitting here with *Dylan*?"

"Of course," Dylan answered for Kitty. Puzzled, he glanced between the two women and noted the faint flush crawling up Kitty's neck. He narrowed his eyes. "What would you like to order?" he asked her.

Kitty's shoulders squared. "Just coffee, Pearl. Thank you."

The older woman's brows rose, and she filled the cup sitting in front of Kitty with an almost belligerent air. Dylan remembered that Pearl was known for her uncompromising manner, but this was something else entirely.

Kitty gave her a swift smile, then focused her attention on doctoring the black stuff with a dollop of cream and the contents of three packets of sugar. By the time she was stirring the ghastly concoction she'd made, Pearl had moved on.

"What was that about?" Dylan asked.

"That?" Kitty picked up the cup between both hands. Her lips, unpainted but lush, went into a full pucker as she blew on the coffee.

Dylan's hands involuntarily squeezed his own mug.

She blew again. "Oh. You mean Pearl?" One bare shoulder lifted. "She's usually okay to me, but now I gather she's unhappy that her husband has become a regular at Bum Luck."

"That place is reopened?" It had been a biker hangout when he was a kid, and the way he remembered it, the whole town had breathed a sigh of relief when the bar closed.

"Mmm." Kitty sipped at her coffee and sighed with pleasure.

Dylan's hands squeezed again. "Still," he said, trying to refocus, "what does that have to do with you?"

She gazed into her cup. "It's my mother who re-opened the place."

The image of the blond woman popped into his mind again. Kitty had her mother's height and straight-arrow posture, but while the older Wilder was undeniably beautiful, she lacked the arresting and innocent prettiness of her daughter. He shook his head. "I repeat, what does that have to do with you?"

Kitty's bare, smooth-skinned shoulder shrugged again; then she lifted her eyes and met his gaze. "You know how it is in Hot Water. The past, the present, the mother, the daughter—we're all inextricably coiled."

She was right. It was the town's charm and it was its bane. It was why he'd left and it was what he missed most. He found himself half smiling. "I tried to explain that to Honor Witherspoon, though I'm not sure she believed me."

Kitty's blue eyes were back on her coffee. "Is that right?"

He remembered the darkness, the palpable taste of Honor's fear. She'd been alone for two weeks when he'd joined her in captivity, and he'd calmed her while they waited for rescue by spinning stories about Hot Water. She'd been distracted, then fascinated by his description of small-town life. To his surprise, he'd not been able to

get the place out of his mind since. It was as if, once released, the memories refused to return to the dim corner
where he'd shoved them when he left Hot Water.

"Honor was scared shitless after two weeks with the
kidnappers," he said. "We thought they'd go for the ex-
change—well, it was worth a try anyhow—but the bastards reneged and threw me in the cellar with her."

"She was kept in a cellar?"

He chuckled dryly. "It was a wine cellar, if that
makes you feel any better. But as you can imagine, she
was pretty shook by the time I showed up on the scene."
Still, she'd struck him as a beautiful woman, one he
might have been interested in if he hadn't met her in his
role as rescuer. Yet even after their release, he hadn't felt
anything more than brotherly toward Honor. "She
whacked me with a magnum of champagne."

"No!" Kitty let out a little laugh. "I know I shouldn't
think it's funny, but—"

"I laughed too, but only because she missed. She had
no idea the FBI was negotiating her release and had decided to take action for herself."

Kitty shivered. Goose bumps broke out across her
skin, miles of pretty, tantalizing skin, from her chin
down to her. . . . Dylan jerked his gaze upward. "You
need a sweater," he said. "A jacket, something." Anything to cover up all that fine-pored flesh.

She shook her head. "I'm not cold. I'm just thinking . . . have you often exchanged yourself for a
hostage?"

"The FBI, in principle, doesn't negotiate. But
Honor's father, Warren, has more influence in Washing-
ton than ten powerful men put together. And then, of

course, there's the little matter of the ambassadorship he's in line for. All that added up to a radical rescue attempt." He met Kitty's gaze. "Bottom line, money changes everything."

At that, she set her coffee cup down. "That's exactly what I've been thinking, as a matter of fact," she said. "I've been thinking about our little problem too."

Dylan froze. *Whoa.* He thought he'd been warming her up with the small talk, slowly working her around to the issue, and she was suddenly throwing it onto the table? "Yes," he said, wary again. "There is our little problem."

Her blue eyes were all guileless innocence. "That's why we're here, right?"

"Right." He drained his coffee, suspecting he might need to be as alert as possible. "Shall I get Pearl to refill us?" Without waiting for Kitty's answer, he looked around for the cafe's owner and spotted her leading a quartet of attractive female tourists toward an adjacent booth.

He saw the moment the foursome spied him. Their eyes widened, and one of the ladies actually cleared the floor by a couple of inches. *Damn.* Resigned to their interruption, he steeled himself to be gracious through the kind of conversation strangers had forced on him lately, thanks to the excessive press attention surrounding his recent cases.

But instead of approaching him, the women whispered frantically in Pearl's ear. Donning a the-customer-might-be-nuts-but-they're-always-right expression, Pearl about-faced, directing the group to a table in the opposite corner of the restaurant.

At a loss, Dylan transferred his attention to Kitty, who also was focused on the women. Then her gaze whipped back to his, her eyes shining with suspicious innocence. A tiny, satisfied smile curved her half-pucker mouth.

"Our marriage?" she reminded him, oozing artlessness. "Are you ready to talk about it?"

"Sure," he said, still on guard. "Talk."

"Okay." She tapped the table with both hands. "Let's get right down to it."

"By 'it,' " he said, just to be on the safe side, "I take it you mean our divorce or annulment or whatever the hell it is we have to do."

"Of course," she answered, as if shocked he suspected she meant anything but. "I completely understand that you want to take care of it."

Dylan pinned her with a stare. "No, Kitty. I want *you* to take care of it."

"Um." Her pink tongue snaked out to lick her bottom lip. "Yes. Well. Of course I will." She scooted forward on her seat and leaned toward him, causing her champagne-glass breasts to rest on the tabletop. "I think you're going to like this."

His gaze on the sweet sight across the table, he let out a soft groan.

"What's the matter?"

Closing his eyes, he ignored the question. "Tell me, Kitty. Tell me so I can get on my bike and get out of here."

"Well, I've been thinking. I believe the easiest way to break off our . . . our . . . association is for me to apply for a divorce on Heritage Day."

He opened his eyes. "Huh?"

She smiled. "I must know a little Hot Water trivia that you don't. Sure, we have that cute little wedding tradition—"

" 'Cute little wedding tradition'?" he murmured. "Tell that to someone who isn't actually married, thanks to the outdated thing."

Her nose tilted a half-inch higher in the air, though she pretended not to hear him. "But on Heritage Day, I can also divorce you just like this." She snapped her fingers.

"Is that supposed to be a threat?" he asked.

She huffed out a sigh. "You're not listening. It's the law, Dylan. Hot Water marriages can become Hot Water divorces on Heritage Day, just another safeguard for those Eastern women who agreed to take on Gold Rush husbands, practically sight unseen."

"Is that true? I don't remember hearing that."

Kitty waved a hand. "Check it out for yourself. The town doesn't publicize any of the potential legalities, you know that. They don't suit the romantic fantasy. But believe me, in just a few weeks you and I won't be Mr. and Mrs. Dylan Matthews anymore."

Mr. and Mrs. Dylan Matthews. Something icy dripped down his spine. Bram Bennett leaped into his mind, the clawing agony on his face when the FBI told Dylan's best friend that they'd found his wife— murdered. Dylan thought again of Bram's deep, still-evident grief as he stood over her grave last night.

"Good," Dylan said hoarsely. "That sounds reasonable. Take care of it on Heritage Day." He looked out the window at the stern brick facade of the I.O.O.F. Hall. "Just give me a call in L.A. when it's done."

She didn't say "Yes."

She didn't say "Okay."

She didn't say "Fine," "Just as you say," or even "Of course."

She didn't say anything at all.

Slowly, so slowly that he heard her take two sharp breaths while he did it, he turned his head toward her. "*Kitty?*"

She swallowed.

"Honey," he said softly. "Have you forgotten all those ways I know to kill people? Have you forgotten number three-thirty-two?"

She swallowed again. "No."

"Well, right now I'm thinking that method is much, much too quick. I know another way, a way guaranteed to take *hours*, and I get to use my bare hands."

"I want you to be the sheriff for the rest of the summer," she said quickly.

"What?"

"You heard me."

He shook his head. "No. I was only teasing you about that yesterday. I'm going back to L.A."

"I was afraid you'd say that." She hesitated, biting her lip. "Here's the deal. If you won't be sheriff, then I won't get the divorce."

He froze. "Say that again."

"We need a sheriff," she said, leaning forward once more. "I don't have a whole lot of choices when it comes to replacements. As a matter of fact, I have *no* choices. And you would be an enormous asset to this summer's success of Old Town. People would come from all over to see you."

He stared at her. "That not what I told you to say."

She gulped a big breath, the move exposing another half inch of softly mounding skin, then hesitated. "Oh, fine," she finally answered. "I said, if you don't do it, I won't get the divorce."

He tried remaining calm. "There are other ways to end marriages."

"Sure, longer and more expensive ways. And unless you cooperate with me, I won't cooperate with you." She bit her bottom lip again. "It's as simple as that."

His blood started simmering. He'd been mad before, and desperate, and coldly determined. But he'd never felt this incredible, burning anger. This . . . this . . . this sweet-faced jade wanted to force him to stay in Hot Water. She wanted to force him to face all the people he'd loved and lost because of what happened eight years ago. She wanted him to stay and face the memories that never let him sleep.

"That's extortion." His voice sounded deadly quiet.

She flinched. "Yes."

"Well, I won't do it," he ground out. "I don't negotiate."

Her blue eyes turned surprisingly hard. "Neither do I, Dylan. That's the deal. Take it or leave it."

He couldn't get over her moxy. Or stupidity. "You expect me to play sheriff to your madam? You expect me to arrest you, drag you down the street, throw you in a cell?"

She didn't back down. "On Saturdays and Sundays, at two and four P.M. The rest of the time you just sit in the jail and answer questions. That's all I'm asking. And if you want a quick divorce, you will."

"Jesus Christ, I want to arrest you, drag you down the

street, and throw you in a cell right now," he said through his teeth.

Her stubborn expression didn't change, and a sick sense of powerlessness made his gut roil. It made him think of that hot, stagnant afternoon when he'd gathered three terrified little kids close while watching Alicia Bennett being dragged into the woods.

That memory was overlaid by Bram again, his tormented expression the day he'd learned his young wife was dead, then his dark figure standing alone in the dusk last evening.

Dylan closed his eyes, trying to shut out the images.

It didn't help. *Mr. and Mrs. Dylan Matthews.* The words whispered rawly in Dylan's head. He opened his eyes to stare straight into Kitty's prostitute-in-the-first-pew face. There was no doubt about it. She was serious. Laughter from the Odd Fellows meeting drifted from the back room, and a weird sense of destiny fell over him like a shroud.

On the wall above Kitty's shoulder, one of the multitude of cherub paintings caught his eye. Unlike the others, the rosy-cheeked, winged baby in this one wasn't blond and blue-eyed. Its hair was dark, its eyes wide and brown, and they seemed to be accusing him and pleading with him at the same time. *Stay,* the cherub seemed to say.

Swallowing, he tore his gaze away. Stay? Let himself be coerced into staying? His gaze was drawn back to the cherub, its expression cheery but stubborn. *Stay.*

Was that what he owed? Was living here for the rest of the summer, reliving the past, the way to clear his debt to Bram and everyone else in Hot Water? His muscles, his mood, tightened.

"I'm going to get you for this, Kitty Wilder," he said.

She swallowed, but didn't look away from him. "Exactly what I want," she answered. "Every Saturday and Sunday afternoon."

Tension coiling tighter, he searched her face one last time for a sign of softening. She had him over a barrel, damn it all, because he'd do anything—*anything*—to sever their marriage, to sever his ties to home. His temper snapped. "Fuck. Fine. Just fine. I'll do it."

Shoving away his coffee mug, he vaulted out of his seat. The four women in the booth on the other side of the cafe gasped. Ignoring them, he stalked out the door.

Kitty followed behind him like some angel-faced, red-dressed devil from hell. On the sidewalk, she caught his arm. Stinging heat lanced his arm. He froze. Amazing how much he could resent her and how desperate he was to do her at the same time.

"Just tell me one thing, Kitty," he demanded, spinning around to face her. "Why? Why the hell did you register the marriage?"

Emotions—yearning, hurt, maybe embarrassment—chased across her face. "Didn't you ever make a mistake?" she finally said.

Those were the precise six words that could shut him up on the subject forever, he thought, gritting his teeth. He couldn't rail at her blunders, not without being the biggest hypocrite on earth. Because, yeah, he'd made a mistake. And someone else had paid for it with her life.

Kitty watched Dylan climb aboard his motorcycle, then do something to make it awaken with a vicious growl.

Without another word to her, he sped off, his black hair waving in the wind.

"Your helmet . . ." she cried out, but he was already leaning around the next corner.

"Excuse me," said an unfamiliar female voice.

Kitty started, suddenly aware that two women were standing outside Pearl's. The strangers were both young, one with very short, dark hair, the other with blond braids. College students vacationing at the campground on Lake Colter, she guessed.

"Can I help you?" Since they were apparently unfazed by her courtesan couture, Kitty also pegged them as repeat visitors to town.

"We were wondering . . ." The dark-haired one began.

The second woman jumped in. "We want to know if that's Dylan Matthews," she said excitedly.

Kitty hesitated.

"Well, is he?" the blonde demanded, obviously a young woman used to getting what she wanted.

A young woman too interested as well, Kitty thought. She opened her mouth, intending to squelch that interest—he *was* married, after all—but another voice took over.

"Why, we thought the very same thing!"

The four ladies she'd met on Aunt Cat's sidewalk the day before were bustling out the cafe's door. "They say everyone has a twin. That must be Dylan Matthews's evil one," a second lady went on to say.

Another of them lowered her voice. "On probation. Ankle monitor. State *and* federal crimes."

"We just watched him inside," the last woman said. "He's a wild animal."

Leaving the others still gossiping, Kitty backed away, shivering.

A wild animal. And she had only herself to thank for unleashing it.

Chapter Six

The following afternoon in The Burning Rose, Kitty served "champagne" to her parlorful of guests following their tour of the upstairs bedrooms. While the hands of the gilt mantel clock ticked ever closer to two o'clock and the player piano cheerfully tinkled out an off-key rendition of "Jeanie with the Light Brown Hair," Kitty's stomach jumped with each sour note. The long skirt of her sapphire-colored costume hiding her knocking knees, she moved among the unisex khaki shorts and athletic shoes, refilling glasses.

Waiting for Dylan to show was like waiting for the touch of the dentist's drill. You knew it wasn't going to be pleasant, but you also didn't know just how *un*pleasant it would be. A tiny buzz or a full-out jaw-rocker?

If his attitude as she'd explained his role that morning was any clue, Kitty guessed jaw-rocker. Though his initial curses had subsided to a simmering silence, when she'd happened to brush his fingers as she'd passed over the jail keys, the look from his eyes had made her heart hammer.

He wasn't happy playing sheriff.

He *really* wasn't happy playing sheriff opposite Kitty.

"Excuse me?" A little girl's voice made Kitty bend down to her and smile. She had immediately noted the handful of children in this group and tailored her talk accordingly. When conducting the brothel tours, she always tried skirting the earthier aspects of The Burning Rose's business, to minimize her own embarrassment and that of the guests. But she was especially circumspect if children were present.

Not everyone grew up with the particulars of sex and sexual relationships explained with the same forthrightness usually reserved for, say, car maintenance.

"Hi, sweetheart," Kitty said. "Would you like some more?"

At the little girl's nod, Kitty tilted the champagne bottle to pour more lemon-flavored carbonated water into the plastic champagne flute clutched in the child's fist.

"You're pretty," the little girl said.

Kitty smiled again. "How funny you should say that when I was thinking the exact same thing. *You're* pretty."

The little girl ducked her head and Kitty's heart squeezed. Once she left Hot Water, she promised herself, she'd have that conventional life she always dreamed of, including a little girl like this one. A little girl whose mother would never leave her, or worse, come back trailing rumors behind her like smoke.

Nor would Kitty pass along the Wilder pragmatic and

unromantic view of love and sex. There was a difference between fornication and tire rotation. She'd tell her daughter the facts, of course, but she would be sure to also mention words like "emotion," "tenderness," and above all, "commitment."

As Kitty straightened, the front door to the brothel banged open. Her stomach jolted and her gaze flew to the clock. Two on the dot.

Dylan—Sheriff Matthews—was right on time.

"Kitty Wilder."

He was supposed to call the name out in a dramatic, playacting sort of way—tourists ate that kind of stuff up—but the way he grimly bit out the words worked too. The guests were frozen as she turned to face him.

Her hand crept up to her throat.

She would have liked to kid herself that it was a touch of her own theatrics, but the truth was Dylan had stolen her breath. He'd gone flat-out uncooperative over the costume, refusing even the tin sheriff's badge that Beau had worn, but the scuffed cowboy boots, old Levi's, and chambray work shirt Dylan had on appeared authentic enough. Especially when the holster buckled around his hips and the badge on his shirt looked so real.

Kitty's breath backed farther up in her lungs. Of course. They *were* real. One hundred and fifty years ago the original Sheriff Matthews had worn them the first time he arrested Rose Wilder.

"Kitty Wilder," this Sheriff Matthews said again, striding into the brothel. The guests fell back to clear a path between them. "You're under arrest."

As she'd done hundreds of times before, she straightened her spine and raised her chin. "And w-why is that?" Before, her question had always come out confident, and not a little sassy, but this time she sounded fearful.

It probably had something to do with the smoldering anger in his eyes.

He grabbed her by the arm, his grip just a teeny painful.

"Ouch," she mouthed.

He merely smiled. "Let's go."

"But . . ." She struggled to remember the script. "But you haven't told me *why* I'm under arrest, Sheriff."

"You know why," he said, his voice low.

"You're supposed to say 'for keeping a disorderly house,' " she hissed.

His gaze traveled over the quiet guests. "Looks orderly enough to me."

"Dylan—" she whispered.

"But you, now *you* are another matter altogether."

She stared at him. He was ad-libbing, of course. She should have guessed he would cooperate only as much as he chose to, but his voice rang with enough conviction to satisfy the onlookers.

Her arm still in his grip, he started hauling her toward the open door. "The good people of this town hired me to keep unruliness under control. And you, Miss Kitty, are asking for unruliness in that dress and with that face."

"What?" Even with her feet sliding along the plank floor, she managed to get a last glimpse of herself in the entry-hall mirror. Though some of the silvering was worn away, in its reflection she could see that she looked perfectly normal. The cut of this costume wasn't any more or less revealing than any of her others, and she didn't have any more or less to reveal than she had on any other day.

As for her face—the only thing that looked different there was its distinct stamp of apprehension.

When she'd dreamed up this big idea, she hadn't considered how much she'd be at Dylan's mercy.

Once she was out the door, her feet dug into the wooden sidewalk. "Hold on!" That wasn't in the script, but neither was the little thrill that his hard palm on her bare skin sent coursing through her body. "Maybe we should rethink this."

He halted. "Yeah?" he said.

The other part of the costume he'd refused was the cliché white hat, and Kitty acknowledged he was right again. With his head uncovered, his long, dark hair gave him a look more authentic to the Gold Rush period. More dangerous.

Movement on the edge of her vision made Kitty suddenly aware of their audience. The brothel guests were pouring out the door and the people in the street were stopped too, their gazes glued on Kitty and Dylan. She swallowed. Not because the attention bothered her—the whole point was to entertain the tourists, after all—but because the way they watched was so different from what she was accustomed to.

Dylan bent close to her ear. "You want out, honey? Just say the word and our little experiment in extortion is finished. I'd like nothing better than to go back to L.A."

"*No.*" She couldn't give up. She wouldn't. It was just that she needed a little time to get control of herself. Her gaze wandering over the crowd, she raised her voice. "I don't understand why you're doing this, Sheriff. I'm just a simple woman trying to earn my living."

The crowd shuffled closer, again surprising Kitty with its avid, serious attention. When she and Beau had played this same game, the tourists had grinned and laughed, enjoying it for the fun that was intended.

"A simple woman doesn't earn a living like you do, Miss Kitty," he said, towing her once more in the direction of the jail.

"Serving champagne?" she questioned, appealing to the crowd. "Playing music? It's not a crime to sit with a man, is it?"

Usually that garnered another grin or two, and often even a plea to the sheriff on her behalf. No one in this group, however, cracked a smile.

"You're walking, talking crime, Miss Kitty. Take it from me."

She dug her feet into the sidewalk again, halting their progress. "Why, Sheriff," she said, " 'take it' from you?" Dylan had wandered so far off the script that her words weren't the least bit planned.

She put her free hand on her hip and a sexy, teasing note entered her voice. "The fact is, I wouldn't mind *taking it* from you. Any old time. Anywhere, even. You just drop by The Burning Rose your next free evening and . . ."

She let her gaze rove around the onlookers and then slowly rove over Dylan's body. Her hand left her hip so her fingers could baby-walk up his hard chest as she added a flirtatious breathlessness to her voice. ". . . and we'll see what we can come up with."

The crowd tittered at that. There was even some actual laughter until Dylan looked away from her face and out at the people clustered around them.

The humorous sounds died.

Kitty didn't blame them, really, because when he turned his face back to her, there was something new in his eyes. The anger was still there, no doubt, but this other emotion was even more disquieting.

Her heart started hammering and words tumbled out of her mouth. "Just joking, Sheriff. Of course I wouldn't presume that you, that I—"

He halted her babbling by wrapping his free hand around her upper arm and hauling her up on her tiptoes. "I'm adding new charges, Miss Kitty."

"New charges?" she choked out. Her heart had crawled into her throat and was still pounding for all it was worth.

"Yes." His eyes bore into hers. "For the temptation of an officer of the law." He lifted his head and surveyed the tourists, as if daring anyone to challenge him. "That's a crime in this town."

Kitty blinked. "It is not."

"It is now." With that, he lifted her up and threw her over his shoulder. One arm clamped behind her rear end to keep her in place.

The people cheered.

They also followed as Dylan strode in the direction of the jail. Her head at his belt level, and stunned into silence, Kitty watched his worn bootheels clomp against the sidewalk's dusty wooden planks, then turn into the entrance to the jail. He shouldered the door open and slammed it behind him. She heard the sound of the lock being set.

The white ostrich feather that had been stuck in her hair worked itself free. It drifted to the scratched jail floor. "You're supposed to let the crowd in," she said, trying to sound dignified with her cheek pressed against the small of his back.

"Not this time," he answered, his voice grim.

She considered stretching down to bite his tight, denim-covered butt.

As if he'd read her mind, she found herself swiftly upended and back on her feet. Breathing hard and aware that her face was likely as red as one of the ripe beef-steak tomatoes growing in Aunt Cat's backyard, Kitty hesitated over which strip of his hide to take off first. She pursed her lips.

His dark gaze went blacker and he focused on her mouth. "You've got to get something straight, Kitty."

"What?" Her surprise at the whole over-his-shoulder episode gave way to anger. "That sounds like *you're* accusing *me* of doing something wrong when it's you who can't get the dialogue straight or the stage directions right. *I* didn't turn *you* upside down."

His gaze washed down her body, then back up. "That's a matter of opinion."

She stared at him. "What are you talking about?"

His jaw hardened. "Kitty, if we're going to continue with this farce, you've got to stop tugging my chain."

She blinked, but that didn't change a thing. He still looked serious, as if he truly believed that she'd been doing something to him. But the plain truth was she could hardly do more than breathe—and even that was difficult—when he was within twenty feet of her.

"You . . ." Her mind blanked out. Trying to reclaim

her thoughts, she slowly ran her tongue against her bottom lip.

"*That's it.*" Dylan grabbed her by the arm again and propelled her toward the cell in the rear of the one-room jail.

Before she could sputter a word, she was behind bars. The cell door clanged shut, and then he locked it with the old-fashioned iron key on the old-fashioned iron ring.

She wrapped her fingers around the heavy bars, positioned lengthwise every six inches or so, and pressed her body against them. "What are you doing?"

He turned his back and swooped down for the feather on the floor. "I'm supposed to arrest you. Put you in jail."

"With the tourists here to witness it," she reminded him, half bewildered again. "If they're outside the jail, what's the point of locking me up?"

He stalked toward her. "The point of locking you up?" The hand holding her feather snaked through the bars and pushed it back into her topknot. Then lingered.

"The point of locking you up," he murmured, his fingers sinking, unwillingly it seemed, into her hair, "is to prevent this." He pulled her head back and leaned his body forward. From the other side of the bars, his mouth lowered.

Dylan jammed his mouth against Kitty's, inhaling the sweet scent of roses and tasting the satisfying fruit of retribution. She deserved his punishment.

For coercion. For forcing him into this dumb, undignified role of "sheriff."

She deserved it because he hadn't slept the past few nights, and instead of the usual nightmare, it was Kitty who'd starred in his dreams.

She deserved it because when he'd walked into the brothel wearing his great-great-granddaddy's star, time had spun backward. Not one hundred and fifty years back, but nine years, maybe ten, when he'd first noticed little Kitty Wilder had developed a willowy body and eyes as blue as the sun streaming through the cobalt glass bowl on the judge's dining room table.

He ground his mouth against hers, tilting her head for a harder, hotter fit, because he hated how her soiled dove's dress revealed the flawless rise of her small breasts and that he'd had to share the view with every Dick, Harry, and Tom Tourist traipsing through the goddamn town.

Angry blood burning through him, he swept his tongue against her pouty lower lip. He roughed it up, lashing against it in short, quick strokes, because she made him want to drag her somewhere, anywhere, and rip off that stupid dress so he could bury himself inside her until he didn't remember who he was or why he couldn't live in the place he loved best.

His tongue grazed her bottom lip again, and as if she couldn't tell this was penance, her mouth softened. He pushed inside.

It was warm and wet and she tasted like honey. Everything fled from his head—why he was kissing her, why he shouldn't kiss her, who the hell he was.

His free hand covered one of hers and she relaxed her grip on the bar, their fingers entwining. He flexed his other hand against her scalp, burying it further in her silky, upswept hair. His heart slammed against his ribs and he pushed his tongue deeper, sliding against the roof of her mouth. She crowded closer.

Through half-closed eyes he saw the tip of her breast brush an iron rail and she moaned. Dylan shuddered, thrusting deep inside her mouth again, as her nipple rose hard and tight against the clinging fabric of her dress.

He lifted his mouth from hers and slid his hands to her waist. Her eyes were sleepy-sexy, her mouth swollen and rosy. Both of them were breathing hard. She had yards of creamy flesh, from collarbone to shoulder to cleavage. He'd never seen anything so pretty as the sight of Kitty's upper breasts rising over the low cut of her gown.

His erection surged against his jeans and he didn't second-guess another kiss. Nothing mattered but tasting her again. "Kitty," he said hoarsely against her mouth. She seemed to know what he was begging for, because she parted her lips and took him in. Her tongue stroked his once, the move so tentative he ached with the hesitance of it, but he forced himself to wait for her next one.

Her hands slid through the bars and grasped his shoulders. The touch rushed through him, along his arms, his torso, his legs, bolting him to the floor. She rose on tiptoe to reach his mouth more easily and he let her take control of the kiss, let her take him into her, that honey-rose taste of her mouth on his tongue, the smell of old wood and old history in his head.

Their mouths fused, melded by a heat that crept upward from the floor their ancestors had walked. Dylan's hands tightened on Kitty's small waist.

He hadn't had a kiss this good in . . . forever.

They were both pressed against the cell bars, but he didn't feel them, didn't feel anything between them. He could only feel Kitty, the texture of her tongue, the warmth of her skin through her dress, the pounding of her pulse that had somehow become the pounding of his.

They were connected. By the past, by home, by . . .

By God. Dylan wrenched away.

"You're a witch," he said, releasing his hold on her. They couldn't be connected. They weren't.

Her hand was shaking as she lifted her fingers to touch her mouth. "W-what?"

He didn't make connections. He didn't want them. They weren't safe, they weren't for him, they were everything he avoided. And for God's sake, the last thing he wanted was to link himself to a woman from Hot Water. To Kitty Wilder, his *wife*.

"Is this part of your game?" he demanded.

She blinked, her eyes half dazed. "My game?"

Damn, she still looked so good. Beautiful, with her golden hair disheveled and her mouth wet and swollen from his. Panic raced through him and he ran his hands through his hair, hauling in long breaths to get another surge of lust under control. "This isn't going to happen," he said. "I won't let you."

She stared at him. That pouty, sexy mouth of hers worked, but no words came out. "You!" she finally said. Her fingers touched her mouth again. "Don't you dare try to rewrite recent history. *You* kissed *me*."

"Hah," he replied, worried like hell because his legs were still glued to the floor, keeping him so close that he could count the number of times her pulse beat in her throat.

Her upper lip curled. " 'Hah'? All you can say is 'Hah'?"

He swallowed. "Hah." It was the best he could do.

Her body quivered. He could tell she was getting mad, but he didn't know a way to stop it, or even if it was wise to do so.

"*You* kissed *me*," she said again.

He shoved his hands in his pockets, trying to get his thoughts back in order. Or just plain back. "That might have been how it started, but—"

"But nothing." Her spine straightened and her blue eyes turned to blue fire. "Just because I'm dressed like this doesn't mean you can treat me like a . . . like a . . ."

"That's not it," he ground out. "And you know it."

She crossed her arms over her chest. "It's been enough for other men."

Something blazed inside him. "We're not talking about other men." Christ, he didn't want to. "There's this—this thing between you and me. It's—"

"A figment of your imagination."

His eyebrows jumped. There were a lot of things you could say about what just happened, about what was between them, but that wasn't one of them. "I think—"

"Well, you can just think again." She looked ready to stamp her foot, and her cheeks were flushed with angry color. "I don't like you and I didn't want you to kiss me and I don't want you to kiss me ever again."

"Okay," he said cautiously.

She was obviously working herself up to a real mad. "You don't have the slightest idea who you were kissing."

He wasn't sure she was capable of hearing him, but he tried anyway. "Well, I think I know you—"

"You don't know *anything* about me." She started pacing around the small cell, agitation rippling off her.

"Okay, but—"

"But nothing." She kept on pacing. "For example, I bet you don't know that I won every handwriting contest in second grade, or that I broke my wrist trying to ride a skateboard, or that I was *this close* to a president's physical fitness award, except I could only do four push-ups instead of ten."

His panic was quickly subsiding in the wake of Kitty's surprising aggravation. If she couldn't do a few girlie push-ups, he thought, what kind of danger to him could she possibly be? "You're right. Four out of ten is definitely 'close,' " he murmured.

She shot him a suspicious look, but then kept on pacing. "And I don't want to be kissed by someone who doesn't know that. I don't want to be kissed by someone who doesn't know that Sue Ellen Moffett didn't invite me to her birthday party in fourth grade because her mother said my mother was a tramp. I don't want to be kissed by someone who doesn't know that I can speak French like a native—well, like a native with a bad accent—and that I know all the words to every song New Kids on the Block ever sang."

The last of his unruly emotions now completely dissolved, he pressed his top molars against his bottom ones, trying not to laugh in the face of all these hotly spoken, sweet, and earnest facts. "Kitty—"

"But you're not interested in those things, are you? You don't care that my favorite flavor of ice cream is butter pecan, my favorite chocolate is semisweet, and my favorite car is a Chrysler Town & Country minivan, but I almost like the Honda Odyssey better because it comes in snazzier colors."

He looked at her with fascination. "I didn't know *any* make of minivan came in snazzy colors."

With a flurry of skirts, she came to a stop in front of him. "There are a lot of things you could learn."

He shouldn't want to know what they were, but he discovered he couldn't help himself. "Keep going. Tell me more about you."

Her eyes narrowed. "Why?"

He lifted his shoulders in a casual shrug. "Maybe I want to kiss you again."

That galvanized her. "Not in a million years," she declared vehemently. "Not unless you know I'm afraid of hospitals and spiders and that when I swim in the ocean I'm terrified a whale might swallow me whole."

"Interesting," he said, rubbing his chin and trying not to laugh again. "A Jonah complex."

"No." She shot him a look. "A bad experience at a showing of *Pinocchio*."

His shoulders shook. "Ah," he choked out. This was just too good. "What else should a man know who wants to kiss you?"

"My favorite season is fall, my favorite holiday is Halloween, and I stopped believing in Santa Claus when I was four years old because the presents he left under the tree I'd found the week before in Aunt Cat's hall closet. I like the snow but I can't ski, and the truth is I don't do any sport very well that requires a piece of equipment between my feet and the ground."

"I guess that lets out sledding too," he murmured.

Her eyes widened and then her face brightened. "No. I'm actually an okay sledder." She paused. "Well, of course, that's behind to the ground, which is probably why."

Dylan suppressed another impulse to laugh. Just like that, his mood was the best it had been in days. Weeks. Years. Why the hell he'd let himself get worked up over kissing Kitty was a mystery. Despite the fact that she'd made them legally married, she was harmless. Incredibly sweet, but harmless. He even wanted to kiss her again right now.

He smiled. "Come here," he said, crooking his finger and stepping up to the cell door.

Her face sobered. "Why?"

"So suspicious?" he asked.

"Wilders learn that early," she said.

He thought of the older woman they'd seen the other night, her posture upright, her arms swinging in confidence. "When did your mother come back to town?"

Kitty's chin lifted a notch. "Six months ago."

"Would you mind my asking why?"

"Why she came back?" At his nod, Kitty shrugged. "You'd have to ask her. I don't know."

"She hasn't said?"

Kitty shrugged again. "Not to me. I haven't spoken with her."

Uneasiness feathered up his spine. *Kitty's harmless*, he reminded himself. He thought of butter pecan, New Kids on the Block, Pinocchio. Never boring, but harmless. "Come here," he said again.

She hesitated.

Reaching for his ace in the hole, he held up the cell key and dangled it. "It's time to go."

The door swung open with a rusty creak, but still she hesitated, which made him guess his desire was written all over his face. Pissed at himself for having made her so wary, he reached in and tugged her out by the arm. "I'm not going to bite." Or, he decided with a sigh, kiss her either.

Because with just his palm to her wrist, another electrical surge of attraction was already sparking between them. Kitty tickled his funny bone, and she probably was as harmless as he thought, but it wasn't smart for him to get close to her again. Not when the passion between them was mutual—no matter what she said—and so hot.

It shouldn't be hard to keep apart. He was famous for his detachment, after all. He dropped her arm.

She didn't move away. "I'm serious," she said. "I don't want you to kiss me."

"Fine." He didn't know why she had to repeat it.

"I don't even want you *thinking* about it."

"*Fine*." He didn't know why that pissed him off even more. She was harmless, remember?

"Ever," she concluded with a scowl. Then she turned away from him.

Battling rekindling resentment, he watched her walk toward the door leading out to the street. The cut of that damn dress accentuated the straightness of her slender shoulders and the tantalizing, slight sway of her hips.

Harmless.

She paused, her hand poised to throw back the door's lock; then she whirled. Her breasts rose over her dress, dangerously high, on a deep, serious breath. "Just so you understand, Dylan. I won't let you make love to me and walk away again."

She was gone before he found out he was still capable of movement. He hadn't heard a word she'd said, stunned as he was by yet another punch of lust. Just one look at her angel's body in that wanton's dress could knock him flat.

Harmless? Shit. Harmless as a heart attack.

Chapter Seven

On Monday, the only day of the week the living-history district was closed, Kitty left her small house around 1 P.M. to pick up Aunt Cat from her weekly hair appointment. She drove her 1969 T-bird—well, Aunt Cat's, actually, until she'd given up driving the year before—slowly through the streets of Hot Water. Navigating the T-bird was like steering a boat, Kitty thought as she floated through the intersection of Empire and Nevada, then grinned to herself. Why not a boat? Wasn't she the captain of her life?

The first two weekends with Dylan as Sheriff Matthews had been a smashing success. Even before her jubilant advertisements had run in the entertainment sections of the targeted newspapers, local word had spread. The first weekend had been busy. The next, the streets were downright mobbed.

Even the "arrests" had gone off without a hitch.

Of course, she'd had a few qualms after the very first one, but Dylan had performed the rest competently enough. Sure, she might wish he put a little more oomph into his role, but the truth was the visitors cared about looking at him, not looking at him doing anything in particular. He was a hero. A celebrity.

The icing on the cake was that he'd been very careful not to touch her, let alone kiss her. While she wasn't crazy about the handcuffs he whipped out to clamp on her wrist, at least it was better—safer—than his *hands* on her. She had enough trouble just putting the memory of his touch and those kisses from her mind.

But she kept the entire incident in perspective by remembering those iron bars between them. No matter how spectacular the kissing, they were locked apart by who they were. A Matthews man married a pedigreed woman like Honor Witherspoon. Maybe at eighteen Kitty had harbored foolish hopes to the contrary. But now she understood. Accepted the reality.

As she approached Locks, Stocks, and Barrels, a parking spot opened up. Under that shop's roof, one could have a haircut, get a key cut, or purchase a handgun or hunting rifle as long as one was willing to abide by the specified waiting periods. A hand-lettered sign posted in the front window clearly spelled these out: "Up to thirty minutes for a free beauty operator, no more than fifteen minutes for a new key, ten days for the firepower of your choice."

Head down as she dug through her purse for her sunglasses case, Kitty strode through the front door of the shop and smacked into a man, her forehead to his chest. Somethings metallic clattered to the linoleum floor.

Kitty jumped back. Then smiled. "Judge," she said. "I'm sorry."

Judge D. B. Matthews smiled back. "Kitty Wilder. My apologies."

He looked so much younger than Kitty remembered that she wondered if he'd just had a new haircut or perhaps a beauty shop application of Grecian Formula on his close-cropped dark hair. But no, the style looked the same as always, and there was still a generous, though attractive, sprinkling of silver at his temples.

"Whatever are you doing here?" she asked.

He shifted his feet—nervously, she thought for a moment—until she realized a selection of shiny keys were scattered across the floor.

"Oh, let me," she said, but they both bent over to gather them up. As they straightened, she poured the two she'd retrieved from her palm into his.

"For Dylan," he said, shaking his fist so the keys rattled like dice. "To the house and his old apartment above the garage. I understand I have you to thank for his decision to stay in town a while longer."

Kitty's smile died. "Well, uh . . ."

"He said you persuaded him that Old Town needs a sheriff."

But not that she'd coerced him into agreeing to *be* sheriff. Whew. "Yes, well, he's a cooperative sort, huh?"

Judge Matthews shook his head. "Not with me. I've been verbally arm-twisting him for the last four years to quit the FBI and open a law practice in Hot Water."

Kitty frowned. "But surely that would mean he'd have to finish law school first?"

"He already did, by taking night courses over several years. That's when I started hoping. When he was younger, he always said he was going to continue the Matthews's practice, but then . . ." The judge looked down. "Well, then he decided to go into law enforcement instead."

Hmm. Dylan had completed his law degree. She supposed he'd finished it because it could be useful in his career with the FBI. But the young man on the banks of the creek eight years ago had seemed adamant about completely and forever rejecting any plans he'd made before the kidnapping.

Yet now he was back, law degree in hand, putting hopes in the hearts of—*Hope* in the *heart* of his *father*. And Dylan was back because Kitty had married him. He was staying because she'd forced him to. Guilt heated her cheeks and she dropped her gaze from the judge's eyes to his chin.

"Well, um, it was nice chatting with you." She started sidling away.

"You too, Kitty," he said. "Good-bye." Before exiting, he slid a lingering glance over his shoulder, to the area of the shop where six or seven women were being serviced by the three beauty operators.

It was that odd, lingering glance that made Kitty peer in the same direction. Her gaze moved past the counter with the cash register, beyond the three beauty-salon chairs one in which Aunt Cat sat, getting her comb-out—then stopped in front of the four hair dryers.

Stopped at the manicurist's table. On the wall above the table, a locked glass case displayed samples of the handguns Erwin Sanderson sold. Directly below that, her back to Kitty, sat Nellie Sanderson, the manicurist and shop owner. Beneath the table was a yellow washtub filled with suds, for the soaking of a client's feet before a pedicure.

And across the table sat Nellie's client. While another woman might not have thought ahead, and would have been forced to hitch her pant hems into untidy rolls in order to slide her feet into those suds, not this one. Not Kitty's mother, who wore sleek cropped pants below a fitted blouse.

In six months, this was the closest Kitty had ever been to Samantha. It might seem unbelievable that in such a tiny town they hadn't run into each other before, but that was because Kitty had run the other way whenever she'd spotted her mother.

It was too late for that now.

Inhaling a deep breath, Kitty averted her gaze and turned to approach the trio of chairs on her right. "Hi, Aunt Cat." She smiled at the hairdresser, Lisa, arranging her aunt's silvery hair. "Hi, everybody." Kitty nodded to include hairdresser Rita and her client, Olive, as well as the women beneath the dryers: Teresa Ha, Virginia Sanger, and Alice Lynch.

Lisa's eyebrows were hidden beneath her short fringe of bangs, her eyes were so wide. "Go ahead and sit down, Kitty," she said, nodding toward the free chair beside Aunt Cat. "It'll be a few more minutes."

As if she didn't have a care in the world, Kitty hopped onto the vinyl seat, ignoring the sick rush of awkwardness invading her belly. Her eyes met her aunt's in the mirror.

"Are you okay?" the older woman asked quietly.

"Fine, fine," Kitty hastened to say, aware that not only every eye but every ear in the place was turned her way. She tried to meet Aunt Cat's gaze in the mirror again, but Samantha was reflected there too, her perfect profile, her shoulder-length blond hair.

Kitty's chair squeaked as she rotated a half-turn to avoid the sight, but there was another mirror plastering this wall as well. In it Kitty had a perfect view of Nellie Sanderson holding up a bottle of nail enamel for Samantha's approval.

Ironic that they should meet over nail polish, Kitty thought. When she was a little girl, studying the photos in Aunt Cat's house, she'd pictured her absent mother as some exotic combination of Rapunzel and San Francisco flower child. She'd had the requisite long golden hair and dreamy, sad eyes. Though there'd never been any doubt that Samantha was her mother—Aunt Cat, as a true Wilder, had been plain-spoken in matters pertaining to sex and procreation—Kitty had regarded Samantha with the status of a mysterious, beautiful big sister.

In fifth grade, the girl who sat beside Kitty had a sister who was a trans-Atlantic flight attendant. She'd showered Kitty's classmate with foreign dolls and unfamiliar candy. Best of all, after her big sister's visits, the other girl would come to school smelling of sophisticated perfumes and showing off shiny silver tubes of cast-off lipsticks.

Kitty would inhale the delicious scents and gawk at the creamy colors rising out of the elegant tubes, all the while imagining that any day her beautiful big sister-mother would bring her gifts too. Or even send them. The idea of a package in the mail would cause her heart to pound. Inside would be something only this glorious creature would know Kitty longed for, before she even knew it herself. A two-layer makeup kit, perhaps, complete with a dozen tiny brushes and a rainbow of nail polishes. Maybe a bazooka-pink phone for her very own or a fancy curling iron to make waffle waves in Kitty's stick-straight hair.

Of course, the gifts never arrived. Occasionally she'd talk to Samantha on the utilitarian beige phone in Aunt Cat's kitchen, but after a while she avoided the stilted conversations. Aunt Cat never pressed, accepting Kitty's decision in the matter. It was another Wilder custom not to censure others' choices, because, Kitty guessed, they'd never wanted anyone to censure their decisions to become prostitutes, bootleggers, and the like.

Chair squealing again, Kitty swung back toward Aunt Cat and caught the entire shopful of people staring at her. She saw them all reflected in the mirror, including Rita, whose scissors remained poised over her client's iron-gray hair, and Teresa, Virginia, and Alice, who had abandoned their celebrity magazines for the more interesting event-in-progress. Even Nellie had one eye on Samantha's nails and one eye on Kitty.

Only Samantha wasn't looking.

Kitty faked a smile. "What's up?" she said to the room at large.

Nobody looked away. Lisa flushed, however, and

made some comment about the previous busy weekend in Old Town.

"We're expecting even more visitors next week," Kitty called out, her voice bright. The shop's not-so-subtle study didn't ease, however. She suspected everyone was cataloging similarities between her and her mother.

There were some, she acknowledged, surreptitiously comparing their two reflections in the mirror. Their height, blond hair, blue eyes. Kitty didn't mind getting any of those attributes from her mother. As a matter of fact, when she was eighteen, she'd actually lost her resentment toward Samantha altogether. A teenage Hot Water resident herself, Kitty had understood how stifled, not to mention stigmatized—though Wilders were used to that—unwed mother Samantha would have felt if she'd stayed.

More, since Kitty herself didn't specifically recall insisting on using protection on her wedding night with Dylan, she'd realized she couldn't cast judgment on an unplanned pregnancy either.

No, after that night with Dylan, the abandonment hadn't bothered Kitty anymore.

The door to Locks, Stocks, and Barrels suddenly swung open. Kitty and everyone else glanced the newcomer's way. The room hushed, going so quiet that Kitty swore even the hair dryers held their hot breath.

Pearl stalked into the shop, the ties of her apron—its front embroidery declaring "Eat at Pearl's Café or Dic"—fluttering behind her. If she noticed anyone but the woman she was after, she gave no sign.

"Samantha Wilder," Pearl snarled.

No, Kitty thought as another rush of nausea poured into her stomach, Samantha's having left town didn't bother her.

What bothered Kitty was that Samantha had come back.

"Samantha Wilder," Pearl snarled again. Her angry strides ate up the floor between the door and the manicurist's table. "What have you done with my husband?"

Another woman might have felt vulnerable in such a situation, with her fingernails freshly painted and her bare feet up to the ankles in water. Samantha looked like she felt nothing. Nothing at all. "I haven't done anything with him, Pearl."

Kitty closed her eyes. Off and on through her whole life, rumors had circulated about Samantha and where she was and what she was doing. Regardless of that, until six months ago Kitty had made it her mission to live down the "wild" Wilder brand. She'd vowed to stick it out in the town she loved and strive to make people view the Wilders differently.

"Kitty." A hand touched her shoulder and she opened her eyes to see Lisa standing beside her. "Go home," the hairdresser said.

In the mirror, Kitty watched Pearl angle close to Samantha's ear, her posture stiff and her face angry. Kitty swallowed. "Aunt Cat—"

"Right now she wants to stay for Samantha. We'll get her home when she's ready." Lisa half smiled. "Let me do this for you, okay? Don't forget that Spenser's my husband's grandfather. We owe you a few for bending backward to get him some extra cash by working in Old Town."

"But—"

"Go, Kitty," Lisa insisted, her gaze darting to the manicurist's table. "This isn't about you."

Kitty slipped out of the shop without another protest, though she knew Lisa was wrong. Once Samantha had returned to Hot Water, so had the rumors, with a vengeance. Professional escort, call girl, gangster's moll. People had started to look at Kitty out of the corners of their eyes too, forcing her to realize she'd made no progress at all. Why, she could live like a nun—she nearly had—and the people of Hot Water would still see what they wanted.

Kitty reached for her car keys. Just a few minutes before, she'd been considering herself the captain of her life. What a joke! Instead, like her mother before her, she was what the town saw her as—just another wild Wilder.

Lisa was definitely wrong. The truth was that anything to do with Samantha was all about Kitty too.

At Monday morning's first light, Dylan hopped on his bike, desperate for time away from Hot Water. Even after a mere two weekends playing sheriff, the free day felt like a reprieve from a prison sentence.

For hours he roamed through the Mother Lode, randomly following country roads that led through towns with names like Dewdrop, Confidence, and Moccasin. In front of him, heat shimmered off the black pavement like the sinuous, beckoning movements of ghostly fandango dancers. He followed them without thinking until suddenly realizing he was on a direct path toward home.

He eased off the throttle. It was only early afternoon. He couldn't go back so soon. Not when the engine's drone had yet to flat-line his restless thoughts.

Not when damn Kitty Wilder wouldn't leave him alone. Not awake, not asleep, not aboard the Harley.

From the instant she'd flounced out of the jail on that first Saturday afternoon, she'd taken up permanent residence in his mind. He itched to know what made her tick. Why did she like minivans? Why didn't she speak to her mother? Why did she so vehemently deny the sexual chemistry simmering between them?

He spent most of his days bewitched by her mouth. Staring at it, remembering its honey-hot taste, he was always a hair away from locking out the crowd again to dive in for another sample. But even partly aroused, he dredged up enough good sense to keep clear of her. He couldn't afford the complication—especially not when he was married to it. Sex and Kitty were two subjects he was determined to keep separate for the rest of his stay in Hot Water.

But as he leaned into the next curve, he caught sight in the distance of a slender figure walking along the road toward him. Shit. Separating *himself* from Kitty didn't seem possible. He eased to the narrow shoulder and braked.

Head down, she strode along the edge of the road in her heavy sandals and cut-off overalls. His gut tightened. The overalls—with nothing beneath. No! As she drew nearer, his reeling mind registered the presence of a pinkish, skinny-strapped tank top and he breathed again.

Her head lifted, as if she scented danger, and she almost tripped in her haste to stop when she spied him.

Yeah, he thought. *Beware, honey.* He unclipped his helmet and lifted it from his head, then shook his hair free.

She started walking again.

He waited to speak until she was abreast of him. "I don't suppose this is a pleasure walk. You're pretty far from town."

Her hair was pulled back in a ponytail, but tendrils of it were plastered to her sweaty forehead. She scowled at him. "I'm in a very bad mood."

"I can see that." He wished the sweat or the scowl made her less tempting. He also wished her ill temper didn't tick him off, because for some unfathomable reason he'd been almost stupidly pleased to see her. "Kemper's Market out of butter pecan ice cream?"

Her scowl deepened. "I need a ride." She dangled what looked like a broken fan belt in front of his face. "Unless you happen to have a spare on you?"

He shook his head. "Where were you headed?"

"Before the fan belt broke, I was out for a mind-clearing drive. After that, the Wal-Mart in Colter," she said, naming the larger town a few miles south.

He frowned. "Jesus Christ, Kitty. Did you think you were going to walk the whole way?"

She rolled her eyes. "Since I left my wings in my other pants, yes. Colter is closer than hiking back to Hot Water."

"Speaking of pants . . ." He had no idea why he wanted to. Except that her legs were long and bare and her skin was creamy-smooth. "You're, uh, not dressed for a motorcycle ride."

It was the best he could come up with.

"Fine." She started trudging past him.

"Sheesh." He grabbed her arm. "You *are* in a bad mood."

She glowered. "I warned you."

"Want to talk about it?" The words just slipped out of his mouth.

"No."

"Good." The instant rebuff didn't offend Dylan in the slightest and had nothing to do with why he bit out, "Get the hell on," then scooted forward on the leather seat and handed his helmet to Kitty.

She couldn't get the thing buckled. After a few minutes of watching her struggle, all the while sucking in her sweet, full lower lip, he cursed at her once more and took care of it himself.

"Get on," he said again.

With a hand braced on his shoulder, she gingerly lifted one leg to swing it over the Harley's bulk. The ragged hem of her shorts slid high, and he saw the long inner muscle of her thigh flex from knee to near crotch.

Jesus.

Seated with her feet on the passenger pegs, she curled her fingers in the belt loops of his jeans. There had to be eight miles of air between them. "I guess I'm ready," she said.

He sighed. Then he reached behind him and flattened

his palm against the small of her back. Without a word, he hauled her forward, gluing her front to his back.

The helmet thumped the back of his skull. She squeaked in his ear.

He had the first instant hard-on of his life.

"Wrap your arms around my waist," he said, once he could talk.

As she moved to obey, he made sure to grab both her wrists and guide her arms high enough on his torso to avoid her detection of his altered state. "Right there." His voice was gruff.

"Okay," she said, bouncing a little on the seat. "I'm ready now." Her voice turned cheerier. "Hey, this might be fun. I've never been on a motorcycle before." She bounced again.

"Stop that, damn it."

"Sorry," she said. But she didn't sound sorry. Her linked hands pressed against his lower chest. "Lead on."

He didn't know if he could. Nothing was going right. This was supposed to be his day off. His day off from *her*. Yet here she was, plastered against him, her crotch to his ass, and it had turned him on so hard, so fast, he wasn't sure he could ever move again.

Her hands dug into his diaphragm once more. "What's the matter?"

Kitty's voice was so annoyingly upbeat, so irritatingly unaffected, that he set his jaw and thumb-started the bike. It roared to life and she squeaked in his ear again. The noise saved him. He made it to the sanctuary of Wal-Mart with his sanity half intact by picturing a mouse behind him instead of a long-legged, creamy-skinned Kitty.

The store's automotive section appeared like an oasis after the disturbing motorcycle ride. By tacit agreement, they didn't hurry through the shopping. Dylan welcomed the frigid air-conditioning to cool him off and Kitty seemed content to browse the long aisle. He made sure to keep to the end with the turtle wax, leaving the antifreeze and fan belts all for her.

Thirty feet separated them, and he was so intent on ignoring her that it took him a few minutes to notice a pair of twenty-something men talking to her. For an irritated instant he thought she was flirting, but then he looked more closely.

The two had her backed up against the fake lamb's wool car-wash mitts and "almost like real" chamois. Each man carried a twelve-pack of beer that didn't appear to be his first of the day. "C'mon, Miss Kitty," one said. "We're staying at the campground by the lake. It's party time."

"Sorry, guys, I'm busy," she answered.

The man talking looked put out. "No! We took a break from waterskiing last week and went through that whorehouse. We know you. It wouldn't be a real party without a Wilder."

The other man snickered. "Wouldn't be a *wild* party."

Kitty's lips lifted in something that no one with half a brain could think was a smile. "Good for you. Wild, Wilder. That's new."

Both dolts grinned back at her.

"So you'll come," the first man said, taking hold of her arm.

Dylan hated the big, ugly paw on her smooth skin.

He strolled down the aisle. "What's up?" he asked, reaching them. "Is there a problem?"

"No problem," one of the bastards answered without taking his eyes off her. "We're just getting this cute Miss Kitty to come with us."

"But she's with me," Dylan said, his voice mild.

The man glanced over his shoulder. "Oh? Well, we're going to a party. There's plenty to go around, if you want to come." His grin was sloppy. "I bet Kitty shares."

Dylan went cold. "I don't think so."

"Sure she does." His jovial tone didn't disguise the mean-drunk look in his eyes. "What do you have to say about it anyway?"

"Lee! David!" Two young women hurried over, one with long braids and the other with short dark hair. "What are you doing? Everybody else is ready to go back to the campground."

"We're going to bring Miss Kitty with us." The other man took Kitty's free arm.

She pulled away. "No."

"*No*," Dylan affirmed.

The first jerk swung around to face Dylan, his stance combative. "I asked it once and I'll ask it again. Who the hell are you to say anything about it?"

"Oh, my God," one of the young women said. She stared at Dylan in sudden recognition.

Dylan got ready to acknowledge his identity—"FBI agent" would probably end David and Lee's drunken bravado—when he noticed both young ladies shudder in what looked like fear.

"Let's go," the short-haired girl said, her voice gone

high. The other whispered in David's ear, then in Lee's. The two men jumped. Within moments all four of the young people were fleeing up the aisle.

Dylan stared after them. "What the hell . . . ?" But the question disappeared as he looked back at Kitty and saw the stricken expression on her face. He stepped closer to her. "Are you all right?"

She turned, inspecting a display of car fresheners in the shape of pine trees, lemons, and daisies. "Sure."

He couldn't stop himself from closing his hand around her ponytail and running his palm down its smooth length. "They were asses."

"I know." She picked up a rearview-mirror replacement and bent her head over it, apparently examining the plastic frame for minute flaws.

His palm itched to touch her again, so he gave another long stroke to her hair. "Does that happen often, honey?"

She hesitated, then shook her head.

"Strange men don't mix up the brothel fantasy with reality?"

She shook her head again. "Not so often, not when I'm outside of The Burning Rose itself, anyway."

He remembered the group of rugby players on the tour he'd taken. She'd handled them pretty damn well. He'd been annoyed with her that day, but he'd admired her poise too.

Still, despite her denials, he could tell she was upset as she selected the appropriate fan belt, then made her way to the registers. All through the purchase and as they headed back into the heat toward his bike, she avoided his gaze and gave only the barest of responses to his several attempts at small talk.

Finally, he slowed. "Kitty. Honey."

She kept her head down.

Alarm thickened his blood. "What is it?" he insisted. "Did something happen that I didn't notice? Did they hurt you or—"

"No. Of course not." She continued on toward the motorcycle.

He couldn't leave it at that. When they reached the Harley, he put both hands on her shoulders and forced her to face him. "Look at me, Kitty," he ordered. "Tell me what's wrong."

"Dylan . . ."

His fingers squeezed her shoulders. "Spill it, Kitty."

Her chin came up. "I'm embarrassed, okay? Are you satisfied now? It's humiliating to be treated that way, and it's especially humiliating for you to witness it."

Shit. He grabbed her around the back of her head and pulled her against him. "I'm sorry."

She fit so damn well, her cheek in the hollow of his shoulder, her silky hair sliding between his fingers as if it had a thousand times before, that he closed his eyes to savor the sensation. For a few minutes she let him hold her, leaning into his body.

It wasn't until they were back on the bike, however, that she completely blew his mind. Her body was plastered against his. He hadn't started the Harley yet, so though she spoke softly, he heard her words loud and clear.

"It's not strange men who bother me so much," she

said. "It's Hot Water. It's the way people there look at me sometimes."

He winced. *Jesus.* She might as well have reached down his throat and pulled his guts out. It was exactly the same way he felt. Dylan's town identity rubbed him raw too.

But he didn't know what to say to her. What he *should* say to her that wouldn't serve to strengthen the bond between them. Dylan released a long sigh. His connection with Kitty was like one of those woven-grass Chinese finger tortures kids got in birthday-party treat bags. The harder you tried to pull free, the tighter you found yourself stuck.

Chapter Eight

The hot wind dragged back Dylan's inky hair and Kitty turned her head to keep it from whipping against her face. Her arms circled his waist and her breasts pressed against him. She hoped he couldn't hear her thudding heart beating over the rumble of the motorcycle, but surely he had to feel it knocking against his backbone.

It frightened her to be this close to him.

Not physically close—though he looked dangerous enough with his hair wind-tossed and a stubble of dark beard on his face—but letting him see inside her. For as long as she could remember, she'd hidden her shame from everyone.

Wilder Women Don't Wed And They Don't Run. They didn't bleed either. On the outside, anyway.

Dylan steered the motorcycle into a curve and her body followed the lead of his, leaning into the movement, leaning into him. When the bike straightened out, she scooted backward on the seat, breaking their contact.

Dylan instantly released one handlebar and reached behind to press her close again. "Safer," she thought he shouted.

But what he really said must have been lost in the wind. Nothing was "safer" with the two of them wrapped together like yin and yang.

A few minutes later Dylan swerved across the empty road to park in front of the T-bird. Kitty hopped off the bike, stumbling a little in her haste, and he grabbed her elbow before she went down. She fumbled with the helmet until he had to help her with that too.

He flicked a glance at the powder-blue T-bird. "Forget the minivan," he said. "This is you."

She flinched as his fingers brushed the tender skin beneath her chin. "It was Aunt Cat's," she said.

"Still, I like it." He pulled the helmet free, then brushed her hair off her forehead with a small frown.

Her scalp prickled and she stepped back. "Well, uh, thanks very much. You're free to go. I can take it from here."

"Kitty, I'll fix the fan belt for you." He set the helmet on the motorcycle seat before walking over to lift the car's hood, which she'd left unlatched.

"No, no. You've done enough. I don't ex—"

She broke off. He'd gone rigid, his arms raised, his hands still gripping the edge of the hood. His face was turned to the left, his gaze on the weedy roadside next to the car.

Her mouth suddenly dry, Kitty dipped her head to

look beneath the hood and across the engine at what had captured Dylan's attention. Her stomach flipped over.

Half covered by the short, dry weeds was a tangle of objects. The shredded remainder of a helium balloon. A tattered and flattened teddy bear whose fur had once been brown, perhaps, but was now a muddy shade of purple. A length of fishing line, still bearing the withered remains of one or two flowers, probably part of a lei. The balloon, the bear, the lei, all three were anchored to the ground by a weathered wooden cross that had long ago yielded its upright position and now lay belly-up against the dirt.

A name was written in black along the crosspiece, still visible after all these years. Eight years. *Alicia.*

Kitty swallowed. "I didn't see that when I stopped. This must be—"

"This is where Alicia's car was." He let out a harsh laugh. "Funny how I didn't notice right away."

"Well," Kitty said quickly, "who would remem—"

"I remember *everything.*"

She swallowed again, aware he hadn't released his grip on the T-bird's hood, aware the muscles of his arms were bunched with tension. "I can take care of this, Dylan. Go on home."

He inhaled a long breath. "No." His head turned toward her and Kitty thought she'd never seen such . . . absence. It was as if he'd taken his emotions somewhere and left only the shell of himself behind.

"Dylan." Without thinking, she reached out and touched his arm.

He threw off her hand with a rough movement. "I'm fine," he snapped. "I can handle this."

"Of course you can," she said, retreating a few steps. God, but could she? He'd been declared a hero the day he'd rescued the children, but obviously his memories cut another way. She dug her fingernails into her palms, trying to distract herself with her own pain.

Turning his back on the remains of the memorial, he stripped off his T-shirt. "It's like hell out here," he said.

But Kitty couldn't completely agree. Broiling sun or no, she was suddenly frozen by the sight of Dylan's heavily muscled shoulders and chest. His abdomen rippled with muscle too. She'd never considered herself capable of being riveted by the male form, and she'd attributed her attitude to those practical, pragmatic Wilder genes that made the Wilder women capable of using men but perhaps not enjoying them. Yet something about *Dylan's* male form. . . .

"Kitty?"

She didn't want to look away just yet. His gold chain and its "church lady" medallion were partly obscured by a dusting of black hair that feathered beneath his collarbone and circled his light brown nipples. A thin line of the same stuff bisected his hard belly and disappeared beneath the waistband of his worn jeans. The masculine backdrop was made only the more fascinating by the tattoo adorning the skin covering his left pectoral.

Dylan cleared his throat. "Uh, Kitty?"

Her gaze lifted. "Your tattoo," she said, randomly choosing just one of the many things worth mentioning.

His right hand clapped over it. "Oh."

Her brows rose. "Oh?" Small enough that her own palm could cover it, a red heart permanently decorated

Dylan's chest. A red heart wrapped—protected—by coil after coil of barbed wire.

He turned back to the car. "I applied for the Bureau's Hostage Rescue Team. Five of us were accepted that year, and in the, uh, ensuing celebration we let the rest of the team talk us into tattoos."

He bent over the engine, then grunted and swung the gold medal and chain around his neck so that it lay against the skin between his shoulder blades.

"And what's that?" she asked.

He grunted again.

Curious, she walked closer. Her bare shin met the front bumper's chrome, its heat searing her skin. She yelped.

"What happened?" In a heartbeat, Dylan was looming over her, frowning.

"Nothing." Just inches away from his hair-covered chest, she tried to appear composed. Her hand crept up to her throat, where her skin was smooth and his . . . wasn't. "I just burned my leg on the bumper."

"Let me see." Before she could protest, he was kneeling beside her and touching her calf with his hands.

She quivered. "No!" She spun away from him, astonished by her immediate need to touch back. To smooth his tangled black hair and feel his rough beard against her hand. To touch the heavy muscles of his shoulder. To slide her palm beneath that chain around his neck and drag him up to her. Her skin flushed. She could see herself tracing that heart tattoo with her tongue, tasting his skin, his heat, his desire.

He rose to his feet and narrowed his eyes. "What the hell is wrong with you?"

She bit back a round of hysterical laughter. If he didn't know, then he wasn't suffering from the same case of instant lust that she was. "I'm going for a walk."

Setting his jaw, he hesitated, then shrugged. "This shouldn't take long. Don't go far."

She could hike all the way back to Hot Water and still not recover, she admitted to herself, so she didn't disobey him. After grabbing up a sturdy stick to scare off snakes, she headed along an animal trail through the scrub manzanita and oaks toward the brighter green cottonwoods promising the presence of water.

In the notch between two mild slopes, a stream trickled, its banks lined with young trees. Beneath the shade of their thirst-quenched branches, she spotted a flat-topped boulder on the opposite side of the creek. Insects hummed and blue-winged dragonflies zigzagged through the hot air. Kitty jumped the five-foot-wide stretch of creek to take a seat on her chosen boulder. With a sigh, she slipped out of her sandals, set them beside her, then dangled her feet in the cool inches of water.

She rested her elbows on her knees and her chin in her hands. Sighing again, she wondered where this sudden sexual appetite had come from and how hard it was going to be to stuff it back where it belonged. Wherever that was.

It worried her that her newfound lust might be a previously untapped byproduct of the Wilder genes. Maybe she'd been wrong all along, and her predecessors had actually *enjoyed* their sexually free lifestyles instead of merely falling into them. *Argh*. A sudden ripening of latent concupiscence would blow her plans for conventionality right out of the water.

Except she'd sexually craved only one man. Dylan.

That thought didn't make her any happier.

"You went too damn far."

His deep voice intruding into her thoughts and privacy nearly sent her sliding into the water. She scrambled to stay on her rock and glared at him across the creek bed. "You almost gave me a heart attack," she said.

He acted as if he didn't hear her. He leaped off the muddy bank opposite her, then waded into the shallow water as if he wasn't aware of it. His hand was rough on her bare arm as he pulled her off the rock so she was standing in front of him, her wet toes to his wet boots.

His nostrils flared as he stared down at her. "I was calling your name, damn it." He gave her a tiny, controlled shake. "Why didn't you answer?"

Kitty swallowed. "I—I didn't hear you." As dangerous as he looked with his unshaven face and untamed hair, more disturbing was the something dark and desperate in his eyes. "Dylan, I'm sorry."

He dropped her arm and swung away from her. "You scared the shit out of me, okay?"

This was near where Alicia had disappeared, of course. And though he'd rescued those three children, there hadn't been a rescue for Bram's wife. The details of the tragic story were as indelibly etched on Kitty's mind as they were on that of anyone who had been around Hot Water that summer. With three terrified preschoolers clinging to him and no safe place to leave them, he had been forced to watch Alicia being dragged into these very hills.

Kitty's hand trembled as she reached toward him. "I'm sorry," she whispered again and stroked the pads of her fingertips down the warm, bare skin of his back.

He froze. Then he looked over his shoulder at her, his eyes intent. The water splashed as he slowly turned toward her, the cheery sound at odds with the stark need on his face.

His breath swelled his chest and she stared at all that male skin, once more fascinated, once more hungry for what she shouldn't want and could never have. The insects buzzed the sound of that ever-present sexual tension that always ran between them. Kitty couldn't seem to break it and she couldn't look away from Dylan.

A dragonfly darted by, then around them. Kitty thought perhaps it cast a magic circle about her and Dylan, because with that insect's orbit time stilled and the world dissolved. There was only the cool creek beneath them and the green leaves surrounding them. That insistent, sexual Morse code continued pulsing between them, telegraphing need, passion, need again. When Dylan caught her hand and drew it toward him, she already knew he was going to place her palm against his chest.

He inhaled sharply at her touch.

The dragonfly swooped down in a flutter of its incandescent wings, almost landing on Kitty's nose. Despite the bewitchment of the moment, she laughed, delighted rather than bothered.

Dylan's mouth turned up in a faint grin. "He's jealous."

Kitty tilted her head. "Jealous?"

"His wings don't come close to the beautiful blue of your eyes."

Her fingertips flexed into his skin. "Oh, Dylan." Heat rushed across her body.

"Don't move," he whispered. "Don't go anywhere."

As if she'd want to. A kiss was coming. And yes, she'd told him never to do it again. She'd believed she didn't want him to. But at this moment she couldn't deny her own sexual craving, or the emotional one that was probably a thousand times more dangerous.

He cupped her face with his palms, keeping her head angled just so, and then he leaned forward. Tears pricked Kitty's eyes, and she hated herself for having to close them as he neared, but it was too much.

He brushed her mouth with his. Gentle, soft, dragonfly-wing sensation that made her heart shudder in her chest.

"Oh," she said. "It was like this before." Not in the jail cell, but on that night eight years ago. She flattened her other palm against his chest. No wonder she'd never wanted another man.

"It was never like this," he whispered. His palms cupped her shoulders as his mouth dragged across hers again. "Never."

Needing more, Kitty slid her hands up his chest. He shivered beneath her touch and she opened her eyes to see that his were closed and his jaw looked rock-hard. She clasped her hands behind his neck and pulled him down to her.

He resisted. "I'll rub you raw," he said against her mouth. "I didn't shave this morning."

"Please," she said, pulling harder. Her body was throbbing, clamoring for something more.

He groaned—then gave up.

Against the pressure of his lips, Kitty instantly parted hers. His tongue thrust inside and her body went liquid with relief. This was what she wanted. Her knees sagged.

His hands scraped down her back to catch her hips. He drew her against him, and she slowly slid her bare arms along the ridge of his shoulders. She moaned as the ordinary flesh between her elbows and her underarms proved to be previously uncharted erogenous zones.

Dylan hauled her even closer and angled his head. His tongue thrust deep again and she leaned into the kiss, feeling the hard bulge of his erection against her belly.

Her heart was riding high in her chest, buoyant with excitement. She smoothed her hands across his back, widening her fingers to touch as much of him as she could. He shivered again and, groaning, lifted his head.

His nostrils flared in and out with his labored breaths. Kitty's lungs were working overtime too, but she didn't want to stop. She needed this.

Going on tiptoe, she fitted her mouth to his.

He drew back and she tried following his lips, but he eluded her again.

"Kitty," he said, his voice raspy. "Wait a minute."

Frustrated, she fell back onto her heels, her body dragging along his. He groaned and clutched her hips, pressing her against him. Still sucking in air, he rested his forehead against hers.

"Kitty, I . . ." He lifted his hand and ran a gentle finger around her mouth. "I hurt you already."

"I don't care," she said. Her body was awake, still throbbing, still demanding he *do* something. No more soft touches, sweet kisses. Without even thinking, she turned her face into his neck and bit the underside of his jaw.

His muscles bunched beneath her hands. "Damn." He jerked her a few inches away.

Kitty stared at the red, twin arcs from her teeth marks against his skin, fascinated. "I did that," she said. Her eyelashes rose and she met his burning gaze. "I want to do it again."

"Yeah?" He didn't look away from her eyes while he pulled her arms off his shoulders and then brushed the straps of her overalls down. "You're a bloodthirsty little thing."

She blinked, absorbing the notion. "I think maybe I am."

He smiled faintly, though it didn't soften the planes of his face, which were suddenly harder, sharper. "Then I'll make you a bargain. You can bite me as often as you want, honey, as long as I get to do this." His palms covered her breasts.

Kitty jerked. "Oh." She looked down at his big hands. Then she glanced back at his face to see that he was looking there too, apparently captivated by the sight. The small mounds that she'd always considered disappointing, if she considered them at all, suddenly swelled. They tingled. She sucked in a sharp breath, trying to stop herself from pressing into him.

His thumbs moved, rotating along the outside curve of her flesh. They passed across the hard, jutting tips.

Kitty jerked again. "I'm not wearing a b-bra," she whispered, as if that could explain her body's jumpiness.

That faint, maybe-not-even-amused smile of his lifted the corners of his mouth. "I know." He rotated his thumbs once more and she almost screamed when they touched her nipples again—and then moved on.

"I'm not very big," she said.

His thumbs halted before they'd even made it to the best part, and she almost bit him again. "Maybe they're not very sensitive, then?"

They were so sensitive that she was shaking with desire. "Maybe . . ." It was the only word she could manage to force over her dry tongue.

His mouth kicked up in another half smile and he cocked an eyebrow at her. "Maybe I should make a full examination?"

Her eyes widened; her face went hot.

"Oh, Kitty." He closed his eyes and leaned forward to give her a hard, fast kiss. "How the hell do you do it?"

She trembled. "Do what?"

He took his hands off her breasts, then curled his fingers under the spaghetti straps of her tank top. "Make me feel like I'm making out in church."

Before she could digest that, he yanked. With the straps at her elbows, her breasts popped free, the spandex-and-cotton material of the top bunching beneath them.

"Damn," he whispered, his gaze burning her naked flesh. "Making out in church and loving every minute of it."

She inhaled, her breasts pushing forward. His gaze didn't move. *He* didn't move.

She was throbbing all over now. Her nipples, her breasts, in her belly, between her legs. This was desire, she thought. This craving, this need, this crying out of her body that was desperate to be assuaged.

Her whole life she'd wondered why men had visited The Burning Rose. Now she knew.

And didn't. Because any touch wouldn't do. It was Dylan who could lift this frustrating spell, only Dylan.

And still he didn't touch her.

"I'm going to bite you again," she said through her teeth.

"Sorry," he murmured. "But it's my turn now." He bent and took her entire breast in his mouth.

Kitty gasped. She arched into the heat, the wet, and he caught her. She bent backward over his arm, totally lost in the sensation of her flesh inside him, of his tongue sliding over sensitive skin. He curled his tongue around her nipple and she rose up on her toes, trying to keep connected there. *Right there.*

But the sensation feathered away and she heard a sound like a sob. His eyelashes flew up and his gaze flicked to her face. Assessed her expression. Then he let her breast slide out of his mouth until he held only the nipple. It rested against his tongue and Kitty thought she might go mad with the feeling of his hot breath blowing across her wet skin.

Then he sucked.

She thought she screamed.

But she didn't know what to believe, because she thought she'd been upright too, yet now she was pressed against the flat-topped boulder, shoulders to knees. Dylan was standing between her legs, bent over her bare breasts. He sucked the other nipple into his mouth.

Bit down.

A flaming arrow of pleasure shot from her breast to her womb. Her hips arched up and her ankles hooked the back of his legs. "Dylan," she choked out.

He bit again, and another arrow burned through her.

Her hips lifted once more. "Dylan." She grabbed at his shoulders, pulling his mouth toward hers.

"I'm not through—" His protest died as his bare chest abraded her damp breasts.

Kitty fisted her hand in his hair and held him against her mouth. She thrust her tongue between his lips, needing to take something, to take back control.

He sucked on her tongue.

Hot shivers erupted over every inch of her skin. She thrust against the pressure of his mouth. He groaned and her head spun as the sound vibrated against her tongue. Her heels dug into the backs of his hard thighs.

Finally, he tore himself away, resting his weight on his elbows, one on each side of her head. Trying to catch her breath, she made a face at him. "I really hate how you keep doing that."

One corner of his mouth lifted. It was almost worth losing his lips on hers to see that he had lost some of his earlier desperation. "Hate that I keep doing what?" he asked.

As if he didn't know.

She tried glaring at him. "Stopping like that. It's not fair. It seems so *easy* for you."

He laughed, his chest rubbing against hers. "This hard enough for you, baby?" He lowered his hips to press against hers.

Kitty closed her eyes to savor the delicious sensation. Her hip joints loosened, her legs splaying wider to accept more of his weight. "How could I have forgotten this?" she whispered.

"Hmm?"

She opened her eyes to find him studying her face. "It was the very first and very last time I ever drank beer, you know."

His dark brows scrunched into a single line. "What? When?"

"That night. You know." She blushed. "The Odd Fellows were selling beers and I nabbed a couple of six-packs when I saw you leaving the park." She'd followed him, and when she'd found him sitting on a fallen oak branch, she'd sat down too. And handed him a beer. Taken one herself.

Dylan shook his head and the ends of his long hair brushed her cheeks. "I'm sorry, sweetheart. I knew you were pretty out of it by the end of the evening. You must have had one hell of a headache the next day."

He kissed her temple, her forehead, the bridge of her nose. Anticipation shortened Kitty's breath. Then, under her hands, the muscles of his back tightened with renewed tension. Dylan's lips found hers, and he grunted in satisfaction. As he settled his weight on her, she opened her mouth for his tongue and this time he didn't pull away or stop too soon.

This time he devastated her with his kiss, thrusting his tongue in a slow, steady rhythm that he mimicked with his lower body. He pressed against her wide-open thighs and Kitty pressed back, lifting off the rock to meet him. She moaned and her hands touched him everywhere she could reach—sifting through his hair, spreading across his shoulders, sliding down his spine.

The throbbing intensified. As if he sensed it, he slowed the rocking rhythm, then stopped altogether. Using his weight to hold her down, he rubbed his hips against her, little movements that focused on the one point of her body that throbbed above all others.

Kitty shivered, but she couldn't stop herself from wriggling against the rock, instinctively trying to get out from under him, trying to get away from the sensations that were so much and yet not enough.

"Shh." He drew his wet mouth from her lips to her ear. "Stop squirming, honey—you'll scrape all that pretty skin off your back."

But she couldn't control her body. It was moving without her will. "I can't . . . I can't . . ."

"Shh," he repeated. "I can. I will." He slid one palm over her breast.

Kitty froze, then bowed into his touch. "Dylan." She thought she was begging. "Please."

"Yes."

His hand moved away from her breast and then he pushed off the rock, all the delicious touches gone as he stood over her. Half nervous, half excited, she watched his hands rush to the buttoned fly of his jeans.

His gaze on her body, he ripped two of the silver buttons open. Then he hesitated, shaking his head.

Kitty's heart pounded in her ears. The start-stop wasn't curbing her desire, but coiling it tighter, escalating its power.

"How do you do it?" he whispered, his voice hoarse.

"How can you lie there like that, yet look so damn innocent? So untouched?"

Her breathing labored, Kitty stared at his hands, willing them to get on with it. To get on *her*. She wanted to experience it again. Really remember it this time, instead of just as some half-hazy memory of this same pulsing desire. "You know I'm not," she said, hoping to hurry him along. "Eight years ago you and I . . ."

He froze. "Damn it!" His hand left his jeans and he smacked himself on the forehead. "*God damn it.*"

A chill washed over Kitty's heated skin. "W-what?"

He looked down at her, his expression savage, but no longer savage with desire. "What the hell are we doing? What the hell am *I* doing?"

Kitty slowly sat up. Without thinking, she pulled at the straps of her overalls and slid her arms through them, so that its bib covered her nakedness. "Well, um . . ."

He pointed an accusing finger at her. "Don't answer that. I don't want to think about it. I don't want to be tempted. Shit."

With vicious splashes, he waded out of the creek, then turned back, glaring at her from the other side. "You stay away from me. Eight years ago you were trouble I didn't see coming. I'm not going to let it happen again."

He kicked at the water, droplets arching into the sky, then falling like shooting stars. "Damn, damn, *damn*. I don't have a condom on me and I can't even say for sure that would have stopped me." With one more smack to his forehead, he was gone, though she could still hear him thrashing and cursing as he headed for the road.

She followed more slowly, desire still throbbing in her

body. It took her a couple of minutes to find her sandals—
they'd been flung into the creek in two different directions—
and then she had to pick her way back carefully in her
bare feet, holding her dripping sandals in one hand.

Just over a week ago she'd ordered him never to kiss
her again, yet she'd been dying to do that and more today. *Begging*.

Her face burning with embarrassment, she slowed
her steps, giving him plenty of time to reach his motorcycle and leave.

Except that he hadn't left. Looking angry and as dis-
solute and desirable as ever, he was sitting sideways on
the motorcycle seat, his legs stretched out in front of
him. He kept his gaze on the sodden toes of his boots as
she approached.

Her keys came flying through the air. She caught
them in her free hand. "Thanks for fixing my car," she
said, heat crawling up her neck again.

He grunted. He hesitated. He grunted again. "I'm
sorry, Kitty. I don't blame you for what just happened. I
shouldn't have made it sound like it was your fault."

But he should blame her. It *was* her fault. If she
hadn't married them, really and truly married them eight
years ago, he wouldn't be in Hot Water right now. She
thought of his face when he'd seen the ruins of Alicia's
impromptu memorial. There was no doubt he hadn't
wanted to come back.

But then she thought of his touch on her body, of his
smile when he'd teased her about her breasts. Oh, yes,
he should blame her.

Because it was so darn hard to regret Dylan's return.

Slowly she opened the T-bird door and tossed her

sandals onto the passenger seat. Obviously he wasn't going to leave until she did. Knowing Dylan, she figured he'd probably follow her back to town, just to make sure she and the new fan belt arrived safely.

The car started up just fine. She rolled down her window and looked at him. He was astride the motorcycle now and reaching for his helmet. Guilt gnawed at her. She owed him something—explanations—but some she couldn't make. This one, though, this one she could.

"Dylan."

"Yeah?" He flicked her a glance.

"I'm sorry about . . . earlier. Of course it was partly my fault. A lot my fault."

"Kitty—"

"Let me finish." She stared out the T-bird's dusty windshield, trying to be as honest as she could. "The truth is—the truth is I don't remember that night eight years ago all that clearly. I told you about me and beer. So I . . . I think today I just wanted to gather all those long-ago impressions and make them more . . . real."

Confession made, she was so embarrassed she hit the gas and steered the T-bird into a spectacular U-turn that spit gravel in every direction. Now even more embarrassed, she didn't hesitate to press down on the accelerator again and head for home.

Chapter Nine

Samantha Wilder led the way into the kitchen of her small house behind Bum Luck. In one smooth movement, she pulled out a chair for Aunt Cat, then swept the white pharmacy bag on the nearby countertop into the utensil drawer. Tucking a strand of hair behind her ear, she smiled at the woman whom she'd named her daughter after, the woman who had raised her daughter. "Iced tea?"

"Thank you," Aunt Cat said. "And thank you for taking me home from the beauty shop."

Samantha turned toward the refrigerator. "You'd be home already if I didn't have to meet Sylvia here to pass over the bar receipts. But I promise to get you there in half an hour or so."

"I'm in no hurry. It gives me a chance to spend some time with you."

Samantha hesitated. "Maybe you shouldn't." Then, without meeting her aunt's gaze, she set a tall glass of tea on the small kitchen table.

"If you're talking about that silly business with Pearl, you know that kind of talk has never bothered me."

Samantha reached for the sugar bowl and put it down beside the glass. As she opened the drawer for a spoon, the white paper bag inside caught on something and crackled loudly. Her heart jumped. Hoping her guilt didn't show, she shoved the bag farther back and picked up a spoon, which she placed beside the glass of tea with more force than she'd intended.

"I'm not involved with Pearl's husband," she said. "He just visits the bar on occasion."

Aunt Cat sipped at her tea. "How is Bum Luck doing?"

Samantha almost laughed. Of course, the laugh would have sounded high and hysterical, but it was still funny how little some things changed. Aunt Cat was as imperturbable today as she had been so long ago when Samantha told her she was three months shy of becoming an unwed teenage mother. Samantha swallowed hard, forcing down another bubble of hysteria.

"The bar is doing fine. Great." Three years before, when she'd hit forty years old, she'd begun thinking of changing occupations. She'd already gone longer in the business than anyone she knew, and despite long hours at the gym, her body had started showing its age. Hysteria threatened to rise again, and Samantha pressed a fist against her stomach.

"It was a good choice for you then," Aunt Cat remarked.

"Maybe." Though buying a bar *had* been a good choice. If there were two things Samantha did well, they were serving drinks and pleasing men. "But perhaps I shouldn't have come back here."

Aunt Cat gave her a look that was part exasperation, part fondness. "But you did. That should tell you something, Sammy."

Hearing that long-gone nickname made Samantha want to scream and cry at the same time. Was that why she'd come back? To a place where someone remembered that once upon a time she'd been Sammy? No. That was too close to seeking a second chance, and Samantha didn't believe in those at all.

"I wish Kitty hadn't been there today." The words slipped out. She hadn't been planning to bring up Kitty. She tried never to think about her, and she'd become expert at it after so many years.

"You could try talking to her," Aunt Cat said.

But that was like asking for a second chance too. "I don't really think she wants me to."

Aunt Cat took another sip of iced tea. "Kitty . . . Kitty is still trying to figure herself out."

Samantha grimaced. "Join the club." Except a woman of her age should already know who she was. What she was. The most she could ever be. A woman her age should be contemplating the second half of her life with serenity, with grace. She certainly shouldn't be forced to contemplate—

The doorbell rang and she hurried toward it, glad to escape her thoughts. When she pulled the door open, a tiny, chubby whirlwind rushed past her knees. Sylvia

Kula came next, waddling like a duck that had swallowed a beach ball.

Samantha almost cried at the sight of her, the pregnant woman appeared that beautiful.

Sylvia groaned. "How can you look so cool and fabulous when I feel like a squat mushroom?"

Samantha laughed. "And here I was thinking you looked like Mother Earth come calling."

Sylvia rolled her big brown eyes. They were bright and her skin and hair had a healthy, fecund sheen. That unmistakable evidence of fertility fascinated Samantha, she supposed because in her previous life pregnancy had been something abhorred and avoided at all costs.

"Where's Mother Earth's little Earthlette, then?" Sylvia said. "We better find her before she eats her way through your cookie jar."

They headed for the kitchen, where they indeed found Sylvia's three-year-old daughter, the whirlwind Amalie, seated at the kitchen table beside Aunt Cat, the cookie jar before her.

Aunt Cat looked up. "Amalie says you make the best chocolate chip cookies in the whole world, Sammy."

Amalie only nodded, a chocolate smear at one corner of her mouth. Samantha's heart twisted. The little girl was so . . . everything Samantha had missed before. So everything that was too late for her now.

She poured two glasses of lemonade and set one in front of Amalie. The other she handed to Sylvia. "Come in my office and I'll get you what you need."

She'd converted the second bedroom of the house into an office, though it couldn't hold much more than a desk, a computer, and a fax machine. She didn't even need those, really, because she farmed out the bookwork to Sylvia.

Samantha rummaged through a stack on a corner of the desk. "I received something from a new supplier that I wouldn't mind getting your opinion on."

"Sure, just put it with the other stuff and I'll look at it when I get home." Sylvia flopped down in the room's one chair and lifted her legs straight out to stare morosely at her ankles. "Swollen," she declared. "Everything about me is swollen. My breasts, my stomach, my ankles."

Samantha bit back her grin. "I'm sorry, Sylvia."

"My *knees* are swollen." Sylvia looked up at Samantha. "Amalie pointed that out to me. And then five minutes later said she hoped her little sister would be blond and blue-eyed like you."

Samantha couldn't help smiling now.

Sylvia groaned. "The truth is, I hope she is too. What am I saying? Every time I come over here *I* want to be tall and blond. Nobody wants to be a short, tubby brunette like me."

Sobering instantly, Samantha dropped the papers in her hand. "Oh, no. Don't say that. I don't mean to make you feel bad. I won't see Amalie anymore, or you, or . . ." She paused when she noticed Sylvia staring at her. "Or whatever you want."

"Samantha . . ." Sylvia slid to the edge of the chair and grabbed one of Samantha's hands between her own. "I didn't mean it that way. It was the pregnancy blues talking, with a tad of self-pity mixed in. It was the kind of babble a woman friend can only share with another woman friend."

"Oh." Samantha's eyes stung. She blinked, embarrassed by this strange new tendency to get teary-eyed at the drop of a hat. "I'd . . . I'd like to be your friend, Sylvia." She couldn't remember having a woman friend before. Rivals, yes. Friends, no.

Sylvia smiled. "Why, Samantha, we already are. Don't you know that?"

"Yes," she whispered. She'd felt comfortable with Sylvia right away, but she hadn't seriously considered that the other woman would want her friendship.

Clearing her throat, she released Sylvia's hand and turned back to the desk. Finding the right papers at last, she swung around. "Here you go," she said. "I—" She broke off, noticing that Sylvia appeared asleep.

Sylvia opened her eyes. "Don't worry, I'm still breathing."

Samantha frowned. "But you look done in. Why don't you go home and take a nap? Leave Amalie with me and I'll drop her off after I take Aunt Cat home." The instant the words were out, she wished she hadn't said them. Friends or not, Samantha was a woman who hadn't taken care of her own daughter. And with Pearl stirring up gossip all over town . . . She'd just placed poor Sylvia in one hell of a position.

"You're an angel."

Samantha gaped. "Y-you're sure?"

The other woman was already heading for the kitchen. "Amalie will think it's a great adventure. I warn you, she'll be begging you to dye her hair or something, but I promise not to hold it against you if she badgers you into agreeing."

Samantha couldn't help laughing. "I think I can promise she won't go blond."

In the kitchen, it was decided that Sylvia would drive Aunt Cat home now and that Sylvia's husband, Tony, would pick Amalie up after his workday ended. That way, Samantha needn't rush around before her shift at Bum Luck. Within a few minutes the house was empty except for Samantha and Amalie, who, as predicted, immediately wanted to know how to make her hair "yellow."

"When you're a grown-up lady," Samantha said firmly, "if you still want yellow hair, you can go to a good beauty shop and pay someone to make it that color. But I hope you keep it just the color it is, Amalie. Your hair is beautiful."

Amalie beamed. " 'Tis?"

" 'Tis." Samantha couldn't stop herself from leaning down and placing a kiss on the little girl's curly, dark hair. Its scent was sweet and light and the name of the delicious fragrance danced on the edge of Samantha's mind.

"What should we do now?" she asked Amalie.

There wasn't a doubt in the three-year-old's female mind. "Paint fingernails and eat cookies."

Samantha's lips twitched. Three? Forty-three? There wasn't much distance between the two. "Those just happen to be my two favorite things to do in the whole wide world."

The hot-pink nail color Amalie chose was a beautiful contrast to her golden-tan skin. She seemed to think so too. She danced in front of the mirror in Samantha's bedroom, holding her fingers out like fans as she admired her reflection. While Samantha watched her, another draft of the girl's sweet fragrance floated past and Samantha wished she could remember what it was.

She smiled. "Well, my beauty, what's next on our agenda?"

Amalie opened her eyes wide. "Cookies?"

"Don't you think we've had enough?" When the little girl looked about to protest, Samantha hurriedly compromised. "I'll send some home with you when your daddy picks you up. How's that?"

"Okay," Amalie said. Her face brightened. "How 'bout ice cream?"

Samantha had to laugh. And, of course, Amalie recognized it for the sucker sound that it was.

"Vanilla," she said, skipping toward the kitchen.

Samantha laughed again. "Which is the flavor you had here last week." Actually, she'd bought it with the little girl in mind, just as she'd baked the chocolate chip cookies for her this morning.

Checking the clock, she decided to make it a very small scoop. As she reached into the freezer, she called over her shoulder, "Can you find the spoons, Amalie? They're in the top drawer by the sink."

" 'Kay."

The ice cream was hard as granite and Samantha adjusted the freezer temperature before tackling it with a metal scooper. The frozen stuff peeled off in thin curls, and it took a surprising amount of time and elbow grease before she had even a small bowl's worth.

"Here you go," she finally said, and swung around to the table. Amalie sat patiently, spoon nearby.

The child had found something to entertain herself with while waiting. The white bag that Samantha had stuffed into the utensil drawer was on the kitchen table. Amalie had dumped out the contents and was inspecting each of the four different boxes inside.

Samantha's stomach heaved. She dropped the bowl back on the counter, then ran to the bathroom and threw up. Standing on shaky legs, she washed her face with cold water, brushed her teeth, then stared at her forty-three-year-old image in the mirror.

She knew she was still a good-looking woman. She was tall and full-breasted and she needed only an occasional touch-up to hide the few strands of gray in her blond hair. Though her physical characteristics had been her stock in trade for over twenty years, she'd welcomed the signs of advancing middle age. A psychiatrist—or even an experienced bartender, for that matter—would analyze her welcome of the aging process easily. Obviously, she'd been more than relieved to finally find a good reason to leave the tawdry business she called a career behind.

That was what was so damn ironic about her new predicament. She'd been *welcoming* middle age, for God's sake.

Sighing, she walked back into the kitchen. Amalie's ice cream still sat on the counter and Samantha half smiled as she placed it in front of the little girl.

"Tanks." Amalie smiled back, and abandoned her found playthings to apply herself to the vanilla ice cream.

As Samantha bent to pick the paper bag off the table, another wave of Amalie's delicate scent struck her. Her fingers froze halfway to the bag. *Oh, God.* She recognized the so-appealing fragrance now. It was baby powder.

Heart pounding, she slowly retrieved each box off the table, refusing to consider the scent an omen. It couldn't be, she thought, redepositing the four different brands of unopened pregnancy tests inside the paper bag. Just as she couldn't be pregnant. Surely one of these tests would give a different result from the first one she'd taken.

A few hours later Samantha saw Judge D. B. Matthews walk into Bum Luck with another man who had to be his son. Standing at the bar, Samantha felt her stomach pitch, but she wrestled it back under control. With shaking hands she ran a glass of cold water and swallowed down some of the liquid. In the mirror behind the bar, she watched the two newcomers stroll through the room. D. B. looked a whisker short of all-out grinning as they paused beside a corner booth stuffed with six young men.

He wore the pride and pleasure he had in his grown son like another layer of skin. Queasiness descended again, but again Samantha fought it off. She swallowed one last sip of water, then forced herself over to D. B.'s usual table, where he was just settling in across from his son.

She gave both men her most professional smile. "Judge, how nice to see you. Your usual martini, I presume. And for you?" Her gaze shifted to the younger man.

"Samantha, this is my son, Dylan." D. B.'s voice was rich with love, and it made her blink back more of those too-ready tears. "Dylan, Samantha Wilder."

The tall young man pushed out of his chair and held out his hand. "Ms. Wilder."

She shook his hand. "Please, it's Samantha." Though his dark good looks were similar to his father's, none of D. B.'s ebullient mood seemed to have rubbed off. Dylan studied her with an intensity that wasn't impolite, but it wasn't understandable either.

Her spine stiffened. Did he know something? Had D. B. told him something?

"I . . . know Kitty," Dylan said.

Samantha felt herself flush. "Ah. Well." She looked away, unsure of what to say. "What can I get you to drink?"

"A beer—no." His expression tightened. "I'll have a whiskey."

"One whiskey, one martini." Samantha surrendered to the urge to look at D. B. again.

He was gazing at Dylan, though, still wearing a faint smile. "You don't know how often I've imagined us sitting here like this," he said to his son.

To his grown son. To the son he'd raised when he'd been left widowed as a young man. On legs gone suddenly heavy, she made her way back to the bar to fill their order.

Their drinks balanced on a tray, Samantha took another sip of her water before delivering them. She met her own gaze in the mirror and nodded, understanding what she was going to have to do. Tonight.

Tonight she had to break off her affair with Judge D. B. Matthews.

The fling had been ill-conceived to begin with, she thought, then almost laughed aloud at her awful pun. God. Ill-conceived.

The whiskey and the martini wobbled on the tray and she hastily rested it on the counter. With both hands she lifted her water glass and drained it, hoping the cool liquid would settle her stomach, as well as settle her mind to do this thing. This very right thing.

Six months ago she'd chosen to return to Hot Water for reasons she still didn't understand. She'd faced just what she'd expected—whispers, innuendo, some barely concealed animosity along with some less-concealed curiosity. Most of the reaction came from typical small-town small-mindedness, though part of it seemed to stem from protectiveness toward Kitty. Samantha doubted her daughter knew how many champions she had in town. As *she* very well knew, living with the Wilder reputation could blind a woman.

Then, soon after she'd opened Bum Luck, D. B. had come in one night. The judge. She'd been nervous at first, which was funny, because men never made her nervous. She'd chalked it up to his high rank in town.

Without even thinking about it, she'd gone straight into vamp mode, adding an extra little sashay to her walk, lightly teasing him without quite meeting his eyes. It was the armor she'd used for more than twenty years, a flirtatious yet touch-me-not attitude to contrast with her please-touch-me profession. Always it had both protected her and driven men wild.

The thing was, D. B. had seen right through it. Sure, she'd noticed that swinging her hips and giving him an extra glimpse or two of her cleavage had made his cock play soldier like every man's before him, but he'd laughed about it.

He'd laughed at her.

She was offended at first. Then embarrassed at how obvious she must seem to him. And then on a subsequent visit, he'd stayed past closing to lift the chairs onto the tables for her. Despite the bulge she could see in his pants, he'd also helped her complete the rest of the mundane closing tasks, then brewed a pot of decaf coffee himself and poured her a cup while *she* sat down.

They hadn't talked about their pasts. Instead, they'd exchanged ideas about running a business, about small-town life, about middle age and all that it meant. He'd been friendly to her, nothing more. Yet after he'd left and she'd locked up, she'd thought about kissing him.

And the next time he stayed after closing, *he'd* kissed *her*. Their affair began.

But she'd always known it had to end. He was a Matthews; he was a judge. She was a Wilder first, and then all that she'd been after.

If there really was a child growing in her belly, D. B. Matthews wouldn't want to be its father. He and Samantha were supposed to be engaged in an affair. No, in something less. A fling.

God, not in forever.

But the more she thought about it, the more that

menopause or premenopause or *something* like that seemed likely—there just couldn't be a child on its way.

Inhaling a deep breath, Samantha picked up the tray and then walked toward D. B. This time he looked up and smiled at her, but she pretended not to notice as she slid the drinks onto the table.

She spoke to the vicinity of his nose. "Would you like a tab, or . . . ?"

"I'll settle up at the end of the night," D. B. said.

She fought off the little shiver rolling down her back. "Fine." That usually meant he was going to stay until after closing. That he was going to stay with her. "Good."

It was good. It would give her time, tonight, to tell him it was over.

The next hours passed in a blur. Samantha supposed she poured drinks and made change and smiled and said good night, because the till was full and she had dozens of dirty glasses to wash when the clock read closing time. Dylan had taken off after nursing his first whiskey and half of another, leaving his father contemplating two of the three fat olives she always put in his martinis.

After locking the door, she poured two mugs of decaf. Then, plastering on a sophisticated, if-only-you've-seen-what-I've-seen smile, she seated herself opposite D. B., setting one mug of coffee before him.

"Hi," he said softly. He took her hand in both of his. "You look tired."

He was a beautiful man. His body was lean and the lines on his handsome face were made by years of smiling, of laughing, of caring about other people. Steeling herself, she slipped her hands from his and gave them two brief pats.

His eyes narrowed. "What's going on?" he asked.

Damn, he was smart. She stared into her coffee mug, thinking this shouldn't be so hard. "D. B. . . . I . . . we . . ."

The legs of his chair screeched against the parquet floor as he scooted close to her. "What's the matter, sweetheart?" He ran the knuckles of one hand down her cheek.

She almost lost it right there. She wanted to put her head down on the table and cry. Worse, she wanted to climb onto his lap and weep against his warm neck that she knew smelled of shaving cream and sandalwood.

Instead, she lifted her head. She thought of all the times she'd had to pretend, night after night, years and years of pretending, and looked him straight in the eye. "I don't think we should see each other anymore."

"What?" He didn't even blink.

She let one eyebrow arch, as if she were slightly annoyed by his inattention. "We're not going to see each other anymore."

"Bullshit." Now he blinked, but only in the most natural of ways. Not as if she'd stunned him, surprised him, or even disappointed him.

Uneasiness trickled down her spine. "I said—"

"And I said bullshit."

Samantha sat, frozen. For twenty years she'd been able to wear next to nothing and direct men to do her bidding. It had been a gift, considering her business. She'd been able to maintain her dignity, to be touched in ways that only she allowed, because of this certain air of command she possessed that had never failed her.

She swallowed. "D. B. . . ."

He leaned forward. "I've missed you," he said against her mouth. He parted her lips and slid his tongue inside. It rubbed against hers like old friends rubbing shoulders.

Samantha shuddered, her resolve slipping too easily away. As if he'd read her mind earlier, he urged her out of her chair and onto his lap.

She had no idea why she went so willingly. But his mouth tasted like vodka's dry heat and his hand was so soothing when it trailed down her back, then not soothing at all as it edged under her sleeveless turtleneck and then inside her bra to cup her breast.

"Let's take this off, sweetheart," he said. In seconds he'd bared her torso, and her hard nipples were poking against the soft cotton of his sport shirt. He squeezed one between his thumb and forefinger.

Samantha moaned. She didn't want to. She was supposed to be . . . He squeezed again and she couldn't remember whatever it was. No man, ever, had made her respond so quickly, so easily.

"You're so ready tonight," he whispered, his eyes full of praise. His tongue filled her mouth and she melted into his body at the same time that she arched into the hand on her breast. He touched the waistband of her long black skirt. "Let's get this off too."

"Yes," she whispered back. Then froze. No! No, she was supposed to be stopping this. Ending this. But his hand gave a parting tweak to her hard, tingling nipple and she couldn't hold onto her resolve.

He helped her stand, and as he unfastened the buttons of her skirt she told herself maybe it would be better this way. Why, yes. She'd always been at her best telling men what to do when she didn't have her clothes on.

As if to prove her point, when her skirt dropped to the floor, he groaned. "You're going to kill me, sweetheart."

Some habits never died. Under her long black skirt she wore a tiny triangle of gauzy black panty and a black garter belt and stockings. The first time she'd been with D. B., she'd discovered how much he liked her bad-girl underwear. And as the saying went, if the shoe fit—or in this case, the lingerie . . .

Then she couldn't think anymore, because he brushed his big hand between her thighs to push her panties aside and slide his long middle finger inside her. She was already wet—how had he known?—and her body bowed.

"D. B. . . ."

"Shh." He positioned her in front of him, that finger still penetrating her. "Let me look at how pretty you are."

Pretty. "Pretty" was for young girls. Sammy had been pretty. Samantha was beautiful, sexy, she made men—

D. B. slid another finger inside her. She moaned. "So pretty," he said. He cupped her breast and rubbed his thumb across the nipple. His other thumb found her clitoris and he rubbed that too.

Samantha gasped. "D. B., let me, let's . . ."

"Shh. This is for you."

She braced her hand on his shoulder. Oh, God. For her. When had a man done something *for her*?

His thumbs continued to strum her. Her head fell back. He was good at this, Samantha thought, as good as she had always been at pretending for men. Hundreds of them. Thousands of them.

But their nameless faces spun out of her thoughts when D. B. touched her. She didn't need to pretend for him. She couldn't pretend with him. She'd tried to pretend she wanted their affair to end and he'd seen through that just as he'd seen through her mantrap-vamp posturing.

He was twisting his fingers inside her. She could hear the sexy, arousing sounds of her own wetness, and her nipples budded impossibly tighter. Her knees softened and she bore down, into those knowing, almost-good-enough fingers. Her orgasm was rising, swirling, a tornado, a hurricane; it was something big and scary and she didn't want to be in it alone.

"D. B.," she murmured, so close she was desperate. "Take your clothes off, your pants . . . please. Please."

Again he didn't obey. "This is yours, sweetheart." He thrust his fingers high, then pulsed his thumb against her throbbing clitoris. "Take it, sweetheart."

Samantha screamed. Her muscles spasmed and he groaned as her body locked onto his fingers and she spun into the storm.

The next thing she knew, she was on his lap again, still shivering in reaction. He held her close against him, soothing her with long, comforting strokes of his palm. She lifted her mouth and kissed his chin. "Thank you," she said.

He shifted her closer against his chest. "I think I'm the one who should be grateful."

She kissed him again. "I can make you *very* grateful."

"Not tonight." His cheek rubbed the top of her hair.

"Tonight was just for you. But I'll help you put the chairs up and then walk you home and tuck you into bed."

"But—"

"No. You look too tired." He lifted her chin with his finger and looked into her eyes. "You need your sleep if you're going to be your pretty self in the morning."

Pretty. There it was again. Giddiness rose inside her, glittering bubbles of effervescence that were like nothing she'd ever felt before. It wasn't power. It wasn't sex. She knew what both of those felt like.

It was something only D. B. gave to her. Like how he made her feel pretty. Pretty and young and sexy and . . . in love.

That giddiness was love. She was in love with him.

Closing her eyes, she rested her cheek against the strong, thudding beat of his heart. Behind her eyelids, tears stung. The affair would have to end soon, of course, because of her possible pregnancy and because of the past she'd never told him about. But not just yet. She needed a little more time, just a little, because she'd never been in love before. And since she didn't believe in second chances, she knew she'd never be in love again.

Chapter Ten

Dylan might have imagined that the note Kitty left him on the desk in the sheriff's office smelled faintly of roses, but there was no doubting that was the fragrance beckoning him through the open front door of The Burning Rose. Steeling himself against its lure, he stepped inside.

"Kitty," he called out.

Her voice drifted down the stairs. "Up here."

He hesitated. It was half an hour before the living-history district opened. While soon they'd be mobbed by the weekend visitors, now the brothel was quiet. He'd be alone with Kitty.

Since last Monday on that rock on the outskirts of town, he'd been keeping himself sane—and away from her—by remembering she was trouble. Trouble that had brought him back to Hot Water, where he was forced to play sheriff. Trouble that meant painful, twilight glimpses of Bram Bennett, who had once been his best friend. Trouble that brought him face-to-face with other old friends, coaches, and schoolteachers who couldn't wait to tell him they hoped he'd come home to stay.

But the note he'd found, saying "Aunt Cat asked me to invite you to dinner tomorrow night. I'll be there too," must be addressed. The invitation must be refused. Kitty tempted him too much.

He mounted the stairs slowly, trying not to think of all the men who had walked this way before him. But the wooden treads were worn in their centers and his boots slid into the depressions naturally, like a man slides into a woman. The morning air outside had been pleasant, but as he climbed the stairs of the brothel, the temperature spiked and the atmosphere thickened like breathless anticipation.

How many sex acts had been performed within these walls? Ghosts of copulations past seemed to swirl around him and the hairs on the back of his neck rose. He hesitated again.

Superstitious, horny fool. Scoffing at himself, he stepped on the top stair. The old wood groaned like a man in the final throes of orgasm and he almost leaped out of his skin.

"Is that you, Dylan?" Kitty's voice emerged from the first bedroom on the right. "Are you all right?"

No. He was haunted by the past, in more ways than one. And he was frustrated, both situationally and sexually, but damned if he was going to let Kitty know any of that. Instead of speaking, he grunted, then entered the bedroom.

She looked up. "Bad mood?"

Her instant read might have made his bad mood even blacker if he could have worked up any thought at the moment besides one. But with Kitty sitting on the crimson-colored bed in the crimson-colored room, the only thing on his mind was sin. Wicked sin. The dress she wore was the shade of raspberry sherbet, and like all her other costumes, it left her shoulders and the tops of her breasts bare. That wasn't what riveted him. He'd almost gotten used to seeing all *that* skin—liar, liar, pants on fire—but what snared his attention now was that she had her skirt lifted.

Above her knees.

Kitty sat on the edge of the bed with the front hem of her skirt pulled up as she worked on it with a needle. Her legs were modestly crossed and she was mending. Common, ordinary mending.

Yet, as Dylan stared at her legs, his pulse started a heavy chug-chug through his veins. Though he'd seen her wearing shorts, there was something about this view of her incredible legs, framed by the froth of ruffles in her lap, that made it seem forbidden. Nasty. Tasty.

"Did you want something?" Her gaze on him, she leaned down and bit off a hanging thread.

He wanted her to bite *him*. Bite him again. His hand rose to his throat and he rubbed his knuckles over the place she'd marked him on Monday. The signs of her teeth were gone now, but the memory of their stinging pleasure hadn't left. Nor had the memory of her face once she'd done it, her eyes wide in aroused awe at her own daring.

"Dylan?"

He shook himself. "Hmm?"

"Did you get my note?" Kitty asked.

Her note. Thinking back, he ran his hands through his hair. The note. Her note. The invitation. His refusal wouldn't surprise Kitty. She'd made that point moot by clearly indicating she'd be dining with her aunt then too. The last thing the two of them needed was more togetherness.

"Right," he started. "I—"

"Kitty Wilder, I've been looking for you everywhere." Mrs. Shea, of Shea's Dry Goods, bustled through the door of the small room. The space her plump body required forced Dylan a few feet closer to the bed.

Surprised, Dylan stared at the older woman. As stocky as she was, she must have moved up the stairs like a cat, or else he was even more distracted than he thought.

Kitty looked surprised too. Pausing in her stitching, she raised her eyebrows. "How can I help you?"

"We're *not* going to hold another sharpshooter contest on Heritage Day," Mrs. Shea declared in ringing tones. "I won't have it." She crossed her arms in agitation, and her enveloping gingham dress billowed out, then fell with all the grace of a gunny sack around her.

All the female reenactors—Mrs. Kelcher of Kelcher's Boarding Rooms; Claudia Lee, who gave tours of the Joss House; and Laura Phipps, who worked in the Wells Fargo Office, to name but a few—wore similarly styled dresses. His gaze drifted toward Kitty. The high-necked, voluminous things the other women wore only served to make her look that much more . . . undressed.

He quickly averted his eyes, deciding he better go ahead and take care of his business. "Kitty, I just came to say—"

She talked right over him. "I never said anything about another sharpshooter contest, Mrs. Shea."

The other woman harrumphed. "Then why is Spenser talking about one?"

Kitty's forehead pleated. "I don't know why—"

"What's wrong with a contest?" Wheezing, but with a militant glint in his eye, old Spenser limped into the room, propelling Mrs. Shea forward, which in turn pushed Dylan up against the bed.

Spenser hooked his thumbs in his assay-officer suspenders. "Remember, we held one once and—"

"And thanks to that ridiculous idea of Kitty's, my husband, John, is now missing an earlobe!" Propping her hands on her hips, Mrs. Shea turned her wrath on Spenser.

Kitty grimaced, then looked up and caught Dylan's eye. She dropped her needle and thread and pushed her small pink ears forward with her palms. "They stick way out," she mouthed, then gave him a guilty grin.

Dylan knew John. Less ear could only be an improvement. "Well, Mrs. Shea," he said innocently, holding Kitty's gaze, "maybe this would be a good time to even them—"

Kitty reached over and gave a ruthless pinch to the back of Dylan's thigh. His suggestion ended in a strangled groan and he fell to the mattress in pain.

The dizzying scent of roses filled his head as she leaned over him and smiled with saccharine sweetness.

"Charley horse?" Under her breath, she added, "Watch it. She's mad enough as it is. Next time it's the needle.

"I promise," she said, turning back to Mrs. Shea. "I don't have any plans like you're worried about."

The older woman still appeared unappeased. "Then where did the rumor come from? It had John practicing on tin cans last night and he put holes in the laundry your mother had on her line."

Kitty stiffened. "M-my mother?"

"I saw it myself. I don't know where we're going to find scandalous underwear like that to replace it, but I caught John staring at those things over the fence. Not white underwear like God-fearing women wear, but red, purple, even black!" Mrs. Shea harrumphed again. "You should have seen the guilt on my husband's face. On one set he'd shot the fabric between the legs and over the basooms clean away!"

Dylan slowly sat up. Out of the corner of his eye he saw Spenser rubbing his silver-whiskered chin, his bushy eyebrows drawn together. Dylan didn't dare look at Kitty. "Um, Mrs. Shea, did John, um, *admit* to the, um, desecration?"

The woman's eyes widened. " 'Desecration'? It was hardly sacrilege."

"That could be a matter of opinion," he murmured, then raised his voice. "So he said he did it?"

Her eyebrows slammed together. "Of course he didn't. What man ever admits to anything? But he was all puffed up and red in the face, just like I will be if I have to knock on Samantha Wilder's door and ask where she purchases such things so I can replace them. Kitty, you'll have to do that for me."

"I'm sure my—Samantha won't expect you to . . . to replace anything," Kitty said.

Dylan turned his head to stare at her. Instead of sounding like she was about to bust with laughter as he was, her voice was wooden and so was her expression. "You don't even need to tell her what happened," she added. "We can keep this whole thing between us."

"Well, it's too late for that," Mrs. Shea said. "I already told Amy Byer about it. Lisa Thomas and Pearl too. Your mother is going to hear sooner or later."

Spenser winked at Dylan. "Make that the whole town." He turned toward the door. "I still think a sharpshooter contest is a good idea."

Galvanized once more, Mrs. Shea hurried after him. "You'd better let the entire subject drop, Spenser Marsh!"

Their argument and their footsteps clattered down the stairs, leaving Dylan once again alone with Kitty. In a brothel. On a bed.

He shifted toward her. "Kitty, about tomorrow night . . ."

Her face was averted from his as she looked out the room's small window. He followed her gaze, tracing Hot Water's rolling hills and its residential streets that followed the old, twisting miners' paths. Among the heavy foliage of long-established trees he spotted the white cupola of his father's big house and the tall spire of the Methodist church.

"Do you ever miss it?" she asked.

He swallowed.

"Believe it or not, I wi—would." She closed her eyes and her curly lashes fanned against her cheeks. "Mrs.

Shea, Spenser, Pearl. The past, the present, the good, the bad. No matter what, it's still home."

He nodded. Kitty's voice held all the ambivalence that he also felt. "There's no place else in the world like it. Your roots are here."

She opened her eyes and looked at him. "Yours too."

"I . . ."

"Admit it, son."

Dylan jumped, startled to find his father now in the room. "Judge. I didn't hear you come in." Christ, whenever he was around Kitty he was either so lost in lust or so lost in figuring her out that the street skills he'd trained so hard for deserted him.

"I don't think either one of you would have noticed an elephant tromping through." His father's face was watchful.

"Were you looking for me, Judge?" Kitty asked.

Dylan rose off the bed. "I have something quick to tell Kitty and then—"

"Sit down, sit down." The judge gestured with his hand. "It's you I was looking for."

Dylan narrowed his eyes. "Me?" He studied his father. The old man—hell, he appeared to get younger by the day—looked as successful as a small-town lawyer-turned-judge had a right to, dressed in Saturday khakis and a sport shirt. A hundred years ago Dylan had expected to be that same small-town lawyer and then a judge as well. His fingers curled into fists as pain shot through him, as vicious and biting as on the day he'd left Hot Water.

"A call came to the house this morning after you left," the judge said, slipping his hands into his pockets.

"I promised Nick I'd get back to him today after I talked to you."

Dylan went instantly wary, his training finally kicking in, better late than never. His father's pose was too casual, his voice too laid-back. "Get back to Nick about what?"

"You know the camp for underprivileged kids the Odd Fellows run outside of town." At Dylan's nod, his father's gaze slid away from his. "Nick was wondering if you could come out and give a couple of talks to the kids. Morale boosters, that kind of thing. On the, uh, nature of heroism."

Christ Almighty. "No."

His father pulled his hands from his pockets. "Dylan—"

"No." On the nature of heroism. Shit.

The judge frowned. "Don't say th—"

"No." Dylan was aware of Kitty, wide-eyed beside him. Of his father's tension, now undisguised. Neither mattered.

The judge sighed. "C'mon, son. At least talk to Nick. There's an Odd Fellows meeting coming up and he's hoping to see you there. Come as my guest." He hesitated, then looked Dylan straight in the eye. "Do it for me."

That pain stabbed Dylan again, sharp and deep. Get sucked into the Odd Fellows? Get corralled into talking on the "nature of heroism"? He couldn't do it. He wouldn't do it. And yet the man he'd loved and admired his whole life, the man he'd disappointed as deeply, probably, as he'd disappointed himself, was the one asking him. "When's the meeting?"

"Tomorrow night."

Dylan almost laughed out loud at the irony. But his gut told him that evading the fire for the frying pan was the lesser of the two evil options he had to choose from. "Sorry. Previous engagement. Ask Kitty. I'm spending the evening with her and her aunt Cat."

Kitty supposed she had no right to be angry with Dylan for accepting Aunt Cat's invitation. But as she passed the mashed potatoes to him on Sunday night, she *was* mad. And worried. Barbed wire didn't guard *her* heart and he was getting way too close. Every time they were together he managed to uncover more of her.

Take yesterday morning, for example. Just when she thought she could look at him without the cravings beginning, without remembering the texture of his fingertips stroking her skin, the rough surface of his tongue on her nipples, and wanting those sensations all over again, he'd seen her stripped naked.

By Mrs. Shea and her mother's underwear. With Dylan as witness, that humiliating story had peeled away yet another layer of Kitty's hard-won dignity. As had happened over and over during the past six months, every time Kitty relaxed, every time she thought she had the Wilder notoriety safely closeted for the moment, Samantha had managed to throw open the doors. This time exposing her kinky lingerie in the process.

"I can't remember the last dinner I had this good, Ms. Wilder," Dylan said.

Aunt Cat beamed. "I thought we owed you something for taking over the sheriff's job."

Dylan glanced at Kitty. "The truth is—"

"That I owe him something, Aunt Cat," Kitty said, flashing him a look of warning. "And I've promised to see that he gets it."

"The truth is," Dylan repeated, ignoring her interruption, "I'm glad to have something to do."

Kitty lifted her head. "Then you're not mad at me anymore . . . ?"

"Don't push your luck, kid," he murmured, then gave Aunt Cat a rueful smile. "I wouldn't know how to fill all the vacation time otherwise. In L.A. or here."

"There's a lot of people in Hot Water who might have some ideas about that, including your father," Aunt Cat answered.

Dylan's expression closed. "Maybe that's just another reason I'm glad I have the sheriff's job to do."

The forkful of roasted chicken turned to dust in Kitty's mouth as she recalled the awkward tension between Dylan and the judge the morning before. His father had tried to draw him into the community and Dylan had nimbly but doggedly sidestepped the gentle noose. At Dylan's refusal to attend the Odd Fellows meeting, the patent yearning on Judge Matthews's face had disappeared, to be replaced by an acute disappointment.

She looked across the table at Dylan. "Your father wants you to stay." Appalled at her own words, she tried apologizing. "I'm sorry, it's none of—"

"I won't," Dylan said, his voice matter-of-fact. "I . . . can't. The judge remembers I once thought about practicing law here, but that plan died when . . ." He cleared his throat. "It died a long time ago."

Kitty dropped her gaze. The tines of her fork clinked against her plate as she stabbed another bite of meat, though she really wanted to stab Dylan. Darn him. No. *Damn* him.

"You have something against that chicken?" His expression had eased into amusement.

She had something against *him*. She didn't want to see inside to his soul, any more than she wanted him seeing inside hers. But she could, she did, she saw through him to the truth that he missed Hot Water just as much as Hot Water missed him. He could flatten his voice and clear his throat and say "I can't" and "I won't" from now until kingdom come and Kitty would still know what he really wanted. Oh, boy, did he want to come home!

It was Aunt Cat who saved the meal. She might be eighty years old, but she hadn't lost the Wilder charm when it came to men. Despite Kitty's clumsy start, Aunt Cat soon had Dylan laughing as she reminisced about her younger days. When Kitty began clearing the plates, Aunt Cat segued into stories about her own mother, Margaret Wilder, who had owned and operated a notorious speakeasy.

"I never knew how much of those Wilder stories to believe," Dylan said, grinning. "But you're telling me she really made her own gin? And avoided the authorities by paying them off in barrels of the stuff?"

Kitty smiled grimly as she lifted his plate off the table. "Don't forget, those 'authorities' would be some of *your* ancestors."

He smiled back and winked. "Naah. My ancestors

were smarter than that. A Matthews would have exacted more interesting payoff from a Wilder than still-stew."

Aunt Cat laughed. "You'd be right, Dylan. There's always been a little something going on between the Matthews men and the Wilder women."

Kitty rolled her eyes. "Not enough to rub off a little of the Matthews respectability."

"But, Kitty"—Aunt Cat turned in her chair to catch her before she escaped into the kitchen—"that's what you've never truly understood. The Wilders never needed respectability."

But I do. Kitty bit back the words and ducked out. In the kitchen, she tied an apron over her jean shorts and white, sleeveless blouse. Aunt Cat had raised Kitty with love and with honesty, passing down the Wilder history as well as trying to pass down the Wilders' legendary indifference to love and marriage.

Kitty shook her head, because she still didn't get the Wilder women, even after all these years. It was the old saw of the chicken or the egg, but which came first didn't matter when the result was the same—Kitty couldn't understand their indifference because she longed for the traditional.

As she rinsed the plates, then stacked them in the dishwasher, she could hear Aunt Cat continuing to talk, punctuated by Dylan's deep laugh. Probably at some Wilder woman's expense, she thought sourly. What else was new?

A few minutes later, any more of the conversation between the other two was lost in the loud drone-and-clatter of the dishwasher. Once the pots and pans were hand-washed, Kitty started coffee and stepped back into the dining room. "Who wants—"

Her mother looked up from the place at the table beside Dylan. "Hello, Kitty," Samantha said.

The room was silent until Aunt Cat's voice broke through the sudden tension. "Samantha brought a chocolate cake. She made it herself."

Kitty looked over at her great-aunt. "She bakes?" she said, as if Samantha weren't in the room. It was a stupid thing to say, but she felt stupid. Surprised and stupid and graceless.

And Dylan was witnessing her vulnerability once again.

"I have to go," Kitty found herself saying. A mirror hung on the wall opposite her and she could see her reflection in it. Her face looked dead, her expression numb. Her gaze met her aunt's. "Thank you for dinner."

Aunt Cat nodded, unflappable as always, a quality Kitty supposed one gained when raising an infant at an age when most people were contemplating retirement. Kitty was always the flappable one, and that was exactly how she felt right now. *Flap, flap,* she thought hysterically. She wanted to move her arms up and down and fly right out of there, but her shoes seemed stuck to the floor.

Dylan stood up. "I'll see you home," he said.

Kitty stared at him. See her? *See* her? That was *not* what she wanted. "You don't need to. I'll be fine."

"Of course," he answered, but kept on coming. His hand enclosed hers in a firm, warm grip. "Thank you for dinner, Ms. Wilder. Good night." He squeezed Kitty's fingers. "And nice seeing you again, Samantha."

Then he guided Kitty out the front door, his touch firm but impersonal. On the sidewalk, he ignored his motorcycle and set off in the direction of her house on foot.

"You don't have to do this."

"Shut up," he said. But he said it pleasantly.

They walked in silence for a few minutes. "You've met her before?" Kitty finally had to ask.

"Mmm. At Bum Luck. I went there for a drink with my father."

"Ah."

The warm night air washed over Kitty's face, bringing her numbed skin back to life. As they turned up the next street, a butterscotch-colored dog woofed, then galloped up to a front fence. Kitty slipped her hand out of Dylan's, pretending she needed both hands free in order to properly pet the Murphys' Labrador, Chaos. Which, if you asked Chaos, was probably true.

Both she and Dylan admired the dog and stroked his fur. When Chaos presented them with his slimy green tennis ball, Dylan took it without complaint and gave it a toss. In response, the dog regarded Dylan with good-natured incomprehension. Dylan slanted Kitty a quizzical look. "The Murphys used to have a dog named Nugget," he said. "She was the smartest dog in town."

Kitty smiled, petted Chaos a final time, and headed off down the street again. "That's her son. And in case his name and his retrieval prowess aren't enough of a tip-off, he's *not* the smartest dog in town. But we forgive him for it."

Hearing herself, she grimaced. "Come to think of it, he's probably the only one in Hot Water not expected to follow in his family's footsteps."

Dylan's arm bumped against her shoulder. "You could try to see some good in it."

She didn't pretend not to understand. "That's easy for

you to say. You don't know what it's like to be a Wilder."

He tugged on her ponytail. "It's not that easy being a Matthews either. People see what they want to."

"It's not exactly the same thing," she retorted. "They look at me and see a long line of lawless women. They look at you and see over a hundred years of lawmen, as well as your personal stack of athletic trophies and college scholarships. You're the town's pride and I'm the town's pr—"

"Shh." He took hold of her upper arm and turned her to face him. "Don't say that. Don't say any of it. I never asked to be Hot Water's . . ."

"Golden Boy?" she supplied.

"Whatever." Then he released her arm to push both hands through his hair. His gaze moved off her face to stare into the summer night. "My reputation's a goddamn burden for me too."

The pain and frustration in his voice peeled away another layer of her own protection. She stared up at him. "Then why do we still love it here?" she whispered.

His eyes closed. "You said it yesterday. It's home."

They didn't speak again until they stood on the front porch of her little house. The bulb beside the door had burned out and she couldn't discern Dylan's face in the dark. "Well," she said, battling another wave of awkwardness, "thank you for walking me home."

He hesitated. "I wish you weren't so hard on yourself, Kitty." Somehow his hand found her cheek, and he cupped it with his palm. "I can't stop thinking you have the wrong perspective on all this. About who you are."

She held herself still, refusing to lean into his touch.

"In Hot Water I'll always be a Wilder. No matter how I behave, no matter what I do or don't do."

His thumb stroked across her cheekbone. "Then why not look at it from another angle?" His thumb stroked again.

Goose bumps ran down Kitty's neck, tumbling over themselves toward her feet. She swallowed. "What do you mean?"

He lazily brushed her skin once more. "Stop worrying that you have something to prove. Instead, do what you want."

Suddenly the night seemed to close in around them. It was darker, warmer, more intimate. Dylan's voice hushed. "Do something, say . . . bad."

Her heart started to pound and she swallowed again. "How do you know I don't do, um, bad things all the time?"

He laughed, the sound low and seductive. "Your face, Kitty. You couldn't have that gospel-choir face and even be one-quarter as wild as your Wilder genes. But maybe you should let them out to play a little. Don't they— you—deserve it?"

Let them out to play a little. In an instant, that recently awakened greediness came alert. Her body swayed toward the heat of his and when she breathed, she breathed in the smell of him, a masculine smell that was leather and denim and . . . not enough. "Dylan." She froze, the yearning in her own voice scaring her.

She stepped away from him, and her shoulder blades hit her front door. She pressed her palms against the solid wood. It wasn't smart to let him get too close. She knew that.

Apparently, he didn't.

He moved forward, bracing his hands against the door so that his arms caged her. "Come on. Admit it. Don't you want to break out sometimes, Kitty?"

What he didn't understand was that she'd done that eight years ago. Broken free of the Wilder mold and wedded him. But what had that youthful, rebellious impulse achieved? She crowded back, closer to the door, and tried to gain control of her heartbeat and her breathing. "Break out and do what?" she asked, pretending not to know exactly what he was talking about.

He lifted one hand and touched her face again, trailing the backs of his knuckles from the outer corner of her eye to the outer corner of her mouth. Her lips throbbed. "You can see in the dark," she said, just to prove to herself she could still speak.

"I can see you," he answered.

But he wasn't supposed to! And he wasn't supposed to get any closer to her either, but now he was leaning into her. His denim-covered leg brushed her knee, the touch burning like hot metal against bare skin.

She gasped. "Dylan—"

"I'd love to see you do something bad, Kitty. Go all-out Wilder and do something really, really bad." The raw edge to his voice grazed her flesh. Another jolt of greedy desire shot through her.

"Something really bad?" she echoed faintly.

"Say an affair." A sinful smile entered his voice. "You could have an affair with . . . hmm . . . How about an affair with a married man?"

Of course, the married man he was talking about was himself. She sagged against the door. "Dylan . . ."

"Why not, Kitty?"

He seemed to have forgotten about telling her to stay away from him. "That's too tempting," she whispered.

"Too tempting? Why?"

The words slipped out. "Our wedding night . . . I've always wondered . . ."

His knuckles brushed across her bottom lip. "Wondered what?"

There was a pulse in her lips. Amazing but true. All of a sudden she couldn't quite remember why being this close to him was dangerous.

He brushed her mouth again. "You've wondered what?"

He continued tracing her mouth even as Kitty spoke, his touch drawing the words from her. "That night . . . the beer . . . I don't remember it."

Dylan's hand dropped and his body shifted back, no longer touching hers. "You don't remember 'it'?"

"What happened after the 'I dos.' " That he learned one more of her secrets wasn't such a big deal, Kitty suddenly decided, blithely kicking away another of her protective walls. She cared only about his coming close again, his doing something to assuage the needy pulse at her lips, in her chest—everywhere. "After the wedding, I remember we went to your house. Then the next thing I knew, I was waking up in your bed."

She gulped a breath and let the truth break free. "I don't remember what it was like when we made love."

Chapter Eleven

Befuddled, Dylan stared down at Kitty, trying to make out the details of her face in the darkness. Standing on her doorstep, he'd been bewitched by her again. In the space of one breath, it seemed, he'd gone high on lust, playing word games while stroking her incredible skin. He'd actually forgotten all about their marriage at that moment. He'd forgotten they should keep apart. In horny-teenager mode, he'd been thinking no further than getting his mouth on hers once more.

Teasing her, talking about sex, always seemed to tip her off-kilter, and so he'd used it to lower her defenses. To get a little nearer to all that rose-petal softness and rose-sweet fragrance. There were a thousand and one reasons for him—them—not to indulge in any sexual play, but against his desire for her, they stacked up like a bag of sand against an armored carload of bullion.

Now she said she didn't remember their making love on their wedding night. She remembered nothing between the wedding itself and waking up the next morning in his bed. By then he'd already been on his way to Quantico.

He didn't know whether to laugh or to cry. He groaned instead. "Kitty—"

"I've felt cheated for eight years," she whispered, "that I don't remember."

"Kitty—"

"I just have these vague impressions, you see. Your kiss, your bare chest—" She broke off and her hand reached out and ran down his torso.

He groaned again, trying desperately to hold himself back. "Kitty—"

"You're right. I deserve this. Let's do it, Dylan." Just inches away from his, her body quivered with sexual tension.

Shit. His cock was screaming with the need to press against her. Her intoxicating, heated-rose scent was in his head, making him sex-drunk again. Still, he tried to wrap his mind around the situation. To think it over clearly. They'd been married for eight years and she couldn't recall their wedding night.

Yet she wanted to be with him . . . again.

A true hero would—

He stopped himself and sucked in another breath of that dizzying, delicious rose fragrance. Wasn't a "true hero" exactly what he knew he wasn't? So why should he be hesitating when Kitty was convinced she deserved a wedding night? Since she didn't remember the one eight years ago, he didn't need to worry that having sex now would make them any more married in Kitty's mind.

Christ, and then there was that! A spurt of anger spiced his clamoring desire for her. She'd *married* them. Made it legal. Made him come back to Hot Water.

When he remembered that, when he remembered it was because of her that he was back in Hot Water, tortured by memories, tortured by his lust for her . . . when he remembered *that*, maybe he too deserved this night.

"Give me your keys, Kitty," he said, his decision made.

"Why?"

"Because I want to get inside as soon as possible so I can strip you naked."

"Oh." She shivered. "This is Hot Water, silly. It's not locked."

Immediately his hand found the doorknob, turned it. Kitty stumbled backward into the living room, made shadowy by the meager light coming from a room—her bedroom, probably—down the short hallway. He caught her around the waist so she wouldn't fall.

Then he kicked the door shut and took her down to the hardwood floor. She gasped as he settled on top of her, his elbows on either side of her head.

He closed his eyes as his cock found the shallow, heated niche between her clasped-together thighs. His hips arched against hers and she gasped again. "You don't remember this?" he asked.

Her thighs opened a fraction. "It was the beer—*ah*." She bowed when he flexed against her once more.

He lowered his head toward her and his hair fell forward. Kitty touched it, tucking one side behind his ear. "I want yours free," he said, his voice sounding harsh and needy. He reached behind her neck to tug at the rubber band confining all the long, silky stuff that fascinated him.

Once it was liberated, he lifted a handful of her hair, letting it fall through his fingers like water. He scooped it up again and then mingled it with his, rubbing the dark and the light together between his palm and fingers. In that instant, his anger disappeared, overrun by another wave of hot lust. "We're going to be just like this, honey," he said. "Dark and light, rough and silk, male and female."

Her pupils were dilated, her blue eyes now almost as dark as his own. "Was it like that eight years ago?"

Breaking their gazes, he wound her hair around his wrist and stared at the golden band it made against his tanned skin. "You were sweet then too. I felt alone as hell, but I was sure I didn't want anyone's company that night."

"Except mine." She trailed her fingers down his cheek.

He released her hair and dipped his head to catch her fingertips and nip them. "If I recall, you wouldn't go away."

"You looked like you needed a friend."

"You looked all grown up." With calculated deliberation, he pressed into Kitty's body again and watched her eyelashes flutter closed and felt her thighs open even more. "I noticed you all summer."

"You did?" Her eyelashes lifted and her ripe mouth opened in surprise.

"Mmm." He traced her lower lip with his forefinger. "Long hair, long legs, those blue, blue eyes. What wasn't to notice?"

"You never looked twice at me."

"You just never caught me at it."

She absorbed that remark for a moment, then frowned. "Why didn't you want me to? Was it because I'm a Wil—"

He covered her mouth with his hand to quiet her. "It wasn't that. It was a lot of things that summer, Kitty."

She opened her mouth to talk again.

But he was tired of talking. So he took advantage of her parted lips and bent his head to slip his tongue between them. The heated, honey taste of her exploded like fireworks in his head and sparks shot through his bloodstream. His cock surged forward in its tight niche as Kitty's thighs relaxed and opened. Dylan settled between them.

Oh, yeah. Heroic scruples were cold comfort compared to sex with Kitty.

He angled his head and fit himself, his mouth, his hips, more tightly against her, reveling in her response. Moaning, she bucked beneath his weight, then sucked on his tongue.

He tore his mouth away.

Her hands linked behind his neck, trying to pull his head back down. "Kiss me again."

"In a minute." He hauled in a desperate lungful of air.

"Kiss me now."

She surprised the hell out of him by pushing him over and rolling on top of him. She looked surprised too, so surprised that her blue eyes went wide and she sat up.

Her eyes went wider still as the place between her legs met the hard ridge of his cock. His hands clamped down on her hips to prevent her from lifting off him. "Stay," he muttered. Gritting his teeth, he used his hands to coax her to rock against him. She moaned, and her head fell back, the movement lifting the hem of her shirt to reveal the plane of her belly and her tight navel.

Her long hair tickled the tops of his hands, and that erotic touch alone almost set him off. He squeezed her hips to get her attention. "Kitty, we need to slow down."

Her head came up and her eyes opened. She looked dazed. "Okay," she said. Then her gaze focused and she plucked at his collar. "Take this off."

He half laughed, half groaned. "Kitty—"

Her fingers wormed their way beneath his shirt. "The Wilder genes want this *off*."

He choked out another laugh. "Have I created a monster?" But when her fingers brushed against his bare nipples, he surrendered to this sexy, demanding beast and struggled out of the fabric.

The back of his head hit the floor as her gaze roamed over his naked belly and up toward his throat. "You're pretty," she said. The fingers of one slender hand spider-crawled up the center of his chest to pick up his medal.

"You always wear this. Why?"

He tried gaining control of his breathing. "It's a St. Barbara medal. She's the patron saint of prisoners. Miners too, as a matter of fact."

"But why do you wear it?" As she leaned closer to inspect it, her hair feathered over his chest.

He sucked in a breath, his brain hardly able to concentrate on her question. "The mother of the first child I ever found gave it to me. I wear it for . . . luck." The last word turned into a groan when her hand moved from the medal to find his tattoo. He flinched.

Her hand jumped away and her gaze flew to his. "Does it hurt?"

He shook his head. She was going to kill him. "It doesn't hurt. When you touched it, the heel of your hand . . ." He groaned as she did it again. Tracing the outline of the tattoo with her fingertips, she brushed her palm across his nipple once more. It went even harder.

"*Okay.*" In one movement he jackknifed up, coming to his feet and bringing her with him. "It's my turn now."

He grasped the edges of her shirt and pulled it over her head. Her hair fell around her like Lady Godiva's, covering the lacy cups of a flesh-colored bra. He stepped back to admire the beauty of her smooth flesh covered by the long, golden hair. Then he touched her shoulder, drawing a line toward her wrist. She shivered.

"I don't remember this," she said, her voice thready, almost uncertain. "Was it . . . was it like this?"

He should feel guilty.

He didn't.

"Like what, honey?"

"I feel hot and cold and anxious and eager all at once." She swallowed. "Was it like that?"

He caught her hand and brought it toward his mouth. "Some of those things," he murmured, kissing her fin-gertips. "It's better now."

"Better how?"

"Such a talker," he scolded. He tugged on her hand to bring her a step closer, then distracted her by toying with the front clasp of her bra. Her heart thudded against his knuckles as he slipped one finger beneath the clasp and rubbed it against her skin.

She inhaled and her breasts swelled. He withdrew his finger.

Her air expelled and she instantly swayed toward him. He smiled. The men before him must have almost ignored her breasts, because her response to his lightest caress was as immediate as it was unschooled. They might be small, but they were so sensitive that he wondered how close he could bring her by touching only them alone.

Trying to avoid any skin-to-skin contact at all, he used his thumb and forefinger to twist open the bra's clasp. The cups parted a few inches, but he avoided touching her breasts again by brushing the straps away from her shoulders. The bra fell to her feet, leaving her hair still covering the sweet mounds of flesh.

"Dylan," she whispered. She shivered, and one taut, rosy nipple poked through the long strands.

All the muscles in his body went rigid. Holding tight to his control, he clasped his hands behind his back and leaned close to the nipple still hidden. His gaze transfixed on where it should appear, he blew out a stream of warm air.

The responsive little nub popped into view.

"*Dylan.*"

"Hmm," he said, straightening. Without taking his eyes off her, he slowly pushed her curtain of hair behind her shoulders, inch by inch revealing her bare breasts. They took center stage, the pale flesh crowned with the tightest, pinkest nipples he'd ever seen in his life.

His cock surged against his belly, pushing against the buttons of his fly in its need to get out, get in.

"Dylan," Kitty said again. "You're taking too long."

The urgency in her voice was the only thing that saved him. With Kitty on that fine edge, he could draw it out, keep control. He swallowed. "I was thinking maybe, just maybe, if I take my time you'll remember, honey."

"Remember?" Her breasts were quivering under his gaze.

"You know, that night." He leaned down and licked one nipple. It was hard and hot against his tongue. He licked it again.

Around them, Kitty's delicate rose scent swirled like steam. "I remember it," she said quickly. "I do."

"You do?" He stood up and she moaned softly. "What is it you remember, Kitty?"

Her hand lifted away from her side, dropped. "This. You. You know." Her breasts rose and fell with her unsteady breaths.

"This?" He leaned down again and kissed the tip of the other breast. Sucked it inside his mouth.

She arched toward him and he curved his hands around her slender rib cage. "I remember, Dylan," she said, her hands in his hair. "I do, I do, I do."

She tasted so good. It was something *he* would never forget, the soft, warm skin against his cheek and the satisfying sensation of her nipple against the roof of his mouth. He was good at sex. The women who'd complained about his emotional distance had never complained about his performance in bed. It had seemed only fair, after all, just another application of the Golden Rule, to do unto women as you wanted women to do unto you.

But with Kitty, he wasn't even thinking about the do-unto-him part. It was arousing enough to hear her gasping for breath and to feel the bite of her fingers in his scalp. He switched to her other nipple and sucked that too, taking the free breast in his palm and kneading it gently.

"Please," she whispered. "Please."

He lifted his head. "Is it all coming back to you, honey?"

Her eyes were entirely serious. "Yes, it's coming, all right."

He almost choked, but instead pulled her against him. Her breasts pressed against his chest and they both shuddered. His mouth found hers and she slid her tongue along his. He groaned.

"The bedroom," he said against her lips, and started walking her backward. But he tripped over her slower feet and nearly sent them both crashing to the floor, so he lifted her. Finding her mouth again, he carried her into the bedroom, their lips fused, her feet dangling.

In the dim light of a bedside lamp, he saw the room was small but uncluttered. Though her bed was small as well, and covered with throw pillows, it would do, he thought. He didn't want anything more than their skin between them anyhow.

Without taking time to finesse, he pulled the bedcovers back, shoving aside the extra pillows to lay her against the pristine sheets. He flipped off her heavy-soled sandals, then sat on the edge of the mattress and kissed her deeply, one hand working on the fastening of her shorts. Her belly muscles jumped when the zipper slid down, and he insinuated his hand into the denim's open vee to soothe them. She tore her mouth away from his.

"I don't remember this," she said, that uncertain note sounding again.

"It will come back to you," he answered, then smoothed off her shorts and panties in one movement.

Her thighs clamped together. "Dylan . . ."

He forced his gaze away from the pretty hair between her legs, his temperature rising with the kind of single-minded fever that only a descendant of a forty-niner could truly understand. "Kitty," he whispered. "Honey. It's going to be all right."

He slid his hand up her body to cup her breast again.

She arched into his touch. "It's going to be good."

"More than good." He stroked his thumb across her nipple. "You want this, right?"

Her eyes glazed as he thumbed her other nipple. "Yes, now, hurry."

He laughed, then stood up and shucked off the rest of his clothes. She scooted over to make a place for him on the bed and he edged in next to her, lying on his side so he could trail his fingers from her throat to her belly button.

Her thighs relaxed and she turned toward him for a kiss. It heated instantly, their tongues fighting for dominance. Her hand brushed his cock.

. He groaned, caught her fingers, pressed them to his hard length. She grasped him, tentative but interested. He groaned again as she moved her palm against him, up and down, up and down.

"Kitty, stop." He lifted her away from him by the wrist, then held it against the pillow beside her head. He grabbed the other wrist and pinioned that one too. Half lying across her, he went about arousing her as high as he could, as high as he felt himself. He kissed her lips and licked her ears and bit gently on the sweet nipples that must have been created for his mouth.

Not until she made needy noises at the back of her throat did he move one hand from her wrist to her thighs. They parted for him easily, and he ran his palm along the smooth, warm skin, pushing them open. He lifted his head to watch his darker-toned hand dip between them.

The folds of her body were already half unfurled, blossoming and dewy. He touched them with a fingertip and they bloomed even more. Delving deeper, he found the heart of the flower and gently flicked it with the pad of his forefinger.

"Dylan?" Kitty's eyes were closed and her face and breasts were flushed. She bit down on her puffy lower lip.

His chest tightened; it was such a damn pretty sight. "Shh, honey."

"I don't remember this," she said, her eyes still closed but her forehead pleating. "I don't remember you touching me like this."

He circled the little protrusion, his anticipation jumping as it pulsed against his fingertip. Her thighs fell apart and the sight of her open body, open for him, backed up the air in his lungs. He painted the pretty petals with her own wetness and felt her tension start to coil. His cock hardened—impossibly more—against the outside curve of her leg and he couldn't stop himself from rubbing it against her sleek skin.

She moaned and he dipped in the entrance to her body. Just one finger, halfway, but the tight, heated grip almost unleashed his control. She moaned again, her hips pressing into the mattress, and he pushed his finger a little farther.

Their breathing sounded loud and harsh in the room, but inside Kitty's body it was soft and slick. He leaned down to suck at her breast again, his finger gently moving inside her. His cock surged like his finger wanted to, but instead, he kept the rhythm slow and steady, the intrusion shallow.

Kitty was closer. So close.

"Dylan." Her voice was soft and hoarse and needy.

"Getting there, honey. Almost there." Her body was gripping his finger like an erotic vice. He clenched his teeth to keep his lust where it belonged—second to Kitty's pleasure.

"Please," she whispered. Her body was quivering with tension and her eyes were wide, her gaze glued to his face. "Dylan, please."

"Take it," he urged her. "It's yours." His thumb circled the nub between her legs.

Her hips made a restless roll. "It's too much," she said, then shook her head. "No. Not enough."

He eased his finger out, then placed two together, pausing at the entrance to her body.

She was trembling with passion. "Dylan," she said, "it's hot . . . I . . . What are you doing?"

His two fingertips just breached her body, the way wet but tight. "It's the burning rose," he said. "And I'm going inside." He thrust his fingers in to the hilt.

Her hips rose off the bed; her hoarse cry echoed in the room. For long moments she shook with desire fulfilled, then desire sated. Dylan hadn't seen anything so beautiful in eight years.

He gathered her against him until all her shivers stopped. It took more long moments, but then she finally opened her eyes and looked at him, the blue still nearly eclipsed by the dark pupils. "It wasn't like that before, was it?" she asked, her face still flushed but suspicious.

He bit the inside of his cheek. "Not exactly."

"How 'not exactly'?"

He lifted an eyebrow. "Are you complaining?"

She pursed those half-puckered lips, which made him want to kiss them, so he did. Her mouth opened for him and she rubbed her body against his. He slid over her and without the slightest bit of encouragement, she opened her legs for him.

His cock touched against her plump, damp softness.

Her breath caught. "The Burning Rose?" she asked.

He nodded his head, knowing exactly what she meant. "The Burning Rose. You didn't realize?"

"I feel like an idiot. I thought it was a reference to Rose Wilder and her . . . prowess or something."

Dylan's lips quirked. "I guess it was, in a way." He pressed harder against Kitty's body and she gasped again. "And you don't feel like an idiot to me."

Her eyes closed and she tugged him down to her mouth. "Make love to me," she said against his lips.

He usually shied away from the term "make love," but this time he just smiled and lifted his head. "But that's what we've been doing, honey."

Then he went about proving that to her, kissing her,

caressing her, building the fire between them again until she was panting and there was only one way to quench it. He turned away to roll on a condom and then came back to the cradle of her body, holding himself above her with straight arms, poised to enter the ultimate pleasure.

Her ankles hooked the backs of his thighs and she pulled him down. He had just touched her wet, open softness when his gaze snagged on another pair of eyes staring at him from the jumble of throw pillows to Kitty's left.

It took him a moment to realize the big browns belonged to a stuffed animal. A stuffed bear.

A memory seared his brain. Alicia's memorial along the side of the road. A bear just like this one, but weather-worn, its eyes scratched and lusterless. Dead.

Brown eyes like this bear's. Brown eyes like those of that cherub on the wall in the cafe. Brown eyes like Alicia's own.

"Dylan?" Kitty's plea sounded uncertain while his conscience wrestled with his passion. Could he take his pleasure in this bed, in Hot Water, when not far from here Alicia had died? When Bram was somewhere out there tonight, alone and grieving, thanks to Dylan?

Kitty's hands traveled down his spine. She lifted her head off the pillow and nipped at his chin. "Come back," she whispered.

With her touch, the memory, the doubts, dissolved. He closed his eyes, savoring the feel of her beneath him, the sweet anticipation of the release he'd find in her body. He smelled the scent of flaming rose petals. His body found the entrance to Kitty's, pushed partway in.

The first burst of pleasure shot, hot and addictive, through his bloodstream. He opened his eyes to look at Kitty. Her gaze was fixed on his face and her mouth was parted. He took another inch of her tight body. She shivered and her lashes dropped.

Dylan couldn't stop himself from glancing at those other eyes, the still-open brown ones, looking for censure or benediction or . . . forgiveness. Kitty's body pulsed hotly around his, but the fires of hell seemed to burn inside his soul. Did he deserve something that felt so damn good?

Of course you do. It was Alicia's quiet voice, the one he heard in his nightmares. *Make something good here, Dylan.*

But that was what he tried to do every day! It was why he'd left Hot Water, why he'd joined the FBI, why he'd worked his ass off the past eight years to bring home every single missing person he could, because he hadn't been able to bring home *her.*

"Dylan?" Kitty was still breathless, still needy, still blue eyes full of sensual power and passion he couldn't deny.

Make something good here, the voice said again.

Dylan stopped thinking and with one movement— because it was where he just had to be—thrust home. Kitty gasped. Her face crumpled and Dylan's mind spun as she stiffened in obvious, untried discomfort beneath him.

"Kitty, damn it, Kitty—" Without volition his hips flexed again, her body was just that tight, that compelling. She gasped again.

"*Kitty.*" He groaned, trying to gather his will to back

out. But then her face eased, her muscles relaxed, and she lifted her hips.

He closed his eyes at the goodness of the counter-move. It seated him deeper, and he drew out again only to find his way once more into the center of Kitty's burning rose. Now she caught the rhythm, and their mouths fused as they strained together for release, then strained against it, wanting it now, wanting to anticipate it forever.

She made a sound deep in her throat and he caught her hips in his hands, tilting her a crucial few degrees. He thrust in, she thrust up, and then she flew, shaking like oak leaves in a summer wind.

He thought—nothing. He only followed her, losing everything but the feel of Kitty beneath him, around him, with him.

Their recovery was as long as the climax was high, but after a time he realized her closed eyes and limp body were no longer evidence of recuperation, but evasion. Heads on one pillow, they lay side by side, facing each other. With a short sigh, Dylan grimly lifted his hand and tapped her on the shoulder.

After a long hesitation, her eyes opened. "Yes?" She might as well be taking his fast-food order.

He sighed again, this time with less resignation and more frustration. "Well, sweetheart? Don't you have something to say to me?"

Her body stiffened and her eyebrows jumped together. "Wait just a minute, Buster. You sound mad. It's not *my* fault I was a virgin." She glared at him. "The fact is, *you* should have told *me*."

He narrowed his eyes and spoke through clenched

teeth. "Give me a break. How the hell should I have known?"

"Obviously you knew we didn't make love that night, which is more than I did!" She grabbed the end of the sheet and pulled it up to her chin, her mouth stubborn. "Furthermore, you *also* knew we were married."

Forcing himself to stay calm, he tried putting it all together in some logical sequence. She'd been eighteen years old when they'd indulged in what he'd considered almost a prank—a harmless one—and married. A last Hot Water hurrah. That she hadn't had sex with anyone before that time wasn't such a surprise, he supposed. And yes, he'd known they hadn't slept together that night. But who could imagine she wouldn't have had sex with anyone in the eight years since!

And why not?

A cold feeling of dread crawled up his naked back. He reached down to draw the covers around his own neck, barely resisting doing something completely childish like pulling them over his head.

Or running away. That sounded appealing too.

But he was a man. A federal agent. A lawyer, the son of a judge, Hot Water's Golden Boy. A husband who had just gone to bed with his virginal wife.

Shit.

"Kitty," he said, trying to sound calm and reasonable, "exactly why were you still, uh . . . untouched?"

She squirmed against the sheets, her knee almost taking care of any future encounters he might have hoped for himself. "I told you, I didn't *know* I was untouched."

Remain calm and reasonable, he told himself. He

drew in a long breath. "Kitty, exactly why haven't you had sex since that time when you thought we did but you didn't remember?" He winced at having to ask such a convoluted question. Christ, everything she did caught him in tighter and tighter coils.

"I don't believe in it," she said promptly. Too promptly.

He thought he moaned. Whatever you would call the noise, it was a sick, distressed sound. "Don't believe in what, exactly?" he asked, hoping she wasn't going to say what he thought she was going to say.

She blinked those big blue eyes at him. With those damn heavy-lashed things and her wide brow and fine-pored skin, if you forgot about the whore's mouth, she looked exactly like a cross between the big sister on *Little House on the Prairie* and an earnest heaven-dweller from *Touched by an Angel*. A scary thought, which proved he needed to a) start sleeping more and b) cancel his cable subscription.

"I don't believe in breaking marriage vows," she said, then frowned at him. "Why are you looking like that? You should be glad about my fidelity, I'd think. I am, after all, married to you."

When words continued to elude him, she frowned at him again. "What's the matter? Oh." She reached over and gave a kind pat to his shoulder. "You needn't feel bad about *your* other relationships. You didn't know we were truly married then, so they don't really count."

She hesitated for a moment, then spoke again, just a knife-edge of sarcasm sharpening her voice. "So, of course, I forgive you."

Dylan's cold dread turned to pure . . . there wasn't a

name for it, though "insanity" might do. "Kitty Wilder, I've said it before and I'll say it again."

He flopped onto his back and stared up at her sky-colored ceiling. "I'm going to kill you."

Chapter Twelve

At the Odd Fellows monthly dinner, the pinkish chicken on D. B.'s plate appeared to have enough life left in it to squawk, so he gave it a chance to run by leaving his knife and fork on the table. By nine-thirty, when the meeting was over and his plate was back in the kitchen, where his chicken presumably escaped, he was starving and desperate to pass some time before heading to Bum Luck and Samantha.

He wanted to see her, he needed to see her. But there were only so many hours a man could nurse his vodka martini in a bar on a Sunday night without attracting un-wanted attention, so he took the on-ramp to Highway 49, going south. Halfway between Hot Water and the larger town of Colter, he turned into the crowded gravel parking lot of the best Chinese restaurant in the area, The China Chef.

A little won ton soup, a little chow mein, and he'd handle the vodka better, as well as the wait until he could be alone with Samantha.

Her recent attempt to end their relationship was worrying the hell out of him. He'd bulldozed right through the moment—how easy it had been to flatten her effort somewhat mollified him—but that didn't mean he'd squashed her doubts.

For God's sake, he had them himself. Where was this relationship going? How was it going to end? But Samantha made him feel young again, so he clung tenaciously to a youngster's ability to stride forward into an uncertain future.

He knew only that he needed her. Especially tonight.

Inside the dimly lit waiting area of The China Chef, the delicious smell of vegetables sautéeing in hot sesame oil made his mouth water. From the kitchen came the loud clatter of pots and pans as the cooks tried to keep up with the orders from the full dining room as well as with those from walk-ins like himself.

D. B. made his selection at the take-out counter, paid, then took a seat on the red vinyl bench placed against one of the foyer's walls. As he leaned back, he realized someone else was waiting there, sitting in the darker shadows at the far end of the bench.

"Samantha." Surprised, he wondered for a moment if he'd imagined her there.

But her half smile appeared very real. "Judge. Good to see you." Her guardedness was also very real.

He glanced at the cashier, then slid down the vinyl so that his thigh kissed hers. "You're not working tonight? I was planning on stopping by later."

She shook her head. "I had Andy take my place."

"Is something the matter?" Not that she didn't deserve time off, but he knew she worried, even on Sunday nights, about the crowd getting too rowdy if she wasn't there to supervise. That attention to her business, that acute sense of responsibility, only made her more attractive to him. His gaze ran over her pale face. "You look tired again," he said, reaching out a hand to touch her cheek.

She flinched away. "That's why Andy's on tonight," she answered lightly.

D. B. still didn't like it. "Have you seen a doctor?"

"Yes. Friday, as a matter of fact." She hesitated. "There's nothing for you to worry about."

That didn't sound quite right. "Samantha . . ."

She put her hand on his thigh, only an inch above his knee, yet just that gentle touch sent his mind skittering and blood rushing to his groin. "How was your Odd Fellows dinner this evening?" she asked.

He tried gathering his thoughts. "What?"

One corner of her mouth twitched and she drew her hand away. "I asked how your dinner was tonight."

"Long." With Samantha here beside him, his concern switched to the other person who had been worrying him. "Disappointing. I was hoping to persuade Dylan to go with me, but he refused."

She touched the back of his hand. "That bothers you."

D. B. took a long breath, released it. "The truth is, years ago—the summer Dylan left—I think I failed him." It felt surprisingly good to finally speak his fear out loud.

"Something to do with the kidnapping?"

His eyebrows rose.

She shrugged. "When the town's favorite son returns, so do the stories about said son. I've heard all about him and all about it."

Not all of it. Nobody knew, not even D. B., how Dylan had been affected by the kidnapping. He knew only that his son had changed afterward. Dylan's future plans, his natural optimism, his love for the place where he'd been born and raised, had been leveled by the events on that one fateful day.

And maybe by the things D. B. hadn't said . . . and the things he had. "He was only twenty-three years old. Christ, I was forty-two and *I* didn't know how to react to the tragedy."

"No one could be prepared for what happened, D. B."

He let his head fall back against the wall. "We were all so *damn* frustrated. Grateful, ecstatic that the children were safe, but Alicia Bennett was missing. We'd all watched her grow up. The whole town had been to her and Bram's wedding."

"She sounds like another favorite."

He nodded. "But not like Dylan. More like Kitty. Everyone watched out for Alicia. But then . . . she was gone." D. B. stared straight ahead. "It wasn't fair, but who other than a judge should be able to handle that? Instead, I lashed out against my own son, who was already hurting."

He looked at Samantha and took her hand, because he had to touch her. "We had always been close, Dylan and I. I screwed that up."

She squeezed his fingers. "If you think I'm going to pass judgment on how a parent behaves toward their child, D. B., you're looking at the wrong woman."

Her clear empathy relieved the ache in his chest. He lifted their linked hands to kiss her knuckles. "Right back at you, sweetheart. When you had Kitty, you were just a kid yourself. You did the right thing."

She glanced away. "Did I?"

"Uh-huh. It's not easy raising a child under the best of circumstances. I know I wouldn't want to go through it again."

Her chin lowered. "No, I didn't think you would."

"I just wish being home didn't make Dylan so miserable."

"I stopped by Aunt Cat's earlier this evening and saw him there." She disengaged their hands. "He didn't seem all that unhappy, if you ask me."

D. B. gave her a sharp look. "Really? How did he seem?"

She cocked her head, as if thinking back. "Almost . . . relaxed. Aunt Cat was dragging all the Wilder skeletons out of the closet and he was egging her on."

D. B. smiled, heartened by the thought of his son enjoying himself. Maybe Dylan was finding home palatable after all. God, that made him feel better. That, and the fact that the woman who fascinated him more than any other he'd ever known was no farther than an elbow away. He lifted the one closest to Samantha and gave her a gentle poke in the ribs.

"Maybe I need to make a visit to Cat myself," he said. "It's hard to envision the Wilder skeletons skulking in closets. Stripteasing in the sunlight, maybe, but not skulking anywhere." He grinned down at Samantha.

She didn't laugh, as he had expected her to.

New worry dragged at his lifting mood. "Samantha? What's wrong?"

Her gaze met his, but in the dim light he had to let his imagination paint the blue of her eyes. She half smiled. "I'm just tired."

He thought of going back to her place—no, to his. They could open both sets of French doors in the master bedroom suite and the night breeze would blow across them while they ate their Chinese in bed. Afterward he would tuck the covers around her and guard over the sleep she so much deserved.

No one need know about it. That was the one good thing about having a nearly estranged son. If Dylan discovered that Samantha stayed the night, he wouldn't say a word on the subject to D. B. or anyone else.

"What did you order?" he asked her.

"Vegetable fried rice and cashew chicken."

"Soup, broccoli beef, and chow mein for me," he said. "They would be good together, yours and mine."

She hesitated.

That worry tickled the back of his mind again. "Damn it, Samantha," he said, not sure why he was swearing or even why he suddenly felt so anxious, "*we're* good together."

Her mouth opened. He tensed, but then the front door of the restaurant opened, and a foursome entered. A familiar foursome. Without thinking, he jumped up from the bench and stepped away from Samantha.

She moved too, sliding further into the shadows.

"D. B.!" Bob Byer hailed him. D. B. walked forward to greet the other man, his wife, Amy, and Pearl and Red Morton.

The men had also attended the Odd Fellows meeting, though they had sat at a different table. D. B. shook their hands and kissed Amy and Pearl on their respective cheeks. "You people are hungry too?"

Bob grinned, then shot a teasing look at his wife. "Not us. It was Amy and Pearl."

D. B. chuckled at Amy's sputters of mock outrage, while warily eyeing the more subdued Pearl and Red. Word around town was that the Mortons had hit a troubled patch, and if their demeanor was any indication, the word was right on the money.

"But I'm glad we bumped into you, D. B.," Bob said, rubbing his hands together. "The Park Committee came up with an idea tonight that we wanted to run by you."

"Oh?" Out of the corner of his eye he checked on Samantha. With her legs crossed and her arms wrapped around herself, she appeared cold, or closed off.

"Why don't you join us for dinner?" Amy suggested. "We can talk then."

"I already ordered takeout . . ." And he had plans for tonight. Plans for taking Samantha home with him. He darted another look at her huddled figure. It seemed suddenly imperative to have her in his house, in his bed, where she couldn't get away from him.

"They'll serve it to you at the table," Amy insisted. "Go over to the cashier and tell her you've changed your mind and are eating in, D. B."

He hesitated, trying to think of a gracious refusal.

"While you're deciding," Bob said, "let me tell you what our committee discussed tonight. With Dylan home, it got us thinking . . . maybe it's time we named the park."

D. B.'s gaze flicked toward Samantha again. "The park?" While the Odd Fellows owned and maintained both the town park and the adjoining cemetery, neither of them had ever been officially named.

"It's been eight years." Bob put an arm around his wife and hugged her close. "With Dylan back, it made us realize that Hot Water hasn't really had any—" He broke off and looked at Amy. "What's that Oprah word?"

"Closure," she answered.

Bob nodded. "That's it. The town needs closure. We're considering planting a tree in the park in Alicia's memory, with a nice brass plaque."

"That sounds good . . ." D. B. half turned his body so he wouldn't lose sight of Samantha.

Bob was still talking. "We'll make a ceremony out of it on Heritage Day and at the same time name the park in honor of our town hero."

"Town hero?"

"Dylan, of course."

D. B. grimaced, remembering his son's vehemence when he'd brought up just such a topic. "Bob, I really don't think—"

"It's her!" Pearl suddenly exclaimed, her attention riveted on the shadows at the far end of the red bench.

D. B. froze.

"Her who?" Amy looked around. "Oh."

"I won't be able to eat if *she's* here." Pearl sent a venomous look at her husband, whose face flushed the color of his nickname, even to the tips of his ears.

Red Morton shifted on his feet. "Pearl, I've told you. There's nothing—"

"So you say," she hissed in an even louder voice. "But I know where you've been at night and I *know* what kind of woman she is."

Jesus Christ, D. B. thought. "Pearl—"

"Don't bother," Amy said in an undertone, putting her hand on his forearm. "Nothing anyone says makes one bit of difference."

Pearl's voice went strident this time. "Forget *Kitty* Wilder. I'll tell you who should be working in that brothel."

D. B. flinched. "*Pearl—*"

"I'm telling you." Amy squeezed his arm. "It won't help."

"Oh, shit." D. B. glanced toward the restaurant's exit, his legs turning to lead. Amy was right. He *couldn't* help. Nothing he could say would make a difference now. Not for Samantha. She'd just run out the door.

"She's left," Amy told Pearl.

Cursing again, D. B. closed his eyes. He had a feeling, a very bad feeling, that she'd just left *him*.

Kitty gazed at Dylan, who lay flat on his back, staring at the bedroom ceiling. Biting down on her lower lip, she studied his profile. Even this partial view of his face was so gorgeous—the dark brow, the black lashes, one high cheekbone, and the right half of his finely etched, full mouth—that it could easily distract her from their current sticky situation.

Until she noticed the vein pulsing at his temple.

She swallowed. He'd just made love to her and now he'd said he was going to kill her. But really, maybe he already had.

It was certain, at least, that she would never be the same.

Between her thighs she felt both sore and sated. Her skin—shoulders, breasts, belly, everywhere—tingled, nerve endings roused and still alert after their sexual awakening. A little shiver shook her body and the muscles inside her clenched, as if they were still wrapped around Dylan, as if they could recapture that fabulous pleasure.

His head rolled on the pillow and his eyes were so dark she couldn't read anything in them. "You're cold," he said.

"No."

He hesitated. "Hurt?"

"No." Except she thought she might cry anyway. "You can go now."

"I can go," he repeated, his voice expressionless.

"Yes." She wanted him to, while she had a shred of self-possession left.

"Well, I'm not going anywhere. Not until you fully explain what the hell happened here tonight."

"Dylan—"

"Now, Kitty."

She hesitated, searching for an answer, for an attitude, that would make this awkward afterward easiest for both of them. "Hmm. Let's see." She pursed her lips, as if casting her mind back.

"*Kitty*—"

"Now I remember," she said hastily, keeping her voice light. Uncaring. "You talked me into trying out my Wilder genes and taking *off* my blue ones. Then we had sex. I liked it."

"That part I know," he said, his voice tight. "But I want the complete truth about why I came to be the one to . . . deflower you."

The burning rose. Kitty clamped her thighs tight against another betraying shiver. "I already explained that too."

He rolled onto his side to face her. "Indulge me with the details, please."

"Fine." She drew her knees up to her chest. "That night, eight years ago, I drank too much beer. The next morning I woke up in your bed wearing your T-shirt and nothing else. I had a hangover, of course, and every inch of me throbbed from my toenails to the crown of my head." But now that she'd really made love with him, she knew that kind of throbbing was entirely different. "The last thing I remembered was marrying you, so naturally I concluded we'd . . . shared a wedding night."

" 'Naturally'? Jesus Christ, Kitty." He scowled. "What kind of man did you think I was? When I figured out how drunk you were, I tried to sober you up with a cold shower. For the record, *you* decided to strip out of your wet clothes and then you promptly passed out on my bed."

He rolled onto his back again. "I sure as hell didn't take advantage of your condition. Even if I hadn't realized you were drunk and I *had* gone to bed with you, you can't have seriously thought I would have left town without saying anything to you."

Kitty shrugged. "Why not?"

He turned his head to look at her. "Because . . . because . . . hell, Kitty, because that's not what a man should do."

"It's what men have always done to Wilder women."

He blinked. "*Fuck.*"

"Well, of course, that too," she said flippantly.

With another curse, he squeezed shut his eyes. "I don't like this."

She sighed in relief. "Me neither. So why don't we stop the post-game analysis and get dressed." She scooted toward the edge of the mattress.

His hand clamped down on her shoulder. "We're not leaving the bed until we get this straightened out."

She tried wiggling away from his hand. "There's no tangle in my mind."

He tightened his grip. "If you move one more inch, I'm going to flay you alive."

Didn't he know he already had? Her stomach flipped over in panic. If he went any deeper, her heart would be exposed, and she couldn't survive that. "Please, Dylan. I need to . . . to shower."

His hand on her shoulder didn't move. Any second now he'd detect the embarrassing, goose-bumping, sexual reaction his flesh against hers was detonating. She licked her lips. "Just a few minutes alone in the bathroom. At a time like this, a woman could use a little, um, privacy."

In an instant his fingers moved to her chin and tilted it up. "You *are* hurt." His gaze roamed her face.

"No. Not really." Not in the way he thought anyhow.

"Let me see." He grabbed the sheet as if to push it down.

Kitty clutched it to her breasts. "No!"

He gave her an impatient look. "I'm an FBI agent."

She stared at him, not daring to relax her grasp on the sheet. "Give me a break, Dylan. FBI file or no, I really don't think my private parts fall under the federal government's jurisdiction."

"Honey, I hate to break it to you, but your private parts fall under *my* jurisdiction now," he said grimly. "And I meant that I'm trained in first aid."

"Me, too," she countered. "I know it all. Direct pressure, tourniquets, the whole shebang."

He lifted an eyebrow. "Promise me you don't think a tourniquet is necessary."

She glared at him. "Only on *your* private part, unless you let me out of this bed."

The corner of his mouth twitched, but his hold on her shoulder loosened. "You're scaring me, babe."

"Close your eyes." She slid one leg over the edge of the mattress.

"What?"

"Close your eyes so I can get to the bathroom."

"I've already seen everything." He looked amused.

She squinted at him. "Tourniquet."

Laughing softly now, he finally obeyed.

She dashed for the door. He wolf-whistled just as she reached it.

Under the shower's hot spray, she let a few tears fall. Then she tried coveting the thought that he might be gone when she left the bathroom, but even for someone who'd managed to avoid the problem of her marriage for eight years, it seemed a pretty lame hope.

So Kitty wasn't surprised to find him propped up against the pillows when she walked back into the bedroom. He was wearing his jeans and nothing else. She pulled her blue chenille lapels of her bathrobe a little closer together. It was too bad she hadn't left an armored robe hanging on the hook in the bathroom.

He'd turned up the light, and as Kitty approached, she couldn't help but notice his solid pec muscles, his rippling abdomen, and that when he crossed his arms, his biceps bulged. The medal he wore around his neck glinted from its place against his dark chest hair. He looked so . . . male against the butter-yellow sheets of her bed. Her mouth gone dry, she gestured behind her. "Did you want to . . . you're welcome to use the shower."

He shook his head. "No, thanks. I smell you on me and I like it that way." His hand patted the mattress beside him.

Another little tremor shook her body. She moved forward to disguise it, filing away the unexpectedly sweet, arousing idea that he liked her scent on him. "I've been thinking, Dylan . . ."

He smiled. "And what's been going on in that pretty head of yours is exactly what I've been sticking around to find out."

"Well, first." She took a few more steps toward the bed. "There's no need for us to go into any apologies or recriminations or . . . whatever."

His eyebrows came together. "Apologies or recriminations for what, exactly?"

She waved toward the bed. "You know."

"For this?" He inserted two fingers in the fist of his other hand and moved them in a vulgar imitation of lovemaking.

Her lip curled. "That's crude."

Shaking his head, he laughed. "You're a prude, Kitty. But don't worry, honey, I'm not about to apologize for what we did in this bed. I've been doing some thinking too. The undeniable fact is, you turn me on. The way I see it, you're twenty-six years old. You wanted to have sex with me, and boy-howdy, I wanted to have sex with you. It doesn't matter what didn't happen between us before."

Kitty released a pent-up breath she hadn't realized she'd been holding. She turned him on. That little nugget she also filed in the back of her mind, ready to savor some other, less crucial time.

"Exactly. It doesn't matter." She reached the bed and sat on the edge of the mattress. "Whatever didn't happen in the past . . ." With a casual gesture of her hand, she waved the whole messy business away.

"So now we just have to discuss what *did* happen." His dark, implacable gaze pinned her. "In the past."

"*What?*" Swallowing, she shoved her suddenly trembling hands in the front patch pockets of her robe. "What do you mean?"

"I think it's time you told me exactly why you registered our marriage."

Kitty's heart stopped beating, already preparing for sacrifice. "It was a mistake," she tried anyway. "My one silly mistake."

Dylan didn't blink. "I once got a man to confess where he'd hidden the ransom money a family paid to get their son back," he said softly. Pleasantly. "It was what we needed to convict the man and we couldn't convict without it. It took me twenty-two minutes, Kitty, and I never laid a hand on him."

With that, he reached across the mattress and took a firm hold of hers. "Seven minutes later, just to get away from my company in the interrogation room, he agreed to a prison term of thirty years without the possibility of parole."

Kitty swallowed to wet her dry mouth. "You're trying to intimidate me."

"Yes." He stroked the top of her hand with his thumb. "Is it working?"

She swallowed again, and then the words just tumbled out. "The Wilder women don't wed and they don't run."

He stilled. "The motto in The Burning Rose?"

"The family motto." Kitty looked down at their entwined hands. "From Rose to Clara to Margaret to Rosanna. Then to Samantha, then to me. Those words have been passed on to all of us."

"And no Wilder woman has ever done either. Is that right?"

She nodded, her head still lowered. "I guess you could say that Samantha ran for a time, but she's back."

Dylan was silent for a moment. "So registering that marriage, really wedding someone, was your rebellion?"

Startled, Kitty jerked her head up. "Yes." She'd never expected him to understand that part of it so clearly and so quickly. "I didn't see it exactly that way at the time, but in hindsight . . . yes."

"How, exactly, did you see it at the time?"

Kitty dropped her lashes to hide her eyes and hoped the heat crawling up her neck wouldn't make it past the collar of her robe. "I'm not sure I remember, exactly," she told him. "When I woke up it hurt to blink. My head was pounding and my stomach . . ." She shuddered. "In the midst of all that physical misery, I assumed . . ." (and had been angry that she couldn't remember the details) "I assumed we'd . . ."

His mouth twitched.

"I assumed we'd had sex. Okay, I said it. Satisfied?"

He nodded. "And then . . . ?"

"And then I got dressed. I found the marriage certificate on the floor. I was a young and foolish eighteen. And I stood there, looking at that certificate, thinking how a Wilder had kinda, sorta wedded after all."

"And 'kinda, sorta' didn't seem good enough?"

"Well . . ." It *hadn't* seemed good enough, not when it was Dylan whom she'd wed. "But I didn't think about making the marriage legal until I was walking home."

One of his eyebrows lifted. "I sense we're getting somewhere."

Kitty shifted on the bed and stared down at her lap. "Do you remember Ned DeBeck?"

"I remember some DeBecks. I don't know a Ned."

"The family's moved now, but Ned was my age. I ran into him as I was walking home that morning. Through high school he'd been . . . persistent."

"He liked you?"

She shook her head. "He liked the idea of how easy Wilder women were supposed to be."

"Asshole." Dylan spit out the word and his hand tightened on hers. "So what did he say to you?"

She cleared her throat. "He'd seen us together the night before, and I looked pretty rumpled that morning."

"So he assumed I got what he'd been after, I suppose?"

Kitty nodded, focusing on a pulled thread of her robe, rubbing it with her free thumb. "I felt cheap and dirty and hungover and mad and I thought . . . I thought . . ."

"You thought you'd show him."

Kitty shrugged, then met Dylan's gaze. "Yes."

He frowned. "But you never told anyone what you did?"

"Right."

"But that doesn't make sense, Kitty. What was the point of rebelling when nobody, including the asshole DeBeck, knew about it?"

"*I* knew about it. Do you see? It's what *I* thought that mattered."

He was silent for a few moments. "Yeah," he finally said. "I get that." He let go of her hand.

Kitty's fingers curled into the tousled bedspread. "I just wanted to be like everyone else," she whispered. "For once to be normal, conventional."

"And marrying a near stranger, then keeping it secret

for eight years, will certainly do that for you," he said dryly.

She looked at him. "It's easy for you to be sarcastic. But how would you like to be a Wilder? To be me? I've only wanted a normal family my whole life. To have a husband, children, to be in love and be loved like everybody else. What chance do I have for that in Hot Water?"

Dylan looked away. "Maybe you have a chance to live without the kind of pain Bram has."

Kitty stared. Bram. Bram? "What does he have to do with this?"

Dylan shrugged, his expression cold, his voice flat and faraway-sounding. "Think about it, babe. That's where all that 'in love and be loved' can take you. Staring at someone's grave night after night after night. I don't want that for myself and I wouldn't wish it on anyone else either. Even you."

Kitty shivered. Not at the image of poor Bram, but because of the sudden absence of Dylan. Sure, he was still on the bed, but it was as if he'd turned himself off and was detached from her, from the room, from the world.

"And now that we've"—he seemed at a loss for the correct description this time—"consummated the marriage, Kitty, I hope to God you don't have any crazy ideas that I'm your ticket to conformity."

A Wilder and a Matthews? Truly married? Long ago she'd accepted that it was a fantasy which could never come true. He would end up married to someone with a pedigree. Someone like Honor Witherspoon. Kitty released a short laugh. "I know my place, Dylan."

At that, he came partly back to life. "Fuck, Kitty."

"See? You know it too."

"Damn it." He pushed away from the pillows and started toward her.

She jumped off the bed and backed away. "It was your idea, Dylan. And you're right."

He stilled. "Exactly which of my ideas am I so right about?"

Her heart was aching, but, by God, it was still beating and she thought she finally knew how to protect it from Dylan. "Forget about normal. Who cares about conventional? I'm going to stop wishing for something I can't have and embrace my heritage. From now on, I'm letting all those Wilder genes out to play."

Chapter Thirteen

Kitty woke up late Monday morning, alone in her bed. Dylan had left following their discussion the night before, apparently silenced by her declaration that she'd decided to toss away her need for the conventional and was going to release her Wilder genes. He'd looked at her, shaken his head, then given her mouth a gentle kiss on his way out the door. She hadn't touched him at all.

It hadn't seemed wise.

"Wise" had seemed like stripping the bed linens. Then she'd gone out her back door and into the dark to gather the clean sheets she'd left hanging on the clothesline that morning before work. Though her single-wide garage held both a dryer and a washer, she liked to hang the sheets in the fresh air. The summer temperatures in Hot Water made them dry just as quickly anyway.

But burying her face in them had provided little solace. Yes, they'd smelled fresh, but they'd also smelled like home—warm air, tangy manzanita, and just a hint of the lavender growing in the garden next door. Sheets wouldn't smell like this when she moved to Seattle. At the prices she'd heard tell of, she wouldn't have a prayer of affording a place big enough for a potted plant, let alone a yard.

To drum the thought from her head, she'd hurriedly made up the bed, then attacked the financial work she'd let stack up again. After an hour, she'd sat back in her chair and stared at the computer screen, waiting for the expected elation.

Thanks to Dylan's presence as sheriff, their Old Town admission receipts were up. Way up. And while she'd realized that the living-history district had definitely been more crowded lately, Dylan's presence had distracted her from absorbing exactly *how* crowded. They'd taken in oodles of money.

The reenactors' portion would set a new record. By summer's end, Kitty's share would easily cover all she owed Aunt Cat.

Funny, though, the elation had continued to elude Kitty. Finally giving up on it, she'd gone to bed. The birds were starting to twitter when she at last fell asleep.

They were in full song now as she dragged herself up from the twisted covers and went about her usual day-off activities. In the morning she accomplished a week's worth of errands, and then after lunch she chauffeured Aunt Cat to her usual appointment at Locks, Stocks, and Barrcls. Later, when she went inside to pick her up, she steeled herself in case she found her mother there.

Samantha wasn't present, but the shop went quiet as

Kitty walked in. There was a time when she wouldn't even have noticed the silence or been suspicious. In general, people liked her and she liked them right back. Furthermore, for all her licentious ancestry, she'd never done anything worth gossiping about—at least anything that anyone knew. But once Samantha had returned, Kitty began to feel every citizen's eyes on her, their breaths collectively held. It was as if they were waiting for her to finally show her Wilder ways. And if she did, she knew the townspeople would look at one another and nod, telling themselves they'd expected such behavior from her the entire time.

Last night Kitty had told Dylan that being a Wilder was exactly what she planned on doing.

Yeah, right.

Acknowledging her own falsehood didn't make her feel any better. Still miserable, she floated Aunt Cat home in the T-bird, then slowly sailed the few blocks back to her house. Catching sight of a man on her doorstep, she nearly drifted into a mailbox. But then she saw it wasn't Dylan.

Thank goodness she'd turned off the engine before seeing who it really was. And what he carried.

In the summer, high schooler Eric Hardin made deliveries for his mom's florist shop. He held a box of flowers addressed to Kitty. A big box filled with two dozen long-stemmed red roses.

Eric's beat-up Volvo was long gone, but Kitty remained on her porch, staring through the cellophane window at the beautiful flowers. Traditional. Classical. Romantic, even. But best of all . . . conventional.

They were the conventional flower a man gifted to a woman.

Finally, fearing the heat would prematurely wilt them, Kitty let herself into the house, still somewhat dazed. She didn't have a vase tall enough, and she hated cutting them down too much—*long-stemmed red roses!*—so she settled on using a wide-mouthed cut-glass pitcher that had once belonged to Aunt Cat. The roses still towered over their container, but Kitty considered it fitting.

Long-stemmed red roses for a Wilder woman weren't a perfect match either.

She carefully flattened the box the flowers had arrived in. She scooped up all twenty-four pieces of trimmed stems and deposited them in the garbage. The vase looked best on the narrow coffee table in her tiny living room. No, it was better on the kitchen counter. Uh-uh. She was right the first time; it belonged in the living room.

After stalling some more, she had nothing left to do but open the small envelope that had come with the flowers. Staring at it as if it might bite, she dried her suddenly sweaty palms on the front of her shorts. Then, throwing caution to the wind, she snatched it up.

The same slanted, masculine handwriting that spelled her name on the envelope filled the card inside.

Thank you for last night. Whenever you're ready to walk on the Wilder side, call me.

The words drove her out of the house, because all at once the walls seemed too confining. The roses were too red, their scent too tantalizing, the possibilities of what Dylan proposed too dangerous. A long walk would return her to normal.

She must have been fiddling with the flowers for hours, because the sun was going down while she strolled through the streets of Hot Water. Passing the cemetery, she wasn't surprised to spot Bram there, standing at the foot of Alicia's grave, his head bowed. Kitty paused, watching him.

It made her want to cry sometimes, and at other times it made her want to yell at him like Alicia surely would have if she could. Bram had been grieving too hard for too long. Kitty didn't doubt that he'd loved his wife, but sometimes she wondered if he mourned the loss of control over his life just as deeply. Bram had always been one to order things just so.

Losing your beloved young wife to a random kidnapping had to wreak havoc with that.

Without thinking, she headed for the ironwork gate leading into the cemetery. As she slipped inside, she wished she'd brought one of the roses, but then she spied something she thought Alicia would like even better. Carrying it in her hand, she made her way to the grave site with the simple marker that read, "She loved well/She was well loved."

Kitty stifled a shiver of sadness when she came to stand beside the man already there. "Hi, Bram," she said softly. Without waiting for a reply, she bent down.

"Hey, Alicia," she whispered. On the close-clipped grass sat a small box carved from stone. It was said to have been Bram's first gift to his wife when she was alive. Under one of its corners, Kitty tucked the bluejay feather she'd found. "I like to think of you flying, friend."

"Thank you."

Kitty looked up, startled. It was Bram who owned the living-history-district property, so technically he was her employer. They'd talked on many occasions over the years, but she was shocked he would choose to speak to her now. Here. He always seemed to disappear inside himself when he visited the cemetery.

"You're welcome," Kitty replied, standing.

"She liked birds." His voice had a raspy quality that had first appeared on the night they'd found Alicia dead. It made his voice sound like that of someone who had screamed loud and long—or of someone who hadn't allowed himself to scream at all.

From the corner of her eye Kitty caught movement in the adjacent park. More ironwork fencing separated the two pieces of land. It was only a decorative divider, really. On busy days the sounds of children and the squeak of the swings could be enjoyed by the laid-back residents of the cemetery. Likewise, a child could escape the boisterous atmosphere of the park by taking a quiet walk among the gravestones.

The figure in the park moved again. It was Dylan. Dylan watching Bram.

Kitty swallowed. "I'll see you, Bram." She paused for another moment. "You too, Alicia."

Gravel scuffed beneath her sandals as she headed along the cemetery path toward the park. A warm wind picked up, then tossed a handful of browned oak leaves against a pocked, scarred marker that read only, "1852."

Whoever lay beneath it had been one of the very first to live and die in Hot Water.

She shivered again. Not because she was walking among the dead, but because, as she neared Dylan, she could tell he was still focused on Alicia's grave. On Bram.

"How are you, Dylan?" she asked.

He stood on the other side of the chest-high wrought-iron fencing, his hands stuffed into the pockets of an ancient pair of jeans. He wore a sleeveless white undershirt that was so thin she could see the outline of his gold medal beneath it. St. Barbara, the patron saint of prisoners. On his feet were the rattiest pair of running shoes she'd ever seen outside a garbage can.

She wanted to lick him all over.

"You should go talk to him," she suggested instead.

He blinked, as if suddenly coming back to the present. "Kitty," he said. He smiled, slow and full. His hand lifted palm-upward and the fingers curled. "Come here."

Her heart vaulted the fence; her feet shuffled slowly toward it.

He leaned over and caught her by the ponytail, dragging her closer. When she was near enough, he bent his head and kissed her.

Her mouth went soft and so did her knees. For support, she gripped a rail of the wrought-iron fence in one fist and let her other hand cup his head. His hair felt sleek and alive against her palm.

His tongue pushed inside and she welcomed it with hers. Dylan crowded closer, then, groaning, broke off.

He glanced down at the fence post he'd nearly impaled himself on, its finial shaped like an arrowhead. "We've got to stop meeting on opposite sides of bars," he muttered. "Climb over, honey."

She moved to obey, then remembered why she'd approached him in the first place. Not to kiss him. There was still so much separating them. "Bram's over there. You should go talk to him."

Dylan's expression turned wary. "No."

"Have you spoken with him at all since you came back to town?"

Wary went stony. "No."

"But he was a friend of yours!" she insisted. "A good friend." Everyone knew the two had been as close as brothers until Alicia's death.

Dylan took a step back from the fence and shrugged. "I've been avoiding a lot of my friends. Ask anybody."

She frowned. "Well, why is that? Everyone is thrilled to see you and all you do is make excuses or flat-out ignore them."

"Maybe there's someone else I'd rather spend time with." She could tell he was changing tactics to sidestep her questions, but still her skin goosebumped when he stepped close again and ran his fingertips down her cheek and under her chin. "Did you get the flowers?"

Kitty flushed. "Thank you. They're beautiful. But, Dylan, I think you need—"

"Did you read the card?"

Her face went hotter. In fact, all her skin went hot and prickly and she started to feel that amazing pulse in her bottom lip again. She ran her tongue over it.

"I love when you do that."

"Do what?" She nervously licked her lip again.

The corners of his mouth twitched. "That. Man oh man, those Wilder genes are just popping up all over, aren't they?"

Kitty tried to hang onto the more serious issue, but was losing ground fast. "What do you mean by that?"

One long finger reached through the fence to flick the crown of her breast. Kitty gasped, and looked down to see that her nipples were standing up against the fabric of her spaghetti-strapped summer top, tight and needy, showing as clearly through the thin cotton as . . . as his did.

It was a Wilder instinct that suddenly awoke. It was a Wilder hand that insinuated itself through the bars. It was a Wilder voice, throaty and sexy, that came from her mouth as her finger stroked his hard point in return. "I think that's the pot calling the kettle black."

He smiled. His eyelids went to half-mast and the look he gave her with them could ignite asbestos. "I don't care what you call me, honey, as long as you promise we're both going to be simmering soon."

Kitty's newfound daring collapsed. This morning she'd admitted to herself that she'd lied about embracing her Wilder-ness, right? She wasn't any less interested in the conventional today than any other day. Except now she was more interested in Dylan. The man who didn't wish being in love on himself or anybody else. The man whose name was linked with a beautiful heiress.

Kitty's heart squeezed. She honestly didn't think she had it in her to be casual about sex. At least not with Dylan. Not now.

Swallowing, she took a quick step back. "S-sure, Dylan. When I'm ready to simmer again, you'll be the first to know."

After eight years, Dylan was used to sleepless nights. After nearly a month in Hot Water, he was even used to sleepless nights thinking about Kitty Wilder. But it was too much, by God, to bear them after knowing the sweet, tight heat of her body.

Almost a week had gone by since he'd encountered her in the cemetery the day after they'd had sex. Though she'd claimed she wanted to go Wilder, she'd run away from him then and every day since. He was starting to worry.

She'd *said* she didn't take their marriage more seriously now that they'd been in bed together.

She'd *said* she didn't see him as her ticket to becoming conventional.

She'd *said* she'd given up on all that and was going to enjoy being a wild Wilder.

But as of this moment, he'd not seen any evidence of that.

At first, he'd promised himself to wait her out. Let *her* come to *him*. But now, as he set off on foot Sunday morning, determined to waylay her on the route between her house and Old Town, he was planning her surrender. By dusk, they were going to be on their way back to bed . . . and into an affair.

It made perfect sense. First, they wanted each other, there was no doubting that. They'd been trading steaming looks all week. Second, she owed him something for playing sheriff. Third, it would be freeing for both of them. She would indeed come to appreciate the release of her sexuality. When he became accustomed to her in bed, he would be able to recover his usual detachment.

Perhaps he'd thought he needed only that one time with her. So he'd been wrong. So what? A few more nights with her should appease his lust.

To that end, he wasn't going to let her retreat from him anymore. No more shared, sizzling glances that led to shared, heated memories that led to Dylan ready to strip paint off the walls from midnight to 4 A.M. To satisfy his Kitty addiction the night before, he'd contemplated ordering pay-per-view porn so he could toggle between naked women and *Little House* reruns. That was how desperate the situation had become.

Hence his plan was to heat her up in order to cool himself down. As he said, it made perfect sense.

His watch read four minutes before 8 A.M. while he loitered on the first corner she usually passed on her way to work. He leaned against the squat U.S. mailbox planted there, amusing himself by opening and shutting its squeaky door. As the seconds ticked by, he struggled with his increasing impatience, hoping he hadn't already missed her. He planned a full-court press on her resistance and that meant beginning first thing in the morning.

Waiting outside her house had seemed too obvious, however. But as more time passed, he wondered if that decision had been a mistake. With a curse, he slammed shut the mailbox door and the blue metal quivered in reaction. Damn it. Just one more offense to chalk up under Kitty's name. He hated second-guessing himself. He'd embraced FBI training for the very certainty of sticking to prescribed procedures in a crisis.

And thinking back to his sleepless night, his body hard and aching, he knew this was definitely a crisis. He opened the mailbox door again, then slammed it shut once more.

A woman's alarmed exclamation jerked his head up. It wasn't Kitty, but three female strangers—tourists, by the look of their fancy athletic gear—frozen in mid-power-walk stride.

They were coming from the direction of Kitty's house. Perhaps they'd seen her.

He smiled at them. With charm. "Good morning, ladies."

They exchanged anxious glances. "H-hello," one woman said, but all three kept their eyes down as they started to cross the street.

"Excuse me," he called out, "but I'm looking for someone."

Their power walk had slowed to a skulk, their cautious movements like those someone would make when hoping to escape the notice of a rabid dog. Dylan looked around him. Behind him. But there was no one—nothing—on the corner except him and the fairly harmless-looking mailbox.

He tried again, stepping off the curb and projecting his voice. "She's about five-foot-eight, long gold hair, blue eyes—"

"Another victim," one of the women said hoarsely, her eyes going wide.

All three gulped and their skulks sped to a scurry pace. Then another woman paused, her spine stiffening as she whirled to face him. "We won't tell you any-thing!" she cried, her eyes and her voice fierce. "Your looks don't fool us. The truth is all over the B and B. We've been warned about you."

Dylan's jaw dropped. "Warned about what?"

Kitty spoke from behind him. "That you're danger-ous, of course. Have you been harassing innocent women again?"

As he spun to confront her, from the corner of his eye he saw the tourists rush off. He shook his head. Some-thing wasn't right. But the thought disappeared when he took in his first look of the morning at Kitty's flawless skin and pouty mouth. "The only innocent woman I want to harass is you."

A flush rushed up her neck and she glanced away. "It's Sunday. You'll get your wish, Sheriff, at two P.M. and at four."

She carried her plastic-wrapped costume, and he took it from her, looping his index finger around the hanger. "That's not the kind of wish I want, honey," he said softly. Leaning closer, he ran his thumb over her bottom lip.

Her "Oh" came out like a hiccup and he smiled to himself. It wasn't going to take much to turn up the angel-face's heat. He'd been foolish to wait this long, but he suspected the prolonged tension had primed her as much as it had him.

"Let's go." He took her hand, entwining their fingers, and set off in the direction of Old Town.

She made another hiccup-like sound and tried break-ing his hold. After a moment he let her, resisting just enough so that the inner flesh of their fingers dragged against each other's on the long slide apart.

"Stop that," she demanded.

"But, honey—"

"Stop that too." The glance she gave him was stern.

"But that's how you taste," he said. "And I can't get it out of my mind."

A sound like a growl came out of her mouth.

"Sexy," he murmured, then had to leap away when she suddenly kicked out. "Hey, what's that for?"

She stopped and put her hands on her hips. "Okay. What are you up to?"

He was prevented from replying when someone called Kitty's name. They were in front of one of the many bed-and-breakfasts in town, and Mrs. Meeker, the proprietor of this one, hurried down the wide, front steps of her two-story, mint-green Victorian. Casting one suspicious glance back, Kitty moved to meet the other woman, leaving Dylan on the sidewalk.

Whistling lightly through his teeth, he prepared to wait. It didn't take a genius to figure out that Kitty was already teetering on the sexual precipice, and he didn't have the slightest compunction about being the one to give her the gentle nudge over. Hell, he'd make sure the fall was good for her, right?

An older couple exited the B and B through its beveled-glass door, then crossed the painted plank porch. They watched their feet as they descended the front steps, looking up only when they reached the sidewalk.

Feeling nearly at peace with the world for the first time in days, Dylan smiled at them. "Good morning."

The little old lady emitted a small gasp and clutched her husband's arm, her fingers digging into the sleeve of his lemon-colored Arnold Palmer sweater. Without a rejoining pleasantry, they made a wide berth around him and hurried off down the street.

Dylan turned to stare after them. "Well, a good day to you too," he muttered. He was so surprised by their lack of courtesy that he almost missed the fact that Kitty had ended her conversation and was already heading down the street in the opposite direction of the impolite pair.

He jogged to catch up with her. "It's the weirdest thing. Since I've returned, half the strangers I meet recognize me."

"What's so weird about that? Didn't some magazine name you Man of the Year or some other ego-inflating title?"

"It's the other half. They seem to recognize me too, but they also seem afraid of me, as if I'm a criminal or something."

Kitty choked.

Which meant he got to pat her on the back, the touches turning into a lingering caress from her shoulder blades to the small of her back. It was the sweetest little dip and he planned on exploring it in more detail as soon as possible.

She glared at him over her shoulder. "I'm fine."

"I'm not."

He should have known she'd stop at that, looking at him with genuine concern. "Whatever's wrong?" she asked.

The sincere words, the look, seemed to shorten the distance between them. As solid and caring as entwined hands, they connected Dylan to Kitty in a way he hadn't let himself connect to anyone in eight years. Ignoring the sensation, he smiled down at her with the slow ascent of one eyebrow—the wolf looking at Little Red Riding Hood and licking his chops. "I'm starved for sex."

A blade of shame stabbed him, but, damn it, he had to extinguish that soft light in her eyes.

Kitty stiffened. "And I'm supposed to be your banquet?"

He shrugged. "We're married, after all."

She narrowed her eyes. "And we both know how thrilled you are about that."

"That doesn't mean we can't have some fun with it. C'mon, Kitty. You said you wanted to let those Wilder genes out to play. Prove it." *Prove it to me so I'll be able to walk away.*

He wasn't surprised when she tossed her head, but he saw the betraying flush on her cheeks. She ignored him for the rest of the walk to work, but at her two o'clock arrest, her cheeks flushed pink again the moment he threw open the door of The Burning Rose. When he heaved her into the jail cell, witnessed by a gaggle of tourists enjoying the show, he reached through the bars and pulled the feather from her hair.

She tried to snatch it back, but he evaded her grasp to brush it under her chin. "All over you," he mouthed, his back to the audience. "I want to stroke this all over you."

Gooseflesh rose on her throat, then waved across all the bare skin exposed by the neckline of her dress. He swallowed, so distracted by the sight that he didn't react when she grabbed the feather from his suddenly lax hand and jammed it back into her hair.

"Behave yourself," she whispered, glowering.

Then he grinned, slow and confident. "Not on your life."

At precisely 3:58, he left the jail to make the day's coup de grâce arrest—the one designed to heat her up so hot that tonight she'd set his sheets aflame. It was 4:00 on the dot when he threw open the front door of The Burning Rose and it crashed against the wall.

Kitty's eyes went wide as his booted feet rang against the waxed plank floor.

Even wider when, instead of pulling out the handcuffs and clapping a manacle on one of her wrists, he ran his palm up her bare arm and cupped her by the back of the neck. "Miss Kitty Wilder, you're under arrest for the crime of keeping and maintaining a house where men and women of evil name and fame are drinking and misbehaving themselves."

"M-misbehaving?" She tried edging away from his hand on her neck, but he tightened his hold.

"Definitely misbehaving. Come along with me. There's a fine to be paid."

Her eyes narrowed suspiciously. "A fine? My usual punishment is a night in jail."

The crowd in The Burning Rose was enjoying the entertainment, but he could feel Kitty quivering beneath his hand. He smiled. "The sheriff has a fine he wants to discuss in *private* with you."

Her quivering became an all-out tremble as the people around them laughed knowingly. "Then the sheriff can *pay* for my private time like all the other gentlemen in town," she said, her smile sweet but sharp. "Now release me, sir."

Instead of obeying, he hauled her close against his body. "We're talking about what *you* owe, honey. Let's go."

Followed by the usual Sunday afternoon mob, he marched her toward the jail, congratulating himself on having found the surefire way to achieve the upper hand with her. The front of his body rubbed against her back as they moved down the street, his hips brushing the high, round curves of her butt.

"Give me some room," she said through her teeth.

"Can't give you a chance to get away," he murmured beside her ear. His body scraped against hers again. "You feel good."

Her spine steeled, and what he could see of her face, her neck, and one cheek, burned bright red.

Dylan smiled to himself, feeling the satisfaction of a man on the way to regaining dominance over his world. When she suddenly halted, standing firm in the dusty road, he was so surprised he almost plowed her over. "Wha—" he began.

"Sheriff," she declared, whirling to face him, "I've had enough of this inconsiderate treatment. I challenge you to a duel."

"A duel?" he echoed, feeling for the fake guns in the stupid holster he was wearing. Then he thought of John Shea and his missing earlobe. Christ, they *weren't* real, were they?

"A duel." Kitty confirmed, eyeing him with such hostility that Dylan was pretty sure that if it did come down to a shoot-out, she wouldn't be aiming for something as innocuous as his ear.

The crowd was circling them, Old West style.

The hot sun beat down on his head, and Dylan started to sweat. "Miss Kitty, I, uh . . ."

Without looking away from him, she held out a hand. "Spenser! Jeremy!" She snapped her fingers. The ostrich feather in her hair waved imperiously.

Over the crowd, Dylan caught sight of Spenser and Jeremy, who—unlike him—didn't appear caught by surprise. Traitors. One of them should have given him a heads up! Jesus, what was the point of being the town hero if no one treated him with proper respect?

He unfastened the button at his throat, doing his best to fake unconcern. "What exactly are the, uh, terms?"

Just then the people closest to him parted, and Jeremy and Spenser were let into their circle, each dragging long cloth-and-metal contraptions—*hoses*?—behind them.

"The terms?" Kitty repeated. "The terms are fire hoses at forty paces."

Uh-oh. Bad news. When he'd been making his plans, so had Kitty.

She smiled at the crowd as she grasped one of the wide-mouthed hoses with both hands. "In 1861, Hot Water held its first 'bulletless duel.' The sheriff thought then that it was a fine way to settle differences without bloodshed." She lifted an eyebrow Dylan's way. "So how about it?"

Oh, the sneaky little thing was full of surprises. Secret marriages, sex appeal, fire hoses. And she didn't leave him any choice, as usual. Dylan squared his shoulders. "I'm all for handling disagreements with nonviolence," he replied, reaching for the hose Jeremy held out.

He'd kill her later.

Method four-thirty-two.

As Spenser paced off the necessary distance, Dylan tried to figure out what he was going to do. Depending upon the pressure, he might hurt Kitty or, at the very least, sweep her too roughly off her feet with the force of the water.

"Don't worry, sir," Jeremy assured him as he showed Dylan the brass fitting that would release the water. "We've held duels like this during the last five Independence Day celebrations. The hoses are hooked to two old pump trucks. No one will get hurt."

Last July fourth, Dylan had spent the day at the Witherspoon estate, letting Honor pry out of him more stories about Hot Water, its eccentric people, its old-fashioned traditions. He looked down at the hose in his hands. Some new traditions had started without him.

Shaking off a weird sense of loss, he faced Kitty. The crowd was lined up closely on either side of them. It was roasting outside, so the tourists probably hoped for a little cooling overspray.

"Sheriff Matthews." Kitty's voice traveled easily through the hot, dry air. "Do you accept the challenge? Whoever's left standing is the acknowledged winner?"

"Just a minute," he yelled back. "If you're the victor, you get to stay out of jail. If it's me, what do I win?"

She tossed her head, and her hair slid out of the bun on top of her head and fell to her shoulders. Gold threads shone brightly in the sunlight. "Why, me, of course."

The crowd cheered. He barely managed to stop himself from doing the same.

"On three." Good ol' Spenser held his red bandanna in the air. "One . . . two . . . *three!*"

Unwilling to chance Jeremy's assessment of the water pressure, Dylan aimed just short of Kitty's feet as he twisted the nozzle. Not as considerate, her hose was pointing straight at him.

Water started trickling out of his first, with just enough force to jump a foot or so.

She grimaced and twisted faster.

The first spurt from her hose kicked up a splash of mud onto his cheek. His adrenaline jumped and he twisted again. Water leaped from his hose . . . another disappointing three feet.

Water from Kitty's hose suddenly sprang forth, catching him squarely on the knees. The crowd cheered again, she whooped, and he dug his heels into the new mud at his feet.

His hose continued to sprinkle like an elephant with a leak.

Wearing a triumphant grin, she played her spray over his body. The water was strong, enough to sting if he wasn't clothed, but he grimly stood fast, vainly twisting at his hose's fitting, which now seemed frozen.

He—wasn't—going—to—let—her—win. But she was concentrating on his knees and ankles now, and the mud beneath his boots was getting squishier and squishier.

"Give up, Sheriff?" she called out gaily.

His hose was still operating at watering-can force. "Never!" He gave the fitting a vicious twist, and water suddenly gushed.

It caught Kitty full in the chest, instantly soaking the front of her dress.

She gasped. He might have felt satisfaction, except that between the soaking and the gasping, the neckline was gaping dangerously. Within seconds, she was an eyelash away from exposing to all her pretty, for-his-eyes-only breasts.

"Kitty!" He threw the stupid hose down and rushed toward her.

To immediately lose his footing and fall flat on his ass in the reddish, sticky mud.

The onlookers went wild.

So did his temper.

He was still lying there, staring up into the mocking blue sky while the wet dirt worked its way into every pore of his body, when Kitty walked up to him. Gingerly. He thought it was because she feared his reaction, but then he saw the gleeful grin on her face and realized she was merely trying not to slip in the mud.

"Are you okay?" she asked. In one fist she held the sagging material at the front of her dress. She tried biting back her grin, but it broke out once again.

"You owe me," he said as laughter—laughter at his expense—rolled through the street. She owed him big, damn it. When he'd meant to heat her up, she'd succeeded in cooling him down. Dylan Matthews, a cool fool.

Her mouth turned serious, as serious as her puckery, kiss-me mouth could look. "I know," she said, her eyes wide. He could tell that, inside, she was laughing too.

He sat up. There was mud in his hair, under his fingernails, and somehow, some way, between his toes. "I'm warning you," he told Kitty. "You're going to regret that." Then he flopped back in the mud, unable to face the uproarious tourists.

Sinking down beside him, Kitty giggled.

He shot her a venomous look, then finally surrendered. No one liked a sore loser. He laughed.

Chapter Fourteen

Sitting in the bar Sunday night, D. B. admitted to himself he was a coward. It was a hell of a thing for a fifty-year-old man to know about himself, but it was the truth.

He'd dragged his one and only son to Bum Luck for a drink because he wasn't brave enough to face Samantha alone. Not after virtually ignoring her in The China Chef last week once his friends arrived.

There was also Dylan and the Odd Fellows' plan. He should warn his son that they aimed to name the park after him on Heritage Day. But D. B. knew he was going to be yellow-bellied about that too. He suspected that telling Dylan would drive him away, and D. B. already had enough trouble getting people he cared about to stay close by.

Hell, Samantha wouldn't even come to the table to take their order.

"Well, Judge, should I go to the bar to get our drinks?" Dylan asked after another few minutes without service.

"No!" Damn it, D. B. wasn't going to let the woman ignore him the entire night. Then he narrowed his eyes at his son, his frustration spilling over. "Didn't you used to call me Dad?"

Dylan's eyebrows rose. "What's eating you?"

Over his son's shoulder, D. B. could see Samantha leaning close to George Gilbert, who owned a real estate office in the next county. The old coot had arrived after D. B. and Dylan, and she'd already brought him his drink. Now she was personally delivering a basket of pretzels, when most customers retrieved their own from the stack on the bar. D. B. glowered.

Dylan turned his head and looked in the same direction as his father. "You forget to pay your bar tab or something, Judge?"

D. B. didn't take his eyes off Samantha. Christ. How could he begin to make it up to her if she wouldn't come near him, if she instead chose to fawn over some paunchy fool who looked ready to swallow his dentures because of her attention? "Women," he said with a disgust he really felt toward himself.

Dylan's eyebrows shot upward again. He turned his head once more, turned back to look at D. B. "Women?" he asked.

"Women," D. B. confirmed. "And some are a hell of a lot more trouble than others."

Dylan leaned back in his chair, an odd smile curving his mouth. "Wilder women."

"The worst."

Dylan rubbed his chin. "I'm running into my own lack of cooperation," he murmured after a moment, looking more amused than frustrated, "if that makes you feel any better."

It didn't. D. B. stared at the empty tabletop. He had to make Samantha understand that what had happened in the Chinese restaurant wasn't because he was ashamed of their relationship. Sure, it might surprise—fine, *shock*—a lot of Hot Water to discover their judge was seeing Samantha, but it wasn't anyone's business but hers and D. B.'s.

That was why he hadn't broadcast it. That was why he always waited until everyone else left Bum Luck before touching her. At least that was what he always told himself.

"You two look thirsty!"

D. B. looked up to find Dylan's old friend Tony Kula standing beside the table, a full pitcher of beer in one hand and three empty mugs in the other. "May I join you?" he asked.

Before either Dylan or D. B. could respond, Tony set the glassware down with a clack and drew over a chair from a nearby table. Its wooden legs creaked as he settled his impressive poundage onto the seat. He grinned at the other two men. "My wife and my daughter are having a girls' night out, so I'm a free man."

It took him only a moment to pour three foamy-headed beers. One he shoved toward D. B., the other toward Dylan. He lifted his. "To women!"

Catching each other's eye, D. B. and his son both groaned.

"Let's drink to anything but that," Dylan said. "You're talking to the walking wounded here."

Tony grinned. "I heard about today's duel."

Before D. B. could pursue what he meant by that, Tony launched into a recounting of the previous year's high school football season. He followed that with a detailed analysis and breakdown of the team's—the Argonauts—upcoming chances.

D. B. spent half of his first beer watching his son relax, then laugh, then finally join in an enthusiastic reminiscence of his and Tony's own championship season. Something inside D. B. relaxed too. At least he had one thing to be thankful for. This was what he wanted for Dylan—an opportunity to reconnect the ties he'd severed so abruptly and so finally eight years before.

Despite that, D. B.'s tension over Samantha continued to coil as she persisted in ignoring him. He tried catching her eye a half-dozen times, but she kept her chin lifted and all her smiles for her other customers. After draining his second mug of beer, he couldn't stand it any longer.

Slapping the glass on the table, he swore not to cower another minute. He was going to corner her somewhere, anywhere, on top of the bar if he had to. Damn it, she was going to listen to him. He shoved his chair back.

"You can't leave now, Judge." Tony poured the remainder of the pitcher into D. B.'s mug. "Not when I've saved the best story for last."

"I'll be back—"

"It's about John Shea," Tony said, then leaned across

the table and lowered his voice. "And Samantha Wilder's underwear."

"Oh, shit," D. B. thought he heard his son mutter.

"What kind of story is this?" he asked slowly.

Tony grinned. "Funny as hell. Scoot in and let me tell it to you."

"Tony," Dylan interjected, "maybe Bum Luck isn't the right—"

"I want to hear it," D. B. said, scraping his chair back to the table. "Go ahead."

It seemed that John Shea had been transfixed by the sight of his neighbor Samantha's underwear on the line. It seemed that John Shea's wife had leaped to the conclusion that John had shot away some of the strategic parts of the risqué next-to-nothings, in a session of target-practice-gone-awry. It seemed that everyone in town was having a good laugh over Mrs. Shea's naïveté and John Shea's bad luck in getting caught gawking.

And last but not least, it seemed that the residents of Hot Water were also speculating wildly about Samantha and for whom she wore her triple-X-rated underwear.

"Makes you wonder if all those rumors are true," Tony concluded, shaking his head and grinning.

"What rumors would those be?" Behind D. B., Samantha's voice cut like the blade of a cold knife.

Tony's hand jerked, toppling his near-empty beer mug. He flushed. "Oh, my God. I'm sorry. For the mess, for . . ."

Without hesitation, Samantha smoothly moved forward. She re-righted the mug, then cleared up the mess. In seconds, their table was clean and dry and their pitcher and mugs were stacked on her tray. Her frosty gaze ran over them. "Good night, gentlemen," she said.

They were being thrown out.

All three of them gaped at her. She appeared as elegant and untouchable as always, her blond hair twisted at her nape, her straight dancer's posture unbowed. But D. B. noticed the telltale rapid pulse at her throat. She was upset and he felt sick.

"Samantha . . ." he began, trying to project both his apologies and his concern for her into her name.

She turned and walked away.

Dylan stood. "Well, men, this rat is taking the hint and running for the door before she calls in rodent control."

"Sylvia's going to kill me," Tony said, also standing. His round, usually jolly face looked mournful. "Samantha's a friend of hers. I bet I sleep on the couch tonight." He looked down at his enormous frame. "And it's a small couch."

Dylan cast a considering glance at D. B., then grabbed his friend's arm. "Give me a ride, Tony. I'll help you prepare some appropriate groveling on the way home." He clapped his hand on D. B.'s shoulder as he passed. "G'night, Judge. And good luck."

D. B. sank into his chair, bloodied but determined. He wasn't leaving until Samantha forgave him.

No one approached him for the rest of the night. When Samantha locked the door behind the last customer, he wasn't even sure she was aware he was still inside.

In the quiet of the now-closed bar, Bob Dylan's "Lay, Lady, Lay" pulsed through the speakers. As Samantha walked back toward the bar, D. B. stood up to confront her. "We need to talk."

She surprised him by nodding coolly. Her arms folded over her chest. "Yes, we do."

He hesitated, unsure of how to start, where to stand, if maybe they should be sitting somewhere comfortable. His hands and feet felt too big and his Adam's apple was the size of a grapefruit.

He was fifty years old, and with that composed, cold expression on her face, she made him feel fifteen.

"If you weren't so damn beautiful . . ." The words slipped out, along with a rueful laugh. He shook his head. ". . . maybe I wouldn't make such an ass of myself."

Her eyebrows rose. "I think you're acting as you should. As a respectable citizen of the town, one who holds a position of great responsibility." The words were reasonable—understanding, even—but her tone cut like a shard of ice.

He winced. "Why does that sound like the precise definition of a pompous ass?"

Samantha spun away. "We always knew this wouldn't last."

"What?" He strode toward her and caught her arm. "What the hell are you talking about?" He tried to turn her toward him, but she resisted, pretending an absorption in the parquet tiles of the floor.

"I tried to tell you before," she said. "You have to see it now. It's time we . . . stopped."

Something desperate and angry released like bile into his gut. "Stop what?" He shook her arm. "Stop having sex, stop caring about each other?"

She faced him. Cold again. Angry. "Both, of course."

He stared at her. For over four—five, now—months he'd been having an affair with this woman. While he'd not known where it would lead, he'd never imagined this moment. Maybe it was because he'd never planned there would *be* such a moment. Maybe he'd thought he'd found something to keep him young for the rest of his life.

"Samantha," he said softly.

Her calm almost crumbled at his tender tone. "No," she said, taking a hasty step away from him. "No." She shook her head.

All his earlier awkwardness disappeared as a notion clicked in his brain, a notion that had already clicked in his heart. "Sweetheart, I'm sorry," he said. "I screwed up the other night at the restaurant. I don't know . . . I think part of what I've liked about us is that it's been ours alone. No one else's. But I never meant to make you feel . . ."

"As if you didn't want to admit knowing me?"

He winced again. "I'm sorry if that's how it seemed to you."

"It did," she said, her eyes glittering. "But hell, I understand. You're a judge, and I'm a—"

"Successful, beautiful woman. Samantha, you have nothing to be ashamed of. And I swear to God, I'm *not* ashamed of you."

She put her hand over her eyes, and when she took it away, there was pain in them. Pain, and pity. "You should have seen your face after Tony told you about John Shea and the underwear."

D. B. tried shrugging off the accusation. "I don't like the idea of everyone talking about you." Then he gave her a sheepish grin. "And I feel kind of possessive about your underwear. I especially don't like the idea of another man imagining you in it."

For a long moment she stared at him. Then she laughed. "Oh, D. B., what do you think I did before I returned to town?"

The laugh, the question, they both scared the hell out of him. He lifted a shoulder. "I don't know. You worked in a bar, owned one, maybe. I don't care."

She laughed again. It wasn't a pleasant sound. "Oh, yes. You will."

He smothered another unmanly sense of panic. "What are you talking about?"

Her expression was unreadable. "For over twenty years I was a stripper."

"No!" The denial burst out. "That's just a rumor."

She nodded. "I admit there's been plenty of those too. I was never a prostitute. Nor a gangster's moll, or some politician's girl on the side either. There was an occasional man in my life, but what I gave, I gave away for free. However, the truth is, I *was* a stripper."

D. B. closed his eyes. "I don't believe you."

She laughed again, the sound bitter. "You don't want to believe me. You want to think I left here when I was seventeen years old and found some kind of job you consider acceptable."

Her arms crossed over her chest again and her mouth pursed. "How would you like this little fiction to go? Oh, I've got it. You'd like to think I worked for minimum wage somewhere ... a diner, maybe, or a toy store. On my nights off, you'd like to think I went to a community college, where I earned a degree in business—no, home ec. On Sundays I attended a church service, followed by a walk in the park before cheerfully tackling my homework."

"I'm not so parochial as that," he said, stung.

She smiled, a smile that wasn't soft and warm, but hard and cynical. "No, you're right. You thought perhaps I worked in a bar, or owned one. On my *days* off, I went to college."

D. B. didn't believe this—any of it. That he'd so royally screwed up, that she was looking at him with this disturbing mix of sadness and contempt, that Bob Dylan's music was still chugging through the speakers as if nothing catastrophic were happening to what had been, just a few months ago, a well-ordered, middle-aged life.

"All right, then," he said with resignation. "Tell me how it was, Samantha."

"My mother died when I was sixteen. She was hit by the train as she walked home from her cocktail-waitress job, the job that was right here in this bar."

D. B. nodded, though he hadn't known about her mother working in Bum Luck.

"A few months later I was pregnant by a college boy who breezed into town for the weekend and who swore he'd love me forever. He didn't give me his real last name." She spoke the words with cool matter-of-factness. "I gave birth, decided I didn't know one damn thing about being someone's mother, then left Hot Water to find my fame and fortune."

"And to forget," D. B. interjected.

She froze, then gave him a stiff nod. "Score one for the judge. But now, where was I? Ah, yes. Fame and fortune. I fancied myself a dancer, you see. One of my Wilder ancestors performed a mean fandango, I believe. I bought a bus ticket to Las Vegas and found that diner job. I also took classes—not academic ones, but dance classes at a nearby studio."

"And then?" He still wasn't sure he believed her story.

"And then it was a remarkably short leap to the local strip club. Two of the girls I took classes with stripped, and they kept telling me about the great money, that I'd have more free time to practice my craft, that it really didn't *mean* anything." She shrugged. "I was a Wilder, after all. I wasn't exactly shocked by the idea. And in reality, it *didn't* mean anything. It didn't mean anything at all."

D. B. tried to take it in. He'd never deluded himself by thinking she was inexperienced, of course. Part of the appeal of their relationship was that they were two mature people with mature attitudes about each other, about sex. Though she made him as horny as a boy, they came to each other with the confidence of adults who'd been around the block a time or two.

But this? That she'd spent more than twenty years taking her clothes off for other men?

"I still don't believe it," he said.

Pity returned to her face. She hesitated, and then she closed her eyes for a moment. The music changed and the downbeat of Steppenwolf's "Born to be Wild" throbbed like a pulsating vein through the room. Samantha started swaying.

The swaying turned sinuous and she opened her eyes,

her expression suddenly dreamy, almost orgasmic. Her tongue sneaked out to wet her lips and D. B. took an involuntary step back. She didn't even acknowledge him.

Instead, her hands went to the long row of buttons marching down the knee-length black dress she wore. They were fastened to display a modest amount of cleavage, but not for long. Her hips rotating in a slow, sensuous circle, she unbuttoned one after another after another, as if the vibrating, sultry music made her too hot for clothes.

D. B. couldn't look away. His mouth went dry, and, shameful or not, his shaft hardened. She peeled off the dress, letting it drop to completely reveal a set of her sexy underwear.

The underwear that John Shea had seen hanging on her clothesline. The underwear that barely covered the good parts of the most luscious body he'd ever seen in his life. The body that dozens, hundreds, thousands? of other men had seen over the years.

She kept right on dancing, as if he weren't there. As if he, like all the other men she'd ever taken her clothes off for, didn't matter.

Still swaying, she shut her eyes. Her hands fluttered to her thighs and then crawled slowly up, just like he wanted to do. Sweat broke out over D. B.'s skin. His breath wheezed in his chest. He felt rooted to the floor, the thudding drums of the song commanding his heartbeat, until she cupped her breasts in her own palms and offered them to someone neither she nor D. B. could see.

God, he *was* a coward. Because that was when he turned and ran.

*   *   *

From the upstairs back bedroom, Kitty heard the front door of the brothel bang open.

"Kitty Wilder!"

It was past closing time in Old Town and she was on her hands and knees, picking up something that looked and acted a lot like dandelion fuzz from the antique carpet. Though a service regularly cleaned the restored buildings, The Burning Rose wasn't on its schedule again until next week.

"Kitty Wilder!" It was Dylan's voice.

She sighed. "I'm up here," she called back, wishing she didn't have to. In the past few days, her resolve to keep a safe distance from him hadn't changed. She knew releasing her Wilder-ness with Dylan would be courting heartbreak.

Yet it was obvious his intent hadn't changed either. Every look, every word, every one of his breaths seduced her . . . and he knew it. His dousing two days ago might have temporarily cooled him down, but she didn't fool herself it would last. How would she protect herself against his next sexual onslaught?

"Kitty." Looming in the doorway, a piece of paper in his hand, Dylan didn't look at her as if he had seduction on his mind. Strangulation, maybe.

He shook the paper in his fist. "Well, Kitty?" He was wearing his standard jeans, cowboy boots, and chambray work shirt. But the shirt was pulled free and unbuttoned to reveal a thin white undershirt like she'd seen on him before. "What the hell is this?"

Recognizing the paper, she sat back on her heels. "PR?"

"PR? You mean public relations?" He stepped into the room. "That's BS."

A few days ago Spenser had proposed the idea of slipping into the souvenir passports a half sheet detailing the pretend Sheriff Matthews's real FBI-agent exploits. The papers had come back from the printer yesterday and been handed out for the first time today. "Is there some factual error?" she asked innocently.

His brows slammed together. "Aren't the banners you have strung up across the streets enough?" He looked down at the sheet of paper in his hand. " 'Hometown Hero,' " he read from it, his voice filled with disgust.

Okay, Kitty did feel a bit guilty about passing out the Dylan Matthews fact sheet. But Spenser had been gung-ho about the whole notion and truly, there was merit to it. The whole point of Dylan's playing sheriff was to capitalize on his notoriety. Not to mention that she'd learned even more interesting details about him when composing the bio. "Did Honor Witherspoon's father really offer to buy you a security company in gratitude for saving his daughter?" she asked.

That was what some of the regular newspapers opined. As Aunt Cat had said before, the tabloids contended it was Honor herself whom her father had offered to Dylan.

"He has offered me the position of head of security in *his* company," Dylan said shortly. "Among other things."

Kitty let the "other things" lie, not sure she wanted to know how much truth there was to the tabloid rumors. The idea of Dylan and another woman still made her feel betrayed. Sure, it was unfair, but it was still true. She cleared her throat. "Are you going to accept the job?"

He lowered his brows again. "Don't try to change the subject, Kitty."

"I'm just wondering if you're burned out with the FBI. When I did the research for that bio, I couldn't help but notice that for several years you've been involved in very tense, very high-profile cases back-to-back."

"That's the nature of the job." Then he let go a humorless laugh. "And if it's the truth you want, I'm effing sick of the FBI."

Kitty blinked, stunned by the unexpected confession. "Then you're going to take Warren Witherspoon's offer." And maybe his daughter too? Another pang of jealousy stabbed her heart.

"No." He rattled the paper ominously. "What I'm going to do is find some special kind of torture designed to pay you back for circulating these."

His gaze raked over her, and he suddenly stilled, the atmosphere in the room just as instantly changing. The heat in the air jacked up several degrees—and its source didn't seem to be Dylan's temper. His nostrils flared and his eyes narrowed, the anger in them having somehow converted to an emotion distinctly more . . . carnal. "Kitty," he said, his voice raspy and notes lower than before.

Nerves pinging in alarm, Kitty swallowed. "What?"

"Maybe not a torture after all," he said softly, cat-footing closer. "But a trade."

"What kind of trade?" Kitty edged backward, her knees catching in the long skirt of her costume.

He let out a soft groan, his gaze glued to her breasts. "You're killing me."

Kitty looked down. Her blue dress was as low-cut as the others, but in this position her knees were pulling the bodice lower. Indecently lower. The top rise of her breasts was completely exposed and the outer rim of her right nipple was peeking over the lace.

She should move. Pull up the dress. Stand. Something. But the expression on his face paralyzed her. His nostrils flared again and his cheekbones appeared to be pushing against his tanned skin. As had happened before, those dangerous cravings ignited inside her, growing all at once to a greedy, physical hunger to touch him, taste him, *know* him.

On the wall over his shoulder, a hand-lettered sign proclaiming "Satisfaction Guaranteed" reminded her of all that had happened in this room. Men had come here, full of passion and sexual excitement. Night after night, satisfaction guaranteed, they'd been at the mercy of Kitty's foremothers, ready to pay whatever it took to experience a woman's touch.

She wanted that power for herself.

The idea shocked her, rocked her with its seductive force. But it didn't shake the sudden conviction that she could regain some control of her life, of her desires, by taking charge. Right here. Right now.

Sinking back against her calves, she licked her lips.

"Maybe I don't want to trade," she said, her voice hoarse now.

His glance flicked up to her eyes.

"Maybe I want to torture *you*."

A pulse in his jaw jumped. "You're doing that already."

"Poor baby." She swallowed, trying to keep up her courage. "What could I do to make it better?"

"Let me see your breasts."

A shiver coursed through her. "It seems to me you're looking at them."

His voice was guttural. "All of them."

She shivered again, liquid heat rushing between her thighs. The idea that he appeared desperate to see body parts that she'd always dismissed as inadequate not only excited her but gave another boost to her feminine confidence. Wetting her mouth with her tongue, she lifted her hands and took just a moment to tug down the neckline of the dress and lift one breast free. Then the other.

They sat on the shelf of the bunched bodice, the nipples hard and turning brighter pink under his unblinking stare. They trembled with every beat of her heart, and his breath turned loud and rasping in the quiet of the room.

"Come here," he choked out.

She nearly obeyed, but then halted. This was about *her* power, *her* desires, *her* needs. She shook *her* head. "You come to me."

His gaze jumped to hers. She could tell he was resisting her command, wanting to keep all the authority for himself. With the backs of her fingers she traced the outside curves of her bare breasts.

"Kitty . . ."

She did it again.

He stepped forward, reaching out for her. "Let's go somewhere."

Kitty stayed where she was. The power was here, in The Burning Rose, in the spirits of the women who had worked this room. Kitty thought she might understand them now, as much as someone from a century and a half later could, the shame she usually felt when thinking of them diminishing. Here in Hot Water it might have been the Wild West, but in other parts of the world it had been Victorian times. For women of that era, choices had been limited, and the dominion—and opinions—of men had been the norm.

So between these walls perhaps they had found an independence of sorts. Within this room, Kitty recognized that her ancestors might have found pleasure in a man's pleasure. More, they had established a not-so-subtle aura of female dominance that had protected them against degradation. Here, in The Burning Rose, a woman could lie with a man without bringing her heart into it. And oh, that was what *she* wanted to do with Dylan.

"Kitty." Dylan stretched his hand closer. "Let's go."

She ignored him and reached for one of his belt loops instead. Rising to her knees, she pulled him closer.

"What are you doing?" His voice grated.

"You wanted to see me," she said. "Now I want to see you." The top snap of his jeans popped open.

He shuddered. "Shit, Kitty."

The zipper rasped loudly.

He shuddered again.

She'd never felt so powerful in her entire life. So in control.

Pushing aside the edges of the jeans, she widened the vee made by the zipper. He sucked in a breath through his teeth as she used her hand to trace him through the silk of black boxers. The hot hardness jumped against her palm.

"I must be dreaming," he muttered.

Thrilled by her boldness, she slid both hands inside the loosened denim to cup the cheeks of his hard, round rear end. Her movement parted the slit at the front of the boxers, exposing a tempting glimpse of smooth flesh. Squeezing the taut muscles in her hands, she leaned forward and gave a delicate lick to the bared skin.

He groaned, his hands spearing into her hair. She licked again, taking her time with an upstroke and a downstroke, intrigued and excited by the steeliness covered with such sleek, hot skin.

Her skin was hot too, and there was another rush of wet heat between her thighs. She moved closer to him, and her naked, tingling nipples brushed against the denim of his jeans. She closed her eyes, rubbing her breasts against the fabric again.

"Kitty." His voice sounded strained. "Let's . . . let me . . ."

"No." She stared up at his face and thought the stark neediness there was the most beautiful thing she'd ever seen. He'd been the man of her dreams, the golden idol on a pedestal nearly all her life, but now that she was truly at his feet, it was as if they were for once on equal footing.

With a slow, deliberate movement, she pushed down his jeans. Then she looked up to catch his gaze once more, and holding it, eased his boxers away.

His breath hissed. Kitty licked her lips, then broke their eye contact to focus on what she'd revealed.

It was huge and potent-looking and it startled her for a moment to think she'd managed to take it inside her body. It jutted toward her as if wanting to intimidate her, to dominate her, but Kitty knew it was only posturing . . . like barbed wire wrapped around a heart.

It was vulnerable. *He* was vulnerable.

To her.

Kitty leaned forward and took him in her mouth.

He groaned and it surged against her tongue. It seemed to grow larger, but she wouldn't let him get away. She painted it with pleasure, tasting his skin, grasping the backs of his hard thighs and feeling the shudders that racked his body. His hand cupped the back of her head and she felt his fingers trembling too.

In this game of desire, she was winning.

Or so she thought.

The world suddenly spun. He pushed her down onto her back, shoved up her skirts, moved his hand between her legs, and tugged aside her panties. "Dylan." She panted, resenting the sudden change in positions.

"Be quiet." He used his other hand to hold her shoulders down as he came between her knees.

"Not without a condom," she said, the last word ending in a moan as one of the stroking fingers between her thighs brushed high, teasing the pleasure center of the rose. There was still a chance to bring him back to her mercy.

Cursing, he reached down to the tangle of denim around his ankles.

She rose up on her elbows. "You have one with you?"

"Only every moment for the last two weeks." He cut her a look at the same time that he drew a foil-wrapped package from his pocket. "Call me psychic. Hell, call me hopeful." It took just a minute for him to slip the condom on.

Then he turned back to her, his eyes hot, his mouth grim. "Now," he said.

"No." Kitty remembered this was supposed to be hers. For her. "This is mine."

He laughed, his teeth flashing white. "Hell, yes." His body lowered.

"Dylan." She braced her hands on his shoulders. "I'm not kidding. I—" He brushed the tip of his arousal against the wet petals of her body. She moaned.

When he pushed inside, she couldn't protest. It felt too good.

"And you're mine," he said.

He slid so deep, she thought he'd found her heart. For that instant before surrender, she worried that there was no such thing as making love to Dylan without it.

Chapter Fifteen

Late the next afternoon, Kitty stood in the small pharmacy section of an air-conditioned aisle at Kemper's Market. She avoided all thoughts of past, present, and future by giving her complete focus to what type of headache remedy to buy. Aspirin? Ibuprofen? Did she want time-release capsules, caplets, or tablets?

Undecided, she shoved her hands in the pockets of her overalls. Even the easiest of decisions didn't seem so clear-cut anymore.

After hesitating for another few moments, she reached toward the time-release ibuprofen. As her fingertips touched her choice, she glimpsed the top of a dark, glossy head above the goods on the aisle's highest shelf. In guilty reaction, her hand jerked, sending the boxed bottle of ibuprofen and four larger boxes of whatever was stacked beside it sailing.

The box of capsules belly flopped to the floor. Three of the other four items fell beside it without further incident. The remaining box launched by her sudden panic took a more unfortunate trajectory, dropping into another shopper's unattended cart. The force of the landing of the bonus-sized box of condoms—yes, that was what it was, size large, heavily ribbed—rocked a roll of paper towels. As the roll swayed left, the condoms slid into the newly revealed niche beneath them, snuggling a carton of eggs at the bottom of the basket. Then the paper towels fell to the right, completely covering the surprise item.

Kitty cast a nervous glance in the direction of the adjacent aisle, then scooped up the condom boxes on the floor to shove them back on a shelf. When she stepped toward the additionally burdened cart, she recognized another body part—Dylan's foot—turn into her aisle. Leaving the last box of condoms where it lay hidden, she whipped around the end display, and from there into the aisle he'd just vacated.

She couldn't let him find her.

If he did, he'd realize she'd made up the excuse about a mega-important, not-to-be-missed Hot Water Preservation Society meeting. After readjusting their clothing the day before in The Burning Rose, he'd told her of a planned evening out with his friends. They'd finally roped him into a social event and he'd asked her to accompany him.

But she'd thought not. No way. Uh-uh. It was bad enough that she couldn't resist him sexually, but she wasn't going to start seeing him socially. That wasn't smart. Besides, Kitty and Dylan? The people of Hot Water would split their sides at the very idea of the town's legendary hero spending time with a Wilder.

She moved quickly to the end of the aisle, eyeing Kemper's automatic doors and the freedom they promised. Deciding to make a break for it, she darted into the open area by the registers just as those doors went *whoosh*. Judge D. B. Matthews stepped through.

Argh. Coming face-to-face with the judge would be nearly as bad as bumping into Dylan. If he mentioned to his son that he'd seen Kitty, the jig would definitely be up. Kitty leaped back.

"Careful," a sharp voice said.

Kitty turned to face Pearl Morton, pushing a cart and frowning at her in like-mother-like-daughter disapproval. Despite the censure, Kitty smiled in apology. "Sorry."

Pearl didn't soften. "Watch where you're going," she said, edging her cart to one side of the aisle, nearly running over Kitty's foot in the process. She turned her back to inspect a row of hair products.

"Sorry," Kitty murmured again. She loitered, pretending to survey whatever was on the shelves in front of her, biding her time until the exit was clear. *One . . . two . . . three . . .*

After counting to thirty, she strode forward at the same moment that Pearl pushed her cart ahead. The metal wheels caught Kitty's bare heel and she yelped, spinning. Her elbow swept some items off the shelves, and they hit the floor with a *thwack*. Sighing, Kitty knelt to retrieve them. Without a word, Pearl sailed by, her gaze trained on the grocery list in her hand.

As the other woman's cart passed, Kitty noticed the

eggs on the bottom, the bonus box of condoms next to them, the roll of paper towels on top of that. And on top of *that*, an expensive bottle of hair tonic—guaranteed to cure female baldness. Kitty looked down at one of the items she'd knocked to the floor. The exact same bottle.

"Pearl . . ."

The other woman ignored her and turned the corner. The last thing Kitty saw was the baldness tonic, which she'd accidentally but most certainly knocked into the cart, sliding down the plastic-wrapped paper towels to disappear beneath the shampoo that Pearl had probably just ticked off her itemized list.

Okay, lately Pearl's treatment of Kitty had been lousy, but in a small town the contents of your grocery cart were as closely scrutinized as the new color you were painting your house or the new perm you received at Locks, Stocks, and Barrels. To avoid such intense surveillance during Kitty's high school years, the other girls had driven to the bigger stores in the next town to buy things their moms would disapprove of.

Or they'd asked Kitty, with no reputation to lose, to make the purchases at Kemper's for them.

Squaring her shoulders, Kitty followed Pearl, prepared to confess in order to spare the older woman embarrassment at the checkout counter. The next aisle over was empty and she strode to the end of it quickly. Standing by a display of diapers and baby wipes, she looked to the right. Nothing. Then to the left.

Oh, holy havoc, Batman. Standing in the store's back corner, where the cases of soft drinks were stacked, was Samantha.

And Pearl's husband, Red Morton.

The two were close together, talking, and they might have been at it for some time, because the only items in Samantha's cart so far were a box of saltine crackers and what looked like raspberry leaf tea. Kitty swallowed. She had to waylay Pearl before she caught sight of Samantha and Red.

Doubling back, she cringed to find the woman in question heading purposefully down the aisle. If Pearl made it to the diapers and baby wipes, she'd be certain to see the pair. Kitty girded her loins. "Uh, Pearl," she said, blocking the woman's cart.

"What?" she answered impatiently.

The condoms and the baldness tonic in Pearl's cart, though unseen, seemed to Kitty to glow like radioactive material. "Uh—well—" she stammered, trying to think of a delicate way to bring up the items.

"I don't have time for this." Pearl changed course, pushing her cart around Kitty, though a back wheel managed to crunch over her little toe.

Silenced by the pain, Kitty hopped on one foot after her. As Pearl reached the end of the aisle, Kitty caught her shoulder, causing Pearl to bump the corner of the cart into the rows of shelving. The older woman turned, and behind her back, Kitty saw something teeter on the topmost shelf and then topple into the cart. Still gasping from the pain in her toe, Kitty, flamingo-legged, just pointed.

With an impatient sigh, Pearl turned around. "Oh, thank you," she said ungraciously, adjusting her accordion file of coupons that were threatening to spill from the cart's child's seat, where they'd been placed. Then Pearl accelerated her pace, turning right without ever glancing to her left.

Momentarily relieved that Samantha and Red remained undetected, Kitty hopped forward. She gazed up at the shelf to ascertain what type of product had fallen into Pearl's cart this time. Her relief turned to horrified resignation. Oh, heck. It was a purse-pack of bladder control pads.

More determined than ever to track the café owner down, Kitty took a breath and limped forward. Glancing to the left, she saw Red and Samantha still deep in conversation. Nerves jangling again at the potential catastrophe, she swung right, then swayed backward as her nose almost met Judge Matthews's chest.

His gaze locked on her mother and Red, he didn't seem to notice as Kitty ducked around him and turned down another aisle. Oh, this was getting worse and worse. Now one of the county adjudicators was paralyzed with shock at her mother's behavior!

Pearl wasn't in the canned goods or the cereal aisle. Not by the pet food either. To give her sore toe a rest, Kitty paused by the small selection of books and magazines. But then she thought she caught a glimpse of dark hair at the end of the aisle, so she snatched something from the nearest rack. Opening the book in the middle, she buried her face behind it.

Unable to stand the suspense, though, she peeked around it. She was alone. *Whew.*

"Kitty?" a voice said behind her.

She froze, then realized the voice was Pearl's. Taking a deep breath, she shut the book and turned around.

Pearl's cheeks were red. "I wanted to say . . . I know I haven't been . . ." She looked down into her cart as if searching for inspiration.

If it was inspiration for an apology, Kitty didn't believe Pearl was going to find it among the embarrassing items hiding there. "Pearl—"

"No, let me say it." But then Pearl's head jerked up, like a retriever spotting something falling from the sky. "I hear Red's laugh."

And the name of this bird was disaster.

"Your mother's too." Pearl's mouth in a grim line, she made as if to swing her cart around.

Envisioning a one-cart pileup—into two bodies—Kitty grabbed it with both hands, despite the book she was still holding. "Pearl, no . . ."

The other woman wrenched her cart away. Kitty's half grip on the book was broken, and it fell amongst the other items in the basket, wedging against the metal mesh. As Pearl whirled an about-face, Kitty glimpsed the book's title, scrawled in blazing, self-help scarlet: *Finding Your G-Spot After Fifty.*

Then Pearl and the cart disappeared in a flash of riotous indignation, leaving Kitty to brace herself for the impending earthquake.

"Well, well, well," another voice sounded behind her. "Fancy seeing you here, when you're supposed to be all tied up in a meeting."

Kitty closed her eyes. Of course. What else could go wrong? "Hello, Dylan."

But then a new, happy thought struck. She twirled on her one good foot to face him. "You're an FBI agent, right?"

"Ye-es." He narrowed his eyes. "Why?"

She grabbed him by the arm. "You need to arrest someone. Now, before they really need to be arrested."

He resisted her forward pull. "What?"

She tugged again. "Arrest somebody. You can do that, right? I don't care who it is. Pearl, Red, Samantha. Just get one of them out of here before some laws are really broken."

This time he let her drag him to the end of the aisle. When she pointed, he obediently took in the scene ahead. Red and Samantha in the distance, still standing close, still talking. With his arms crossed over his chest—an oddly belligerent pose, Kitty thought—D. B. Matthews also was where she'd left him.

And driving toward them slowly, menacingly, was Pearl, the cart with all it shouldn't have in it before her. Wronged woman and metal cart bore down on the unsuspecting couple like a steamroller.

Kitty squeezed Dylan's forearm. "See? See? You need to stop it. There's going to be trouble unless we do something. And this time I'll never live it down."

Dylan hesitated for a moment, then took her hands in his, turning her away from the coming conflagration. "Kitty," he said. "Honey." He looked down at their joined fingers. "There wasn't any meeting, was there?"

"No, no, of course not," she replied impatiently, glancing over her shoulder. "Forget about that. We have to do something. You need to fix this."

He caught her gaze with his. "You want me to fix this?"

"Yes!"

The expression in his eyes looked serious but kind. "Do you trust me, honey—do you really trust me to do the right thing?"

She bit her bottom lip. "Of course I do."

He brought her hands to his mouth and kissed them. Then in one movement he slid his arm around her shoulders and swept her away from the impending scene and toward the exit.

"Hey—" She dug her feet into Kemper's linoleum, but the move didn't deter Dylan. "You said you were going to fix it!" she cried.

"And I will," he promised. "I will."

Kitty tried to think clearly as she tightened her arms around Dylan's waist and leaned into the turn in the road. She didn't know where they were going and yet she'd told him she trusted him. But obviously she shouldn't. This wasn't the way to stave off the disaster happening back at Kemper's.

She sighed, her mind refusing to remain totally focused on the Red-Samantha-Pearl problem. It was hard to dwell on debacle when the summer almost-evening was so beautiful. Though it was nearing dark in the Gold Country, the day's heat radiated up from the road. Dylan's large body blocked most of the wind, but his hair streamed back like black ribbons trying to catch Kitty and bind her to him. He should be wearing a helmet too—as before, he'd made her wear his—but it wasn't as if she could insist he buy a second one.

Not when they would probably never be together like this on the motorcycle again.

The road curved left and Kitty once more followed the lead of his body. Despite what they had left behind, the speed, his closeness, the delicious mingling of the scents of day and night lifted her mood.

The road they traveled turned onto Highway 49 and the traffic increased, then increased again as they neared the big town of Colter. Kitty still couldn't guess where he was taking her, not even when he pulled into a massive car dealership just outside the town.

Huge floodlights lit the lot brighter than day, illuminating row after row of pickups, SUVs, vans, and cars. Kitty blinked as Dylan helped her remove the helmet, trying to adjust her eyes to the faux sunniness. "Is there something wrong with the bike?" she asked.

"No." He hung the helmet on one handlebar and then took her hand, leading her in the direction of the salesman already hurrying their way.

"Good evening, folks," the man said, the overhead lights bouncing off his bald pate and the gold nameplate saying, "Jimmy" pinned to his short-sleeved dress shirt. "What can I do you for?"

"Well . . ." A small smile quirked the corners of Dylan's mouth. He drew Kitty closer and slung his arm around her shoulders, hugging her close. "We're looking for something special."

Kitty frowned. "We are?"

"Let me guess," Jimmy said, stepping back and cocking his head. "I'm usually very good at this. I can tell what suits a couple from a block off. Hmm." He rubbed his chin.

Kitty frowned again. "But—"

"A sports car," Jimmy said, his gaze on Dylan.

"Nope." Dylan shook his head.

Jimmy's eyebrows came together and his eyes shifted to Kitty. He snapped his fingers. "Something old that's new again. One of the PT Cruisers or a new Volkswagen Bug."

"No," Kitty said, still unclear as to their purpose here and wondering what Jimmy would think of her T-bird, something old that was still old. "I don't want—"

"Either one of those," Dylan finished for her smoothly. "We'd like to look at minivans."

"Ah." Though Jimmy obviously tried to appear unsurprised, the three inches his eyebrows gained on his forehead gave him away. But then he pasted on a glib salesman's smile. "Please, folks, follow me."

"Dylan, I . . ."

"Shh." Leaning down, he planted a swift kiss on her lips that sent her brain cells spinning off into the overlit night.

Within seconds they were standing in paradise, between two long rows of gleaming minivans in every color of the rainbow. Kitty's jaw dropped in amazement. Dozens upon dozens of sliding doors gaped open in invitation, each providing tantalizing glimpses of comfy interiors with cup holders and headphone jacks and ceiling-mounted VCRs. Kitty twirled, astonished and delighted, feeling like Dorothy touched down in the Land of Ozzie and Harriet.

Leaving Dylan to listen to Jimmy spouting the boring details of hp, mpg, and APR, Kitty danced from van to van, her mood sailing even higher as she peeked inside one, sat in the driver's seat of another, and played with the seat releases of a third. She'd waltzed her way down one row and was headed up another when Dylan stuck his head inside the passenger window of the van she was currently drooling over.

He grinned at her. "Like what you see?"

From the farthest seat, Kitty looked up at him, awed. "Check this out!" One quick flip and the seat beside her converted to a tabletop sporting two cup holders and a magnetic checkerboard.

He whistled soundlessly. "A true suburban Shangri-la. I hoped this little excursion would cheer you up." Then he tossed her something, and she automatically grabbed for it—a set of keys. "Wanna take a test drive?" he asked.

Belated embarrassment kicked in. Kitty grimaced, knowing this wasn't the usual woman's idea of an evening's entertainment. "Oh, I don't know . . ."

"Come on." He opened the door and leaped into the passenger side, then patted the driver's seat. "Jimmy insists."

Still feeling foolish, Kitty ducked into the spot behind the steering wheel. She looked over at Dylan, noting the contrast between him, with his powerful body and rebel's hair, and the vehicle's built-in babyseat, powder blue, vinyl-and-faux wood-trim interior. "Are you sure?"

"Kitty, it was my idea, wasn't it?"

The minivan didn't have nearly the float factor of Aunt Cat's T-bird, Kitty noticed as she took a right-hand turn out of the auto dealership. In the rearview mirror she could see their salesman waving them off, and she returned a tentative half salute. "Guess we surprised Jimmy, huh? He never pegged us for an interest in minivans."

Dylan grinned. "A fact for which I'm truly grateful."

Embarrassed again, Kitty bit her bottom lip and fumbled around to find the knob that operated the headlights. "I suppose you are. But . . . thanks." She took the first exit off the highway, driving onto a narrow rural road that led them farther away from the town of Colter.

They rode without speaking for a few more minutes until Kitty couldn't stand the silence any longer. She glanced over at Dylan, his face unreadable in the blue dashboard glow. "This isn't exactly fixing the situation between my mother, Pearl, and Red."

"Nope, though I was hoping this might get your mind off it," Dylan admitted. "Kitty, you've got to realize that some calamities can't be prevented. It's not your responsibility or your fault, no matter what happens."

"But it will reflect on me," she insisted.

"I know you think so," he said. "But I wish you wouldn't. Hell, Kitty, you're sweet, you're beautiful, you've been a loyal friend to Hot Water and everybody in it. What do you have to be ashamed of?"

She shook her head. "You've been away for too long. You've forgotten how it is at home."

"Maybe. Maybe I have been gone too long."

Her stomach lurched and she squeezed the steering wheel. "Do you mean that?"

There was a moment of silence before he barked out a laugh. "No." His voice changed then, going softer, deeper. "But I'm not so sorry I came back for this visit."

Kitty swallowed. "Why is that?"

"I'm glad I got to know my wife."

The words wrapped around her like a warm blanket. "Oh, Dylan. I'm glad I got to know you too."

"Then why did you give me the brush-off tonight?"

Oops. She'd forgotten all about that. "The brush-off?"

He wasn't buying her feigned bewilderment. "I believe you said you had an important, *long* meeting of the Preservation Society tonight. Not fifteen minutes after you claimed it was to start, I find you meandering around Kemper's. If you didn't want to be with me, Kitty, you could just have said so."

"No!" She took a breath, then quieted her voice. "It wasn't that. I mean, it wasn't you. But all your friends were going to be around and I just couldn't see how the two of us—how I was—"

"How you were what?"

"How I was going to pretend we were just . . . acquaintances." Hours of watching him without touching him, longing to be close but making herself stay clear, had sounded like that torture he was always threatening her with.

"Why the hell would you pretend that?" He sounded sincerely baffled.

"A Wilder and a Matthews—"

"Could certainly be attracted to one another and act on that attraction. For God's sake, Kitty, I know I wasn't planning on keeping away from *you*. Believe me, by the end of the evening I'm sure everyone would have known how things stand between us."

Which was exactly *how*? Before she could voice it, he answered the unspoken question.

"We're married. Nobody needs to know that but you and me. But the fact that we're . . . spending time together needn't be a secret. You're not ashamed of *me*, right?"

"Of course not."

"And you said you don't have a reputation to ruin, not that I think a twenty-six-year-old woman has to apologize for having sex. So what's the big deal?"

Kitty didn't like the turn this conversation was taking. "You're using logic and reason to confuse me," she complained.

He chuckled. "No flies on you, honey. So you'll say yes the next time, right?"

"The next time for what?" she asked warily.

"My old friends are going to be ticked that I didn't show up tonight after promising I would. They're going to set up something else for sure. Next time you'll come with me?"

She hesitated.

"Kitty?"

Of course, with any luck, that next time might never come. "O . . . kay."

"Tomorrow night, then."

"*What*?" She was so startled, she pulled to the side of the road and turned off the engine. "What are you talking about now?"

In the dashboard light his eyes were dark pools and only his cheekbones and mouth were illuminated. "A barbecue at Tony and Sylvia's tomorrow night. It's already planned. We'll go together."

"Dylan—"

"What's the problem? I'm starting to think you only like me in bed." He sounded amused. "Show me you love me for my mind too, Kitty."

Love. That was the problem. That was the heartbreak she was trying to steer clear of. Looking over at him in doubt, she sucked in her bottom lip.

He groaned. "Start the car and drive back to the dealership," he said. "Quick."

Startled, she immediately twisted the ignition key. "Why?"

His arm reached out and he traced the curve of her cheek, then ran his finger across her damp lower lip. "I've been trying to play the gentleman, honey, but something about seeing you bathed in blue light and surrounded by squeaky vinyl is obliterating my good intentions. We either get going, Miss Kitty, or we do it on the checkerboard back there."

The air instantly pulsed, alive with that sexual buzz that always ignored every barrier between them. Heat surged through Kitty's blood. She welcomed it, though. This was safe, this greedy lust that overtook her thoughts, her worries. Dylan was right. What was the big deal about being together? For now, for this time, couldn't he be hers? She spun the steering wheel to make a U-turn, her pulse starting to pound.

"You wouldn't have actually done it on the checkerboard, would you?" she said, her mouth dry.

His voice was silky. "Stop the car and find out."

"No!" She bit down on her lower lip. "I mean, someone, Jimmy, would know—"

"I'm not going to tell him."

"But on a *checkerboard*," Kitty protested. "It seems almost sacrilegious."

"Well, there is that," he said, amused again. "But, Kitty, I'm so hot for you right now, I'd do it on a Twister mat with a Monopoly game shoved under your hips and Scrabble letters in both my hands."

Kitty's heart knocked against her ribs as she pictured

the scene. She frowned. "But what's with the Monopoly game?" she asked.

There was a heated silence. "That's it," he said, his voice deadly. "Pull off the road."

Kitty could only obey, her heart no longer knocking, but pounding inside her chest.

"Now, Miss Kitty," he said softly when the engine and the headlights were turned off, "tell me all your minivan fantasies."

She choked. "I don't have any sexual fantasies, exactly."

"Good. Then we'll just go with mine." With one swift movement he pulled her onto his lap and kissed her, his mouth moving hard and hot against hers.

Kitty melted against his chest, opening her mouth to stroke his tongue in welcome. She wound her arms around his neck and wrapped her hands in his hair, reveling in the feel of the glossy stuff between her fingers.

He shoved down the straps of her overalls and shoved up the shirt she wore underneath. Without interrupting the kiss, he adjusted her position so that she faced him, her knees on either side of his hips. "Bless the 'wide, comfortable seating,' " he murmured against her mouth, then brought her up and forward to suck her nipples through her bra.

She arched, twisting her hands in his hair. He sucked harder, and hot shards of pleasure arrowed from her breasts to her womb. She lowered herself onto his lap, grinding against the hard bulge she found there. His hips shot upward and she gasped when the pressure found her sweetest spot.

The windows of the van started to fog as he played

with her. Finally he lifted his head. "Let's get in the back," he said, his breath ragged. He opened the door beside him.

She tumbled out of the van, but then he pushed her right back in via the sliding door and followed. To make room for him, she lifted the armrest of the two-person-wide middle seat, and scrambled along it until he caught her around the waist.

"Uh-uh," he said. He pulled down on her cut-off overalls, tugging them below her hips. Her panties came off too; then she was naked from waist to ankles, except for her heavy-soled sandals.

Kitty's breath sounded loud in the plush interior of the van. "Don't you . . . don't you think we should shut the sliding door?" she said, clamping her thighs together. Though the country road was deserted, the overhead light was burning, her bra and shirt were pushed up under her arms, and the rest of her clothes were in Dylan's hands.

He reached up and turned off the interior light. "Flip down the seat by the window," he said, his voice grating in the new darkness.

Trembling with excitement, she fumbled with the levers, finally managing to fold the seat forward so that the back lay against the bench. Dylan was kneeling on the floor of the car, his feet sticking out the sliding door while she had the middle seat to herself. "Dylan . . ." she said, suddenly uncertain.

Without answering, he turned her on the seat, so that her bare legs faced the open door and the small of her back rested against the folded seat behind her. She could hear him breathing, the sound fast and heavy.

"Dylan . . ."

He ignored her again, instead pulling on her ankles so she slid forward until her knees bent over the side edge of the seat. Then he pushed her legs wide and shoved her clothes beneath her bottom.

She was open to him, vulnerable. *"Dylan—"*

"Shh." He ripped off his shirt and pushed that beneath her too, tilting her hips even higher.

Then he leaned forward, his powerful, naked shoulders hot against the insides of her thighs. His breath grazed her with heat, and then he used his thumbs to open up the petals of her body.

"Just like a rose," he said, each word sending a puff of air against her private flesh, each puff of air sending a flight of goose bumps winging across her skin.

Her breasts were rising and falling with her uneven breaths, and her gaze was fixed on the view she had between them—of her bent knees and his dark hair. His head dipped, and she felt something moist and soft lick her.

She jerked, trying to back away, but the folded seat behind her prevented her movement. He licked again, and she didn't want to move at all.

He licked once more, his tongue moving higher, finding some spot that was so sensitive she wanted to scream, and she lifted her hips toward his mouth. With a murmur of approval he opened her wider, and then he set her on fire.

His mouth was at turns hard and soft, his tongue gentle, then demanding. Her body dissolved into his, her thighs falling open to let him find every secret, to let him discover every vulnerability.

He whispered words of praise; he whispered raunchy,

naughty words that made her moan. And then he made her come, his mouth sucking on her until her whole body shook with the power of it.

After making sure every atom of pleasure had been wrung from her, he lifted his head. "You're so sweet," he said. "God, I could do this all night."

Kitty sighed, so languid and so . . . his that her open pose didn't embarrass her any longer. "But I need you inside me," she said. "I want you."

And he obeyed, moving inside so hard and so deep that she cried out, and cried again in sadness when it was over.

Afterward, he laid his head against her breasts, gasping. She stroked his hair, thinking of all that he'd done for her that night. Not only the sex, but the way he'd rescued her from Kemper's with their trip to the amazing Valhalla of vans. Who else would have thought of such a thing to distract her? No wonder she couldn't resist him.

Tears stung her eyes. "Thank you," she whispered. "Thank you for understanding me."

He rubbed his whiskery cheek against her breast and her nipple jumped to attention. He laughed and lifted his head to kiss it, the St. Barbara medal he always wore around his neck brushing coolly against her skin.

Kitty sighed again, wondering exactly who understood him.

Chapter Sixteen

Dressed and ready for Tony and Sylvia's party, Kitty swallowed hard when she heard Dylan's knock at her front door. On a long breath, she took a final look in her bedroom mirror, smoothing the short skirt of her sundress and then slipping her feet into high-heeled, strappy sandals.

He knocked again. She blew out a sigh, before dragging herself toward the door. Her mood shouldn't be so bleak. Tonight might not be so bad. Look at what happened when she'd predicted disaster yesterday. Word had it that Dylan's father had averted the crisis at Kemper's by heading Pearl off. More amazing, it was also rumored that Pearl and Red had left Kemper's together—smiling!—despite the scandalous contents of Pearl's cart.

Still, notwithstanding that happy outcome and everything Dylan had said in the minivan the night before, she was dreading this evening. Even though one glance at the calendar should tell her all this worry was for nothing. With Heritage Day nearly upon them and everything it would bring—their divorce, their opposite paths away from Hot Water—she shouldn't be concerned that Dylan could do serious damage to her heart.

There simply wasn't enough time left for Kitty to fall in love with him.

Clinging tightly to that thought, she swung open the door. And was forced to catch her breath. With his shoulder-length black hair, and wearing black jeans and a black silk T-shirt, he looked dangerous enough to conquer hearts, worlds, time itself.

"Kitty." The soft tone of his voice was deadly sweet. "I like you in red."

"Scarlet." It was the color of the polished cotton sundress that crisscrossed over her breasts and fell just short of her knees. Her sandals matched.

One dark eyebrow rose. "A statement of sorts?"

He *did* know her well. But while he probably thought she was claiming her Wilder, scarlet-woman heritage with the color, she'd actually chosen it as a reminder of who she was and what she couldn't have.

Him.

He took her hand and pulled her across the threshold. "I like the lipstick too. You have a mouth made for that color."

It was scarlet as well. As he leaned toward her lips, she turned her face so his kiss landed on her cheek. "Don't muss it, now," she said lightly.

His eyes narrowed. "I take it back. I like your mouth naked. I like *you* naked."

She tried not to squirm inside her dress. "You had me naked all last night." After the minivan test drive, they'd barely made it back to her bed before pleasuring each other again. She'd given, he'd given, they'd both shattered together before falling asleep and waking in each other's arms that morning.

"It's the best I've slept in years." He shut the door behind her and tugged her in the direction of her car. "I'll have to bottle you and take you back to L.A. with me."

Struck dumb, Kitty untangled her fingers from his under the pretext of fishing her car keys out of the small purse she carried. Whatever little distance from him she could find was imperative. Not that she thought he meant the teasing comment about taking her to L.A., of course, but there was no reason to put her wise intentions at further risk.

She wouldn't stand a chance against him if he wanted to join her in her bed tonight again. She wasn't so foolish as to believe she could—or would want to—prevent that. But when it came to sex, she could keep her perspective about him. Lust, after all, was lust. She could enjoy it, indulge in it, for the time together they had left. For once in her life, she was grateful for the pragmatic attitude toward men and sex that Aunt Cat had always expressed.

It was when they *weren't* in bed that Kitty felt the most threatened. So, just to be on the safe side, she wouldn't keep too close to Dylan at Tony and Sylvia's.

After their arrival, however, when someone in the Kulas' driveway tossed Dylan a football that he caught one-handed instead of letting go of hers, she quickly realized that he wasn't on the same page of the playbook. "You don't need to stick by me," she whispered.

He pretended not to hear her, his grip tightening on her fingers as they walked up the long driveway to the large house sided with rough timber and large river rocks. The front lawn was shaded by spreading oaks and dotted with colorful flower beds and children's toys—a plastic slide, a tricycle, one of those inflatable clowns that popped up when you pushed it down.

Add a minivan and, to Kitty, it would be heaven.

Once they were inside the house, the crowd swarmed over them, obviously thrilled by Dylan's arrival. The sound of mingled voices rose to riot level and Kitty had to mime a greeting to Sylvia and Tony.

Somehow Dylan managed to maintain his hold of her hand, although a dozen people approached to hug him, kiss him, or clap him on the back. Then, without Kitty even moving her feet, it seemed, she and Dylan were propelled toward the back of the house and led to a couch in the large, skylighted family room.

The people already sitting on the long piece of leather furniture hailed Dylan and obligingly moved to create a scant seat. Keenly aware that sitting on his lap was no way to keep her distance, Kitty instantly took a perch on the couch arm, leaving the cushion to him. Though he slanted her a look from under his brows, a man whose name she couldn't recall distracted Dylan by dropping to the floor in front of him and starting up a conversation about some mutual childhood adventure.

Sylvia arrived to put a glass of white wine in Kitty's hand and pass a sweating bottle of beer to Dylan. The pregnant woman's gaze landed on Kitty's other hand, the one Dylan refused to release, even though she'd tried to slide it away several times.

Sylvia's gaze rose to Kitty's face. "Oh, my," she said.

Kitty tried not to wince. Of all the people in Hot Water, Tony and Sylvia probably knew Dylan best. All three had been high school pals, and Tony and Dylan had roomed together at Stanford. "It's nothing," Kitty said, feeling her cheeks flush.

"I'm just surprised," Sylvia said quietly. "Not that it's such a bad idea."

Whom was Sylvia kidding? "It's a *terrible* idea," Kitty whispered fiercely. "I know it."

As if he sensed her distress, Dylan looked up. His gaze flicked from Kitty to Sylvia and back. "Is something wrong?"

Kitty shook her head. "Of course not."

With a last look at them, he went back to his conversation. Tony wandered up, and soon several men were engrossed in a loud, good-natured argument.

Someone left his nearby seat and Sylvia snagged the free chair to position it beside Kitty. "Let's talk a minute," she suggested, settling her pregnant body with a sigh of relief.

Kitty composed her expression, trying not to appear guilty. "How's the pregnancy going?" she asked, hoping to direct the conversation away from why the town madam was holding hands with the town sheriff.

Sylvia gave a mock groan. "It's going too long. My mother told me to stop complaining, that elephants carry their babies for almost two years. Well, I *feel* like an elephant, and for the first five months I had the kind of morning sickness that defies any quantity of saltine crackers and raspberry leaf tea."

Kitty smiled, seeing right through the other woman's

grumbles. "But then along comes a little one like Amalie."

"Yes." Sylvia smiled back. "It's God's reward." Her gaze narrowed. "Which leads me straight back to you, Kitty Wilder."

"Me?"

"Mmm. I meant what I said. You and Dylan. It's not a bad idea. Not a bad idea at all. He deserves some kind of prize after all these years. Maybe you can give it to him."

Kitty cast a swift look at Dylan. He was still deep in conversation with his old cronies, his face relaxed and his dark eyes alive instead of haunted. She turned back to Sylvia. "It's being home that makes him happy, not me."

"Maybe you can keep him here long enough to realize that."

Kitty shook her head. "Don't count on it."

Someone urgently called Sylvia's name and she rose from her chair. "Excuse me, I think I need to go be hostess." She paused, putting her hand on Kitty's shoulder. "Maybe you should be careful, then. Don't count on *him*." Her gaze flicked to Dylan.

"Of course not," Kitty answered, her spine straightening beneath the scarlet dress. "I'm a Wilder, after all. We don't count on any man."

With a last troubled look, Sylvia left. Sighing, Kitty remained lost in her thoughts until a burst of shared chuckles drew her attention back to Dylan and his circle of friends. Grinning, Tony leaned forward and muttered something for Dylan's ears only and he stilled, then threw back his head and laughed.

And laughed some more.

Kitty swallowed hard against the sudden ache in her

heart. It was as if she could see the present as it should have been, would have been, if Dylan had stayed in Hot Water.

He'd relaxed his hold on her hand, but she left her fingers in the cup of his for another moment. She savored his nearness, simultaneously enjoying the bittersweet pleasure of what should be, and what could never be.

But then one of the Sutherland brothers approached, his gaze on Dylan, and when he was near enough she caught his eye. One point of her forefinger to her place on the couch arm, one swift slip of her hand from Dylan's, and Connor Sutherland took her spot. When she looked back, Connor's large frame completed the circle of old friends and she could no longer see Dylan.

As she wandered away she heard him laugh again, and despite another ache in her heart, she smiled.

People crowded every room of the house. Kitty chatted with a few, but tried to keep circulating, not feeling up to a real conversation. After almost dropping her empty wineglass when a passerby jostled her elbow, she headed for the kitchen to stash it somewhere safe.

Men clogged the kitchen entry, though, and through a chink in two pairs of stocky shoulders, Kitty glimpsed a group of gray-haired Odd Fellows. She was about to excuse herself through them when a comment floated out the door. "Everything's taken care of." She recognized the voice of Bob Byer, who headed the Odd Fellows Park Committee. "As far as I know, Dylan has no idea we're naming the park after him on Heritage Day. The mayor has titled his speech, 'From Hot Water Up Bubbles a Hero.' "

Several people groaned at the half-baked pun, and

Kitty would have, too, if the idea of Dylan's being honored on Heritage Day didn't set off a three-alarm-fire's worth of warning bells ringing. He'd hate it, she thought in panic. He'd hate it, and just as certainly as she knew that, she also knew that he'd blame her for it.

She had to tell him what the Odd Fellows planned to do.

Her skin went cold and she shivered, aware of what would happen once she did. Dylan would hop on his motorcycle, married or not, divorced or not, and immediately leave Hot Water behind for good. And Kitty.

And more important, much more important, he'd leave without that happy light in his eyes, that easy laughter, that appreciation of home.

With a few more days here, maybe he *could* overcome whatever pain the place brought him. Maybe she could engineer an opportunity for Dylan to run into Bram, and he could say what he obviously longed to.

Maybe she wouldn't have to give him up quite so soon.

She didn't know what to do. Biting her lip, she turned from the kitchen just as little Amalie wormed her way through the doorway, something in her hands. Apparently on an important mission, the child scurried down a hall and slipped into another room.

That's it, Kitty thought. *Sylvia*. The other woman knew Dylan. Like Kitty, she'd seen the love Dylan had for the town. Kitty would ask her what to do.

Figuring Amalie would be the quickest route to her mother, Kitty headed in the direction she'd seen Amalie disappear. The open doorway led to two rooms, what looked like an office and beyond that, through an arched entry, a small room with a couch and a TV.

There, Sylvia sat on the couch, her arm around
Kitty's mother, her expression full of sympathy and
concern.

Kitty froze by the desk in the adjoining office, her
gaze fixed on the two women. A premonition set the
hairs on the back of her neck rising.

"You should have said something, Samantha," Sylvia
scolded. "Here I've been jawing your ear off for weeks
with my moans and groans, and you haven't been feeling well either."

Kitty frowned. Samantha *did* look green around the
gills. For weeks?

From outside Kitty's range of vision, Amalie skipped
into view, a plastic-wrapped tube of crackers in her
hand. "This what you wanted, Mommy, right?"

Sylvia smiled and took them from her daughter.
"Yes, sweetie. Thank you." She held them out to
Samantha.

Samantha eyed the crackers dubiously. "They don't
work."

"Raspberry tea?"

Samantha shook her head. "No good either. Worse, as
a matter of fact."

Saltine crackers? Raspberry tea? Kitty had seen them
in Samantha's cart yesterday. Sylvia had mentioned
both to Kitty just a few minutes ago as a morning-
sickness remedy. For pregnancy. Kitty's mind slammed
to a halt, backed up.

For pregnancy?

No! Yes?

Her mother was pregnant?

She looked at Samantha harder, taking in the definitely greenish cast to her skin. Samantha held a cracker to her mouth, then dropped it into her lap with a sigh. "I don't remember feeling this way when I was pregnant with Kitty," she said.

Her mother was pregnant.

Kitty whirled, and ran smack into Judge D.B. Matthews. She'd been doing a lot of that lately, she thought hysterically. Just like yesterday, his gaze was fixed on Samantha, and he looked a trifle green himself.

Without blinking, he steadied Kitty. Then he murmured some sort of excuse in a strained voice and strode back into the hall. The poor man, Kitty thought. He'd lived his whole life within moral and legal boundaries, and for the second day in a row, her mother had scandalized him. Kitty was scandalized too, for that matter. In the past six months there hadn't been one legitimate rumor about a lover for Samantha, but presumably someone in or around Hot Water had fathered her baby.

A choked sound from the TV room made Kitty whirl around. Samantha's eyes were on her and she looked even sicker. "Kitty," she said, her voice as strained as the judge's. "I didn't want you to find out like this. And I don't want—"

"This baby either?" Shock was drowned by a wave of shame and anger that rose, then crashed, flooding Kitty's entire being. Suddenly she was five feet eight inches of trembling, humiliated outrage. "Well, sorry, but you better face facts," she spit out. "Aunt Cat is too old to do your mothering this time. And we both know *you* can't—or won't—do it."

"Kitty!" Both Samantha and Sylvia called her name as she spun toward the hall and ran.

The first door she found led her outside, to Tony and Sylvia's backyard. It was full dark now, but there were people standing in small groups beneath Japanese lanterns strung throughout the trees and along a walkway beside the creek meandering by. Kitty ran past them all, along the creek, then over two small bridges until she was alone and the Japanese lights were just twinkles among the oaks. From here, the only voices she heard were the ones that kept replaying in her head. *Her mother was pregnant.*

Disregarding her new dress, she dropped to the leaf-covered dirt and leaned back against a tree trunk. She drew her legs up and hugged them with her arms, resting her cheek against her knees.

Her mother was about to set tongues wagging again, more Wilder fodder for a raging fire of small-town gossip. Would nothing ever change?

"Kitty." Through the darkness came a familiar voice. A worried-sounding voice.

She squeezed shut her eyes. "Go away, Dylan." She wanted his comfort, yes. Desperately. But she couldn't let herself get used to it.

"I've been looking everywhere for you." A tall, inky shadow emerged from behind a nearby tree.

"Go away." A hot tear rolled from the corner of her eye and channeled along her nose to catch in the corner of her mouth.

"You know I can't do that." Before she could move or protest, he was somehow sitting in her spot against the tree, Kitty cradled in his arms. "You're my wife, after all."

The words struck like a blow. Kitty couldn't move, she could barely breathe, and it left Dylan free to push her head against his chest. He started stroking her hair. "This stuff fascinates me, you know," he said softly. "All the amazing things you do with it. Those knots, for example, baffle me. My shoelaces untie at the drop of a hat, but not your hair. And then there's those mystifying, one-pin-and-it's-over topknots you wear at The Burning Rose. It's become my obsession to figure out how you defy gravity and keep those up."

Her heart contracted, leaking even more pain. She knew he was talking to calm her, to soothe her, but she couldn't find the voice to tell him it wasn't working. That it wasn't ever going to work.

She felt him press a kiss on the top of her head. "I have to say, my favorite way you wear your hair is just like this, though, a sleek curtain down your back," he said. "I think I could get lost on the other side of it and never find my way out of you."

Oh, God. Her heart contracted again and another tear trickled down her cheek. The moment she'd realized he'd come to find her, to comfort her—"my wife," he'd said—the person who had been lost was her. Lost in love with him.

She couldn't lie to herself anymore. How foolish she'd been, trying to imagine that there wasn't enough time for this to happen. Hah! The truth was, on a night eight years before, when *she'd* sought *him* out, her childish hero worship of him had turned to full-blown, full-out, I'm-saving-myself-for-you love.

She'd called her actions rebellion the next day. She'd pointed her finger at the leering, foul-mouthed Ned De-Beck. And both had been part of the answer. But the pared-to-the-essence, the *soul*, of why she'd made her marriage to Dylan legal was one simple thing. She'd been in love with him.

And like everything else in Hot Water, her feelings hadn't changed.

Dylan stroked Kitty's hair, murmuring nonsense until she relaxed against his chest. He inhaled a breath, drawing her delicate rose scent into his lungs. His arms tightened around her and he kissed the top of her head. He hated to see her upset.

On his final Heritage night in Hot Water, she'd found him like this. Alone and nursing his wounds in the darkness, he hadn't welcomed her. Not at first. But then she'd handed him a beer and sat quietly beside her. After a while, he'd started to talk. He'd told her about leaving home. About his acceptance to the FBI Academy and that he wasn't going to tell his father about his decision before leaving town. He'd told her he was getting up the next morning and riding his motorcycle to Quantico instead of to law school.

Her silence had been accepting and her face so damn sweet. He'd kissed her a few times, and over a few more beers, their talk had turned to lighter things—they'd reminisced about Hot Water's entrenched customs and traditions. He didn't even remember now which one of them had suggested a Hot Water wedding, but it had seemed like a fitting farewell at the time.

Now he rested his cheek on the top of Kitty's head, wishing he could give her at least half the understanding she'd given him that night.

"It's your mother, right?" he said. "I saw Samantha inside the house."

For an instant Kitty stiffened, but then she tucked her head beneath his chin and sighed. "I don't want to talk about it."

"Okay." He could understand that. There were things he never wanted to talk about either. Things he hadn't spoken of that night eight years ago. But being in Hot Water again, especially being with his old friends tonight, forced him to confront those unspeakable things over and over again. "Let's go," he said.

She drew away to look into his face. "Are you sure? Tony and Sylvia planned this party for you."

Her face was just a shadow in the darkness, but he didn't have any trouble finding her mouth for a light kiss. "We made an appearance."

"But . . ."

Dylan was already lifting her to her feet. "But nothing." Both of them needed to get away from everyone and everything. He thought of his condo in L.A., wishing like hell they were there. It was sterile and ugly, but at least it would distance them from home and the memories that bcdcviled them both.

He tugged her in the direction of the house, certain

they'd be better off away from the crowd. "Tony and Sylvia won't mind if we leave, not now that I've said my hellos to all the guests."

Except when he and Kitty reached the lantern-lit backyard, there stood a family of new arrivals. Stunned by an immediate, intense rip of new pain, Dylan halted just outside the circle of light. No, he hadn't greeted these particular guests yet. He didn't want to greet them now.

From his place beside the newcomers, Tony's voice hailed him. "Dylan, there you are! Look who's here."

Dylan wasn't able to breathe, let alone move.

It was Kitty who squeezed his hand and propelled them both forward, a smile on her face. He knew his was frozen in an expression of—what?

"Hello, Nan and Tim," she said, acknowledging the adults in the group. Then she made a big play of glancing at the three children beside them and doing a dramatic double-take. "My goodness. It can't be, can it? Micah, Dani, and Willa?"

Dylan couldn't make himself look directly at them. But from the corner of his eye he noticed the three smiled, though it was their mother who spoke for them. "They're thirteen, eleven, and ten now. Can you believe it?" Nan Burton glanced at Dylan. "We moved right . . . after. We live about fifty miles north now."

Kitty nodded, as if Nan had been speaking to her. "But how nice of you to come to Hot Water tonight."

"We're staying through Heritage weekend," Nan said, her eyes again darting in Dylan's direction. "We . . . thought it might be a good time for a visit."

Her husband pushed through the children and held out his hand. "Dylan, I'm glad to see you."

Dylan's voice worked after all. "I'm glad to see you too, Tim. All of you," he said, letting go of Kitty to shake the other man's hand.

Though Dylan still couldn't bring himself to look directly at the children, on some level he *was* glad. Yes, seeing them ripped the scab off the old wound, but knowing that they were growing, thriving, lessened a little of the damage.

He swallowed. "Kitty and I were just leaving." His gaze swept past the kids and he found Tony's face. "Say good-bye and thank you to Sylvia for us."

"Dylan—" Kitty and Tony spoke in unison, but Dylan was already skirting the groups in the backyard, heading in the direction of a side gate.

Kitty trotted to catch up with him, but he didn't slow his pace until they were alone on the dark driveway. Then he leaned against Kitty's car, sucking in long, unsteady breaths while she unlocked the doors. She hesitated before climbing in on the driver's side. "Dylan . . ."

"Take me to your house, Kitty," he said. *Take me away.* He needed to detach, to forget, to find solace somewhere. To find it in her body.

It was as if she read his mind. When they returned to her house, she led him into the bedroom and then initiated a tender lovemaking. But that role was too passive for him, the sex too soft to deaden his memory.

He took over.

To the slamming beat of his heart, his hands were urgent and hard on her body. Arousal inflamed his blood and his mouth was desperate, on her neck, on her breasts, between her legs.

She moaned and writhed and he could feel her passion escalating, he could taste it on his tongue, and his cock surged. Everywhere was heat, burning heat, and that scent of roses. When he plunged inside her, he shuddered, then plunged again, taking her body on a joyride that he hoped like hell would cauterize both their wounds.

His fingers dug into her hips and she cried out his name. But he didn't stop, he didn't slow, he just pushed the pleasure higher and higher until she screamed and he shuddered, pumped, and came.

And then came to discover that the memories, the pain, they were all still there, waiting for him. He laid his head against her breasts, so damn tired.

"Are you all right?" Kitty whispered. Her hand came up to stroke his hair.

"I should be asking you that," he said, squeezing his eyes tightly shut.

"I asked you first."

He told himself to move away from her. To move off her body, to leave her house, to disconnect from her. But he was so fucking tired. "No," he said finally. "I'm not all right."

"The children."

Kitty's heart beat against his cheek. "I should have said something to them, I know," he said.

Her hand stroked his hair again, but she didn't answer. She didn't prompt him or press him, and in the silence his memories welled up, one after another, until he had to speak of them.

"I was out for a ride on my motorcycle. As I came over a rise, I saw Alicia's car on the shoulder of the road. I saw that cowardly little prick pointing the gun in the driver's side window."

Kitty's heart beat steadily against his skin and he focused on its calming rhythm. "I gunned the bike, almost flying along the asphalt, going so fast I didn't see when he noticed me speeding toward them. But by the time I braked the bike nearby, he had Alicia out of the driver's seat and standing on the road. For a minute I thought it was going to be okay, so I started to back away. I thought he'd jump in her car and take off, and Alicia and I would go to town and notify the sheriff. But then she yelled to me that the kids were inside—Micah, Dani, and Willa. She screamed for me to get them out of the car.

"I ran to the passenger door and opened it. They were so scared—hysterical with fear—and so damn little, Kitty. They wanted their mom and they wanted Alicia and there was that gun. As I was getting the little ones out of the car seats, he started dragging Alicia toward the woods. When I looked up, the two of them had vanished."

Dylan sat up and turned his back to Kitty, trying to resist the weight of the next memory. "I ran the kids a distance away and yelled that he could take the car now. That I'd let him leave. That we'd let him go. I yelled and yelled and yelled, but nobody came out of the woods. Alicia never came out."

Kitty laid her hand on his shoulder. "You saved the children."

He turned his head and looked at her. "Damn it, that's what everyone said. They kept saying it. But I didn't save Alicia." He pushed his hands through his hair. "I couldn't leave the kids alone, though. I didn't know if there was an accomplice nearby or if the first man would circle back for the kids if I left them to search for Alicia. I just couldn't leave them, you see?"

"Of course I see that," Kitty said. "Everyone does. It's why you're a hero."

"Hero." The word twisted like a knife in his gut. "Every damn case I've worked since, every child I've looked for, every person I've found or protected has been a way of trying to truly earn that. But I never do. I left the place I love and the work that I wanted and it's still *not enough*."

"Why?" Kitty said. "Why isn't it enough?"

He closed his eyes. That was the one question he hated answering the most. "Because when I went roaring down that hill toward Alicia, I thought I *was* being a hero. I didn't doubt for a minute that Hot Water's Golden Boy could save the day, just as I'd saved the final high school football game. The Big Coach in the Sky was putting me in a life-and-death competition and I wasn't even afraid." He sucked in a long breath, and finally uttered aloud the thought that had tortured him for eight years. "The truth is, my hell-bent-for-leather ride may have escalated the situation. Maybe because of me, Alicia is dead."

"Oh, Dylan," Kitty whispered. She grabbed him by the shoulders and pulled him into her arms. Her chest heaved on a sob.

God help him, he took the comfort she offered. He wrapped himself around her, entwining his hands in her long hair. He could feel her heart beating against his skin, and underneath the barbed wire he'd worn for eight years, his heart joined its tempo.

She always made him feel so damn good.

She always had.

"Kitty." He held her away from him to look into her face. "Come back to L.A. with me."

She stilled. "What?"

He swallowed hard, one hand moving to touch his St. Barbara medal. "After Heritage Day. Come back to L.A. with me."

"Why?"

"I could show you around. We could—"

"Dylan—"

"Don't answer now." Not when he was scared shitless at the thought of what he'd just asked. But he wasn't ready to say it was a mistake either. He brought her back against him, then closed his eyes and rested his cheek on her silky hair. "We'll talk about it later. We'll talk about it after the divorce."

There. That made him feel better. Saying that gave him a little more time and space.

Chapter Seventeen

Two evenings later, Kitty cut through the cemetery on the way from her house to the park. She imagined the at-peace residents of Hot Water were enjoying the annual Odd Fellows barbecue as much as the livelier denizens of the town. The aroma of grilling chicken and hamburgers wafted through the air, and over the excited shouts of children came the cheery twang of the county's famed old-time fiddlers playing "Turkey in the Straw."

For the past twenty years the barbecue had preceded the Heritage Day festivities. This morning when they'd left her house together, she and Dylan had agreed to meet there—an hour ago.

But her tardiness couldn't be helped. Although in the summer months she was supposed to be responsible only for working in The Burning Rose, since she was "head" of the one-person advertising and PR department of the Hot Water Preservation Society, Heritage Day itself ignited a dozen fires that apparently only she could extinguish. At 6 A.M. she'd been unearthing the missing bunting from the city hall basement. At 6 P.M., when she was supposed to be meeting Dylan, she'd made a dash to Kemper's Market for the brass polish needed to spiff up the bells on the wagon horses' halters.

Next year the last-minute errands would be someone else's job, she reminded herself. Strangely, the thought didn't cheer her up.

She didn't know if anything would. Since Tony and Sylvia's party, she hadn't been able to shake the stomach-churning notion that she was strapped to railroad tracks, a train heading straight for her. Yet she had a good reason for it.

Her mother was pregnant by some unknown lover, guaranteeing Wilder infamy for another generation. Kitty had confessed to herself she was in love with Dylan. And as for him . . . well, he'd virtually told her he loved Hot Water but thought he'd failed it. What was left of her heart after that revelation, he'd gone on to completely shred by inviting her to L.A. *After the divorce.*

Atop the nearby rise that was Alicia's grave site, Kitty caught sight of Bram Bennett, and her footsteps faltered. Bram grieved for the loss of control in his life and Kitty couldn't blame him now. She felt exactly the same way. Helpless. Hopeless.

There was nothing she could do about Samantha. Nothing she could do about loving Dylan. And she couldn't make his half invitation to L.A. anything more concrete . . . or conventional.

The only power she had was the power of the secret she'd been keeping, even through another night of tender and passionate lovemaking. The secret that tomorrow the Odd Fellows would be naming the park after Dylan. She still hadn't told him.

She swung open the gate between the cemetery and the park just as the fiddlers stopped playing on the temporary stage set up for the weekend. The park teemed with people, townsfolk as well as tourists already in for the Heritage festivities. Once the fiddlers shuffled off, a strange hush came over the crowd when a spotlight focused on the stage, illuminating a microphone centered there. In the deepening dusk, Hot Water's mayor approached it, the mike's metal stand glittering.

Kitty frowned and glanced at the man nearest her, a firefighter with the county fire department. "Phil, what's going on?" she asked.

He shrugged his beefy shoulders. "Something big, rumor has it. I have no idea."

The microphone squealed and a couple of technicians scurried over for an adjustment. Kitty continued to frown. Had the park-naming been rescheduled for tonight? The mayor of Hot Water traditionally opened Heritage Day at a 9 A.M. ceremony, set for tomorrow morning. Kitty had supposed he'd give his speech about Dylan then.

Anxious to be near Dylan if it happened now, Kitty edged her way around the hundreds gathered in front of the stage, searching for him. But when the mayor eventually started speaking, she still hadn't located Dylan.

"Good evening," Mayor Art Ames boomed, the round

tones of his voice matching the roundness of his Santa-belly. "It's going to be a very special Heritage Day to-morrow, without a doubt. But I have something interesting to tell you all tonight too."

Still looking for Dylan, Kitty joined some people standing on the benches of a picnic table in the rear. But it was almost dark now, and she couldn't pick out individuals. Then, from the vicinity of the stage, a near-blinding light was trained on the throng.

The mayor's nervous chuckle grated through the microphone. "I told you it was something interesting. Even to the media."

It was the light from a professional video camera, Kitty realized, astonished. Surprised murmurs erupted all around and Mayor Ames held his palms out for quiet. "Please. Let me finish. I'd like you all to know that today Bram Bennett finalized a business deal that included selling the piece of land that encompasses our Old Town."

"What?" Kitty said aloud, echoing the loud dismay of many in the audience.

"Shh, shh." The mayor held out his palms again. "Please. While I'm sure we're all sorry that Bram no longer owns that piece of property which is so important to us all, the good news is that the new owner wants to reassure everyone that no changes will be made in its operation or profit sharing."

Kitty blinked, still stunned. How could she not have known Bram was thinking of selling, let alone that someone was interested in buying? No one had come through the living-history district looking to purchase it, she was sure of that. But who would buy it sight unseen?

Mayor Ames was smiling now, gesturing toward the shadows at the bottom left of the stage. "And I'd like to introduce you to the new owner now. It's my honor—" He chuckled. "Honest, that was a pun I didn't see coming, folks. I should say, it's my *pleasure* to present . . . Honor Witherspoon."

Kitty's breath stuck in her throat as an unfamiliar young woman walked toward the microphone. From both sides of the crowd, flashbulbs burst like sparklers in the darkness. The young woman grimaced.

The expression didn't mar her perfection. Even from here, Kitty could see the smoothness of her pale complexion. Up close, one could probably see beneath it to the blue veins carrying all that Witherspoon blue blood too, but at Kitty's distance, most noticeable was its dramatic contrast to her straight, jaw-length black hair. She wore it in a trendy, jagged-bottom cut that probably cost more than the understated little black pantsuit she was wearing.

Which was likely silk, hand-tailored, and in the same dollar range as a mid-priced minivan.

With an inexplicable yet obvious wariness, Honor Witherspoon leaned toward the microphone. It shrieked, much harsher on the ears than the average mild squeal, and she shrank back.

The technicians rushed onstage again, adjusting the equipment. As Honor eyed them with a patient, almost pitying air, Kitty acknowledged that not only was the other woman beautiful, she was also small and delicate, except for the healthy set of curves under her black silk top.

Kitty hated her.

The emotion slightly lessened when Honor was gestured toward the mike again and it let out another ear-splitting scream. Once more the dark-haired woman stepped back, this time dragging the technicians with her. Though they seemed doubtful at first, in a moment they nodded. One man drifted away, while the other held the mike himself, some distance from Honor's mouth.

After a brief moan of feedback, her soft, throaty voice filled the park. "I'm only sorry for two things tonight—my disastrous touch with anything electrical, and that I seemed to have brought the press along with me." She hesitated as another barrage of bulbs flashed. Then she lowered her voice in an intimate, we're-friends-already manner. "Please bear with them patiently . . . or throw them in the nearest creek, whichever suits you best."

Laughter rumbled throughout the park, but then it quieted, the crowd already partly won over by the big-city beauty.

"I know it might feel like an outsider has taken something that belongs to Hot Water, but I want to assure you that I don't *feel* like an outsider. That I don't want to *be* an outsider."

Honor Witherspoon paused, and for the first time, her poise completely dropped. She took a deep breath and started again. "You may know that a few months ago I was kidnapped. Needless to say, it was an experience I don't like to dwell on. But out of that came my friendship with FBI Special Agent Dylan Matthews, and it was he who told me stories about the very unique place where he grew up." She paused again, took another deep breath. "I can't tell you how special those stories were to me after two weeks alone in the darkness. They gave me the courage to hope, to believe in goodness again. So I thank you for that, and for the future."

The people broke into spontaneous applause. Kitty stared, still dumbfounded, as Honor gave a small parting wave and turned toward the stairs. Then her face lit up and she ran across the stage to launch herself into someone's arms. A man's arms.

The arms of Kitty's husband.

Kitty didn't remember leaping off the picnic bench. She didn't remember running toward the gate leading into the cemetery. She realized she was there only when she threw it open, nearly knocking over Bram Bennett.

"Is something wrong?" he asked in his rough voice.

Kitty stared at him. "Of course." It didn't matter that Dylan had asked Kitty to return to L.A. with him. It didn't matter that she'd been tempted to say yes, even though he hadn't added a promise he'd permanently care about her, a Wilder. Neither mattered once Kitty had seen Honor Witherspoon. Not when Kitty had glimpsed the beautiful and well-bred personification of every reason that she would never, ever have the man she loved.

As Dylan combed the crowded park on Heritage Day morning, he was ready to kill someone. Preferably Kitty. This was no time for her to go MIA! She'd stood him up yesterday evening and was nowhere to be found now either. He needed to see her because . . . because he wanted to, damn it.

"I really like you with that sheriff's badge," Honor Witherspoon said, grinning up at him from her place by his side. She'd attached herself to him like a limpet this morning, sure proof that Heiress Honor was nervous about her first day in her new town. "The cowboy boots are a nice touch too," she added.

Old Town was open and free to all on Heritage Day. While no actual tours were given, the reenacters still donned costumes. In fact, most of the rest of the citizens would be in period dress today too.

"Shut up, Honor," he said pleasantly, "and turn your eyes toward something more productive. Look for a tall woman. Long blond hair you'd give your soul for. Probably dressed in something so low-cut I'll want to wrap her in a blanket."

Honor sniffed at the "give your soul for" comment, but obediently peered around the park. Then she put her hand on his arm. "You're wrong. I'd give my soul for just half the length of her legs, let alone her hair." She pointed toward the street entrance to the park, just a dozen yards away.

The sun shining golden on her head, Kitty Wilder was passing through the open gate, a clipboard in her hand. Her attention was completely focused on the papers she was frowning at, so Dylan was able to cut her off before she even knew he was there.

"Damn it," he said, his irritation spiking as he thought of everything Kitty had kept from him—another night of enjoying her wanton's mouth, another night of burying his hands in her hair and his body in hers. He grabbed her by the elbow and hauled her toward him. "I've been looking everywhere for you."

Startled, she jerked her head up and her eyes rounded. "What?" she said faintly. Honor trailed over and Kitty's gaze darted to the heiress and then back to him. "Why?"

He had to have a why? His irritation jumped again. "I—" He broke off, then let her go to smooth his hair with his hands, trying to think of something reasonable to say. "I wanted you to meet Honor."

As he suspected she would, Honor elbowed him aside to make her own introduction. Kitty shook the other woman's hand, then chewed on her bottom lip as they all stood looking at one another in a strangely awkward silence. The incoming crowd streamed around them.

"I—"

"I—"

Both he and Kitty spoke at once, halted. Damn it. She was looking at him as if he were worm meal, and he couldn't keep one thought straight in his head except how pissed he was that he'd missed her so much last night.

A man bumped into his shoulder. "Oh, sorry," the guy said, then paused. "Hey, it's you, Dylan."

Though the man looked familiar, Dylan couldn't place his name. "Good to see you too," he said anyway.

The man didn't move on. "Congratulations on the park. Pretty cool, huh?"

Dylan frowned. "Congratulations?"

The man nodded helpfully. "That the town is naming the park after you today."

"Naming the park after me?" Dylan's mouth went cottony.

The other man nodded again. "You know, for that day . . . because you're a hero—" He checked himself, his gaze drifting to Kitty. "Uh-oh. Is it supposed to be a surprise?" he asked her.

Dylan looked at her too, cold washing over him as the man's meaning sank in. "Yes, Kitty," he echoed slowly. "Is it supposed to be a surprise?"

"It is." A flush rushed up her face as she glanced quickly at Honor, then back at him. "But I . . . I meant to tell you."

"Except you didn't." His words fell heavily between them. "So maybe you'd better tell me now."

The other man backed away. The rest of the world might as well have too, because Dylan saw only Kitty. He could think only about Kitty and the fact that she'd been keeping another secret from him.

Hugging her clipboard to her chest, she swallowed. "The Odd Fellows are naming the park after you because of your heroism. Today. This morning."

He shook his head, anger growing hard and cold inside him. "No, they're not." That was certain. "You're going to stop them."

"Me?" Kitty blinked those guileless—God, the irony—blue eyes. "Why me?"

He stepped closer to her, his voice low and harsh. "Because I can't live with them naming the park after me. I'm not anyone's hero. Especially not Hot Water's. You *know* that." Panic flooded his gut.

"Dylan . . ." She inhaled a breath. "What I know is

that you were a young man who went riding to the rescue like a white knight. That the rescue didn't end the way you hoped. Lord, Dylan, I and everyone else in Hot Water know that. But that doesn't make you any less."

Any less a hero, she meant. Damn it, this was all her fault! His hands curled into angry fists and her betrayal churned like bile inside him. "What made me less was the expression on Bram's face when he was told the love of his life was dead," Dylan retorted. "What made me less is being back in this goddamn place, where I have to remember that. Where I have to remember everything." He didn't even know the next words were coming, but they slid out, cold and slick as ice cubes. "And by forcing me to come home, Kitty, what—who—made me less is *you*."

Maybe he would have wished the words back, maybe he would have even called them back, except he didn't have time. Not when Kitty stepped closer to him, those guileless eyes now glittering. "Well, then, maybe we're even, Dylan, because you've made a fool of me. Here I was, feeling sorry for that younger Dylan, forced eight years ago to realize what the town had led him to believe was wrong. Forced to realize Hot Water's Golden Boy couldn't turn every situation into a total winner.

"But the fact is, you've never realized that, have you?" She laughed, the sound devoid of humor. "You still don't. For all your big talk about disregarding town-conferred identity, you've completely bought into yours. You must truly consider yourself capable of perfection, or else you wouldn't continue to punish yourself with this pointless self-exile."

He thought he should defend himself, but his mouth didn't seem to be working. Kitty's, however, was doing just fine.

"I hate to break it to you, darling," she continued, "but eight years ago you were merely an arrogant, ego-inflated young man with perfect SAT scores and a stack of athletic trophies. You were not God. And nothing's changed since."

Punish yourself. Self-exile. Ego-inflated. Arrogant. The words whirled in his brain, accusation after accusation sounding louder than all the things he'd called himself for the past eight years. He shook his head, shaking the words away to refocus on his icy fury.

"Just fix it, Kitty," Dylan said, grabbing her arm. "You can call me names later, but just fix this, *now.*"

She held her ground. "Dylan, only you can fix this."

His head was pounding. "I'll leave. Take off. Get out of here today. Now."

Her eyes still hard and bright, she pulled her arm very deliberately from his grasp. "Then you'll want to sign this before you go. So I can get our divorce." She held out her clipboard. "Sign it and you'll be free."

The paper was nothing, his signature, the divorce, the marriage, it was all nothing compared to the hammers in his head and the sick, cold feeling in his belly. Without looking at her, he wrenched the clipboard from her and signed.

In another moment she was gone.

"Ouch." Honor's voice was full of sympathy.

Dylan glanced at her, but she was gazing after Kitty. "Don't tell me you feel sorry for *her?*"

"Of course." Honor cocked her head to look past his shoulder. "And I bet the judge agrees with me."

Dylan spun around to find his father standing behind him. The guilty expression on D. B.'s face churned the bile in Dylan's belly. "You. Do you know something about this park-naming too?"

"I know you can't punish Kitty for it."

Punish. There was that word again.

The judge rubbed his jaw and Dylan noticed the shadows beneath his eyes. "I've known about the Odd Fellows' naming the park since the committee dreamed it up," D. B. said.

Dylan didn't want to believe it, so he made a dismissive gesture with his hand. "Well, you didn't know how I—"

"I did. I knew exactly how uncomfortable it would make you. But I didn't want you to run away from Hot Water again, Dylan. I wanted you to give home a chance."

"Run away? I didn't exactly run away, Judge—"

"*Dad.* I'm your father, Dylan. Though God knows I wasn't my best at it eight years ago. But I'd like to start making amends now."

Dylan stared at him. "You're not making any sense. You didn't do anything wrong."

The judge ran his hands over his hair in a gesture of frustration Dylan recognized as one they shared. "I tried not to think so. But I've got to face the truth now, Dylan. I've got to get it right with you, first of all."

Dylan took a hurried step back. "Another time. Right now, I have to get out of here and—" He broke off as his next backward stride had him tromping all over Honor's feet.

Wincing, she pushed him off her and toward the judge. "Give me a chance to stop the park thing, Dylan. You finish this with your father."

"No, Honor—" But she was already gone. Closing his eyes, Dylan rubbed his pounding temples. "It's all spinning out of control."

The judge put his hand on Dylan's shoulder. "Some things are like that. Sometimes circumstances spin away from us. Sometimes we do the wrong thing with all the right intentions. Sometimes we can't decide if what we did was right *or* wrong, and we'll never be sure."

Dylan waved an impatient hand. "I know, I know."

His father half smiled. "I'd like to believe that. I'd also like to believe that what I said to you eight years ago didn't send you running from town. But then, I've been trying to kid myself about a lot of things."

Dylan shook his head. "*You* didn't do anything that made me leave Hot Water."

"No? Not even when I asked you why you couldn't save Alicia?"

Dylan jerked his gaze away from his father's. He looked around at the milling people, old Spenser Marsh resettling his straw hat, a mother spreading sunscreen on a squirming toddler, a father strolling with his young daughter on his shoulders. The little girl suddenly turned her head and looked at Dylan, her big brown eyes focused intently on his face.

His stomach lurched and his hand rose to touch the

St. Barbara medal hanging over his heart. "Don't you think I wanted to save her, Dad?"

The judge sighed, as if in pain. "It was a stupid thing for me to say, Dylan. I can't tell you how much I regret it. Tensions were high, as were emotions, frustrations. It just came out of my mouth."

"It was the same question I'd been asking myself, though," Dylan said slowly, unable to look away from the little girl's eyes. "From the moment I saw Alicia being dragged into the woods. Alicia was staring at me, Dad, and I could hear her panic, her fear, in my head. *And the sound has never gone away.*"

A tear rolled down the little girl's cheek. Dylan squeezed the medal as a second teardrop spilled from those big brown eyes.

"Dylan—" his father began.

"Dylan Matthews!" the mayor boomed through the microphone. "Will you please come up onstage? We have a surprise for you."

Dylan froze, then slowly turned. Shit! While he'd been uselessly rehashing the past with his father, the ceremony had begun. Obviously Honor had failed to call off the Odd Fellows plan.

"Dad," Dylan said quickly, "could you, would you—" But even as he spoke, the crowd that stood between him and the stage parted, leaving nothing separating Dylan from the beaming mayor except a cleared path through the citizens of Hot Water.

All of whom looked at him expectantly.

Temporarily out of options, Dylan started slowly forward, forcing himself through the gauntlet of old friends and neighbors. Someone called his name, and on his left

he saw his first-grade teacher, Mrs. Macy, the first witness to his return to town a few short weeks before. She
held out her hand, and he automatically reached for it,
pressing her frail fingers with his. Another person
touched his shoulder, and then another called his name.
He passed Micah, Dani, Willa, and their parents, their
faces wearing identical, tentative smiles.

Time and again he was forced to pause, shaking
hands with some, returning the kisses of others. It was
like his first day back in Hot Water when his dad had led
him from one old friend to another, but this time their
welcomes didn't hurt so much. This time, strangely,
they started to make the hurt better.

Once he reached the bottom of the stage, though, the
clawing pain resurfaced. The stairs were to his right and
he eyed the distance, gauging how quickly he could run
past them and then out of the park and from there out of
town. *You'll be free*, Kitty had said.

Suddenly a hand appeared in front of his face. Dylan
looked up, right into Bram Bennett's green eyes. The
other man leaned down from his place on the stage. "Let
me help you up," he said.

Dylan almost laughed. Bram was the one person in
the world he couldn't refuse. Grasping his hand, Dylan
leaped onto the stage. He didn't immediately let go of
his old friend, though. "Thanks, Bram," he said, forcing
the words past his tight throat.

There were a hundred memories they shared. King
Arthur—Bram—and his loyal page, Dylan. Rival pi-
rates fighting for dominance in the seas, a.k.a. the grass
field behind the school. Bicycle rides, baseball games,
the day Dylan had been best man to Bram's quietly

happy groom. Among all the other things that hurt, losing his best friend was almost as painful as losing his best friend's wife.

"I'm so damn sorry," Dylan said. He'd told Bram the words before, eight years ago, but he wasn't certain Bram had heard them.

But Bram was listening now. His grip tightened on Dylan's hand. "Welcome back," he said. "I missed you." Then he released Dylan to disappear behind the group of Odd Fellow dignitaries standing at stage left.

With nothing else to do, Dylan approached the microphone.

Turning to the audience again, Mayor Ames launched into his speech. Standing near the older man, Dylan tuned it out for the most part, only vaguely noting when the crowd groaned at the politician's notorious, and notoriously bad, puns.

I'll decline it, Dylan thought. The town would be confused and angry, maybe, but that was better than a Dylan Matthews Park, named in honor of his heroism. In his condo in L.A., or wherever the FBI sent him next, no matter how many hundreds or thousands of miles away, he'd never be able to put Hot Water out of his mind if they went through with this.

Of course, even as it was, he'd never been able to put Hot Water out of his mind. It had always been there inside him, hiding just below the barbed-wire covering of his heart.

That truth was still echoing in his brain when the mayor finally made the announcement. Dylan Matthews Park. The people cheered, and he called Dylan to the mike.

The scant three feet seemed a thousand times longer than the path to the stage had been. Dylan tried forming a polite, quasi-reasonable refusal as he walked forward, but once he was facing the crowd, all the words left his head.

They looked up at him, their faces expectant: his first-grade teacher, his high school football coach, his father. There were others he recognized too, from Mrs. McMahon, who had tried to teach him piano, to Mr. Ha, who had sold him his first motorcycle. Dozens of people who had watched him grow up, who had fashioned and shaped his life.

People who had watched Alicia grow up as well. People who had grieved and maybe, like him, had never gotten over her death.

Another pain squeezed in his chest and he fumbled for his St. Barbara medal. Wasn't she supposed to be protecting him? Then, at the back of the crowd, a small hand waved. The movement caught Dylan's attention and he focused on that little brown-eyed girl again, sitting atop her father's shoulders.

She was staring at Dylan and suddenly he noticed that she held a teddy bear in her arms. A voice sounded in his head. *Accept it for them, if you can't accept it for yourself. The town needs to move on, even if you won't.*

A cold wash spread over Dylan's skin. Everyone in town still hurt, he realized. Bram, of course, but his father, and Kitty, and Mrs. McMahon too. Micah, Dani, and Willa. Everyone.

Beneath the St. Barbara medal, warmth radiated outward, a deep, rejuvenating heat. Swallowing hard, Dylan looked out over the stage, at the people he loved. His gaze moved farther, over the town and to the hills that were as much a part of him as his DNA. Then his eyes lifted, to the blue summer sky that was the exact envy-of-dragonflies shade of Kitty's eyes. *Pointless self-exile,* he heard her say again.

He cleared his throat and leaned toward the mike. "Thank you very much. I can't tell you what this honor means to me." He took a long, deep breath. "But I can't accept it."

The crowd murmured. Dylan turned his head to offer a half smile of apology at the mayor and Odd Fellows on the stage, then spoke to the audience. "I think we know who we should name the park for. And I think I know why she wasn't the obvious choice. We hate acknowledging that she's gone. We're afraid of the constant reminder that maybe we should have done something different to keep her safe."

Dylan suddenly remembered telling Kitty that some calamaties couldn't be prevented. That things happened that weren't another person's fault or responsibility. And Kitty's telling him he wasn't God. He briefly closed his eyes, opened them. "But now I think it's time to forgive ourselves. And it's time to make Alicia Bennett a permanent part of our history and our town, just as she's a permanent part of our hearts."

The little brown-eyed girl was smiling. Then she started to clap, and after a moment the sound of her small hands was lost in thunderous applause as the rest of the audience joined in.

Dylan hesitated, an idea glimmering in the back of his mind. Then all at once he could see it clearly, so real, so brightly shining. His spirit broke free with it, after

eight years no longer imprisoned. Dylan grinned—
exhilarated, grateful, excited, as if he'd just discovered
gold.

There was one more thing he had to say. Dylan
waited until the noise had quieted; then he leaned toward the mike once more. "Thanks again, folks. Thanks
for understanding. And it would be remiss of me if I
didn't take this opportunity to plug a brand-new business in town."

He grinned again, because the idea, the plan, the future, was that right, that good. "Just as quickly as I can
wrap up my federal job, I'll be coming home. I'm moving back to Hot Water and I'll be hanging out my shin-
gle. The law firm of Dylan Matthews, Esquire, will be
coming soon to a corner near you."

Chapter Eighteen

Once the opening ceremony ended, the townspeople started drifting away from the stage, heading for the Heritage Day festivities taking place in Old Town. Kitty, however, didn't move from her spot by the fence between the park and the cemetery. Dylan was still in the park too, standing at the bottom of the stage steps and surrounded by a group of men that included his father and Tony.

She wasn't sure whether to laugh or cry. The man she loved had just committed himself to the town she'd vowed to leave behind.

"I didn't see it coming, did you?" The voice on her left was friendly. And recognizable.

Kitty slowly turned to face Honor Witherspoon. The other woman wore a lightweight flowery dress that should have looked out of place with her bold, trendy

haircut, but somehow didn't. "No," Kitty admitted. "I
didn't see it coming either."

Honor smiled, as if delighted by a sudden thought.
"Hey, that means I'll get to see a lot more of him. I'm
moving to Hot Water myself."

Kitty stiffened. In bed, Dylan had invited her to L.A.
But perhaps Honor had come to Hot Water for Dylan,
and maybe now Dylan was staying for Honor. Gee, it
just went to show the tabloids weren't always wrong.
"Maybe . . . maybe that's why he made the decision."

Honor's eyes rounded. They were a silvery gray and
looked genuinely disturbed by Kitty's words. "Oh,
Lord, I hope not."

Kitty was feeling a bit disturbed herself. She
frowned. "Really?"

But Honor was staring off into the distance, mutter-
ing. "He wouldn't have proposed some sort of bargain
to Dylan, would he? Something Dylan couldn't refuse?"
Her gaze swung back to Kitty.

Kitty cleared her throat. "You're asking me?"

Honor made a face. "Oh. Sorry. I'm talking about my
father. He's been a little . . . protective lately."

"Perhaps with good reason," Kitty pointed out.

Honor waved an impatient hand. "He knows I refuse
to be baby-sat. Who could live like that? It's bad enough
that the press follows me around. Goodness knows, I
don't need a bodyguard watching my every move too."

Kitty found herself nodding. "I suppose I can understand that."

"I just want to live like a normal person," Honor said
fervently. "In Hot Water, with other normal people."

Kitty had to smile. "Well, the 'normal people' part

might be a tall order. We have our eccentricities, you know."

Honor laughed. "I know, I know. Dylan filled me in on all that too. Like you, for example. You're one of the Wilder women who never marry."

"He told you about that?"

"He told me anything he could think of to keep my hysteria at bay. I'd had more than fourteen days by myself and the sound of someone else talking besides my perverted captors and my own panic was manna from heaven."

Kitty cocked her head, studying the beautiful woman who seemed to almost vibrate with energy. "You don't strike me as the hysterical type."

Honor smiled. "Really? That might be the nicest thing anyone has said to me in a long time." Then she sobered. "My father, on the other hand, has leaped from hysteria into out-and-out delirium. I wouldn't put anything past him, including a promise to cure world hunger if he could find some way or someone he thinks would keep me safe."

Kitty shivered. "Are you still being threatened?"

Honor shook her head. "That's what's so crazy. They caught the men who kidnapped me. The FBI is certain they have them all. But you can't tell Warren Witherspoon anything." Like a conspirator, she leaned close to Kitty and whispered, "Since I've refused a bodyguard, he's been looking for a husband to protect me."

"Dylan." Kitty hated that her voice squeaked. After all, hadn't she herself proclaimed Dylan and Honor a perfect match?

"Oh, not Dylan. I'm almost certain Warren's given up on that idea."

Kitty pretended nonchalance. "Really?"

Honor shrugged. "There's just nothing there, you know? Maybe because when we met I hadn't showered in two weeks." Her gaze slid away. "Or maybe because I'd been listening to some creepy goon's sexual fantasies for all that time. But there's no spark between Dylan and me. We're just friends."

Dylan had said that too. Kitty looked into Honor's silvery eyes. The other woman *looked* sincere. Kitty's pulse started to race. If the heiress *wasn't* her rival for Dylan, and Dylan *was* coming home to Hot Water . . .

An image rose in her mind, an image that rested atop a fat fantasy cloud like a cartoon depiction of a dream. Her minivan, glowing white as angel wings under the Gold Country sun. Her fully loaded minivan, with cup holders and seat-back pockets stuffed with picture books and Happy Meal toys. The VCR was running a Disney movie—anything but *Pinocchio*—and to complete this vehicle-in-the-air was the family man in the driver's seat. Dylan.

No. She couldn't dream that. If not with Honor, he would end up with some other appropriately pedigreed beauty. Shaking her head, Kitty stuck a mental pin in the buoyant fancy. Like a balloon, it whined in protest as it deflated, but thankfully shriveled all the same.

Once more back to reality, Kitty looked at the clipboard in her hand and then at Honor Witherspoon. "Excuse me, but I have to be getting to Old Town," she said. "It was nice talking with you."

"Old Town?" Honor perked up. "Would you mind if I tag along?"

"Oh. Well." Kitty swallowed. Honor was the new owner of the living-history district, after all, so was technically Kitty's new boss. Technically the person to whom Kitty should tender her resignation. She steeled her spine and smiled.

"As a matter of fact, that would be very convenient," she made herself say. "I have something I need to discuss with you."

Kitty led the way toward the gate that exited onto the street, all the while reminding herself there was no time like the present to get on with her life. Across the park, the press corps that had been focused on Honor the night before was now pointing cameras at Dylan. Judge Matthews was trying to discourage the reporters, without much success.

"Poor Dylan." Honor said, giving a long mock shudder. "They're particularly rabid this week. The summer doldrums, I suppose. They're desperate to find something salacious."

Even as she spoke, Dylan and Judge Matthews had managed to push past the phalanx of media types and were now striding toward the exit.

Kitty quickened her pace to stay well away from them. "I don't imagine the reporters will find much more than small-town gossip here."

"You're right. I can't see them wasting paper on the Mortons' reconciliation." Honor grinned. "Even though the details of Pearl's realization that rumors of Red's affair might be as mistaken as her need for condoms, baldness tonics, and sex manuals would be a story *I'd* like to read."

Kitty choked back a laugh. "You heard about that?"

She nodded. "And I adore a happy ending. But now, what did you want to talk to me about?"

They were forced to slow as the townspeople funneled through the exit. Kitty took a deep breath, telling herself she wasn't stalling, telling herself she was just taking a moment before putting into words what she'd planned to do all summer. "I hope you'll accept my resignation," she said quickly.

There. It was out. Not waiting for Honor's response, Kitty dove into the rest. "I was hoping—well, I have people covering all the necessary cleanup from Heritage Day, and I spent last night getting up-to-date on the Preservation Society's books." And packing up everything she owned, while ignoring the ringing doorbell and the ringing telephone. "I was hoping I could leave . . . very soon."

Honor's eyebrows rose. "Are you sure you want to do this? I thought . . . Well, it seemed to me Dylan had something going with you."

"Oh, no. Dylan—" Kitty broke off as, unbidden, that gleaming fantasy rose once again in her mind, more vivid than before. It was *The Little Mermaid* on the movie screen and *Goodnight Moon* in the seat pocket. It was Dylan still in the driver's seat, his forearm propped in the open window as he waited for . . . her.

A little dizzy, Kitty tried taking a breath, tried popping the fantasy, tried not wanting it so very much. But it remained in her head, her heart, shimmering like a mirage. As any thirsty person, Kitty was having a hard time believing it wasn't true. That it couldn't be true.

The sound of Aunt Cat calling her name sharpened Kitty's focus, but didn't smother the silly hope in her heart. Glancing toward the rest of the group waiting to leave the park, she spied her great-aunt, accompanied by Samantha. Even upon seeing her mother, her mother made pregnant by some secret lover, Kitty's hope managed to survive.

She turned to Honor. "Can I catch up with you? It looks like my great-aunt wants a word with me." At Honor's nod, Kitty hung back. She saw Honor pass through the gate, and then Dylan. The two walked off together.

Only a few members of the press were left in the newly named Alicia Bennett Park, a cameraman taking footage of the parting crowd and two reporters looking through their notes, when the older Wilder women met up with Kitty. "Did you need something, Aunt Cat?" she asked, keeping her gaze off Samantha.

"Dylan Matthews came by the house looking for you last night," her great-aunt said.

"Oh?" The hope strengthened, in her mind's eye the minivan's chrome glittering, not silver, but gold.

Aunt Cat turned to Samantha. "And D. B. Matthews came by looking for *you*."

Samantha's mouth opened, but her "Oh" didn't make it out.

Stunned, Kitty stared at her mother, not even noticing as one of the reporters jostled her on his way out. Dylan's father had been looking for Samantha? *It . . . it . . .*

"It couldn't be, could it?"

Kitty jumped as her thoughts were spoken out loud in a stranger's voice. Whirling, she took in the reporter—a heavyset man in his late thirties—who had turned back from the exit and was coming toward them.

His gaze was on Kitty's mother. "I heard you'd retired from Vegas, but I didn't want to believe it. Not after twenty years." Without taking his eyes off her, he called over his shoulder, "Max, get the camera over here. Hurry, damn it. This'll be perfect for the weekend show, spliced with some footage from her act."

Her act? Kitty swung back to study her mother. As she watched, Samantha straightened, her features hardening into a colder, but almost more beautiful, version of her usual self. "I'm not available for comment right now," she said, her voice steady and calm.

The heavyset man gave her an unctuous smile and sidled closer. "C'mon. You'll be news."

Without batting an eyelash, Samantha seemed to remove herself even farther from the pestering reporter. "No, thank you."

Kitty had run up against his type a hundred times in The Burning Rose and knew he wasn't going to take the hint. She drew herself up. "Excuse me, sir, but—"

"But nothing." The man's eyes barely flicked her way. "It's my good luck that I ran into the infamous Las Vegas stripper Gold Fever, and I'm not letting it—or her—go."

Las Vegas stripper? *Gold Fever?* One look at Samantha's frozen expression confirmed the truth. A laugh escaped Kitty's mouth and she clapped her palm over her lips to stop another hysterical sound. What a ridiculous name. And how ironic. How deliciously, I-told-you-so ironic.

In just that moment it was done. For once and for all, for now and forever, a Wilder woman had stripped Kitty of any last hope she might have had for a conventional life in Hot Water. "Stripped," she whispered out loud, then giggled again.

As she ran in the direction of the cemetery, she heard both Samantha and Aunt Cat call her name. Kitty ignored them, focusing instead on her minivan as that ephemeral mental image dissolved like sugar in a pool of tears.

Kitty loitered in the cemetery for a good hour, poking around the highest knolls that were the sites of the oldest graves. But she finally headed back toward the park—she'd dropped her clipboard there, she thought. In Old Town there were people counting on her and details to oversee.

Divorces to obtain.

She found the clipboard, and then she found Samantha, sitting at a picnic table in the shade of an ancient oak. Despite all the Heritage Day celebratory hoopla happening elsewhere around town, there were still toddlers playing in the nearby sandbox, their mothers at the ready. Looking up, Kitty's mother called her name, then returned to studying the little kids.

Kitty hesitated, unprepared to face Samantha. But the fact was, she'd gone numb sometime in the past sixty minutes. Perhaps this was the best moment for a confrontation that she sensed she couldn't duck forever.

Still, it was a long walk to that table. Samantha appeared tired, though her marvelous dancer's carriage remained unchanged.

Dancer. Hah.

"I saw you walking through the cemetery," Samantha said. "You looked like Rose Wilder's ghost in that costume. Don't be surprised if the next thing the tabloids mention is specter sightings in Hot Water."

"You mean after they mention you?"

Samantha didn't flinch. "There's not much point in apologizing for that now, Kitty." She glanced away from the children and gazed squarely into her daughter's eyes. "But I'm sorry if you felt I . . . abandoned you."

Kitty blew out a long breath. "I shouldn't have said what I did the other day. Woman to woman . . ." She closed her eyes for a moment, then opened them. "Woman to woman, I don't blame you for leaving me with Aunt Cat. I've thought about what I would have done in your shoes. I can't say for certain it would have been anything different, or anything better."

There was a long pause. "Thank you," Samantha said. "I appreciate you telling me."

"I'm angry that you came back, though." There was no stopping the truth.

"I know, and I've been thinking about that." Samantha linked her hands on the redwood table and stared down at them. "I can't give you a good reason why I returned to Hot Water when I left Las Vegas. But if it will make it easier for you, I'll close up Bum Luck and leave town."

"No," Kitty said. A man was approaching Samantha from behind, and, sick at the thought of witnessing their meeting, Kitty took a step back.

"I will, Kitty." It was the first time Kitty had ever heard Samantha sound desperate. "Let me do this for you. Let me do *something* for you."

The man was coming closer and Kitty took another hurried step back. "It's too late," she said softly. The talk had started seven months ago when Samantha had returned. In another seven months or less, another Wilder would be born without the benefit of marriage. No matter what, Kitty didn't think she could stand to see that. "You don't have to do anything. I'm leaving myself, very soon. Today."

D. B. Matthews had quietly closed in on Samantha. "And besides," he said from behind her, "I wouldn't let you take my child away from Hot Water."

Samantha stiffened, an anguished expression crossing her face. "You know," she said, her voice low. She didn't turn to look at him. "You know."

Her shocking suspicions confirmed, Kitty left the park and Judge Matthews and Samantha behind. She'd half guessed it when Aunt Cat said D. B. had been looking for Samantha, but still, it was a hard truth to swallow.

Her mother's secret lover was D. B. Matthews.

A Superior Court judge.

Dylan's father.

Like father, like son; like mother, like daughter; like the present repeated the past. There would never be anything normal, never anything conventional, between a Matthews and a Wilder.

And Kitty couldn't live with anything less.

"When were you planning on telling me?" D. B. asked Samantha.

She wouldn't look at him, Samantha promised herself, even though he sat on top of the picnic table and put his feet on her bench. "This isn't about you," she said.

"Exactly what do you mean by that?"

It was hard to know what he was thinking without looking at him. He was using his judge's voice, the one that sounded so damn neutral. "It's *my* body, *my* pregnancy," she answered.

"But it's *my* baby, yes?"

Her head jerked up. "Of course it is," she snapped, then realized her mistake. Looking at him hurt. Looking at him and remembering how good it had been between them made her feel lonely. And loneliness was an unsettling emotion for a woman who had been alone for the past twenty-six years. She put her hands over her face. "I can't believe this happened to me."

"What? An unexpected pregnancy?"

An unexpected love. " 'Unexpected' hardly seems to cover it. I should be thinking about menopause, not morning sickness."

She thought he touched her hair, but the sensation was so light and fleeting, she wasn't sure. He cleared his throat. "You've been throwing up your breakfast?"

"Breakfast, lunch, and dinner."

"I . . ." He cleared his throat again. "I read that morning sickness means a lot of hormones are being released. It's supposed to be the sign of a strong pregnancy."

Samantha dropped her hands to send him a withering, sidelong look. "Or it's something a man made up because he thought it might make a woman cheerier when she's hanging over the toilet."

He laughed. "At least you haven't flushed your sense of humor."

Samantha groaned. "You need to limit your contact with the mayor, D. B."

His expression sobered. "I wondered if I'd ever hear you say my name again."

No. She dug her fingernails into her palms. That look in his eye, that hoarse softness of his voice, would kill her if she let them get to her. He was her fling, for God's sake, a past fling, and she wasn't going to let him get close again.

"I said the wrong thing, didn't I?"

See? That was the danger. He was so damn good at reading her that he might easily discover she was in love with him. What would she have then? Her pride was the only thing keeping her upright these days. "I don't want to go backward, D. B."

There was an instant of silence. "I understand. What *do* you want? What are you going to do about the pregnancy?"

It was a fair question. Samantha glanced toward the sandbox and the chubby little ones playing there. "I'm forty-three years old and I don't know any more about being a mother now than I did at seventeen."

D. B. waited for her to continue without saying anything. That impressed her, it did, because his judicial nerves must be screaming. To father a child out of wedlock at his age, and with Samantha, of all people, would likely cause half the county to die of shock and the other half to ignite a recall election.

Too bad. She turned her head and looked him straight in the eye. "I'm going to have this baby."

He didn't blink. "Good." Then he smiled.

Oh, God. It was a smile brimming with joy and excitement. For a moment—a moment in which her own joy bubbled upward—she thought all the dashes to the bathroom were worth it, just for that one expression on his face. But then he ruined it.

"We'll get married, of course," he said.

She gaped at him. "Of course we won't," she finally answered.

His face hardened. "It's my baby."

"Mine too," she retorted. "And my life." And she wasn't going to tie it to someone who felt forced to marry her.

"Samantha—"

"You wouldn't acknowledge me at a Chinese restaurant two weeks ago. You can't tell me you'd even think of marrying me now if it wasn't for the baby."

He nodded shortly. "The baby changes things, I'll grant you that. Speeds things up."

"It changes nothing, not when it comes to talking about marriage."

"You're not being reasonable." He had the gall to look down his nose at her.

She glared at him. "Consult your book. I'm sure some man has written in there that pregnant women often aren't, which in my opinion is just another way to excuse the typical male's boorish behavior."

"I haven't even resorted to boorishness yet."

She was feeling a little panicky at the determined tone of his voice. There was no way she'd marry him. Not when she loved him and he didn't love her back.

"Face it, Samantha. We're going to be married."

She swallowed. "Haven't you heard? Wilder women don't wed and they don't run."

"I don't give a damn about that stupid motto and I don't think you do either. After all, you *did* run away from Hot Water."

"But I came back." Samantha took a calming breath as she stood up and moved away from the table, suddenly remembering the winning card she had yet to play. "After twenty years stripping for a living in Las Vegas. And for your information, that interesting story is going to come out in *Celeb!* magazine next week, and *Celeb! on TV* this weekend. So, D. B., if you still want to marry me after the whole world knows that, then I'll say yes."

Chapter Nineteen

Before the opening ceremony at the park, Samantha had left her car at Aunt Cat's. Now she met the older lady coming out of her house just as Samantha was unlocking her car door. Trying to appear calm and composed, she placed her fist over her stomach and smiled. "Can I give you a lift somewhere?"

Cat was a beautiful woman—all the Wilders were—and she looked feminine and wise in a long skirt and white blouse. "I thought I'd walk to Old Town and check on The Burning Rose. Heritage Day always makes me nostalgic."

A visit to the brothel suddenly sounded perfect to Samantha as well. "I'll go with you."

Aunt Cat lifted one silver eyebrow. "You're feeling nostalgic too?"

"In a way." The Burning Rose would remind her of

the Wilder legacy and help her forget the speechless man she'd left back at the park. They started off down the street, Samantha adjusting her pace to fit Aunt Cat's slower one. "You know, another thing I've always felt guilty about is not doing my penance in the brothel like you and Kitty."

"Penance?" Aunt Cat made a face. "Why would you call working in The Burning Rose a penance?"

"Come on, Cat. You never felt the slightest bit humiliated playing madam for the crowds?"

"Hmm." Aunt Cat seemed to contemplate her answer. "What about you? Did you feel humiliated taking your clothes off for men?" She didn't ask it unkindly, yet Samantha felt hurt by the question all the same.

"Yes," she admitted. "Sometimes. And sometimes I felt sexy and powerful, and sometimes I was just so sick of the whole thing that I wished I'd never started."

Aunt Cat nodded, her usual unperturbed self. "Exactly as I suppose the first Wilder sisters felt."

"So why isn't it a penance, then, playing them?"

"It's an honor, Sammy. It's representing women who found a way to survive, just like you did. Women who survived on their own terms."

"I wouldn't make the same choices today that I made twenty-six years ago."

Aunt Cat snorted, in a ladylike way, but she snorted nevertheless. "Well, I should hope not! What would be the point of experiencing life if you didn't get any wiser?"

Samantha shook her head. "I don't know, Cat, you're making it all sound a little too easy."

"I never said it was easy, Sammy. I'm saying living

your life is like childbirth. Though there's pain, you usually get something worthwhile out of it."

Despite the reference to babies, Samantha laughed.
"You're beginning to sound like a pot holder, Aunt Cat.
We could start a business, embroidering and selling that
homily. The Wilder one too, while we're at it."

Aunt Cat shook her head. " 'Wilder Women Don't
Wed And They Don't Run'? You and Kitty make too
much of that."

They reached the entrance to the living-history district. Since her return, Samantha hadn't been inclined to
visit this part of town, and as she looked up the steeply
inclined street, her breath caught.

When she'd left Hot Water at seventeen, Old Town
hadn't existed. The buildings had been there, of course,
but most had been boarded up and long abandoned.
Still, even then Heritage Day had been a time of celebration, and the Preservation Society had given walking
tours through the original blocks of town. But it was so
different now, the buildings in good repair, the street and
sidewalks filled with people, many in period dress.

A horse-drawn wagon turned out of the stable nearby,
the bells on its harness blending with the tinkling
player-piano music drifting into the street from an open
doorway. A man dressed in a homespun shirt, stained
leather vest, and heavy work boots clomped across the
wooden sidewalk in the direction of the assay office,
carrying a bulging leather pouch.

Holding it up, he grinned. "I had good luck at the
traces today, ladies. Drinks are on me at the saloon." He
tipped his battered hat and continued on his way.

A couple of blocks up, in a niche between two tall

brick buildings, Samantha saw clothing drying in the breeze. A sign painted on a sheet, "Lin's Laundry," hung by clothespins on the line as well. One block past that was the National Hotel, decorated with red, white, and blue buntings. On its second-floor veranda, people sat at small tables drinking lemonade.

At the crest of Main Street, the white-spired, red brick Methodist church presided. In front of the church stretched a long line of couples that disappeared around a corner. "What are they waiting for?" She pointed.

"The Hot Water marriage, our most popular Heritage Day event." Aunt Cat smiled, full of mischief. "Some call it a tourist trap."

Marriage. Samantha frowned. "Trap" was the right word for it.

Shading her eyes with her hand, she ran her gaze over the restored buildings, searching for the Wilders' ancestral home. "Where's The Burning Rose? It's on the right-hand side of the street, isn't it?"

Aunt Cat moved forward. "Follow me."

A half block up from the stable was a two-story, gingerbread-fancy building painted pale pink with red trim. The door of the brothel was thrown open and those player-piano sounds drifted through the entry. "There are no guided tours on Heritage Day," Aunt Cat said. "But we can go inside and look around on our own."

Samantha peered into the dim interior. "I think I remember every story you told me about this place." She walked inside, welcoming the opportunity to focus on the past instead of on her present muddle. Her eyes still adjusting to the darkness, she headed for the sound of the piano, into a room occupied by several other visitors.

Suddenly a harsh light blazed in her face. *"Celeb! on TV* has found her, folks. It's the legendary stripper Gold Fever, right here in Hot Water's legendary brothel."

Blinded by the abrupt switch from dim room to bright camera light, Samantha shrank back, bringing up her hand to protect her eyes.

A microphone was shoved in her face. "Is it true you're related to the prostitutes who ran this bordello?"

Samantha blinked, recognizing the voice of the relentless tabloid reporter she'd spoken to in the park. "Yes," she said. There was no point in denying it.

"So with your career in Las Vegas you were merely following in your family's footsteps?"

"I wouldn't say they were exactly the *same* career," Samantha protested.

The reporter smirked. "Oh, come on."

Samantha sighed. "I'm done answering questions." She pushed the microphone away.

He shoved it right back in her face. "There are thousands of men who think a visit to Vegas will never be the same now that you're gone. Come on, babe, we want to know what Gold Fever is planning to do next."

"She's spending the rest of her life with me," a deep voice behind her answered.

Samantha's heart leaped, but she ruthlessly reined it back.

The reporter couldn't contain his delight, however, and reached the mike over Samantha's shoulder to get to D. B. "And you are?"

"Her lover and her lawyer. The lady's done with you. Cut off the camera and get lost." Without waiting for the other man's response, D. B. put his hand on Samantha's shoulder and turned her toward him. "I need to talk to you."

"*No.*" Samantha noticed the cameraman was whispering in that jerk of a reporter's ear, and any minute now her embarrassment was going to become D. B.'s catastrophe. She lowered her voice. "Listen, you've got to get out of here before they find out—"

"You're a Superior Court judge, is that right? Judge D. B. Matthews?" The camera light blazed again, trained on D.B.'s face. Holding out the microphone, the reporter pushed past Samantha.

She stumbled.

D. B. shoved the man aside to steady her. "I said, get lost," he told the *Celeb!* people. "I meant it."

The reporter merely smiled. "As you should know, Judge, it's a free country."

D. B. smiled back. "And this is private property."

"That *I* own," said a new voice. Honor Witherspoon's voice, the heiress who now owned the district. She strolled into the room, her voice cold. "And you're no longer welcome, Jerry."

"Harry."

"Jerry, Harry, Moe, Curly, Larry. Whoever. It's time for you to leave."

"Listen, Miss Witherspoon." The man resorted to whining. "You—"

"I have the law on my side," Honor said.

Dylan stepped up behind her. He smiled.

Samantha felt the whole room shiver. Within seconds the place cleared out. Then Honor, Aunt Cat, and Dylan disappeared too, leaving her alone with D. B. and the giddy-sounding player piano.

She rubbed her forehead. "It's going to be all over the tabloids, you know. I'll try to find them and deny a relationship, but your goose is probably cooked."

"I don't care what anybody says about us or our relationship." His smile was crooked as he ran a finger down her cheek. "My goose is only cooked if you won't hear me out."

With the greatest of efforts, she held herself still. "Please, D. B. Don't say it again." If he mentioned marriage one more time, she might break down and accept his proposal. She inhaled a fortifying breath, strengthening herself with the idea of Rose and her sister—and all the Wilders after—who had made it through their lives without depending upon a man. "I won't listen."

"Please, Samantha," he said quietly. "You have to give me a second chance to get it right."

But that was easy to answer. "I don't believe in second chances."

"I don't believe *you*. Everything you've done in Hot Water has screamed second chance. A second chance in the town where you grew up. A second chance to know Kitty."

She backed up a few steps. And a few more.

He moved forward. "And the baby . . . you can't tell me you don't see the baby as a second chance too."

Her next backward step brought her smack against the piano. It burped a sour note, then found its place again. Absurdly cheerful music tinkled around them.

D. B. smiled at her. "What I treasured most about our relationship was the maturity we brought to it. I thought it was so good because we were past all that posturing and jockeying for position that younger couples waste their time on." He shook his head, laughing wryly. "I was wrong about it all."

She wet her lips. "What do you mean?"

"It was so good because I love you."

Samantha jerked, and the piano burped again, then went silent. In the quiet, Samantha could hear the heavy beat of her heart. "No."

"Yes, I do. And I was wrong. I'm not above all that posturing and jockeying, because I was scared as any twenty-year-old about my feelings."

"You can't love me."

"Since maybe the first time I saw you cross the street. Or perhaps that night when we shut down Bum Luck and stayed awake until dawn listening to classic rock. But I didn't want to rush the idea. And I wasn't the least prepared for what your years had been like in Las Vegas."

She nodded. This she understood. "Of course you weren't, you're a judge."

He grimaced. "But not of your past, Samantha." His hand touched her cheek again. "I forgot that for a moment. But the one thing maturity *has* given me is the guts to hold onto something special. A second chance—another chance—for the both of us for love and family. So forgive me, Samantha? Love me? Marry me?"

Her heart squeezed. She whirled away from him, biting hard on her lower lip to get control of her spinning emotions. Her gaze landed on the framed needlework on top of the piano: *Wilder Women Don't Wed And They Don't Run.*

But perhaps they'd never had someone like D. B. to

love. A man offering a second chance—no, her first, really. A chance for love, for family.

Maybe every shimmy on stage, every piece of clothing dropped, every time she'd filled her veins with ice and pretended for the audience, had prepared her for this moment. Closing her eyes, she breathed deeply, and turned.

Facing him, she lifted her lashes and let all those years of practiced pretense slip away. She let him see straight into her heart, hoping it was that much sweeter because she'd never allowed it before. As she'd never allowed, she set free her love and desire. It rushed through her, warming her blood. Without looking first, which she hadn't done in twenty-six years, she leaped into his arms. "I love you."

D. B. caught her against him and buried his face in her hair, just as the player piano burst into song. "Thank you," he whispered hoarsely.

She rested her cheek against his shirt. "I don't know anything about being a wife," she cautioned.

He ran his hands down her back. "Me neither."

She laughed. "Or a mother. I suppose you don't know a thing about that."

He kissed her cheek. "Not a clue."

She looked up at him and grinned, the piano's lighthearted tune washing over them like sunshine. "I suppose there's a book . . ."

He kissed her mouth. "We don't need anything but each other."

* * *

"I didn't see Kitty in the brothel," Dylan said, crossing his arms over his chest and bracing his shoulders and one foot against the outside wall of the assay office.

"Nope." Honor gave him a cheerful smile, then went back to studying the crowded streets. "It's just as you described it. It's perfect. The perfect place for me."

He cleared his throat. "What . . . what do you think Kitty thought of my decision to return to Hot Water?"

"She said she was surprised." Honor frowned. "No. I think I said I was surprised and she agreed with me."

He gave her a sharp look. During those days in captivity, and even after, when her father was trying to throw them together, Dylan had developed a fraternal fondness for Honor. He respected her courage and her optimistic outlook on life. "You think I'm making a mistake?"

"Nope. I'm only surprised you were smart enough to figure out what you really wanted to do. I listened to you talk about Hot Water for ninety-six hours straight. I could tell then that you loved it here and longed to come back."

" 'Longed' is a pretty strong word," he said, shifting his shoulders against the wall.

Honor slid her gray eyes his way. "Longed. You think it's a sissy word, but it's the one that fits."

"You're a pain to argue with, do you know that?"

She shrugged. "Who do you think I should get to replace Kitty as the advertising and PR person?"

He froze. "You're firing her?"

"Yes, and while I'm at it, I thought I'd stick a pencil

in my eye." She wrinkled her nose. "You're an idiot, do you know that?"

"She quit?" He gaped at Honor.

"Mmm. And said she was going to leave town very soon."

"She *what*?"

Honor slowed her speech. "Mmm . . . and . . . said . . . she . . . was . . . going . . . to . . . leave . . . town . . . very . . . soon."

The words took even longer to sink in than they did to say. Kitty was leaving? he thought. Why the hell would she run?

But the answer was obvious. She'd been telling him about it over and over. With the return of Samantha, Kitty thought Hot Water would never look underneath the surface of her Wilder skin to the minivan soul hiding beneath. And maybe she was right.

Kitty coveted *cup holders*, for God's sake, and they'd made her play the courtesan for the past seven summers.

But it wouldn't be Hot Water without her. When he'd spoken into the mike, announcing his plans to return, he'd pictured how things would be between them. He'd had an apology or two to make, of course, but then he'd looked forward to more nights in her bed. More days watching the fascinating contrast of her good-girl face and her bad-girl mouth. More . . . more . . .

Just more.

She was taking that away from him, damn it. Without one word to her *husband*, the little witch had planned to up and leave him.

Then, like a death knell, his heart slammed once against his chest.

She'd planned to divorce him first.

Damn, with everything else going on, he'd forgotten all about the divorce.

A pulse throbbing at his temples, he stared up the street at the column of people winding past the church and around a corner toward the courthouse. "Come on. I need you." He grabbed Honor's wrist and jumped off the sidewalk, dragging her with him. "I'll find her faster if we start at opposite ends of the line and work toward the middle."

After experiencing almost three weeks in captivity, Honor knew when to keep her mouth shut. Though her eyebrows disappeared behind her slant-edged bangs, she let herself be towed up the street. "I need to talk to Kitty," he said, that pulse thumping in his head. "If you see her first, you tell her I'm mad as hell at her. Tell her I'm going to update her FBI file and associate her with kinky-sex groups. Tell her I'll fix it so no self-respecting auto dealership will ever sell her a two-door Daewoo, let alone a fully loaded Grand Caravan."

He continued ranting, until halfway to the church he realized Honor was wheezing. Frowning, he halted, then tapped his toe while she caught her breath.

"I feel compelled to point out," Honor said between gasps, "because you saved my life and everything, that you have a lousy way of wooing a woman."

"Wooing?" he scoffed. Paused, then tried again. "Wooing? I can't woo her."

"Why not?"

He looked up, down, right, left, anywhere he could for

an answer. Then he found it across the street, standing in the shadows of the narrow alley beside the National Hotel building. A memory traveled through him like a shudder. "I don't want to care for her that much," he said.

Honor traced his gaze to the lone figure of Bram, watching the activity on the street as if he were a world away. "Oh." Her hand crept up to her throat. "Who's that?"

"You don't know? That's who sold you the ground you're standing on. Bram Bennett." His best friend—his brother in all the ways that mattered—whom Dylan was determined to reestablish a relationship with. For both their sakes.

She didn't take her eyes off the other man. "My father put the deal together," she said absently. "I haven't met . . . Bram."

"That's him."

"The one who lost his wife eight years ago." Honor was silent for a moment. "How bad was it?"

"You mean what happened to his wife, Alicia?" Dylan asked.

She shook her head. "Bram Bennett. How bad was what happened to her for him?"

A cold claw scraped down Dylan's spine. This memory wasn't one of the happy ones. "Think of the van Gogh painting 'Scream.' It was like watching someone turn from a human being into a silent wail of despair."

Honor winced.

The memory of Bram's pain hurt Dylan too. "That's what loving someone can leave a man with. I'm not going to risk it, not even with Kitty, thank you very much."

Honor gazed up at him. He had to look away; there

was something in her eyes that unnerved him sometimes, something that her father claimed wasn't there
before her kidnapping.

He gestured defensively toward Bram. "That's what
could happen, I tell you."

Something flashed in her eyes. She cast one more
swift glance across the street, then looked back at Dylan. "That man's a malingering jerk."

Stunned, Dylan stared at her. "Honor—"

"Life's too short for all that drama," she said briskly.
"So you could be left alone like him. But you're alone
now, aren't you? You've been alone the last eight years."
Her hand touched his arm. "How's that been for you?"

Detached. Impersonal. Lonely. But he smothered the
thoughts and shook off her hand, stalking away from her.

Except he didn't stalk away from the long line leading to the courthouse. Instead, he found himself striding
toward it. Running toward it.

There must have been a hundred people in line, all
waiting to see retired Judge Tierney, who was scheduled
to perform the ceremonies from 10 A.M. to 10 P.M. People stood two abreast, sometimes four, giggling
teenagers, smiling adults. Starting from the back, Dylan
methodically searched for Kitty. Thinking he'd found
her, he grabbed the lace-edged sleeve of someone's
dress, only to find himself facing a gay "bride" in satin
drag. The old judge was in for one hell of a shock.

Moving quickly, Dylan continued to follow the
snaking line as it turned off Main and into Hangman
Way, the dead-end street leading to the city hall. At the
bottom of the building's steps, a flower-trimmed gazebo
had been erected. Beside it sat a table with cash register

and cashier, and even from here he could see the MasterCard and Visa logos. Inside the structure, in deference to his age and to the long hours he'd spend officiating that day, Judge Tierney sat on a massive chair. An ancient leather-covered Bible rested atop his knees.

Dylan slowed. Eight years ago that leather had been smooth and cool beneath his palm. He'd been grinning down at Kitty as he repeated the marriage vows, bemused by the whole idea of one last hometown adventure before he left Hot Water for good.

She'd been grinning too. Drunkenly, he'd realized later, but had he known then, it wouldn't have changed a thing. He would still have wanted to marry her, because on that last night, when he'd been hiding in the darkness and licking his wounds, she'd found him, talked to him, allowed him to brood when everyone else had expected him to celebrate. The summer had been a success after all, they'd told him. Three lives saved. Only one lost.

The line shuffled forward, and up ahead, he caught sight of a waving feather stuck in a one-pin topknot. His pulse surged.

The truth was, eight years ago he'd married her because he hadn't wanted to leave. And since that time, his "marriage" to Kitty had remained his connection to home. His own secret, private link.

She'd been the piece of his heart he'd left behind.

Chapter Twenty

A hot wind was picking up and Kitty took a long drink from her chilled bottle of water, sold by a member of the large Kemper family who walked along the marriage line with an ice-filled cart. Overhead, a loud *slap* caught her attention and she grimaced. One of the banners strung above the street had torn loose from a bottom mooring.

It flapped again, the left corner kicking up to partly obscure DYLAN MATTHEWS KEEPS OUR STREETS SAFE! Unwilling to lose her place in line, she looked around for someone she could ask to fix it.

Instead, she caught sight of Dylan stalking toward her, murderous intent in his eyes.

Without thinking, she backed away, but then the couple behind her started to swallow up her spot in line. She leaped into place again and squared her shoulders. He wasn't going to scare her off. This was what he wanted, wasn't it? What she wanted too.

She faced forward and pretended she didn't know he was nearing. It didn't work very well, because even before she heard his icy voice, telltale goose bumps were chasing each other down her spine.

"Kitty Wilder, I'm going to kill you."

She turned slowly. "Isn't this where you came in?"

He crossed his arms over his chest. "A lot has happened since I returned. All of which gives you no right to do this without talking to me first."

She swallowed. "We already talked." More talking was exactly what might get her to confess she loved him, and then she'd never make it out of Hot Water. She shifted her gaze away from him. "You signed for the divorce."

If he asked her to stay, to continue their affair, to be his lover, she'd say yes. It was just that simple. And simply unthinkable for a woman who had sought to be conventional her entire life.

The couple in front of her moved forward and she did too, hoping Dylan would take the hint and leave her alone to get their divorce.

"Kitty." He stepped into line beside her.

"I don't have anything more to add," she said, staring at the sunburned neck of the young man in front of her. Then she darted Dylan a glance. Okay, so there was one safe thing to discuss. "Except I'm happy for you that you're coming back. It's where you belong."

"I have you to thank for my decision," he replied quietly. "The things you said made me see myself more clearly. I also have to apologize for what I said to you this morning."

"That's okay." She cleared her throat. "And you're welcome." The line moved forward once again. There were three couples ahead of her. An awkward silence settled between her and Dylan.

"So," he finally said, his voice degrees lighter and more friendly, "exactly how does this divorce business work?"

She gave him a suspicious look, but his expression was unreadable. "Oh. Well." It certainly couldn't be disappointment that stabbed her right through the heart. "You signed, I signed. Judge Tierney will sign, date-stamp the certificate, then send it off to the state capital." She patted the pocket of her dress.

"Sounds easy enough."

Her throat felt clogged. She cleared it again. "Yes, well, a hundred dollars and that official Hot Water stamp and we'll . . ." Her heart dipped toward her knees.

"Kitty?"

Heat flared on her cheeks. "I just thought . . . I just remembered. The hundred dollars. I don't have my purse, just the certificate." He'd think she planned this! He'd suppose she was reluctant to get the divorce!

"No problem," he said easily. "I'll loan you the hundred bucks." He slipped his hand into his back pocket and withdrew his wallet.

"Oh. Um, thank you." The line moved forward again. Two more marriages and she'd be a divorced woman.

"A divorcée," Dylan mused, as if he'd read her mind. "Sounds pretty racy, you know. Not half bad for a half-hearted Wilder."

Covering a wince, she made an agreeable sound.

His voice turned silky and gentle. "So where are you going when you leave Hot Water?"

Her attention focused on the second-to-the-last couple who were almost "married," she didn't even think before she spoke. "Seattle. I have a friend who'll give me a job."

"Male friend? Woman friend?"

She stared at him. "Wait. How did you know?— Never mind. Woman friend."

"Ah." His expression didn't change as the two people before them stepped up to the cashier, and then to the gazebo.

Kitty's heart pounded. She reached into her pocket and pulled out the marriage certificate, looking down at it instead of looking at Dylan. On the front was his "wedding" signature, as dark and beautiful as he'd been that night. Hers looked rounder, softer, more uncertain.

The girl who had sent it off had been unsure of so many things. Except that she loved Dylan. Kitty stared at the piece of parchment and admitted to herself one final truth that she'd buried all these years. With Dylan already gone from Hot Water, she'd sent off the certificate with the hope that making their marriage legal would bring him back. To her.

His breath landed on her neck as he peered over her shoulder. She pretended not to notice. "I sent it to Sacramento and then they sent it back to me once the marriage was registered with the state," she said to fill up the silence.

When he didn't reply, she looked up.

And nearly shrieked. He wasn't looking at the certificate but at her face, his dark, deep-set eyes untroubled, yet intent. Kitty swallowed. "What is it?"

One of his eyebrows rose. "Are you sure this is what you want to do, Kitty?"

No. *Yes.* No! Someone tapped her on the shoulder, and she glanced back. The man behind her was gesturing her forward, to the cashier.

"It's our turn," she said.

Dylan didn't move.

Biting her lip, Kitty took a hesitant step forward. Dylan smoothly followed. He plucked the certificate out of her hand. "Why don't I pay the cashier and you go make small talk with Judge Tierney?"

Determined not to appear any less eager than he, she followed his direction. But even before she'd approached the judge, Dylan was beside her again, sliding his wallet into his pocket at the same time that he returned the certificate to her hand. He nudged her forward. "We're paid up. Hand it to the judge, honey."

Looking back at Dylan, she placed her water bottle in Judge Tierney's hand.

"The certificate," Dylan said gently.

Her face burned. "Oh, of course." She grabbed back the bottle and handed over the paper.

Judge Tierney's glasses magnified his faded blue eyes. He looked down at the paper, looked up for a long moment, then signed his name with a flourish. He slipped the certificate between the pages of the oversized Bible. "I'll take good care of this."

It was done.

Kitty clutched her fingers together, hardly believing. "Thank you, sir," she said.

The old judge winked.

Bewildered, but grateful for the friendly gesture, Kitty winked back.

Then Dylan was leading her out of the gazebo and the next couple stepped up.

She disengaged her arm from his hand. "All done," she said, still puzzling over the judge's strange wink.

"Not quite," Dylan answered. "We need to have that talk."

Though still thinking about the odd wink, Kitty recognized the determined look on his face. "No, Dylan." She took three steps forward, then whirled as realization struck. "*Wait.* I don't believe it. I just figured it out!"

His expression turned wary. "Figured, uh, what out?"

"The judge was hitting on me! Can you believe it?" Outraged, she drew herself up and propped her fists on her hips. "The minute I'm not married, that man winked at me."

Dylan pressed his lips together. "Oh, I'm sure you're mistaken," he said, his voice strangely tight.

"I am *not* mistaken. I may be a Wilder, but he's happily married and at least eighty-five years old."

Dylan coughed. "Well, you *are* a Wilder after all, and truly a temptation to him or any man, married *or* divorced, so . . ."

She glared over Dylan's shoulder in the direction of the gazebo. "I think I'll just go over there and give him a piece of my mind."

"Kitty . . ." Coughing again, he moved in front of her. "You have to live here, and—"

"But I'm *not* living here. I'm leaving." She sucked in an energizing breath. "And, Wilder or not, I won't stand for that kind of treatment in Hot Water or anywhere else." Dylan had been right all along. What *did* she have to be ashamed of? She was her own woman. A *good* woman. She blinked, almost dazzled by the sudden knowledge that filled her with an awesome power.

She *wasn't* merely a Wilder. She was *Kitty.* Herself.

"I'm *not* going to take it anymore!" she declared. With that, she stomped around Dylan.

"Oh, hell," she heard him say in that strange, choked voice.

Then a strong arm snaked around her belly and she was tipped over his shoulder. She half shrieked, then half sputtered. "Stop!"

"You're under arrest."

"*Arrt?*" Her voice was muffled by his shirt.

He started striding down the street. "You're under arrest for threatening a member of the judiciary."

She turned her cheek against his warm back and yelled at him. "You're crazy!"

"I know. And it's all your fault."

The people in the marriage line turned as they passed, their faces startled. "Help!" she called. "Help me!"

Someone giggled. "It's the sheriff and the madam." Several more laughed.

"It's the madam and the manhandler!" Kitty yelled back.

Dylan's big body started shaking and she didn't think it was due to the stress of her great weight. As his strides ate up the street below, she closed her eyes to the dizzying view. Voices swirled around her. She considered calling again for help, but everyone seemed convinced it was just another of their for-entertainment-only reenactments.

When he finally halted, Kitty opened her eyes. Even upside down, she recognized the jail. Keys jangled in Dylan's pocket, and then he had the door open. It was dark and cool inside. He slammed the door shut, then grabbed the iron key from the wall and banged the cell door open.

The soles of her shoes thumped against the wooden floor inside the cell as he set her upright. She took hold of a convenient bar and swayed, light-headed from the sudden change in position.

That dizziness was why she thought she was seeing things. It was why she thought she was seeing Dylan step inside the cell and shut the barred door behind him.

She blinked. He was still there. "What are you doing?"

One of his hands slipped through the bars. "What does it look like I'm doing?"

Kitty forcibly retrieved her drooping jaw. "It looks like you're locking us both in."

"Got it in one." Mission accomplished, he turned to face her. Smiled.

Then he tossed the cell key over his shoulder. It flew through the bars and landed on the floor, yards out of reach.

Staring at him, she backed away. "What's this about?"

"It's about you and me, Kitty."

"There is no you and me."

He raised one eyebrow and came toward her. "I know it looks that way, but—"

"You're scaring me, Dylan."

He stopped. "I know."

"You want to break me, break my heart," she said, the words coming straight from her soul. "Maybe you're still mad about the secret marriage, maybe you think you want me right now. But I know where it will end, the same place every other Wilder-Matthews relationship has ended. Nowhere."

· He took another step forward. "Kitty . . ."

She put out a hand to stave him off. " 'Wilder Women Don't Wed And They Don't Run.' "

"You've done one and you're planning on doing the other. Don't let some antique label you've allowed Hot Water to place on you stick."

She swallowed. "A Wilder never gets a Matthews."

"For someone who saw through me so very clearly, you're a pretty dim bulb when it comes to your ancestors, Kitty."

She huffed. "I know everything about the Wilders. Seven summers in their bordello and a lifetime living with their legends have been a darned good education."

"But you missed the whole point of all the stories. They weren't supposed to keep you down or box you in."

He came toward her again, and she tried to stand her ground, but her feet scurried backward. He sighed, as if she disappointed him. "Kitty, the Wilders did what they wanted, they were their own women. That's what that stupid motto means. You're not supposed to live by its letter, but by its spirit."

She shivered. Hadn't she just told herself that? Told herself she was her own woman?

Dylan advanced again, and this time he didn't stop, even when he had her backed into a corner of the cell. He cupped her cheek in his big, warm palm. "Be a maverick. That's what they were, Kitty. Who cares what Hot

Water will say, what anyone will think? Take what you want. Take me."

She closed her eyes. Take him for how long? Her heart would settle for anything, but still her soul needed every convention, every promise that could make her believe in forever. To make her believe she was loved. That was what Kitty Wilder had to have.

"Kitty," he said softly.

Her eyes opened. He was unbuttoning his shirt. Her pulse trilled—shallow, Dylan-skin-crazy beat that it was—but then she saw the piece of paper lying between his shirt and his heart tattoo. His St. Barbara medal swung as he lifted it free.

"Judge Tierney was winking at *me*. He figured out I had pulled a switch."

She frowned, recognizing their marriage certificate in Dylan's hand. "We're not divorced after all?"

"Never, if I can help it."

Kitty thought she heard voices outside the jail, but she ignored them. "What exactly are you saying?"

"That I love you, Kitty. That I want to be married to you, that I want to wash your minivan, that I want to strap our kids inside it and let them watch movies on long car trips that lead to long nights during which we can make long, slow love."

Could this be true? A delicious shiver rolled down her back and curled between her thighs. "But not *Pinocchio*."

With his forefinger, he made an X right over his barbed-wire-covered heart. "Never that."

"Oh." Tears burned the corners of her eyes. He loved

her. Dylan loved her. He wanted to marry her. What would Hot Water think about that?

And why should she care? Dylan had faced up to what people saw in him. He'd moved past it in order to take what *he* wanted. Why couldn't she? Maybe some people wouldn't be shocked at all, but really happy for them. She thought of Sylvia's approval, and then of Judge Tierney's genial wink, and wondered if she hadn't been half blind all these years.

Then something heated inside her, warming her heart and her soul, changing her. Like alchemy, she thought. Dylan's love and her new clear-sightedness transforming something common into gold. "I—"

The door to the jail burst open. "What's going on here?" The authoritative question lost some of its power when the voice of the person asking it suddenly cracked. Reenactor Jeremy, in his stable-hand costume, skidded to a stop halfway into the room. "Oh."

Several more people crowded through the doorway behind him. Mrs. Shea, Spenser, Pearl and Red Morton. The whole group was bumped forward when Honor, Dylan's father, and Samantha pushed into the jail.

Kitty blinked. The last two were holding hands.

Dylan sighed. "What the hell is going on? Can't a man have a little privacy?"

Looking uncomfortable, Jeremy shuffled his feet. "We heard that a dangerous parolee had taken someone by force."

"*Oh.*" Too late, Kitty clapped her hand over her mouth, realizing she'd given herself away.

Dylan's eyebrows raised. "What's this all about, Kitty?"

She hesitated.

He narrowed his eyes. "Method number six-thirty-three, honey. And you don't want to know exactly what that is."

Kitty swallowed, thinking fast. Well, there were some things that Wilder genes were good for, she decided. Wilder survival instincts.

Plucking the marriage certificate out of Dylan's hand, she threw herself into his arms and kissed him. Kissed him silly.

Once she had him dazed, she lifted her mouth and looked at the small crowd. "Tell them he's definitely dangerous, and I'm definitely a prisoner."

She gazed into Dylan's eyes. He still seemed addled. Oh, good. "A prisoner of love," she said.

But he wasn't addled enough not to give as good as he got. As Dylan lifted her against his body and took control of the kiss, a tinge of roses scented the room. Funny, Kitty thought. She'd never worn that fragrance herself.

But the thought disappeared when she felt herself sliding into delight. The marriage certificate in her hand waved her surrender.